The Sleuth Club

I0687068

Welcome to
Stony
Estancia

The Sleuth Club
A Cozy Mystery
Transitions

Mr. Szilard Substitute Teacher Mystery #3

D.R. Oestreicher, PhD

Omega Cat Press — California

COPYRIGHT

Omega Cat Press, independent publishing since 1990

Paperback ISBN: 978-1-954225-30-5
Electronic Book ISBN: 978-1-954225-31-2
Hardcover ISBN: 978-1-954225-32-9

1 2 3 4 5 6 7 8 9

"Youth is wholly experimental." – Robert Louis Stevenson.

Dedicated to Lynn Conway–R.I.P. June 9, 2024

By D. R. Oestreicher

Zarand Szilard #1: The Ecology Club: A Cozy Mystery (and How to Save the Planet)
Zarand Szilard #2: The Library Club: A Cozy Mystery, Representation Matters

By J. Oestreicher and D. R. Oestreicher

Pandemic Mysteries #1: Darwin's Paradox
#2: Plague of Equals
#3: The Two Pearls

Suramarti Saga #1: Kitane, Bull Jumper
#2: The Murders, The Mosque

By Joy Oestreicher

Legends of Azureign #1: Dragon and Oracle
#2: Raka and Secrets
#3: The Pirate Queen
#4: The Compact Shatters
#5: The Mengsee Raids
Legends of Azureign Collection (1-5 box set)

https://www.amazon.com/shop/influencer-20171115075/

BLURB

The Sleuth Club
A Cozy Mystery
Transitions
Mr. Szilard Substitute Teacher Mystery #3

A cozy mystery: Agatha Christie meets Monty Python.
In a privileged Los Angeles suburb, a substitute teacher
solves the mystery of missing students and murder on
campus.

Sherlock Holmes says, "There's nothing more deceptive than an obvious fact."

Ruth Doyle identifies herself as a graduate of Stony Estancia High School, but there's no record of her. Goleta Hardcastle disappears after her 18th birthday. The students organize the Sleuth Club to find her.

All this happens at a top-ranked high school with a five-star cafeteria in a city incubating an artificial intelligence start-up destined for a billion-dollar stock offering.

Retired homicide detective Zarand Szilard keeps busy as a substitute teacher, a dad to his tuxedo cat, and a foodie committed to feeding everyone. All this stops when gunshots interrupt Career Day. College recruiter Wally collapses onto the outdoor stage. Zarand tracks the muzzle flash to the library roof.

A Marine helicopter and the police SWAT squad scramble to the shooter's position along with artificial intelligence drones.

Zarand's invisible sidekick, Fitch, remarks, *'Too many fingers and not enough pie.'* Zarand agrees. He watches the crowd, waiting for the opportune time to act.

Stony Estancia isn't all murder and mystery. There's Dahl, the tuxedo cat; Cerberus, the chocolate lab; Fitch, the sarcastic invisible friend and polymath; Zarand's bottomless backpack; and food, delicious food.

This book is an LGBTQ safe space.

TABLE OF CONTENTS

COPYRIGHT IV

BLURB VI

TABLE OF CONTENTS VII

    PREFACE...X

HALLOWEEN 1

    1.   ACTIVE SHOOTER 2

STONY ESTANCIA MAP 3

TWO MONTHS EARLIER, HOMECOMING 4

    2.   WOMEN IN STEM 5

    3.   EGG DROP CHALLENGE 13

    4.   FAMILY SHELTER...19

HALLOWEEN 21

    5.   GRAFFITI...22

    6.   KWOLEKS 28

    7.   UNMARKED GRAVES.......................................33

    8.   CAREER DAY 39

    9.   ASSASSINATION 45

    10. CLEAN SHEETS...50

    11. SZILARD'S SLEUTHS 52

    12. TRACE EVIDENCE 59

    13. GOLDING'S GYM 65

    14. FOUR RIVERS 75

    15. HALLOWEEN DANCE 79

    16. FIREHOUSE GRAFFITI....................................85

    17. FIREHOUSE BARBECUE..................................87

    18. WHERE'S GOLETA? 92

19. CAUSE OF DEATH 95

20. TRICK OR TREAT 101

THANKSGIVING **104**

21. CORONER'S INQUEST 105

22. WORLD MYTHOLOGY 114

23. ONLY DONUTS 121

24. THANKSGIVING...125

25. BLACK OPS 132

26. PAULI FALLS 140

WINTER SOLSTICE **146**

27. BAD NEWS 147

28. GOOD NEWS 154

29. CALLING IN FAVORS 160

30. TANGIER..167

31. THE KASBAH 170

32. AL MAHAD...175

33. ELIZABETH ON TRIAL 182

34. THE KEYS 189

35. NEW YEAR'S EVE 194

VALENTINE'S DAY **202**

36. PINK BANQUET 203

37. PERSEY'S PUZZLE..208

38. BENFORD'S LAW 216

39. MORE GRAFFITI..222

40. LUNCH WITH VICKI 227

41. SLEUTH CLUB 231

42. EPICUREAN EATS 237

43. CCTV...243

GRADUATION **245**

44. George Holmes.................................246

45. Modern Mythology.........................249

46. Ditch Day......................................253

47. Putting It All Together 258

48. S-1...266

49. Revelations 269

50. Reunions 277

July Fourth **285**

Epilogue – The Future 286

To the Reader **292**

Cheers, Credits, and Easter Eggs...........**293**

About the author **302**

....**303**

PREFACE

The Sleuth Club
A Cozy Mystery
Transitions
Mr. Szilard Substitute Teacher Mystery #3

Let me tell you about Lynn Conway. I met her in the 1970s when Xerox sent me to Caltech. She was a pioneer in the design of the chips that power today's computers, phones, artificial intelligence, and everything.

During the earlier two decades, integrated circuits had evolved from proof-of-concept to large-scale integration (LSI), 20,000 transistors. The industry was looking forward to very large-scale integration (VLSI), a million transistors. For reference, the chips in a smartphone have tens of billions.

Carver Mead of Caltech and Lynn Conway of Xerox led the transition from LSI to VLSI when they published *Introduction to VLSI Systems* in 1979.

A decade earlier, IBM fired Lynn Conway when she revealed her intention to transition from male to female. They apologized 52 years later. At Xerox, she'd learned her lesson and didn't reveal her transition, but I recall hushed conversations about her gender.

Regardless, her career and contributions continued until she retired. She came out after her retirement in 1998. Today, she's remembered as a transgender activist and for her contributions to computer science and electrical engineering.

This book is dedicated to Lynn Conway–R.I.P. June 9, 2024.

Don, Stony Estancia, April 1, 2025

HALLOWEEN

1. ACTIVE SHOOTER

"I'm Walter Fisher, Wally the college recruiter, here to remind you that all careers start with college." He did a shim sham, showing off his green and gold patent leather shoes. That didn't hold the attention of the Career Day crowd in the Stony Estancia High School courtyard. The students were distracted collecting freebies, trying out the Marines' AH-1Z Viper attack copter, and practicing triage at the Fire Department's mobile first-aid facility.

A pop and two more pops interrupted the show. I didn't breathe as my subconscious processed the sounds. They were gunshots.

I tracked them to the library roof. Smoke. Someone dressed in black. A rifle.

Wally grabbed his chest. "I've been hit."

When I returned my attention to the library, the roof was empty.

The public address system announced, "Active shooter."

I'd drilled for this but never expected it to be in Stony Estancia. As a substitute teacher, my responsibility was ensuring student safety and implementing the "Run, Hide, Fight" protocol.

I shouted, "Evacuation," and led my students up the hill to the far side of the football field.

The next sound was the Marine helicopter heading for the library. Three drones followed like kittens trailing after their mother. The Fire Department rushed Wally to their mobile first-aid facility.

The Marines returned empty-handed. It was time for me to come out of retirement. Substitute teacher Mr. S became homicide detective Szilard.

STONY ESTANCIA MAP

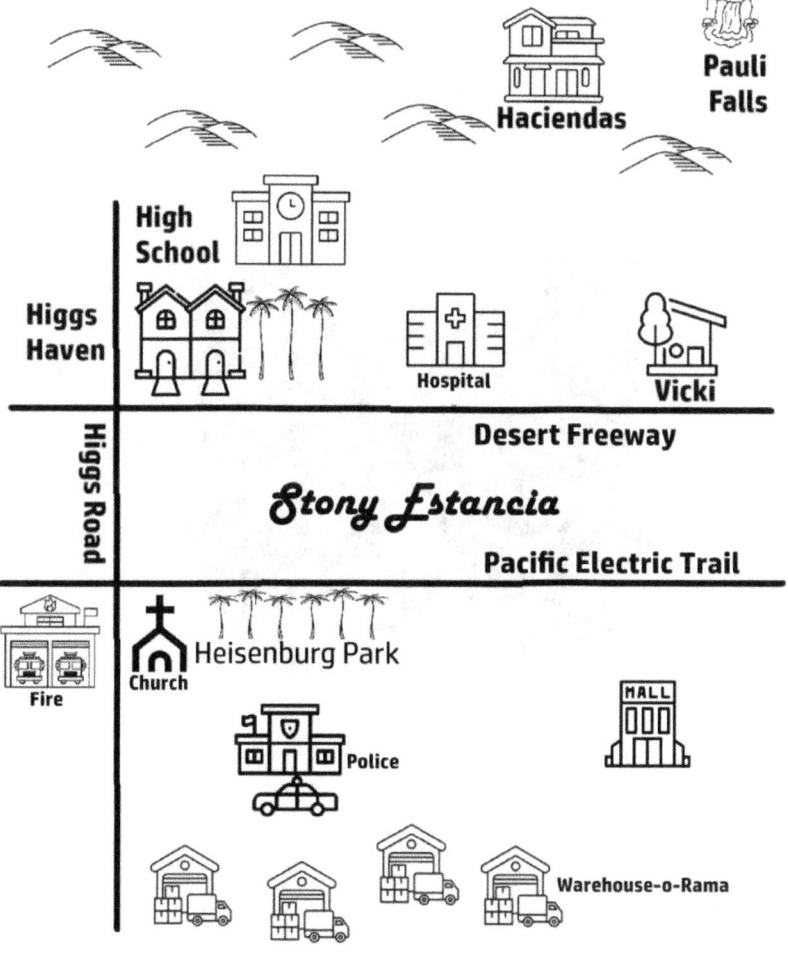

TWO MONTHS EARLIER, HOMECOMING

2. WOMEN IN STEM

I propped my phone against a pint of watermelon gelato and tapped the contact for Vicki. "Sorry, Vee, the Women in STEM Symposium is today."

She sounded upset. "Zee, are you canceling our date to attend a high school event?"

When I didn't respond, she raised the stakes. "Are your honorary grandkids more important than your girlfriend?

I studied her face on my phone. It was neutral, the same expression she used to interview suspects. That was the problem with dating a detective. She was an expert at hiding her emotions, a great poker player.

"Zee, you're a substitute teacher. You don't realize how difficult it is for a Senior Detective to schedule a night off."

'Did you see that? She furrowed her brow. That's her tell.'

Oh, Fitch. You're imagining things, stirring up trouble.

I could count on Fitch to break in at the most inopportune times. He'd been my imaginary friend since college, long before I met Senior Detective Victoria Yukawa. He was usually correct.

Stony Estancia, a posh suburb east of Los Angeles, en route to Las Vegas, wasn't a hotbed of crime. Before retiring, I was a homicide detective in LA and knew the pressures of a serious police department. Stony Estancia was quiet in comparison, but I knew better than to say that to Vicki.

"Please understand, Vee. The students are counting on me to be there. Can't you swap for another night off?"

Her brow furrows got deeper.

I tried another tack. "This is the Women in STEM Symposium. You know how I encourage the girls to consider careers in STEM: Science, Technology, Engineering, and Mathematics."

"Oh, Zee, don't give me more of that honorary grandkid's nonsense. My retired boyfriend is obsessed with teen girls. How do you think that makes me feel?"

"Sorry, Vee. How can I make it up to you?"

"Don't worry about me. I'll be home with a bowl of popcorn and tissues, watching romcoms and reading cold case files."

'Her brow is furrowed again,' warned Fitch. *'Tread carefully.'*

"Are those cold cases for littering or jaywalking?" I kidded her. "Stony Estancia doesn't attract crime like Midsomer County."

'You're making things worse.' Fitch had a long-handled shovel and pantomimed digging a deep hole.

"Two of those cold cases are missing students from your school: Robert Drew and Xanthia Kaldis."

"Okay, Vee. I'll be at the Civic Center to prevent any more of my grandkids from going missing."

The screen on my phone went blank.

Saturday night, I retrieved my suit from the guest closet and laid it on my bed, along with a fresh shirt and my favorite rainbow tie. I wanted to look my best. In front of the bathroom mirror, I trimmed my salt-and-pepper, mostly salt, beard and selected a pink, blue, and white grosgrain ribbon—transgender colors—to tie my gray ponytail.

Fitch approved. *'You're looking good, Mr. S.'*

Thanks, Fitch.

I turned off the bathroom light and headed for my suit when my cat let out a yowl and sprinted from the sofa into the kitchen, ricocheted off the cabinet that held her food, and sprang onto the dining table, the only one in my two-room apartment, and her favorite playground.

"Dahl! What are you doing?"

She knocked a coffee cup to the floor—SMASH—the third one this month, leaped through the doorway, landed on my bed, and eviscerated my carefully selected clothes.

'Zoomies,' explained Fitch.

Don't give me that. I know she can see you. You've been playing chase with her, haven't you?

He covered his face in mock shame. Dahl stared at an invisible spot on the ceiling.

"Now I must find something else to wear, and you've made me late. I tried to sound stern, but Dahl was too cute. She leaped onto the windowsill, licked her paws, cleaned her ears, and purred.

Fitch laughed, *'You should be celebrating. We're a month into the school year, and no one's been murdered.'*

I drove around the Civic Center parking lot searching for an available spot, squeezing my electric car into half a parking slot beside an oversized SUV. Wearing my best jeans and a green Stony High Bruins shirt, I hiked to the colonnade of Tuscan columns supporting a banner proclaiming WOMEN IN STEM SYMPOSIUM.

When they built the Civic Center, the city council spared no expense, paving the plaza with a mosaic of the Stony Estancia emblem in local granites—whites, tans, yellows, and pinks. My high school students, my honorary grandkids, taught me a game. I hopped across, stepping on orange trees and grape vines while avoiding palms and mountains.

The broad plaza was empty. I stomped up the stairs, frustrated to have missed the procession of future scientists. Arriving late wasn't the best way to show support for the women of Stony Estancia High School.

Fitch wore gray doctoral robes with a vertical red velvet panel on each side and three matching horizontal bars on the full sleeves. He topped his ensemble off with an eight-sided doctoral tam hat.

I'm glad no one can see you. What's with that outfit?

'I awarded myself a PhD in Murder—piled higher and deeper.' Fitch celebrated by throwing his tam into the air. When it reached its apogee over the Civic Center, it exploded into green-and-gold fireworks—Stony Estancia High School colors.

I chastised Fitch. *I'm not discussing your educational fantasies. It wastes the time I need to solve murders.*

'Murders. What murders? Show me your stinkin' murders.' A huge sombrero replaced the demolished tam.

Be patient.

Fitch quoted *Alice in Wonderland*, '*But the waiting makes me curious.*'

When I entered the auditorium, Vicki waved to me, flanked by two uniformed officers.

Fitch jostled me with his shoulder. '*I thought this was your date night.*'

I played it cool. "Evening, Detective Yukawa." When she nodded with her poker face, I couldn't resist. "Didn't you have a date with a bowl of popcorn?"

She turned to the uniform on her right. "Officer Tsui, tell this gentleman when our presence was requested for this meeting."

Tsui looked at his phone. "Hard to say. This is an annual event. We never miss it."

She added, "The Stony Estancia Police does more than littering and jaywalking."

'*She fooled you.*' Fitch rolled on the floor laughing, dressed as a harlequin.

I didn't trust myself to say anything. I crossed my arms and pursed my lips.

She jostled me with her shoulder. "Don't pout. I thought you'd like the surprise."

"We had a plan."

"Sometimes it's fun to let the plan go."

'*Round and round you go,*' Fitch was a hydrogen electron circling its proton for fourteen billion years.

I didn't want to win this argument. We were two sides of the detective coin. I was research and planning. She was novelty and improv. Together, we were a team.

Fitch made a heart with his fingers. I forced a smile and gave her a thumbs-up before turning my attention to the stage.

Mayor Cadfael, who campaigned as the Little Leprechaun, introduced the keynote speaker. "Please welcome Dr. Ruth Doyle, a proud Stony Estancia alumna."

'*Who's she?*' asked Fitch. '*I've never heard of her.*'

The mystery woman wore a bold red, black, and green caftan with a matching headscarf. "I'm honored to return to

Stony Estancia. I have fond memories of hikes to Pauli Falls, jogging along the Pacific Electric Trail, and playing softball in Heisenberg Park."

Whoever she was, she knew the city and set the right tone to appeal to the homecoming crowd. Self-congratulatory nostalgia was in the air during Homecoming Week.

"I'm here to encourage girls and young women to pursue a future in STEM." She stepped from behind the podium and approached the audience. "Find something that interests you and follow your dream. In my teen years, my passion was makeup."

'Isn't makeup the antithesis of STEM?' Fitch snickered. *'I don't trust her.'*

Shush. I'm sure she'll bring us back to STEM.

"I studied the arcane jargon like a novice joining an ancient order of powerful women." She reached into her deep pockets and pulled out cosmetics, raising each one above her head like it was a gift from the gods. "Foundation, bronzer, eyeliner, mascara, eyeshadow, eyebrow pencil, lip gloss."

As a teacher, I envied how she had the auditorium under her spell. No one moved as she spoke.

"Soon, my bedroom looked like a medieval alchemy lab with bottles and brushes stacked high. I had no place to do my homework. There had to be a better way, one that didn't consume my entire allowance."

She snapped her fingers, and magically the shiny black and gold treasures disappeared in a puff of smoke. The girls in the audience laughed.

I stood in the back of the room with my mouth agape. Who was this scientist with her fabulous stage presence? I focused my phone's camera on her. An artificial intelligence, facial recognition app, spun its wheels without identifying her.

Dr. Doyle lowered her voice. "I noticed that with all these chemicals—" She signaled the crew to start her video. Ingredient lists flashed across the big screen. "—dimethicone, glycerin, benzoyl peroxide, propylene glycol, sodium lauryl sulfate, dihydrogen monoxide. We never looked like the people in those glossy magazines slipped through the mail slots in our front doors. We never looked the way we wanted. I decided to go back to basics."

The parents cheered.

"To make a long story short, I studied biochemistry and did my dissertation on the biochemical control of skin pigmentation."

The screen showed her commencement procession. I turned back and forth between the video and Fitch in surprise. His robes matched Dr. Doyle's.

How did you do that? I asked him.

'I'm magical, aren't I?'

She held her hands beside her face, palms forward, thumbs under her chin, fingers splayed. "Look at this. Golden caramel. My beautiful color, thanks to my unique combination of eumelanin and pheomelanin, over a hundred genes, my genes, nothing else, without beauty-industry augmentation. Hashtag no makeup."

She received a standing ovation with shouts of "You go, girl," from everyone but Fitch.

'No big deal. I can match her skin pigmentation without studying biochemistry.' Fitch posed wearing black briefs with his arms raised, his biceps flexed, and his pecs on display.

Big whoop. Not much of a trick. You're invisible.

The mayor thanked Dr. Doyle and invited questions.

Leticia, Stony Estancia's favorite internet reporter, walked to the front of the auditorium carrying a shotgun microphone that looked as ominous as its name. Her husband, César, wore a shoulder harness with a steel cable to support his stabilized camera rig.

"I'm from *Stony Estancia Surfs*, the city's premier news site." She handed her mic to César, turned to face the audience, and copied Dr. Doyle's pose. She held her hands beside her face. "Mahogany and proud."

The Hispanics in the audience shouted, "Cree en ti," and "Sé fuerte." Believe in yourself and stay strong.

Dr. Doyle backed away from the podium and stopped smiling.

'What's she afraid of?' queried Fitch. *'Surely not skin colors. Mahogany. Caramel. Tomayto. Tomahto.'*

I turned to Detective Yukawa. "I don't like the look of this."

She rushed to intercept the reporters, halting them before they reached the stage. Vicki held up her credentials and said, "Okay, Tish, that's close enough."

'Your girlfriend showed them.' Fitch laughed, arms crossed in front of a black tactical vest emblazoned with SWAT.

Tish held up a white card. "The First Amendment. Refresh your memory."

Vicki's brow furrowed. "No need. The Stony police support the Constitution." She closed her eyes. "The First Amendment. *Congress shall make no law respecting an establishment of religion, or prohibiting the free exercise thereof; or abridging the freedom of speech, or of the press; or the right of the people peaceably to assemble, and to petition the Government for a redress of grievances.*"

Tish checked her white card. "Well done. You've done your homework."

"I'm not censoring you. I'm keeping you off the stage."

Leticia addressed Dr. Doyle with a clear podcaster's voice. "You tell a great story, but Stony Estancia High has no record of a Ruth Doyle...if that's your name."

My AI search app confirmed Tish's accusation. A notification from *Stony Estancia Surfs* followed: THE KEYNOTE SPEAKER AT THE WOMEN IN STEM SYMPOSIUM IS A #FRAUD.

"That's my name. I have no time to argue with an online reporter." Dr. Doyle, the alleged hometown scientist, turned and left.

The Little Leprechaun took the microphone. "Thank you for joining us and be sure to return tomorrow to see our future scientists compete in the NASA-inspired egg drop challenge."

'I told you she was hiding something,' declared Fitch while making notes in his casebook with an HB #2 pencil left over from state testing.

Fitch's suspicions made me wonder. What could be happening in quiet Stony Estancia? Why was Dr. Doyle hiding her identity and pretending to be a Stony High alumna?

3. Egg Drop Challenge

Vicki and I met at Cocina de Cetto, our favorite Mexican restaurant. I held her chair for her. "What was that about Dr. Doyle?"

"I'm not surprised they ran a background check. César and Tish'll do anything to get clicks on *Stony Estancia Surfs*," Vicki mused while dipping her tortilla chips in spicy salsa roja.

Our food arrived. My carnitas burrito supreme looked neat wrapped in a huge flour tortilla, but I knew that as soon as I bit into the savory pork, crema and guacamole would be oozing everywhere. Vicki's chile relleno was a roasted poblano pepper stuffed with three kinds of cheese, dipped in egg batter, and fried until golden brown, swimming in a puddle of red sauce.

Fitch flipped through the pages of an old phone book. *'Why didn't those internet reporters find Dr. Doyle?'*

I took a chomp from my burrito and pondered this mystery. "Stony Estancia supports education. The parents donated a research library and an observatory. I can't imagine that one of our young women was awarded a PhD without the community celebrating. Tish would certainly have posted something. Nothing escapes her omniscient knowledge of Stony Estancia."

"Well, I'm sure there's a logical explanation. This community has plenty of money. Her parents could have sent her away to a private school." She cut a piece of her chile relleno and covered it with rice and beans.

"Or she could have been homeschooled." After a bite of my burrito, I wiped crema and guacamole from my beard.

"Here's something." I showed Vicki my phone. "She's a full professor, a consultant to the beauty industry, and has her own podcast. How did they convince her to speak here if she had no connection to Stony High?"

"Good question, Zee. I know that the Symposium speakers were volunteers. Why is she here? Why would she pretend to be from Stony Estancia if she wasn't?"

"I love this city, Vee. Still, I can't imagine the attraction for a national figure like Dr. Doyle."

'I wouldn't worry,' drawled Fitch, relaxing on a pink sand beach in Bermuda shorts, wearing a palm leaf hat, and drinking something made with sliced limes and mint leaves.

Fitch might have been unconcerned, but my suspicions kept me up at night. What was her connection to Stony Estancia? Who was she?

'Why is she in this book?' Fitch laughed, holding an Advanced Reader Copy of *The Sleuth Club*.

How did you get that? Don't reveal the ending.

The next day, the WOMEN IN STEM SYMPOSIUM banner was replaced with EGG DROP CHALLENGE. Dr. Chandrasekhar from Stony High addressed the auditorium. "Your challenge is to safely land your egg, the same as NASA landed the Perseverance Rover on Mars. Of course, your eggs only have to survive from the top of the Civic Center, not millions of miles. As inspiration, here is a video from mission control located a few miles west of us at Jet Propulsion Laboratory in Pasadena."

The video showed an amphitheater filled with screens and computers, interspersed with an animation of the rover's landing. Everyone from kindergarten to high school watched and listened intently.

Parachute deployed.

Velocity is 450 meters per second, 12 kilometers off the surface of Mars.

Perseverance has slowed to subsonic speed. The heat shield has separated.

Velocity is 100 meters per second, 6.6 kilometers off the surface.

Priming of the landing engines, 83 meters per second, 2.6 kilometers.

30 meters per second, 300 meters altitude.

20 meters altitude. Sky Crane maneuver.

Tango Delta. Touchdown confirmed.

Pandemonium broke out on the screen and in the auditorium. Girls jumped from their seats and stampeded outside. I joined the women dressed in NASA uniforms, handing out eggs to kindergarteners through high schoolers. With their eggs in hand, the crowd prepared for the Egg Drop Challenge. The eggs stood in for the Mars rover, and the students pitted their ingenuity against NASA engineers.

'With a fraction of the budget,' laughed Fitch, dressed in a T-shirt with a NASA logo and standing in front of an American flag.

20 meters off the surface. *Sky Crane maneuver.*

Tango Delta. Touchdown confirmed.

With that final replay to an empty room, the screen switched back to the Stony Estancia emblem—oranges, palm trees, and mountains.

Only one student remained, Goleta Hardcastle.

I first met her when substituting in Advanced Placement Physics. She wore a green tailored shirt with a gold necktie as if Stony High had school uniforms. It didn't. On that day, I had presented a lesson on momentum to the rows of students in front of the room. She sat in the back, by herself, studying Maxwell's equations from a college text.

I followed her from the auditorium. She picked up three eggs from the deserted table and juggled them. The parking lot had a cornucopia of materials—balloons, cotton, string, glue, paint, rubber bands, and a small mountain of recycling—paper, cardboard, bubble wrap, foam sheets, fast-food containers, and plastic drink bottles.

I'd helped the teachers stack these experimental materials into an attractive display, but the budding scientists' enthusiasm had destroyed any semblance of order.

Goleta shook her head at the chaos. The only sound came from a spool of green thread rolling across an otherwise empty table in response to a gentle breeze. The spool fell off the edge and bounced on the pavement. She pocketed it and walked off into a field, juggling her eggs.

The students gathered on the Civic Center roof and tossed their eggs to the plaza below. Parachutes protected some, geometric structures encased others, and cushioning surrounded them all. Eggs splashed on the plaza when their efforts failed.

The egg-drop-challenge judges were comparing notes to award the age group and overall winners when Goleta returned carrying a rosemary bouquet in one hand and a fist-sized rock in the other.

'I don't think she understood the assignment,' Fitch said sarcastically.

Everyone watched as she held the bouquet over the edge with the rock suspended by a green thread. She let go. The bouquet acted like a colorful parachute. After the rock hit the ground, the bouquet followed, landing on its base. Like magic, the threads binding the flowers unraveled, the bouquet flattened, and resting on a bed of leaves and stems were all three of Goleta's eggs, safe and sound.

No one was surprised when she won the overall honors.

I approached her as she left the auditorium carrying a model of the Perseverance Rover. "I've never seen that solution. Are you planning to study engineering?"

She took a deep breath and pursed her lips. "My father forbids it. It isn't ladylike. My mother has sent applications to small liberal-arts-only colleges. My family only allows pre-law or pre-med."

She appeared dissatisfied with the proposed plan. However, as a substitute teacher, it was not my place to intervene between parents and their children.

She stuck out her chin. "When I receive my trust funds, I'll make my own decisions. Until then—"

A well-dressed Hispanic lady broke in. "Mi hija, why are you talking to outsiders about family business?" She grabbed Goleta's arm.

Goleta didn't budge. "Mi mama, did you forget that I had my birthday? I'm eighteen. I'm an adult."

I backed away.

'Coward,' Fitch chided me.

They don't need an audience, I replied.

I moved farther away, but the argument became louder.

"You're too young. I won't let you make the mistakes I made. I'm a Civil Engineer. I have my Professional Engineer license. Do you know what that got me?"

"Sure do. You've told me often enough," she replied with teenage sarcasm. "Sexism. Discrimination. You went back to school and became a lawyer." Goleta made two tight fists. "I don't want to be a lawyer...or a doctor...or...whatever." Her voice became low, and she snarled, "This is the 21st century. The world has changed."

Her mother snapped back. "Nothing has changed. Civil Rights lawyers like me file Title VII lawsuits every week."

"You're wrong." She pulled her arm from her mother's grasp. "I want to design the Europa lander...or...maybe something with climate change." She ran to her car, jumped in, and sped out of the parking lot, tires spinning.

I turned away, but Mrs. Hardcastle had seen my shocked expression. "Don't worry, Mr. Szilard. She does this all the time. She'll be back in a few days without missing any homework or exams."

I suspected that Mrs. Hardcastle didn't appreciate her daughter's commitment to change, but I gave her a smile and a thumbs-up anyway.

'I wouldn't worry either,' said Fitch, relaxing in a hammock under a palm tree in Hawaiian boardshorts, wearing a coconut leaf hat, and drinking something blue, garnished with pineapple and maraschino cherries. *'That young lady is stronger and more determined than anyone imagines.'*

Fitch was closer to the truth. This was the 21st century, and the world had changed. Dr. Doyle and Goleta were from a new generation of 21st-century women. A new game was afoot. I wouldn't stop thinking about them until I'd uncovered their stories and celebrated their courage and success.

'21st-century women,' Fitch repeated my phrase with disdain. *'Is this book only about women?'*

Of course not, I thought as I drove south on Higgs Road.

I lived in the Higgs Haven Condominiums, an upscale development blending townhouses with meticulously maintained green spaces, a pool, a children's play area, and a health club. I didn't stop for lunch and a nap. I drove by the entrance and continued on Higgs Road to the south side of town. Moving downhill, Stony Estancia became more commercial. I passed the Firehouse Barbecue, the firehouse, and the Stony Estancia Community Church, which occupied a repurposed supermarket. When I reached the flats, the neighborhood transitioned to warehouses, strip malls, and older residences, an area fondly called Warehouse-o-Rama.

Tucked among these nondescript buildings was one of Stony Estancia's hidden treasures, a pâtisserie with no name that created the best confections outside Paris. Since I was early, I relaxed at one of the outdoor tables with French roast coffee, mille-feuille, tarte Tatin, and crème brûlée, pondering if Goleta's teenage angst was about more than her mother's career aspirations.

'*Beaucoup plus,*' said Fitch, wearing a Cheshire Cat smile.

4. FAMILY SHELTER

Rejuvenated by caffeine, heavy cream, powdered sugar, and flaky pastry, I headed west. Even down here in Warehouse-o-Rama, I never saw litter, graffiti, or unhoused people pushing their belongings in purloined shopping carts. This was thanks to the Stony Estancia Family Shelter—a pale yellow single-family house with tan trim and security bars on the windows—not out of place among the modest lawns, flower borders, and mature crepe myrtle trees in this working-class neighborhood.

The shelter was tastefully marked by a small brass plaque above its video doorbell. It was founded in the 1980s as the city's response to federal welfare reform and expanded as nearby houses came up for sale. The other buildings were incognito, blending in with the community.

The aroma of jasmine and the hum of bees harvesting nectar and pollen from rosemary hedges filled the air. I found a parking space a few blocks from the main building and arrived in time to see Mayor Cadfael on the front lawn, standing beside a small, veiled statue, no taller than his leprechaun-like stature.

'You always walk in late during the mayor's speeches. He's going to think you're purposely disrespecting him,' Fitch teased me, dressed in green satin and wearing fine leather boots with large gold buckles.

Surely no one would expect me to leave la pâtisserie before I finished my crème brûlée.

Two young children pulled the sheet from the statue. The mayor smiled for César, the news cameraman from *Stony Estancia Surfs*, and began his remarks, "This statue of Huck and Jim on their raft acknowledges Stony Estancia Family Shelter as a haven for runaways."

I applauded with the crowd, smaller than the one at the Women in STEM Symposium, but no less enthusiastic.

'What's this nonsense about runaways? Isn't this a murder mystery?' Fitch wore patched pants and carried his stuff wrapped in a red bandana hanging from the end of a branch.

Relax. There are missing persons, but also a murder, clever students, cute pets, and lots of food.

'Blah, blah, blah,' Fitch stretched his arms and yawned. *'Let's get on to the action.'*

HALLOWEEN

5. Graffiti

Dahl jumped onto my pillow, landing with a thud. My eyes popped open, and I swatted her. She swatted me back, claimed the warm spot atop my chest, and purred, resting her chin in my beard. The night was moonless, and the room was dark. My hazy mind grasped for the last wisps of a dream. The perplexing Dr. Ruth Doyle and the angry Goleta Hardcastle vaporized. I mumbled, "Let me go back to sleep."

'Wake up, sleepy head. Second dinner.' Fitch wore a bat costume and hung upside-down in the doorway between the bedroom and the combination kitchen and living room.

My stomach growled.

Dahl, Fitch, and my stomach—the hunger trifecta. I threw off the covers and pulled a leather butcher's apron over my PJs.

As Samwise Gamgee said, "Po-ta-toes! Boil them, mash them, stick them in a stew." I sliced my potatoes into the air fryer. My large cast iron pan, the one that I inherited from Grandpa, heated on the stove, filled with sizzling butter, diced onions, and fresh garlic. My mouth watered from the savory fragrances. I slid an aged cheddar cheese block across an antique grater. A sourdough ciabatta au gratin went into the upper oven.

Warm home-cooking aromas filled the room. I was halfway down the stairs, on my way to the deep freeze in the garage, when I rushed back to turn on the oven to preheat. On my second attempt, I retrieved chocolate chip cookie dough preserved in a beeswax wrap. My special recipe doubled the chocolate and added three kinds of nuts. Black cherry ice cream from the kitchen freezer waited patiently for the warm cookies.

Dahl rubbed against my legs, and Fitch sat at the table with a green-and-gold checkered napkin tucked in at his chin.

A Bicycle Built for Two, Vicki's ringtone, disrupted this culinary reverie. I assumed her call was for an impromptu date. "Evenin, Vee. Dahl and I are preparing a midnight snack. Please join us."

Fitch winked at me. I added, "I have warm cookies and clean sheets. You're welcome to spend the night."

"That's tempting, but I'll pass." Vicki's serious tone told me that this wasn't a social call. She continued, "Sorry to interrupt second dinner, but something's happened at your school."

She didn't need to say anything more.

I turned off the stove and put the cookie dough in the fridge. I had retired from an urban police department and moved to the suburbs to dedicate myself to Stony Estancia High School as a substitute teacher and student confidant. Occasionally, I wrote novels and solved murders.

Fitch winked.

And to be near Senior Detective Victoria Yukawa, I admitted.

I rushed into my clothes, ran down the stairs, and headed to school.

I pulled into the barely lit visitor parking lot.

Stony High had recently gotten an observatory, a fifteen-foot dome with a fourteen-inch telescope, and with it came the requirement to reduce light pollution. The campus lights had been replaced with special dark-sky lighting that cloaked the campus in a translucent glow like the fog surrounding Victorian mansions in horror films.

'Dark-sky lighting,' Fitch chortled. *'An oxymoron.'*

The moonless night contributed an extra layer of eeriness. I doubt anyone was frightened by the Halloween atmosphere. Stony Estancia High School, home of the green and gold Bruins, its research library, and the award-winning student dining room reflected privilege and opportunity, not threats or danger.

With my cell phone flashlight, I looked for Vicki. I passed the WELCOME TO OUR SCHOOL, THIS IS A TOBACCO-FREE CAMPUS, and Prop 65 cancer-warning placards on my way to the main gate—a sturdy black steel barrier securing the school. Except tonight it was open.

'An open gate might be ominous,' Fitch intoned in a spooky Halloween voice.

I doubt it. This is Stony High.

Bruin Bistro (the school's renowned eatery), the library, and the academic buildings enclosed a broad courtyard, paved with bricks and sprouting California pepper trees in circular planters. That open space swallowed my phone's feeble glow.

I texted Vicki, **MR S:** WHERE R U

YUKAWA: BEHIND THE LIBRARY.

She wasn't there. An ethereal vision of ghosts—white apparitions—milled around the memorial garden. I repeated my query, and my phone's voice-to-text sent, **MR S:** WHERE ARE YOU?

YUKAWA: I C U [HAHA FACE].

'She's on the hill.' Fitch, enclosed head to toe by white personal protective equipment, like a COVID-19 ICU nurse, blended in with the ghosts.

Foolish Fitch. You're imaginary. No need for PPE.

Vicki stood above the spirits. No PPE for her either. She wore a blazer and neatly pressed slacks. Her straight black hair hung down to her shoulders with the usual laser-straight part bisecting her scalp, a bright line reflecting the dim, dark-sky lighting.

Quiet and calm surrounded us. With my arm around her waist, I kissed her ear and whispered, "Why did you summon me to this romantic rendezvous?"

She ignored my flirting. "You won't believe this." She shone an LED spotlight at the library, not on the white-suited forensic techs, but higher up, illuminating the brick wall. The bright beam revealed graffiti in red spray paint. X MARKS THE SPOT.

"Puppets. Puppies!" These were the strongest expletives I used on campus, where graffiti was the worst transgression I could imagine. "That's disgraceful. I assume you've arrested the perpetrators from San Amano or Alta Mesa. No one from Stony Estancia would do this."

She shrugged her shoulders. "Whatever. The street artists are gone." She panned her light to reveal the rest of the graffiti, U DA BOMB.

I couldn't believe how relaxed she was. Graffiti was unprecedented and threatening. "Puppets. I would take that bomb threat seriously. They defaced Stony High. Such fiends are capable of anything."

'Call the National Guard. Gangs are invading,' Fitch exclaimed sarcastically, carrying a foam baseball bat.

"Calm down, Zee. Let's not blow this out of proportion. Graffiti isn't uncommon."

"What? I've never seen graffiti in Stony Estancia."

"That's thanks to Graffiti Abatement. They remove all traces before they can inspire copycats." She smiled, stood on her toes, and kissed my nose. "You're cute, my naive teacher. We rarely see it on campus, but it's common elsewhere."

I crossed my arms and pushed out my chin. "I've never seen it on the *Surf* website. It would be worth lots of clicks, and they'll do anything for clicks."

"Anything but graffiti." She smiled. "This graffiti was different. I asked the rapid response squad to wait for forensics." She hugged me. "If I hadn't called you, you wouldn't have been any wiser."

I was speechless.

Vicki gave me a half smile and a half nod. "Do you think it's a student prank?"

"Not my students. My honorary grandkids would never do anything like this."

"You're getting too close to them."

"No, I'm not." I took a deep breath and thought like a detective. "Who reported this?"

Vicki pointed up the hill.

"Seriously? You're getting messages from the heavens?"

"Who are you to talk?" she laughed. "You consult with your invisible friend."

Fitch pouted.

She pointed again. "Look beyond the football field."

Past the goalposts was the observatory dome.

'New moon tonight, for millennia, known to be the best time to observe the heavens.' Fitch looked up from grinding a lens in Galileo's workshop.

I got it. "The Astronomy Club," I said.

Vicki smiled.

"Did you interrogate their president?" I asked as a follow-up. "What did she say?"

Vicki checked her notes. "Right. Goleta. She made the call."

"Perfect. You can trust Goleta. What did she say?"

"I quote, 'Someone's violating the dark-sky rules.'"

"It must have been a slow night if the Stony Estancia Police responded to a dark-sky violation."

"Your friend Goleta is very persuasive. She convinced the dispatcher that they were monitoring NEOs and the planet depended on them."

"NEOs?"

"Near Earth Objects, like Chicxulub, the impact that caused the dinosaur extinction. We brought in a special forensic team equipped with night vision so we wouldn't disturb their work."

"You were conned." It was my turn to laugh at the police department's naiveté. That surveillance is automated, Artificial intelligence, etcetera. Did they tell you anything to identify the perps?"

"Not really."

"Right. They're too far away, the bleachers obscure their view, and it's dark. I hate an investigation that begins with no clues, no leads, no ideas."

Vicki gave me an air kiss. "If this had been an easy case, I wouldn't have bothered you in the middle of the night."

I silently repeated, "X marks the spot." This felt like my best clue, my best lead. "What's X? Where's the spot?"

A neon-yellow van skidded to a stop in front of the library. Two larger-than-life smiling faces decorated its side. Metallic gold lettering named the man as César and the woman as Tish, short for Leticia. STONY ESTANCIA SURFS, YOUR HYPERLOCAL NEWS SOURCE. CLICK ON US filled the remaining space, along with a QR code to download their app: Surf SE. They unloaded floodlights, and the moonless gloom deserted Stony High. The handful of students from the Astronomy Club ran across the football field, shouting, "Shut those things off."

Everything came together. Above, the Astronomy Club watched us from the football bleachers. Tish moved through them, collecting eye-witness interviews. Below, crime scene investigators, using night-vision goggles and enrobed in white PPE, collected forensic evidence. High on the brick wall, U DA BOMB. X MARKS THE SPOT, in red spray paint.

César filmed from outside the yellow crime scene tape.

Vicki reminded him of his civic responsibilities. "All graffiti is permanently embargoed."

César muttered, "Someday, someday, I'm producing an award-winning documentary. *Graffiti in Paradise, the full story.*"

Vicki hiked up the hill and spoke to Goleta. "*Stony Estancia Surfs* and their floodlights won't leave while you offer them content. They love posting interview videos. Take your star watchers away, and they'll move on."

"You heard the lady," Goleta spoke with authority. The astronomy club returned to their observatory.

Leticia went with Vicki down the hill. "Will this bomb threat close the school? Who's behind it? Is the bomb squad on their way?"

'*I doubt Stony Estancia has a bomb squad,*' Fitch laughed.

Vicki repeatedly responded, "No comment." I could tell she was seething inside while presenting a calm, in-control façade.

When my phone beeped, I silenced it. I saw no reason to upset Vicki with *Surf SE* notifications. César had posted: #TERRORISM THREATS IN STONY ESTANCIA.

'*What happened to the agreement to suppress graffiti news?*' Fitch silently mocked the reporters.

This is a bomb threat. Something different. I countered.

'*Uh oh. Did you hear that?*' Fitch wore headphones and pointed his dish microphone into the air. When I cupped my ears with my hands, I could make out a faint sound reminiscent of a dentist's drill or buzz bombs from movies about the London Blitz.

6. Kwoleks

"Vicki, can you hear that?" I scanned the sky above Stony High. "Something is flying over us."

"Good. They arrived. Those are Kwoleks."

When she said, "Kwoleks," the noisy spot in the sky lit up like a mini-me of the UFO in *Close Encounters of the Third Kind*, multi-color flashing lights, circles within circles, accompanied by a simple melody.

"Kwoleks? What's a Kwolek?"

"Kwolek is an AI drone," Vicki said as if I could order one online.

I knew about military drones, but my phone AI turned up something else. A cute thing with four miniature helicopter rotors called a quadcopter. "It's a toy."

"Not so loud." She put her arm around my waist and whispered in my ear, "Here comes the inventor."

A short lady, barely five feet tall, stood before us. Her auburn hair was in soft curls. She wore a violet silk blouse with matching baggy trousers. Her phone and video game controller, one in each hand, were psychedelic purple.

"Evenin, Dr. T," Vicki greeted her. "I haven't seen you since the Women in STEM Symposium."

"I've been busy, busy," the lady replied before pocketing her phone and concentrating on the controller. "Evenin, Detective Yukawa. Can you introduce me to this Luddite?"

"This is my friend Zarand. He teaches at the high school. In his earlier life, he was Homicide Detective Szilard." Vicki turned to me. "Zee, this is Dr. Terez Telkes. She's the Stony Estancia Makers Guild's CEO. The Makers Guild is a home-grown startup." Vicki pointed above us where the drones were flying in figure eights and singing *Lucy in the Sky with Diamonds*. "They equipped them with fancy sensors and artificial intelligence."

'Artificial intelligence,' Fitch giggled. *'Another oxymoron.'*

Dr. Telkes added, "Those are my Kwoleks, a billion-dollar market. When we go public, we'll be the biggest company in Stony Estancia."

"Wow! That's impressive, Dr. Telkes." We shook hands. She had a firm grip.

She said, "No reason to be formal. Call me Dr. T."

'Doctor T is formal,' Fitch mocked, wearing his doctoral robes.

I welcomed her. "Thank you for joining us in the middle of the night, Dr. T."

"No problem. I'm always searching for new use cases for the Kwoleks." She fiddled with the controller. "As CEO, my job is to develop billion-dollar markets for our product."

I imagined Dr. Telkes transformed into Rich Uncle Pennybags, Mr. Monopoly, full of herself.

'You have no idea of the pressure on her.' Fitch wore a black turtleneck and jeans. *'If the company succeeds, credit is shared. Otherwise, failure is hers.'*

Mr. Monopoly reverted to Dr. T, Vicki's friend. I welcomed her. "It's midnight snack time. Can I offer you something?"

"Oh, don't bother, tell me what you like. The Kwoleks will deliver it. Food delivery. Another billion-dollar market."

'She's in for a surprise,' Fitch laughed, with a green-and-gold checkered napkin tucked in at his chin. *'Wait until she sees your backpack.'*

Vicki smiled. "Not necessary. Zarand has his backpack. It competes with Dora's Mochila."

'Don't get a big head,' Fitch warned. *'Your backpack can't talk. Dora's bilingual.'*

I set up a table with a white cloth and served savory hot hors d'oeuvres. "It's chilly tonight, isn't it?" I reached both hands into the backpack and pulled out an espresso machine.

Dr. T dropped her controller. "How did you do that? Can I invest?"

"Sorry, it's a one-off. When I moved into my condo, Dahl batted a toy mouse under the fridge. When I slid it away from the wall, I found Dahl's mouse and the backpack covered in dust bunnies."

She gave me a puzzled look.

"I can't explain it. Magical extra dimensions, string theory, or something."

Dr. T laughed and turned her attention to the food.

Vicki had a caffè latte with a bruschetta. The CEO requested a decaf caramel macchiato made with oat milk. She helped herself to stuffed clams and grilled shrimp. I sensed a long night coming. I had a caffè americano and butternut squash potstickers before filling my pockets with dark chocolate-covered espresso beans.

"Just loan me that backpack and I'm sure my engineers can figure it out. A billion-dollar market, for sure."

I ignored that and moved the discussion back to drones. "The Ecology Club uses a drone to survey the mountains. It's more efficient than hiking the terrain."

Dr. T ate a couple of grilled shrimps before answering my implied question. "Kwolek is special. So you don't offend her, she prefers the pronouns she and her. In addition to her regular cameras, she has infrared and ultraviolet sensors, and LiDAR—light detection and ranging."

Fitch stretched out his arms and yawned. *'Boring.'*

I murmured, "That's quite a toy," under my breath.

"I heard that," a Kwolek boomed from above us.

Dr. T continued, "Don't let her size fool you. These Kwoleks are specialized for crime scene forensics. A large language model lives in the cloud, trained on petabytes of crime scene data, conflict data, international data, more than you could experience in many lifetimes. She—"

I'd had enough. "I've seen the hype about AI. It's just pattern matching. No more intelligent than a pigeon in a Skinner box."

'Now you've offended her,' said Fitch.

You're siding with the robot, are you?

Vicki jumped in. "No need to fight. You both have the same goal—to explain the evidence. Zarand uses intuition, and Dr. Telkes likes AI. Neither can claim superiority."

That didn't appease the doctor.

"Let's not jump to judgment. Kwolek hasn't surveyed the scene yet." The high-tech CEO pressed some buttons on her video game controller. "You go, girl. Show them your stuff."

Leticia's omniscient news sense drew her up the hill. She stepped into the middle of our group. "I'm sure the *Stony Estancia Surfs* readers will click on this story."

"I agree, your users will click, and the story will go viral." Dr. Telkes smiled. "This will be a real-life demonstration of Kwolek's power. She's opening billion-dollar markets for artificial intelligence."

Fitch set up an old-time medicine show. *'Come one, come all. Watch grown men make fools of themselves about graffiti.'* Under his breath, he said, *'What a waste of time.'*

While César filmed the quadcopter, Tish treated the CEO like a rock star. "Is it too late to invest?"

That received a broad smile. "Our initial public offering is soon. I'll add your name to the IPO friends-and-family list."

'This should be a good show.' Fitch leaned back in a reclining movie theater seat with a large fizzy drink in one hand and a larger buttered popcorn in the other.

I popped a few espresso beans and waited.

Kwolek stopped playing music and turned off the light show. She traversed the scene, first east to west and then north to south.

"That's a thorough search pattern," I said, offering an olive branch to Dr. T.

'An eleven-year-old could do as well.' Fitch was back in his doctoral regalia.

"Thanks, but that was the gross data collection." Kwolek swooped down and flitted around like a bat pursuing nocturnal insects. "This is the fine data pass."

Dr. Telkes smiled as my head and eyes moved erratically, struggling to follow the hyperactive robots.

After a brief time, Kwolek finished her bat imitations and joined us. "High confidence. Crimes against humanity. The reference sites in my database include Kosovo, Rwanda, and Cambodia. Four shallow graves." She flew over four ovals of fresh dirt. "Perpetrators. Lynch mob. Twenty-seven individual footprints classified by size and brand."

'Shallow graves?' Fitch wore a blue vest and a United Nations refugee worker's cap. *'More likely an AI hallucination.'*

Over the top. Dr. Telkes has lost touch with reality.

Fangirl Tish had a more positive response. "Brilliant. Billion-dollar market, for sure. Best thing since the air fryer."

Those flying cell phones convinced Vicki. She said, "I'm texting Coroner Persephone Paterson to check out those shallow graves." After her phone beeped, Vicki smacked her forehead with her palm. "Oops. Persey, not Peggy. I sent the text to Peggy, the paramedic, not Persey, the coroner. I'm always getting them mixed up."

'Persey for a hearse and Peggy for egg salad,' Fitch laughed.

Egg salad?

'Okay. How about Persey for a horse-drawn hearse and Peggy for an eager rescue eagle?'

Not any better.

I'd heard enough. "Bringing in Persey is crazy. This is Stony Estancia, not some war zone."

"You wouldn't recognize a war zone. Kwolek knows war zones. She has hundreds of them in her training set." The Makers Guild CEO defended her invention. "You're a teacher. Your affection for the students fogs your mind. That's why we need unbiased AI."

When he claimed that his large language model was unbiased, it set me off. "Unbiased! Don't tell me that you believe your marketing hype. That video game learned from the internet, a treasure trove of arrogance and patriarchy. Racism. Sexism. Misogyny."

'Those flashing lights have hypnotized everyone, but at least you have a murder for your book–from those shallow graves, I'd say, four of them.' Fitch put a positive spin on this AI foolishness with a series of fouetté turns.

I was glad Vicki had summoned Coroner Persey. I counted on her to restore sanity.

My *Surf SE* app notified me with: CRIMES AGAINST HUMANITY. AI UNCOVERS #ATROCITIES AT HIGH SCHOOL.

Fitch hid his face in his hands and muttered, *'Over the top. Way over the top. I hope the readers don't throw this book across the room.'*

7. UNMARKED GRAVES

Waiting for Coroner Persey, I served Vicki and Dr. T a second round of snacks, sweet ones. Apple fritters with hot maple syrup, caramelized pineapple with warm fudge sauce, mini strawberry rhubarb pies, and everyone's favorite, old-fashioned rice pudding with fresh raspberries.

'What? No fondue forks?' Fitch complained, fishing out raspberries with his fingers and dipping them in the fudge.

Fitch, you must learn some manners. You messed up my plating.

He had the courtesy to look embarrassed while he licked his fingers.

Kwolek took advantage of her captive audience. She circled the four dirt mounds (alleged shallow graves) and flaunted her AI knowledge. "I can show you many unmarked graves. They aren't as rare as you think." She flashed macabre images, one after another—not what I wanted to see while eating strawberry rhubarb pie. "My training set has petabytes from war zones, hospitals, and schools."

'Can you make that thing shut up?' Fitch put on noise-canceling headphones.

"My beta software can dramatize the reports with generated video. Would you like to see that?" Kwolek projected children playing in front of a one-room schoolhouse, their grisly deaths, and a field of unmarked graves.

I'd closed my eyes and covered my ears. The dataset was extensive, but didn't have anything relevant to Stony High. "Stop! Tell me how many gardens are in your training set. Kew? Versailles? Butchart? Japanese? Botanical?"

"Gardens? Seriously?" Kwolek laughed. "Why would I care about gardens?" She swooped down over the four dirt mounds. "I hope the coroner gets here soon. These graves are off-gassing VOCs, volatile organic compounds, a clear sign of decaying organic matter, and recent burials."

I moved closer. The smell was familiar, but I couldn't place it. Whatever it was, it wasn't pleasant.

The rising sun peeked over the mountains. I'd missed second dinner, and now first breakfast was in jeopardy. Snacks didn't count as a meal. I couldn't imagine what was delaying Persey.

'Dahl is never going to forgive you if you skip two meals. She's an indoor cat. If you don't let her hunt, you must feed her on time. That's the law.' Fitch wagged his finger at me.

With the morning came the groundskeeper, Mr. Mbacke. He approached us wearing a gray twill shirt with an embroidered district patch above the right pocket and his name over the left. He carried a long-handled shovel over his shoulder. "Mornin, folks. I read about this on my *Surf SE app.* They'll post anything for clicks."

He pointed at Kwolek with a shovel handle. "Is that the dang fool thing that generated this fake news? AI hallucinations?"

"Kwolek is set to bring AI power to billion-dollar markets," said Makers Guild CEO, Dr. T. "If you interfere with our IPO, I'll sue for slander. There's a lot at stake with this offering."

Mr. Mbacke stood tall, holding his shovel like a rifle. "Sue me as much as you wish. I rent, the bank owns my car, and its full gas tank is my greatest asset."

"I'll have you fired."

"No, ma'am. I have a union and seniority."

I wasn't surprised that this confrontation drew the reporters from *Stony Estancia Surfs* into the mix. César panned left and right, filming the debate between Dr. T and the groundskeeper—the petite woman and the tall, broad-shouldered man.

"Kwolek's algorithms found four shallow graves. Why should I listen to a gardener?" the CEO asked with disdain. "He's distracting us. He dug those graves. Why aren't the police interrogating him?"

Mr. Mbacke spoke slowly. "I'm going to excavate those mounds and settle this, but while I'm digging, I suggest you think about overfitting, biased data sets, and human errors—common causes of artificial intelligence failures."

'Gobbledygook.' Fitch yawned. *'Boring.'*

Dr. T refused to listen to the gardener. "I have a PhD in Computer Science. I won't have you lecture me with buzzwords that you can't possibly understand." Dr. T put her hands over her ears and repeated, "La, la, la."

I felt embarrassed for them. Two adults shouting at each other like children.

'This is going to be good,' Fitch said with a grin, dressed in his doctoral robes.

Mr. Mbacke stood over Dr. T. "Really? A PhD? Then, I'll assume you saw my paper from the SAIL conference."

"You presented a paper at the Statistics, Artificial Intelligence, and Logic conference? The one in Grenoble? You're that Mbacke?" Dr. T fumed. "You aren't a gardener!"

"Yeah, well— I also garden." Mr. Mbacke went to the first dirt mound and started shoveling.

I joined him. "Can I help?"

"Sure. Dig in."

I found a shovel in my backpack and set to work, but didn't make much progress. "I can't dig down more than a couple of inches."

"Correct. Our dirt is predominantly clay and boulders. I employed a jackhammer to prepare these flower beds in Tiff the Tutor's honor."

'Tiff the Tutor was murdered in The Library Club. Why are you mentioning her here?' Fitch reprimanded me.

"No graves?" I asked. "Then what's that smell?"

"Cow manure. Natural. Organic. Rich in nitrogen, phosphorus, and potassium." Mr. Mbacke summarized, "No graves. No bodies. Come back in a couple of weeks, and you'll find some nice flowers. That hallucinating AI went crazy over my flower beds.

Kwolek landed behind the Makers Guild CEO and let her rotors spin down. Dr. T picked up the quadcopter and said, "No reason to wait around. We have a busy day planned."

"Same here," said Tish as she helped César pack up his equipment.

Vicki let out a long breath. "This is your school, Zee. Do you know why Dr. T and her quadcopters left? Does it have something to do with Halloween?"

'Career Day,' Fitch reminded me, wearing a hard hat and a reflective safety vest.

I explained it to Vicki, "Halloween is tomorrow. Today is Career Day at Stony High. I expect Kwoleks will be flying around to recruit for internships at Stony Estancia Makers Guild, and the Marines—"

Vicki cut me off. "Right, right. I recall. Officer Tsui will represent the police department. He's sharing space with Lieutenant Peggoty Mutai. She's bringing her paramedic team and the fire department's mobile field hospital."

I replied, "I've heard about that. They repurposed an old bookmobile."

Mr. Mbacke added, "The fire department did a great job, but if you look carefully, you can recognize the original bookshelves around the walls."

"I bet the mobile first response unit is the highlight of Career Day."

Mr. Mbacke shook his head. "Sorry, Mr. Szilard, but the Marines are flying in an AH-1Z Viper attack copter."

I kidded Vicki, "How is Tsui going to compete with that?"

Vicki rose to the challenge: "He'll bring the SWAT armored personnel carrier and a team in tactical armor."

'I see your Viper and raise you an APC,' Fitch mocked the militarized police force.

I worried about my Career Day tutorial and wondered how I'd compete with that heavy hardware. I muttered to myself, "I hope someone comes to my talk about the importance of teachers."

Vicki encouraged me with an air kiss. "Cool. I'm sure you'll have a full room—standing room only. Your passion will draw a crowd."

'That's sweet of her, but I foresee vacant seats again this year,' Fitch taunted me.

I hugged Vicki. "I should be going. Will you be okay waiting for Coroner Persey?"

Vicki furrowed her brow and replied, "No problem. I tried to cancel her, but she was on Blackett Street, almost here."

"In that case, I'll stay."

Her brow relaxed.

A chocolate lab jumped up on Vicki, marking her blazer with doggy footprints. "Down, Cerberus."

Cerberus sat at Vicki's feet, mouth open, panting with his tongue out. She scratched his floppy ears. "Good boy."

County Coroner Persephone Paterson, a tall woman with kohl eyes, midnight lips, and black fingernails, followed Cerberus. When she graduated from Stony High, she'd famously appeared in her yearbook as a mortician wearing a black prom dress. Persey spread her arms and announced in a deep voice, "I am Persephone, Queen of the Underworld. Take me to your dead."

'I love this lady's style,' said Fitch.

Just like blow flies attracted to a cadaver, the neon yellow *Surf* van returned.

I apologized to Persey, "Sorry to get you up in the middle of the night. It turns out that we have no graves, no dead bodies."

She laughed. "No problem. My sleep was undisturbed. I have an AI assistant. He delayed Vicki's texts while I dreamed of anatomy classes and Y incisions. Isn't AI wonderful?"

While I contemplated the joys of artificial intelligence, Persey held Cerberus, panting, wagging his tail, and eager for some excitement. "As long as we're here, I'll let Cerberus have his fun." She handed the chocolate lab a treat and said, "Good boy. Go find something."

Cerberus ran around, reenacting Kwolek's search pattern. He settled beside Mr. Mbacke and nuzzled the dirt we dug up from the flowerbed.

"Well, this trip hasn't been a waste. Let's see what Cerberus uncovered." Persey gave him another treat before putting on gloves and getting down on her hands and knees.

"Here it is." She held up a small green circuit board, then another, and another.

Mr. Mbacke examined them. "That's what's left of a flash drive after someone smashed it open and broke off the connectors."

"Is the data lost?" I feared.

"The person who smashed the drive might think so, but no. The data may be encrypted, but either way, Purcell and Associates can retrieve it."

I recalled my earlier encounters with Vinnie Purcell. He was a data encryption wizard. When a secret organization back in Virginia got stuck, they called him.

'Also, you found the granddaughter he didn't know he had. He owes you, like, forever,' Fitch gloated.

Thanks for the reminder. That's from another book.

Now that I knew what we were looking for, I could see lots of tiny green computer boards, looking like St. Patrick's Day mints mixed in with chocolate chip cookie dough.

César filmed the data treasures while Leticia interviewed Mr. Mbacke. "What have we found here?"

He examined one circuit board. "These are 256-gigabyte chips. We have terabytes of data here. Could be pirated video, porn, industrial espionage, or, since this is Stony High, test answers."

Stony Estancia Surfs posted: CERBERUS UNCOVERS #ESPIONAGE AT STONY HIGH.

Tsui put on gloves and filled his evidence bags with smashed circuit boards from USB memory sticks.

'This is unexpected. We have evidence but no crime.' Fitch laughed. *'We're left without a murder.'*

I made my exit. "I have time to feed Dahl and change my muddy boots before Career Day."

At the mention of Dahl, Cerberus wagged his tail.

"Oh, excuse me. Would Cerberus like to visit with his friend?" I scratched the excited dog's ears.

"Good idea. Your first breakfast could be my second," Persey laughed.

Vicki furrowed her brow and made a sad face. "Oh yes, leave the cops to clean up and collect the trace evidence."

I kissed her cheek. "I'm sure you'll find something in this mess."

8. CAREER DAY

California sunshine banished the previous night's dark-sky fog. The forensic ghosts in their white PPE and the ominous red spray-painted graffiti were replaced by multicolored booths promoting life beyond high school. As if it never happened, last night's horror film of graves and bombs was reborn into a carnival.

Middle-aged recruiters enticed students with colorful posters and trinkets branded with QR codes: pencils, tote bags, water bottles, flash drives, chocolates, and the most popular, condoms.

The students mingled, each in their own body spray and deodorant microclimate. Despite diverse backgrounds, they shared a striking similarity in their unisex jackets, ties, and uncomfortable leather shoes—pondering their futures had nudged them towards uniformity.

A green plush bear, Björn, the Stony High mascot, added to the carnival atmosphere.

Fitch mocked Björn while wearing a green and gold jester costume with bells attached to the pointy ends of his hat and shoes. *'What possesses a grown man to dress like that?' I bet he's regretting his life choices. He should have gone to college.'*

Who are you to talk? He's the sales rep for Optimal Organic Produce. That's his job. What's your excuse?

The bear marched around the breakfast buffet playing a lute and promoting his company's offerings. "Gluten-free scones, made with Outstanding Original Products GF flour, protein assets, and no gluten debits. Clotted cream and jam, or jam and clotted cream. Your choice."

Fitch followed, keeping time with a tambourine. *'Does he work for Optimal Organic Produce or Outstanding Original Products?'*

No idea. He never gets the name straight. The kids ignore the question and call him Mr. OOP.

"Mornin, Mr. Szilard." Principal Golding's long white braid wrapped around her head like a crown. Her green dress had a bold pattern of cats and coffee cups. I joined her at a tiny table reminiscent of a Rive Droite café in Paris. A bubble of herbal tea fragrance, cinnamon, ginger, and sweet jasmine, surrounded her. She had a scone with a jam dollop atop the clotted cream. "Have you eaten?" she asked like a good host.

"Yes," I replied. "After Persey uncovered flash drive remnants, I returned home to Dahl and a quick first breakfast: granola with sliced bananas and cream, a toasted bagel with horseradish-dill schmear, and fried eggs, over easy, with Havarti cheese."

Fitch waved his green-and-gold checkered napkin, holding up two fingers.

With that cue, my mouth salivated like Pavlov's dogs. "But...it's time for second breakfast."

"I'll save you a seat," she said.

The Stony High Lunch Ladies, a team of two young Hispanic women, Yasmine and Juana, and an elderly Asian man, Abbu, wore aprons embroidered with their names and the Bruin Bistro logo. They replaced empty serving dishes on the buffet tables adorned with green tablecloths and fresh marigolds. They took turns working the antique espresso machine, a steampunk cross between a samovar and a calliope. Its gold plaque said WE LOVE OUR LUNCH LADIES.

Mr. OOP offered, "Brownies, better than edibles. Freshly made with Old-fashioned Organic Preparations fair-trade chocolate."

"Thanks. I'll take two." I returned to Mrs. Golding with a double cappuccino, brownies, and a scone, heaping my cream atop a thin jam veneer.

Mr. OOP moved through the café serving baklava. "Original Organic Provisions only sells ethical honey and farm-to-table pistachios—the protein with the smallest carbon footprint."

"I'll take two, thank you."

"Vegan or regular?"

"Vegan? I've never heard of vegan honey," I challenged Mr. OOP.

He mumbled. "Okay, butter or no butter."

I didn't mean to embarrass him. I cheerfully said, "I'll take one of each."

He placed the dripping-with-non-vegan-honey morsels on my plate and handed me a bamboo fork. "Would you like peanut butter with those?"

I'd never had peanut butter with baklava. "Yes, please."

I took a bite and gave Mr. OOP a wide-eyed smile.

The Stony High principal laughed at my plate. "Zarand, I see why Vicki says you have a teenager's metabolism."

I took a sip of my coffee and started on my scone. "You know what they say. Working with kids keeps you young."

A Kwolek buzzed our table.

I resisted the urge to swat it. "What's that thing doing here? Is Stony Estancia Makers Guild recruiting?"

Mrs. Golding sat up straight. "Oh yes. They offer internships. My students get to work with AI, the future."

"Really? A waste of time. AI is a fad, a high-tech Beanie Baby, a Y2K sequel. What use is that flying gadget?"

The principal counted on her fingers. "First, just-in-time delivery. Second, deployable CCTV for law enforcement. Third, search and rescue for disasters and combat. Finally, entertainment, she's cute. Billion-dollar markets."

"Wow, Beanie Babies were cute, and where are they now? Does Dr. T pay you?"

"No. Of course, I'm not paid. I've seen those genius quadcopters first-hand. We have a public-private partnership. The quadcopters work back-of-house in the Bruin Bistro. Kwoleks can be heard saying, "Above," instead of "Behind," as they scurry around delivering ingredients."

I challenged her, "I have student safety concerns. How do Kwoleks improve education? I didn't know they were in our school."

Mrs. Golding bristled. "Why should you? You're a substitute teacher. All you need is today's lesson plan."

I didn't want to argue. "Sorry, not my concern."

"That's right," she said with more force than I expected. "You need to keep your distance. I've heard rumors that you get too close to those students. Watch yourself."

Fitch shook his finger at me. 'That's telling you.'

She waved to a group of twenty-somethings on the library stairs. "I gave the Makers Guild that prime location. It's hard to compete with that helicopter and Peggy Mutai's mobile hospital."

"Why give them special treatment?"

She gave me a sly smile. "Full disclosure. I'm invested in Dr. Telkes' startup. She's close to her IPO. When Makers Guild goes public, I'm leasing them naming rights to the Bruin Bistro. How does Makers Guild Gourmet Grill sound? From there, we'll franchise the concept. Dr. T says it's a billion-dollar market."

'Conflict of interest,' shouted Fitch. He changed into a polyester uniform and said, 'Would you like fries with your education?'

I pressed her, "Where are the college recruiters?"

"We have them," she said with a pout, pointing across the courtyard beyond the Bruin Bistro.

'IPO fever.' Fitch shook his head. 'I never expected money to corrupt Stony Estancia.'

I'll keep an eye on her.

'No, you won't. If you upset her, you're outta here, and then, who will support your grandkids?'

A man wearing a green puffer jacket and skinny jeans catapulted himself onto the stage and grabbed the microphone. "Good morning, guys, gals, and non-binary pals. I'm Walter Fisher, Wally, the college recruiter, here to remind you that all careers start with college." He removed his jacket. His T-shirt said, COLLEGE OF HARD KNOCKS. "For example, I have a BFA in creative writing. I'm a barista by day and a stand-up comedian at night. My career wouldn't be possible without college."

The students ignored Wally, collected freebies, tried out the Marine copter, and role-played at the mobile first-aid facility.

Wally did a shim sham, showing off his green and gold patent leather shoes. His taps echoed off the buildings surrounding the courtyard.

The audience acknowledged him with ironic laughter.

'*Where did we get this guy?*' Fitch scoffed.

"Here are some college jokes. Never date an apostrophe. They're possessive."

The crowd rewarded this with a few guffaws, and Mr. OOP played a rimshot on his cymbals.

A woman, sporting a short red haircut and wearing an orange pantsuit, bounded onto the stage.

Wally clapped his hands and shouted, "How about a round of Stony High applause for Sandy?"

The crowd cheered.

Sandy took the microphone. "I'm his better half with better jokes. How many mystery writers does it take to change a light bulb? Two. One to screw the bulb almost in, and the other to give it a surprise twist at the end."

Fitch thought that was hilarious.

Mr. and Mrs. Fisher exchanged good-natured banter. The double act played better than Wally's solo one.

A pop.

Sandy dropped to the floor.

It was a gunshot, a rifle.

The crowd looked around, but my grandkids didn't recognize the sound.

My heart responded to the infusion of adrenaline. I didn't breathe as my subconscious processed the sounds.

I tracked them to the library roof. Smoke. Someone dressed in black. Two more pops.

This time, everyone recognized the noise and evacuated the open courtyard.

When I turned back to the library, there was nothing.

Wally grabbed his chest. "I've been hit." He fell to the stage and his wife hugged him.

The Marine helicopter headed for the library. Three Kwoleks followed it like kittens trailing after their mother. The SWAT armored personnel carrier took up the rear.

The bewildered crowd pointed to the helicopter. Back on the stage, Wally's wife keened, "No. No!"

The public address system announced, "Active shooter."

I'd drilled for this but never expected it to happen. As a substitute teacher, my primary responsibility was the students, implementing the "Run, Hide, Fight" protocol.

I shouted, "Evacuation," and led my students up the hill to the far side of the football field.

From that safe perch, I reviewed the situation. Someone shot Wally from the library. Person or persons unknown were being pursued by the U.S. Marines, the Stony Estancia SWAT team, and the Makers Guild's quadcopters. Wally lay on the stage in the arms of his distraught wife.

Peggy Mutai's paramedics hurried to Wally, carrying oxygen, monitors, and a stretcher.

César panned his camera to record the action. *Stony Estancia Surfs* posted: #GunViolence. Shots fired at Stony High Career Day. Click here for updates.

The paramedics carried Wally to their mobile hospital while he whimpered, "I'm hit. I'm hurt. Am I going to die?"

Fitch, being imaginary, was unthreatened. *'Congrats, buddy. You finally have a murder.'*

9. ASSASSINATION

Vicki put her hand up to block me at the mobile hospital entrance. I stopped, but my eyes continued into the converted bookmobile. Wally lay on the first treatment bed, surrounded by Lieutenant Peggy Mutai and two EMTs. One EMT inserted an IV drip in the back of Wally's hand, while the other wrapped his arm with a blood pressure cuff. Peggy covered his mouth and nose with a clear plastic oxygen mask.

Officer Tsui stood beside Wally's wife, who was resting on the farthest bed. They were ignoring Wally, engaged in a pleasant chat. She had calmed down, no longer hysterical. I wondered if she'd been sedated. The third paramedic sat in the driver's seat, typing on a computer.

Vicki hugged me. "You're on door duty. Don't let anyone in."

I kissed her. "Yes, dear. No problem."

I stood with my legs spread and arms crossed. When Leticia and César approached, "Press coming through...exercising their First Amendment rights," I held up my palm. "Stop, the Constitution just gets you so far. You must report from outside."

Like a football halfback, she faked to the left and reversed to the right, but like a good defensive end, I grabbed her microphone to block her.

The only one who got past me was Fitch, dressed as a paramedic. *'Hey, big shot detective,'* he mocked me, *'Wally was shot center mass. Why was there no blood?'*

I noticed that. Did you see his wife? She recovered quickly from the shock. She was pretending.

'Sure was. No blood. He was never in danger.'

Wally was in tears. He tore off his oxygen mask. "Give me something for my pain. I feel like I've been hit by an NFL defensive line."

"We have aspirin, acetaminophen, ibuprofen, and some paracetamol left over from our trip to aid the Fireys in

Australia. Name your poison." Peggy picked up four bottles from a shelf labeled, COZY MYSTERIES.

'Paracetamol, acetaminophen, gobbledygook, mumbo jumbo. They're all the same.' Fitch ridiculed the EMTs.

"Didn't you hear me? I'm in real pain. I need something stronger," Wally sobbed.

"Sorry. For events like Career Day, where lookie-loos are wandering through the place unsupervised, we leave morphine, other opiates, controlled substances, and prescriptions back at the firehouse where they're secure."

Wally's wife walked over. "Okay. Give him as many ibuprofens as you can."

Peggy put four white tablets in his hand. His wife held up his head and placed a water glass against his lips. He threw the pills into his mouth and swallowed them in one go.

Watching Wally take those pills made me hungry. Fortunately, Mr. OOP appeared. I let him in, accompanied by Principal Golding.

Reporters César and Leticia were unhappy to be the only ones locked out. My *Surf SE* app notified me, COVER-UP AT STONY HIGH. PRESS REFUSED ACCESS TO ASSASSINATION VICTIM.

"Late to the party but bearing gifts. Compliments of Organic Ocean Pirates." Mr. OOP had coffee and cookies. "An international selection. Macarons, macaroons, pizzelles, hamantaschen, and Scotch fingers."

Everyone accepted a coffee, but the cookies sat untouched.

A paramedic called out. "122 over 78. Heart rate 86."

'Those are healthy numbers, nothing like someone who's been shot.' Fitch observed. *'What's going on here?'*

Peggy cut off Wally's T-shirt. Beneath it was a black bulletproof vest. "I see," she exclaimed as she extracted a ceramic plate. "Level III, high-powered rifle safe." She removed the vest and handed it to Vicki. "Evidence."

'Did you see that piece of paper fall when she removed the plate?' Fitch whispered.

Why are you whispering? I kidded him while I hid the card under my foot.

Peggy palpated Wally's chest.

He flinched. "Gentle. That hurts!"

"Don't be a baby. Just fractured ribs." She shouted to the paramedic typing on the computer. "Get him an ice pack."

Vicki examined the vest, taking pictures of bullet holes. "Good thing you were wearing this." She considered that for a minute. "Why were you wearing a bulletproof vest to Stony High Career Day?"

Wally's wife spoke first. "Let him rest. I can explain."

Vicki and I led her to the back of the converted bookmobile. "Thank you. Can you enlighten us, Mrs. Fisher?"

"No need for such formality. Please call me Sandy, short for Cassandra. Everyone does." She took a couple of pizzelles from Mr. OOP.

Vicki helped herself to a hamantaschen. "Why was he wearing that vest?"

"College recruiting is dangerous."

Fitch was incredulous. *'What's the world coming to?'*

"His job is to sell the college." Sandy stood tall. "He's good at it. After listening to him, everyone's excited to attend the school, but his cheerleading gets misinterpreted. The families mistake his enthusiasm for an admission guarantee."

Vicki nodded. "What happens when they don't get accepted?"

"They get angry. You wouldn't believe the threats. Emails. Texts. Memes with decapitated mascot plushies. He's always cautious at big events like these."

When Sandy returned to her husband's side, I reviewed the detective's MMO: means, motive, and opportunity. The means (rifle) and opportunity (Career Day) were obvious. Sandy gave me the motive. My suspects were students who were denied admission. I turned to her. "Give me the list of those unlucky applicants."

Mrs. Fisher shook her head. "We have nothing to do with admissions. We don't know who applied, who was accepted, or who was rejected."

'Nothing is easy. That list would have helped, but it doesn't exist.' Fitch offered me a warm cup of tea and a sympathetic arm.

"No problem." Mrs. Golding had been listening to our conversation. "Our guidance counselors keep a record of applications and acceptances. I'll email you the list, though I suspect the unhappy applicants came from another school. No one turns down Stony High students."

Officer Tsui served himself coffee and pastel-colored macarons before giving his report. "The shooter has disappeared. The Marines checked the rooftops, and the police searched the classrooms."

Fitch dressed as a SWAT squad member. *'No shooter apprehended. It's never easy.'*

Vicki asked Mrs. Golding, "It's your school. Do you want to continue Career Day?"

The principal didn't hesitate. "It takes more than this to frighten the Stony High Bruins." She flexed her muscles, in case anyone had forgotten her side hustle as a stunt woman in superhero movies. "However, I will close the school today, and we'll continue Career Day tomorrow."

Mr. OOP led the crowd outside. He offered the reporters coffee and cookies.

They were grateful for the attention after being refused access. César grabbed a handful of Scotch fingers. Tish took a coconut macaroon. She pointed her microphone at the principal while César filmed. "Do you have anything you'd like to say to the community?"

"Student safety is the number one priority at Stony High." She crossed her arms, showing off her toned and sculpted biceps. "Don't forget our Halloween Dance—right here in the courtyard—open to all—8:00 after tomorrow's delayed Career Day. Dress for success. Wear a costume depicting your dream job."

Leticia pointed her microphone at Mr. OOP, in his green mascot costume. "Is this your dream job?"

"I've had several. After completing my doctorate, my dream job was to become a biochemist. My lab developed bacteria to decompose microplastics—"

Fitch stretched and yawned. *'Boring.'*

"Interesting." Tish cut him off. "Should we call you Dr. OOP?"

"Mr. OOP is fine. Thank you"

I pocketed the piece of paper from Wally's bulletproof vest. "Vee, I need to show you what I found. Dinner at my place tonight?"

"Sure. Are your sheets clean?"

"I'll change them before you arrive."

I didn't have time to prepare dinner for Vicki from scratch. Fortunately, I had leftovers from the Firehouse Barbecue, Four Rivers Chinese restaurant, and Epicurean Eats Greek restaurant. Vicki heated her moussaka in the microwave and accompanied it with pita bread and hummus. I chose ribs and hushpuppies. Dahl selected the head from a whole steamed sea bass.

I showed Vicki the card from Wally's vest. "Do you recognize this?" It had two stylized wings connected by a pair of interlocking M's, with the words Minerva's Mission.

Vicki made a face. "They're a secret group claiming to recover missing and abducted children." Vicki put the card in an evidence bag. "I'll have forensics check it out."

"Minerva's Mission reminds me of Dr. Ruth Doyle from the Women in STEM Symposium. Do you think her name was changed when she was abducted?"

Vicki dipped her pita bread in a bowl of hummus. "A name change is an interesting path to explore. Transgender people also discard their deadnames and take new names and pronouns."

"Dr. Doyle didn't look like a transgender woman to me."

Vicki frowned. "You have a lot to learn."

Fitch hugged Finch, his anima, the manifestation of his feminine side. *'What makes you think you can tell? Gender is about much more than appearance. Did you realize that I was nonbinary?'*

I needed to think about this gender stuff. I went back to basics. "We have a shooter, graffiti, and smashed USB sticks. This feels like a major crime wave."

"I don't think so, Zee." Vicki looked in the refrigerator. "What do you have for dessert?"

I ignore the dessert question. I was thinking of something else after dinner. "Why isn't this a Stony Estancia crime wave?"

"Don't you recall what you taught me years ago as a new Police Academy graduate?"

"Oh yes. Occam's Razor. The simplest explanation is the best."

She smiled. "This isn't a crime wave. It's one crime that we don't understand. We need to fit the pieces together."

"Something else for me to think about."

"You're retired. You have plenty of time."

I ate another hushpuppy coated in honey. "I'm worried about empty seats at my *Education: A Profession for the Future* presentation tomorrow."

"Nothing you can do about that." She ate a forkful of moussaka. "You know what I say?"

"Yes. Don't pay the toll until you get to the bridge."

'With this excitement, I doubt anyone will attend your boring tutorial.' Fitch's bare chest showed off his perfect pecs covered with geometric blackwork ink, recognizing his Polynesian heritage.

Vicki cleared the table. "Do you know what I'm thinking about?"

"Where's the shooter?" I guessed.

"No." She put her arm around my waist. "The clean sheets you promised."

11. Szilard's Sleuths

The next morning, I welcomed my honorary grandkids with fierce "Stony High Bruin" bear hugs. Anything less was awkward and embarrassing. Hugs improved learning and discipline.

My concerns about an empty classroom disappeared. After all the seats were full, more students continued to arrive. I couldn't stop smiling. "Plenty of room. Stand anywhere."

"Mornin, Bruins, you're the educators to inspire the next generation and save the planet." I straightened the collar on my shirt, ran my fingers through my long gray hair, tightened the band holding my ponytail, and wrote "Mr. S" on the whiteboard. That pause worked like a charm. The room was silent. I had everyone's attention. Teacher's Nirvana. "Welcome to *Education: A Profession for the Future*. Today we're going to talk about teaching, a rewarding and honored career, the world's oldest profession."

A screen lowered from the ceiling, and Kwolek projected an image of a cave with aurochs painted on the wall. Cave children sat around and copied the art on flat rocks with charcoal sticks.

"Perfect hallucination," I said, giving Kwolek a thumbs up.

My students applauded.

'That winged widget is your friend now?' Fitch stood in the corner, stuck out his chin, and turned a jealous shade of green.

Not really, my friend Fitch. I love you the best.

While I had the class's attention, I went into my pitch. "Teaching is what separates us from the animals. We make progress by passing knowledge from one generation to the next."

A girl with straight blonde hair stood up, over six feet tall. She wore a peasant blouse with blue embroidered flowers and a long, flowy skirt. When her skirt hem fluttered and let out a loud meow, I pointed to her, "Do you have a question?"

She looked down and said sotto voce, "Quiet, Clouseau," before asking, "What about those Japanese macaques that teach their young to wash their food?"

Kwolek projected a cartoon of monkeys on the beach taking notes while their teacher demonstrated washing sweet potatoes in the surf.

A teen wearing a lavender headscarf didn't wait for me to call on her. She shouted out, "What about those bees that teach the others where to find nectar?"

Kwolek projected a classroom with row upon row of cartoon bees, as far as the eye could see, like CGI armies, sitting at tiny desks watching their teacher dance around a huge map.

A student typing on a laptop with one hand and tapping on his phone with the other added, "Bee GPS for the win."

The class responded, "Go Moe."

Those generated AI graphics derailed my lecture. I'd lost them. As a last resort, I stood silent with my arms crossed.

The girl with long blonde hair raised her hand.

I went over to her desk. "What's your name?"

She stood up.

'She uses her height to her advantage. I see a bright future for her.' Fitch stood beside her, stretching himself to match her stature.

I looked directly into her blue eyes.

She didn't turn away. "I'm Emily, Emily Milhone." She untangled a flame-point Siamese from her long skirt and held it against her cheek. Their eyes matched. "This is Clouseau."

Clouseau meowed.

"What would you like to say?"

"We're not interested in becoming teachers. I'm going to be President, but you can't help with that."

Around the room, students nodded in support.

'You're not much of a detective. You misread the entire room.' Fitch giggled.

The Career Day announcement listed my tutorial as *Education: A Profession for the Future.* Why was the room packed if they weren't interested in teaching?

'Do you need my help?' Fitch taunted, always happy to celebrate my difficulties.

Yes, please, I confessed.

'They're here to learn about your preretirement expertise,' he announced, cleaning his calabash pipe.

I didn't believe Fitch, but to humor him, I asked, "You want to be detectives?"

The group responded with whoops and applause.

"Don't you want to be doctors, veterinarians, lawyers, or a CEO like Dr. Telkes of the Makers Guild, or President like Emily?"

When they gave me that teen stare that meant, *Okay, Boomer, we don't have the time to explain this to you,* I tried again. "Are you afraid that those professions with be automated by AI and only detectives will have jobs?"

They found that very funny.

'Clueless much? Stony Estancia is a city of privilege. Nobody worries about paying bills or being employed.' Fitch pulled out his wallet and fanned his credit cards.

Teenagers can be frustrating. I stood silent.

The boy with a shaved head and a full beard did a relevé before saying, "I'm Louis Rawlins." He shook my hand. "We're here for Goleta Hardcastle."

I fell back on my go-to interrogation technique—silence.

The girl with the lavender headscarf spoke up, "Leeta, that's what we call her, was an excellent student, A's, honors classes, AP Physics, AP Mandarin, Astronomy Club president—"

The Siamese cat yowled, interrupting the girl wearing a headscarf. Emily shushed her cat and whispered to the girl, "That's enough, Hafsa. He gets it."

Hafsa wasn't daunted, "I haven't gotten to the most crucial point." She paused. Everyone waited. "Leeta disappeared."

"Have you gone to the police?"

They gave me that Okay-Boomer stare.

'Oh no. Why haven't they gone to the police?' Fitch stood beneath a freeway sign. AMBER ALERT.

Don't panic, Fitch. No one issues an alert for a tardy high school student.

'This is Stony High. If your grandkids say Goleta's missing, she's missing.' Fitch's freeway sign flashed.

I checked my *Surf SE* app. There was nothing. *Reporter Tish is a clairvoyant. A missing student was a click-worthy topic. Why was the omniscient Surf silent?*

I wasn't ready to believe any of this. "When did you see her last?"

"In the courtyard, Mr. OOP was handing out chocolate baklava for breakfast," Moe said.

'Chocolate baklava,' Finch licked her lips, wearing a Swiss dirndl. *'What a delicious combination.'*

The timeline is important for a missing person case. "She wasn't tardy. You saw her today. When did she disappear?"

Louis spoke, "During the confusion, when we gathered around the espresso machine. We–"

Hafsa cut him off. "She disappeared, like aliens had beamed her up."

Fitch covered his mouth to muffle his laughter. *'They're messing with you.'*

Not my grandkids.

"Are you sure she's missing? She's only been gone an hour."

They gave me another of those you're-clueless, okay-boomer stares.

I switched to information-gathering mode. "I see. What do you want to do? How can I help?"

Emily sauntered to the front. Louis and Hafsa went to the doors, checked that no one was outside, locked them, and stood guard.

Moe went into the teacher's area behind the classroom and returned carrying a box.

Fitch put on his body armor. *'I fear what's coming next.'*

Silly Fitch. This is Stony Estancia.

Emily opened the carton and pulled out a T-shirt. It was Bruin green and printed with Björn, the Stony High bear, wearing a deerstalker hat and looking through a magnifying glass. It said, "Sleuth Club." She gave me the sweetest smile. "Will you sponsor us? Szilard's Sleuths?" She handed me the shirt.

'Miss Hardcastle disappeared this morning. How did they have time to print T-shirts?' Fitch scratched his head.

I'm sure there's a place in town that can rapidly print a box of shirts.

"Are you serious, Emily? I'm a substitute. I can't be a club sponsor. You need to recruit a regular teacher."

The room responded, "We want you."

I was complimented.

Moe moved close to me. "Besides, this won't be an official school activity."

My grandkids chanted, "Mr. S! Mr. S."

She tossed the shirt to me. I put it on. "I'd be honored to advise The Sleuth Club."

We tossed shirts to the excited students until we ran out.

"Oops. You don't have enough shirts."

"No problem," Emily gave me a you-underestimate-us grin. "Moe, can you bring the rest?"

He went into the teacher's workroom and returned pushing a hand truck stacked high with boxes.

"Wow! Now you have too many."

Emily's you-underestimate-us grin widened. "There are more Szilard's Sleuths than are dreamt of in your philosophy."

Fitch shook his head. *'I repeat my objection. How did they have time to print those T-shirts?'*

I didn't worry about Fitch. I had a room full of potential detectives who wanted to learn...from me. "Okay. I'll teach you to be investigators."

'Forget about those hugs. This is what Mrs. Golding meant when she said you were too close to them.' Fitch wore a judge's robe and banged his gavel, *'Guilty.'*

As I walked around the room, I could feel every pair of eyes tracking me. I was in a teacher's Nirvana. "Are you prepared to be apprentices?"

My trainees smiled and nodded. I had the perfect assignment for them. "Find a partner and discover one new fact about Goleta. Uncover her secrets. Who does she talk to? Her favorite foods. What does she dream about?"

The room buzzed with activity. My Career Day presentation was a success. I was a brilliant teacher.

'Don't get complacent. They may be engaged now, but such a trivial assignment won't hold their attention long,' scoffed Fitch.

I'm getting started, I retorted with confidence. To my sleuths, I said, "Contact me whenever you uncover something. I will be your supervising detective."

Fitch was aghast. *'Are you crazy? You're volunteering to mentor a room full of teenagers.'*

'No problem.'

Just to be safe, I added, "Good investigators are self-starters. Here is your first lesson: It's easier to ask forgiveness than permission. Act first. Take the initiative."

In their enthusiasm, they forgot their Stony High manners. Everyone spoke at once. "Do we need reports?" "Will we be graded?"

Emily stood up, holding Clouseau. "This isn't an official school activity. We need to keep a low profile."

'Not much of a low profile,' Fitch put on a Sleuth Club shirt and grabbed one for Finch.

Moe spoke in a whisper. "We're using an electronic evidence board, end-to-end encrypted. Post everything there."

"Can we submit stuff to the forensic lab at the Stony Estancia Police Department?" "DNA for PCR testing?" "Trace evidence for the mass spectrometer."

Emily answered, "That's a big nope."

Moe said, "What part of low profile didn't you understand?"

I added, "Lesson two: Good detectives don't attract attention."

"What about guns? Do we get guns? Body armor?" Louis asked.

'Body armor?' Fitch marched around in chain mail and a jousting helmet. *'How did they hear about Wally?'*

Forget Wally. I'm on to the next case.

Sponsoring an unofficial club was no worse than hugging, but arming them would be over the line. "This is Stony Estancia. No guns. No weapons of any kind."

"Do we have to work with a partner?" Emily asked.

"Yes. Lesson three: The lone investigator is a myth."

"Mr. S, how do we contact you?" Hafsa demanded.

I took out my phone and prepared to share my information.

'Don't do it. It's a trap,' gasped Fitch, fighting off an imaginary opponent with a lightsaber.

Fooled you, I replied to Fitch with a grin.

"You're investigators. Figure out how to contact me. This is where you'll learn lesson four: Evidence is everywhere."

The room burst alive. My most successful Career Day presentation ever. They were engaged. Critical thinking. Problem solving. Creativity. Decision making. This assignment ticked all the boxes. I was destined for Teacher of the Year.

That was the end of my class. My students, trainees, and deputies ran out.

Fitch grinned. *'You released a teenage mob to meddle in a... I don't know... What happened to Goleta? Vicki isn't going to be happy with adolescent sleuths intruding on something that isn't a real case.'*

How hard can it be to find Goleta? She's only been missing for an hour.

12. TRACE EVIDENCE

Vicki joined me as Szilard's Sleuths dispersed to investigate their missing classmate. Together, Vicki and I straightened the chairs and erased the whiteboard.

She hugged me out of sight of the open door. "How'd your tutorial go?" she asked.

The earthy scent of green tea shampoo tickled my nose as I pressed my cheek against her hair. "You were right. It was standing room only. They loved my presentation. Teacher's Nirvana. Better than my wildest dreams."

'Too good to be true,' chortled Fitch, cross-dressed as The Pythia, Oracle of Delphi, wearing white robes and a veil. *'I foresee disappointment.'*

Fitch's negative attitude made me appreciate Vicki. I didn't want her to think I took her for granted. "I apologize for leaving you while Coroner Persey and I went off to breakfast."

"That was long ago, I forgot all about it. It's my job to be with the forensics team. I get better results if I stay with them. The written report leaves out important nuances."

"Did you find anything interesting?"

"Follow me and I'll show you," she said with an inviting smile.

She waved to Dr. Telkes, holding court on the library stairs. Students vying for internships surrounded the CEO. Vicki pointed. "Isn't that man with Dr. T, Wally, the college recruiter, who was shot?"

'They make an odd couple. Computer scientist and comedian. What could they possibly have to talk about?' Fitch blathered on with his irrelevant commentary.

We hiked past the library and through the memorial garden commemorating Tiff the Tutor.

'Tiff the Tutor was murdered in The Library Club. Why are you mentioning her?' Fitch reprimanded me.

We sat up the hill in the same place as that first night. "Are you hungry, Vee?" I didn't wait for a response. "This is to apologize for leaving you without breakfast this morning." I laid out a sandwich assortment on a green-and-gold checkered cloth from my bottomless backpack: roast beef on sourdough, pastrami on dark rye, sliced turkey and Emmentaler on biscuits, roasted veggies on croissants, and the classic peanut butter and strawberry jam on white bread. My pastrami on rye could compete with any deli in NYC.

For condiments, I had mayo made with my secret ingredient (pureed anchovies), dark mustard from the Lower East Side, NYC, banana ketchup from Manila, roasted garlic and basil aioli, and extra virgin olive oil, or EVOO, as the cool kids called it. Plus kosher dill pickles to complement the pastrami.

Vicki helped herself to German potato salad and sarsaparilla with her turkey. "I'm disappointed, Zee. Where's my cranberry sauce?"

"Sorry. My backpack can't hold everything."

'Don't blame your backpack. You didn't think of it.' Fitch wore his green-and-gold checkered napkin.

I thought of it. Jellied cranberry sauce. Whole Berry. Orange cranberry relish. Orange lime. Orange bourbon. Cranberry chutney. With all those choices, I forgot to choose any of them.

I selected a meatless lunch for myself—roasted veggies on a croissant and a green salad dressed with vinegar and EVOO—washed down with matcha tea.

Vicki pointed to the garden, now deserted—the crime scene tape was gone. "What do you see?"

"Graffiti Abatement has cleaned the bricks, and the flower beds are waiting for Mr. Mbacke."

"Exactly. Leave no traces. The crime scene investigators' motto."

Her smile told me that the CSIs had found something. "I'm all ears. Tell me your discovery."

Vicki bit into her turkey sandwich. "I miss the cranberries."

Fitch jiggled a plate of cranberry jelly and thumbed his nose at me.

Even though we were alone on the hill, Vicki moved closer and spoke quietly. "After examining Tsui's evidence bag of data chips, the crime scene techs decided to screen the dirt."

"And?" I asked in anticipation, trying to speed up her reveal.

"Tsui missed the most important evidence."

"Really? The data chips were a good find."

"Maybe—" She drank her sarsaparilla. "Did you wonder what those data chips were doing in Mr. Mbacke's flower bed?"

'You're getting old. Some detective you are. Why didn't you consider that?' Fitch mocked me wearing a deerstalker's hat and puffing on his calabash pipe.

Vicki opened her black satchel embossed with the Stony Estancia emblem and displayed a large evidence bag. "What do you see?"

"Plastic. Splinters and shards. It looks like trash."

"To you..."

I waited patiently.

"They spread them out on a pizza box and took lots of pictures."

"Are you serious? A pizza box? Won't that contaminate the evidence?"

Vicki kissed my nose. "I love you, but you're retired and out of touch." She showed me a photo. "This evidence box looks like a pizza box, but it doesn't compromise the evidence, plus it has a chain of custody log and a seal to prevent tampering."

"Wow, overkill. I like low-tech solutions. Back in my day, a clean pizza box would have worked."

"Forensic tests are more sensitive today. We need to be careful."

"What did they do with the plastic trash pictures?"

"They shook the box and took more, repeating that several times." She took a bite of her sandwich. "Promise me you'll have cranberry sauce next time. Turkey isn't the same without it."

"I promise."

"All the image files were given to an AI program, and it put them together like a 3-D jigsaw puzzle."

"Yes? Yes. What did it reveal?"

Vicki tapped her phone. "This is a virtual reconstruction."

Her screen displayed a parquet jewelry box beside a four-by-four array of wooden USB memory sticks.

It was hard to believe that a computer put those shards and splinters together. "Those USB sticks look identical. Did the reconstruction take a long time?"

'Maybe AI isn't as useless as I thought.' Fitch's mouth was stuck open.

Vickie extolled the virtues of forensic AI. "The first attempts failed, but Vinnie Purcell had some connections to a large data center in Northern Virginia. The USB sticks took the most time because the fine-grained hardwoods, walnut, maple, and cherry, were hard to tell apart."

I admired the image. "Those must have been beautiful before Mr. Mbacke's jackhammer turned the box and its contents into mush." I was ready to believe anything. "Did the AI identify any suspects?"

Vicki proudly reported, "The program found some fingerprints, but they weren't in our database. Dead end, but an interesting one."

I knew what happened. "The data was buried at the school because it was too dangerous to keep close by, a desperate measure taken by a frightened person."

"There you go, making up stories from the tiniest bit of evidence. You're as bad as an AI."

"You can mock me, but I will be vindicated when my buddy Vinnie decrypts the data. There's a gang operating in Stony Estancia, and they're willing to kill to protect whatever was in that box."

Vicki chuckled, "That's a big leap. You're thinking more like a writer than a detective."

'A B-list novelist, at that,' Fitch walked through the hallowed stacks at the Bodleian Library and taunted me, *'Your books will never end up here.'*

Stony Estancia Surfs posted: #PROTECTIONRACKET IN OUR CITY. IS THIS THE END OF SUBURBAN PARADISE?

'What does that omniscient reporter know?' Fitch removed his deerstalker hat and scratched his head.

"I'm not thinking like a writer. If I were, I would ignore the data chips. The better story is about Goleta. My grandkids are concerned. She's missing."

'Oops. They wanted that kept under wraps,' Fitch wagged his finger at me.

Vicki asked, "Is that Goleta, the Astronomy Club president, or Goleta Hardcastle?"

"Yes, they're the same." I played it cool. I didn't want to make things worse by alarming Vicki. "She's tardy." My heart raced. I didn't have the whole story. What were Szilard's Sleuths hiding?

Fitch wore his Sleuth Club T-shirt. *'What makes you think they're not telling you everything?'*

They're teenagers. I'm an adult. I hadn't let Goleta's full name slip. Vicki knew more than she was letting on. "How do you know Goleta Hardcastle?"

Vicki ate a forkful of potato salad. "We've been following Leeta's family. Their daughter has a history of running away." She followed a bite of dry turkey with a gulp of sarsaparilla. "Her mom assured us there was nothing to worry about. She told us about Leeta's visits to an aunt (her sister) in Quincy, California, and an uncle in Edina, Minnesota. Her dad added that the uncle was his half-brother. He also said, 'We raised her right, she's going to a women's college in Massachusetts and is engaged to be married upon graduation.'"

'An arranged marriage?' Finch gasped. *'I don't blame her for running away.'* Fitch marched arm-in-arm with Finch and the suffragettes.

We don't know that she ran away.

Vicki wiped her lips and gave me a light kiss. "You taught me this. The longer someone rambles on, the greater the chance they're prevaricating. The Hardcastles' story was too long, and there were too many details. They're hiding something."

"What do you think it is?"

Vicki whispered. "You may think Leeta's tardy, but the evidence points to missing. Mrs. Hardcastle is keeping a low profile. She doesn't want to admit there are problems." Vicki took a bite of her turkey sandwich with a long drink and threw away the rest. "Other students have disappeared. Unsolved mysteries. Stony Estancia isn't as idyllic as you imagine. Robert Drew. Xanthia Kaldis. Open cases."

"I've never heard of them."

She held her breath for an instant, finger-combed her hair, and tucked it behind her ears. With her hand over her mouth, she revealed, "The investigations have been on a strict need-to-know basis. We're protecting Stony Estancia's reputation. César and Leticia are cooperating."

How was Goleta going to be found if the Sleuth Club and Stony Estancia Police refused to work together? Building on this dilemma, I had a happy thought. What if she doesn't want to be found?

Before I responded to Vicki, my phone vibrated.

HAFSA: HELP [PLEADING FACE].

I tapped a reply, **MR S:** WHERE R U.

HAFSA: GOLDINGS OFFICE [PERSEVERING FACE].

I tapped "omw" and autocorrect sent, **MR S:** ON MY WAY!

HAFSA: KK NO RUSH [RELIEVED FACE].

Hafsa texted, "No rush." I covered up my connection with her and the Sleuth Club by stopping at the Bruin Bistro for a quick first lunch. A Reuben sandwich with kettle-cooked chips on the side, and a chat with Dr. Chandrasekhar, my favorite Physics teacher, who was on cafeteria duty.

"Tell me, Chandra, you're one of the old timers, what do you recall about missing students at Stony High? Robert Drew? Xanthia Kaldis?"

He held an aloo puri, literally potato and fried bread. "I don't count Xanthia Kaldis. She was taken to Greece by her father."

I ate a few crunchy chips. "Okay. Not a stranger abduction."

"Stranger abduction? Of course not. Those stories may get clicks and go viral, but they're rare." He dunked his aloo puri in raita yogurt and took another bite.

"You don't think Goleta was abducted?"

"Goleta, my super physics student? I'll bet she's a runaway. Most children missing from Stony High are."

'Wow. Are there enough to show a trend?' Fitch and Finch stood at the side of the road with a beat-up suitcase and their thumbs out.

"What about Robert Drew?" I asked.

"Robert Drew. Let me think." Chandra sipped some chai. "All I recall about him was that he was also brilliant. That may be the common thread. They were all excellent students."

"Excellent students. Good clue. I read a book about the government abducting intelligent children for a secret project. Could that be it?"

"I doubt it. You'll have to excuse me. Duty calls." Chandra went to settle an argument between two students discussing quantum computing.

After clearing my dishes, I proceeded across the courtyard. The sunny open space, dotted with trees, offered a brief respite from graffiti, missing students, and Wally.

As I passed the library and approached the admin building, Fitch pointed out, *'Finding three smart kids isn't remarkable. Stony High is full of excellent students. Bayesian analysis shows that three in a row is no big deal.'*

We stopped outside the admin building. Fitch said, 'Let's run an experiment. How hard is it to find three super smart people?" He pointed to Mohamed Manuelito and Officer Tsui, who were standing nearby. *'Moe, technological wizard, is number one.'*

I can play this game. There's number two. I pointed to a boy practicing skateboard tricks. *That's Jaxon Chee, he's going to the Olympics.*

Fitch performed an ollie. *'I don't think skateboarding qualifies as super smart.'*

Jax took out his phone, studied it while he walked to the top of library steps. Then he rolled off the top into a complicated combination.

Don't let his style fool you. He uses calculus and physics to invent new tricks, like the Jax 1260 jump.

'Okay. Jax is number two.' Fitch put on his chef's toque. He pointed across the courtyard to two women and a man wearing Bruin Bistro uniforms. *'Can you see the Lunch Ladies?'*

I nodded.

'Yasmine Macapagal has a PhD in Nutrition Science. Number three.'

I was glad that no one was stealing Stony High's brains and was ready to search in a different direction.

Mr. OOP stood at the door. "I have bran muffins—honey glazed, apple, blueberry, and banana—some with cream cheese icing—fresh from the oven and made with Only Organic Preparations wheat and oat bran."

I took a banana muffin with cream cheese. "Delicious. I have a difficult case. Do you have something to make me smarter?"

He gave me an ear-to-ear smile. "Throw away that muffin. I have a few specials made with fair-trade 100% cocoa from Organic Opportunity Pieces, high in epicatechin, which improves your cerebral balance sheet, increasing blood income while reducing brain deficits."

I took a big bite of the chocolate muffin and felt smarter. "You paint a pretty picture there with epicatechin and balance sheets, combining your previous life as a biochemist, and–"

Mr. OOP gave me a self-confident guffaw. "I've had an interesting life. When my son, Robby Junior, was born, I abandoned the long hours in the lab for something more regular. I switched careers to become a CPA."

"Wow! Was that a difficult transition?"

"Not for me. Statistics underlie biochemistry and accounting. Have you heard of Benford's Law?"

"No, but I'll look it up."

You do that,' Fitch wrote in his casebook with a red marker. *'Benford's Law is important in today's fake news world.'*

"Thank you, Dr. OOP. Please follow me and bring the whole tray. I'm headed for a big meeting."

'I doubt muffins are the solution to Hafsa's predicament,' Fitch added, carrying a jail-break toolbox with hacksaws, rope ladders, and crowbars.

I've never known a situation not improved with muffins, I retorted.

Jared Sendak, the substitute coordinator, met me at the door. "Welcome, Mr. S. How can I help you?"

"I have a meeting with Mrs. Golding." I lied.

He wore a purple and pink paisley shirt, loose and unbuttoned, over a tight black tee. "She has someone with her. Do you have an appointment?"

I didn't want to alert him to my rescue mission, and Hafsa had texted, No rush. "No problem. I can wait."

Mr. OOP took his cue. "I have organic bran muffins and free-trade double-chocolate ones."

Jared took a plain muffin lightly iced with cream cheese. After a big bite, he looked disappointed. I could see him looking around for something to drink. I apologized, "We forgot coffee."

'You have coffee in your backpack,' Fitch reminded me.

Not helpful. I have a plan.

After swallowing with difficulty, Jared volunteered, "There's coffee in the staff room. Wait here and I'll get a carafe."

I smiled. "Thank you. That would be great."

Fitch gave me a thumbs up. *'Clever.'*

As soon as Jared disappeared around the corner, I pulled on Mr. OOP's sleeve. "Hurry."

We barged into the principal's office without knocking.

I was surprised to see just Mrs. Golding and Hafsa.

On the weekends, the principal was a stuntwoman. Her office was equipped to keep her in shape—mats on the floor, a rowing machine, and a gym bench with a rack of free weights. Balance balls replaced chairs. Mrs. Golding sat on an orange ball behind a massage table that doubled as her desk. The only other furniture was a trophy cabinet. The walls were decorated with action and science fiction posters.

'Those are her movies.' Fitch's bare chest displayed his perfect pecs covered with geometric blackwork ink.

Hafsa, wearing her lavender headscarf, stood against the trophy cabinet. Mrs. Golding's Taurus statuette, Best Stunt by a Stunt Woman, held a place of pride. It was shown on the school's website, but its size surprised me—twice as tall and three times as massive as the more famous Oscar.

Mrs. Golding's lips curled inward until they disappeared. I'd interrupted a serious talk, but Hafsa's mouth widened into a half-smile.

'Ball's in your court,' Fitch said with glee, dressed in a black-and-white striped referee's shirt.

No problem. I strode across the mats to Mrs. Golding. "Muffin?"

Mr. OOP placed his tray over the massage table face cradle. Principal Golding didn't budge.

Years of interrogation taught me to wait. I helped myself to another chocolate special and sat on a yellow ball, spreading my legs for stability. The muffin was warm, and the savory 100% cocoa coated my tongue. I felt a burst of raw epicatechin-induced intelligence or a spike of sugar.

The principal broke the silence. "Hafsa crossed the crime scene tape and was taking pictures."

She was going to be a great detective. That was lesson one: It's easier to ask forgiveness than permission. I was simultaneously horrified and proud.

'Also, lesson four: Evidence is everywhere.' Fitch added.

Mrs. Golding gave Hafsa a hard stare. "Officer Tsui wanted to arrest you, but you were saved by the school's goodwill with the Stony police."

Hafsa didn't look concerned.

I grabbed the muffin tray and presented it to her. With my back to the principal, I mouthed, "Good job."

She selected a blueberry muffin. "Halal, I assume."

Mr. OOP nodded, "Of course."

'It's from the Bruin Bistro, therefore halal and kosher,' concurred Fitch, who represented the Middle East riding atop a camel.

There was a knock at the door.

'Oh no. Someone else? Too many fingers and not enough pie.' Fitch waggled his AI-generated hands, six fingers on the right and seven on the left.

Mrs. Golding didn't seem happy to have more visitors. "Now what?"

Officer Tsui escorted a contrite Moe wearing handcuffs. He stood beside Hafsa and the Taurus statuette.

Tsui placed a phone on Mrs. Golding's desk. "This is his. He hacked Kwolek and downloaded her surveillance videos."

'Wow. Your grandkids have mad skillz,' admired Fitch, holed up in a basement surrounded by computer monitors.

This was better than Hafsa taking unauthorized pictures.

"Tell me, Officer Tsui," I asked in my most incredulous voice. "How do you know Mohamed Manuelito transferred Kwolek's videos?" I stood close to Moe. "Are you okay?"

Moe rattled the handcuffs. "Sure. No problem."

"We'll have those off in no time." I returned to Officer Tsui. "How do you know Moe stole the videos?"

"Kwolek told me."

'This is going to be good,' chortled Fitch. He played a drum roll. *'Everyone, pay attention.'*

"Let me get this straight, Officer Tsui." I paused for a dramatic effect. "You have detained a Stony High student."

Another pause. "You confiscated his personal property and his private information, on a computer's say-so. Since when is a computer's hallucination probable cause?"

Officer Tsui sheepishly removed Moe's cuffs.

I pressed my point. "You do understand that AIs might sound good, but they're out of touch with reality, don't you?"

Tsui fidgeted with his belt, returning the handcuffs to their holder. He dropped his keys, and when he went to retrieve them, he lost the cuffs.

We watched the sheepish Tsui struggle to get his gear together. The two students had smirks of suppressed laughter. Fitch rolled on the floor with glee.

"Did you have his consent?"

Moe shook his head.

"Did you have a warrant?"

A contrite officer collected the phone from the principal's desk and returned it.

Moe gave him a polite, "Thanks."

Hafsa high-fived Moe. "Score one for Szilard's Sleuths."

The principal narrowed her eyes. "What's this about, Mr. Szilard? I've already spoken to you about getting too involved. Can you please stick to the lesson plan?"

I said, "Yes, Principal."

'So much for maintaining a low profile.' Fitch was back in his jester's costume with bells on the hat and toes.

I backed away into the open door. My heart raced. It was a familiar, grassy green tea aroma. I took a deep breath to be sure. Vicki's shampoo. I turned. She had a student in custody. Louis, wearing his black hoodie with a white skull, but no cuffs.

Louis lay back on the gym bench and did triceps extensions with the dumbbells. "I need my strength to lift my pas de deux partners."

I waggled my fingers at Vicki.

She stuck out her chin. "You didn't answer Mrs. Golding's question. What's Szilard's Sleuths?"

A snarky Fitch mumbled, *'Do you need to know?'*

I sidestepped the questions. "Welcome, Vee. Would you like a muffin?"

Mr. OOP carried the tray around the room.

Vicki took a honey-glazed. "Do you have coffee?" Her need for caffeine distracted her.

I called, "Jared, did you get that carafe?"

He arrived so quickly that I suspected he was listening at the door. "Right here." He rolled in a trolley with coffee, cream, milk, sugar, and green ceramic cups embellished with Björn, the Stony High Bruin, in gold.

'No disposable cups going to landfills from Stony High,' Fitch cheered, wearing his green Sleuth Club T-shirt.

"Thanks." Vicki finished her muffin before repeating, "What's this about Szilard's Sleuths?"

"They're like the Baker Street Irregulars," I said with a laugh.

Vicki replied, "You employ this ballet dancer? What was his assignment?"

Louis did a quick fouetté and removed his hoodie to show off his green Sleuth Club T-shirt.

I deflected Vicki's request. "What's his offense?"

"Louis, this is your fifteen minutes of fame," she said. "Tell them why you're here."

"You get nothing from me without my lawyer." He stretched the sleeves of his T-shirt with biceps curls.

'Does he have a lawyer?' asked Fitch with disdain, bench pressing a barbell with massive weights.

Absolutely. Stony High students have lawyers, agents, accountants, and lifestyle coaches.

Vicki broke the impasse. "Louis found Walter Fisher's jacket."

'Who's Walter Fisher?' Fitch asked. He pantomimed getting shot. 'Oh, you mean, Wally, the college recruiter cum comedian.'

Louis put down his dumbbells and picked up a green jump rope. "This place is better than my home gym."

'He hasn't learned lesson two: Good detectives don't attract attention,' observed Fitch, wearing his jester outfit and banging on a tambourine.

Detective Yukawa held up two evidence bags in her gloved hands. "He stole Wally's jacket. There's an epinephrine autoinjector in the zippered pocket. The other pockets were empty, but we found these in Louis's backpack: Mr. Fisher's wallet, phone, and a driver's license for a female minor."

"A driver's license for a female minor," The principal repeated with surprise. "Seriously? Does that mean what I think? Is it a forgery? Is Walter Fisher part of a student abduction ring?" She did a forward flip over the massage table and stood in a kung fu attack stance. "Is this the break we've been waiting for?"

Vicki ran over to Mrs. Golding. "Calm down. This isn't one of your action movies."

Mrs. Golding looked around the room before whispering to Vicki, "With this evidence pointing to Wally, we should release those students."

Vicki gave a thumbs up, and the three teens walked out.

The principal said, "Mr. Sendak and Mr. Drew, you can also leave." Jared and Mr. OOP headed for the door.

'Oh no, there goes the coffee and muffins,' Fitch moaned, wearing his green-and-gold checkered bib.

I said, as politely as I could, "Please leave the coffee and the muffins."

Mr. OOP returned the muffin tray to the principal's massage table, and Jared abandoned his trolley.

Mrs. Golding pointed to me. "What about him?"

Vicki picked up another muffin. "He's okay."

'Finally, you're part of the inner circle.' Fitch cheered.

It's about time, I grumped.

My phone beeped, and I showed Vicki the *Surf SE* notification. The omniscient *Surf* had posted: SHOOTING VICTIM WITH FORGED DOCUMENTS #ILLEGALIMMIGRATION.

Vicki smiled. "Good cover. No mention of missing children. Glad to see the reporters are keeping a lid on this story."

"Is that a real driver's license?" I pondered.

"We'll send it to forensics," Vicki replied, "But it looks real enough. I don't recognize the name—Emma Marple. Tsui, is she in our database?"

Tsui tapped on his phone. "No record. Could it be a forgery?"

'Isn't Marple a famous Agatha Christie detective?' Fitch searched through the Bodleian Library. *'Yes. In many translations. Agatha wrote better books than this one,'* he chuckled.

Mrs. Golding suggested, "Do you think Mr. Fisher is connected to Stony High's missing students?"

Vicki refilled her coffee cup. "I doubt Wally had anything to do with the missing students." She thought for a minute. "I've briefed you all. Let's work together to solve this." She turned to me. "We. Need. To. Talk."

I could tell she didn't approve of Szilard's Sleuths. I put on a happy face. "How about Four Rivers? I've been craving dim sum."

"See you there at seven for dinner." She forced a smile. "First dinner."

<hr>

Vicki asked Mrs. Golding, "How about another coffee? I want to hear about that parkour chase in your last movie."

The principal did a little shimmy. "That was mostly wire work. The harnesses didn't fit right. With friction and chafing, I couldn't sit for a week, and I had to wear dresses with loose bloomers."

"That must have been awful. I hate baggy underwear."

When Vicki mentioned underwear, I took that as a dismissal. I exited to the courtyard where Career Day was finishing.

Mr. Mbacke had a crew helping the decoration committee prepare for the Halloween Dance. The Lunch Ladies were putting away the leftover food.

Wally, the college recruiter, had recovered from his injured ribs and was on stage. "Let's have a round of applause for the Lunch Ladies."

Scattered groups clapped.

Lieutenant Peggy and her paramedics were securing their mobile medical unit.

I asked her, "Are you finished for the day?"

"I wish. We'll leave our equipment here to be on hand for the Halloween Dance."

Wally shaded his eyes with his hand. "Do I see the famous Bruin Bistro Baklavas? I can't believe any were left over." He put his hands together and pleaded. "I'd trade my life for one. Vegan, please. They're my favorite. I look forward to Career Day at Stony High for these sweet treats."

Louis grabbed a tray from one of the Lunch Ladies and chasséd up to the stage.

Wally took a bite, spraying flaky pastry everywhere.

I joined him. They were delicious.

I dumped the rest into my backpack and headed home for a nap before my dinner with Vicki.

Fitch murmured, *'Maybe we're fortunate not to have a murder to solve.'*

I doubt that. I shook my head. *This is a murder mystery.*

14. FOUR RIVERS

Vicki and I met at the Four Rivers Restaurant. Gold Chinese characters...

四 川

...spelled out Sichuan (literally four rivers) on a red circular door. A pungent Sichuan chili aroma welcomed us into the cavernous dining area. Circular tables occupied the center of the room, while red-upholstered booths lined the periphery. The walls were adorned with brush paintings illustrating Li River karst formations, contributing to a Chinese aesthetic despite depicting scenery from Guangxi Autonomous Region rather than Sichuan Province, after which the place was named.

A lady in a red cheongsam embroidered with dragons showed us to a corner booth. She bowed, poured tea, and said, "Lieutenant Yukawa, Mr. Szilard, welcome back."

Trolleys circulated around the busy restaurant. We had spareribs with rice noodles, crispy spring rolls, turnip cakes, and duck wings from one trolley. Another trolley served us chicken feet, fried pork dumplings, shrimp pot stickers, and sautéed string beans. The chicken feet were for Vicki. For me, they were too much work for too little satisfaction.

It had been a long couple of days, starting with the graffiti, and then Career Day, and the attempted assassination of Wally. The next day promised Career Day part two, the Sleuth Club, and missing children. The only sounds at our table were the hungry clicking of chopsticks and the clacking of our lazy Susan, which sounded like it was missing a few bearings.

When we stopped taking food off the trolleys, the lady in the red cheongsam poured us more tea and counted the plates to calculate the bill.

Fitch pulled a chair to the table and tied a red napkin around his neck. *'She's preparing to chastise you for getting those teens involved in police work. It's time to change the subject. Otherwise, this is going to be an uncomfortable postprandial discussion.'*

"Here comes a sweet cart," I exclaimed with enthusiasm. I selected fried red bean balls and coconut milk pudding. I noticed Vicki's favorite. "Would you like some thousand-layer cakes?"

"Don't give me that big smile. Just tell me how you're going to disband Szilard's Sleuths." She scraped her chair across the floor, drank her tea in one gulp, and slammed the cup on the table. "I won't have those privileged students interfering with the police."

I flagged down another dessert trolley. "Sesame seed ball?"

"Thanks." She frowned. "I want that Sleuth Club gone."

"Easy peasy." I leaned back and clasped my hands behind my head. "You see, I've solved the case. With no case, there's no Sleuth Club. Problem solved."

"What case?" She took a spoonful of my pudding. "The graffiti, the shooter, missing Goleta, or those smashed USB sticks?"

'Still no murder,' Fitch giggled.

Patience. I've got this.

I smiled and held up my open palms. "All of them."

"I hope this isn't another one of your fantasies. You're worse than AI, making up things." No smile.

I signaled the lady in red for more tea. "The case centers around the Fishers. Wally and Sandy aren't what they appear. Silicon Valley venture capitalists hired them to steal the Kwolek design plans."

Vicki picked up a sesame seed ball and took a big bite. "How did they do that?"

'Well done,' Fitch congratulated me. *'She's not convinced, but she's curious. Give her your best.'*

"The bomb-threat graffiti was to keep you occupied while they kidnapped Goleta to be their mule to transport stolen Kwolek plans up north to San Francisco. The Makers Guild struck back by assassinating Wally."

'The worst mystery plot ever,' Fitch declared. *'Why didn't they simply transfer the documents over the internet?'*

Shush Fitch. Just shush. Listen and learn.

"Paper plans? Carried by a high school girl? Are you serious?" Vicki took another sesame ball.

'You're going to have to do better than that,' Fitch laughed. *Challenge accepted. Buckle up and hold on.*

"Yes. They stole more than paper plans. They had models and prototypes." I paused to let Vicki and Fitch consider physical models. There's more to engineering than virtual design. "You should take Wally into protective custody and put roadblocks on highways 1, 101, 5, and 99 to intercept Goleta before she turns everything over to Dr. Telkes's competition."

Before she could respond to my latest plot twist, the red cheongsam arrived with the bill and leftovers in takeout containers. Vicki must have been thinking about what I said, because she allowed me to tap my card on the mobile payment terminal without asserting it was her turn to pay.

She cleaned her hands, wiping each finger with a wet towelette. "I don't believe a word of that nonsense. You've lost your edge. You should do what other retired detectives do. Write novels."

"That's an ad hominem argument. Do you have any real evidence to counter my explanation?"

"You want evidence?" She slid back her chair. "I'll give you evidence." She opened her black satchel embossed with the Stony Estancia emblem and placed a folder on the table. FORENSIC REPORT.

"What does it say?"

"Our best crime scene people didn't find a single trace of the shooter on the library roof. Therefore, he was a professional. Only a professional could fire three shots without leaving a trace. Not some amateur from Stony Estancia Makers Guild, as you *hypothesized*." She folded her arms when she emphasized the word hypothesized.

"That shows your lack of understanding. There were no human traces because Dr. T sent a robot to assassinate Wally. Robots have no fingerprints and no DNA."

'One point for your team.' Fitch wore his black-and-white referee's shirt.

When she didn't snap back at me, I knew she hadn't thought of that. I enjoyed my coconut milk pudding while she pondered a robot shooter.

The *Surf SE* app posted: #ROBOTASSASSIN AT STONY HIGH. THE AI TAKEOVER AND ANDROID UPRISING ARE HERE.

'You should be careful what you say. Tish is omniscient,' Fitch warned me.

Vicki checked the notes on her phone. "You said the graffiti was a diversion to cover Goleta's kidnapping, right?"

'It's a trap,' chortled Fitch.

I stepped into Vicki's trap. "Yes, that's what I said."

"Well, then, how do you explain the graffiti tonight at la pâtisserie south of town?" She paused. "And at Factory and Farm Foods, an hour later." She gave me a satisfied smile. "And now at a warehouse west of that pâtisserie. Three more graffiti sites, all announcing, X marks the spot." She crossed her arms and pursed her lips.

'Gotcha!' Fitch mirrored her stance, puffing out his bare chest, perfect pecs, and tribal blackwork ink.

I had no response. I changed the topic. "What will you wear to the Halloween Dance? I'm going as G. K. Chesterton's detective, Father Brown."

"That matches your fantasy approach to crime solving, a fictional investigator."

"Do you have a better costume?"

"Easy peasy. I'm going as Hedwig Eva Maria Kiesler, also known as Hedy Lamarr, inventor of frequency-hopping spread spectrum technology. If they had had a Women in STEM Symposium when I was in high school, I would have been an engineer, not a detective."

'Can't argue with that,' Fitch said.

15. HALLOWEEN DANCE

I met Coroner Persey in the Stony High parking lot.
Dressed in my Father Brown costume, a long black clerical
robe, a shirt with a white Roman collar, and a black Saturno
hat. I opened her van door. "Bless you, daughter. Welcome to
the All-Hallows' Eve celebration."

She responded with an evil cackle.

I jumped back. She was wearing white makeup, blood red
lipstick, and a horned headpiece. Cerberus wore a black tux.

She read my name tag. "My pleasure, Father Brown. I am
Persephone, Queen of the Underworld. Take me to your
dead."

"No dead tonight. Only a Samhain celebration"

We entered the courtyard where the decoration committee
had augmented the spooky dark-sky lighting by draping black
crepe strips from the pepper trees. The stage and food tables
hadn't been moved since Career Day.

Her voice echoed with a spooky reverb. "How about some
vittles and potions?"

I led her to the snack tables where the Lunch Ladies had set
out sweet and savory Halloween snacks. They were dressed in
Halloween black with gold aprons and green toques.

Persey helped herself to black rice sushi rolls, while I went
for the espresso martini fudge. We met Hafsa, who wore a blue
and white headscarf. Her name tag read, Mother Teresa,
Secretary of Health and Human Services.

I greeted her, "Evenin, Hafsa. I expected you to come as a
brain surgeon."

"Good guess, but I prefer to be in charge of something
bigger than an operating theater."

From across the room, Louis called, "Hafsa. I love your
costume." He wore an orange NASA spacesuit. His name tag
read, Sally Ride, Secretary of Science and Technology. He
closed the distance between us with a couple of ballet chassés
and a grand jeté.

"What are you doing in that getup? Aren't you destined to join a big-name dance company?" Hafsa asked.

He performed a pirouette. "I wasn't thinking about me. My costume is in Leeta's memory. She wanted to be an engineer."

He referred to Goleta in the past tense, and a look passed between Louis and Hafsa that I didn't understand.

'They have a secret,' chortled Fitch, wearing white robes. His tag read, The Pythia, Oracle of Delphi.

Emily joined us in a long, dark dress with a white shawl and cap. Her tag said, Sojourner Truth, Secretary of Transportation.

'A blond Sojourner Truth. She took some liberties there.' Fitch appeared as Fredrick Douglass, the 19th-century orator for civil rights.

I loved these free interpretations and how they updated historical women to be in the U.S. Presidential Cabinet.

The Stony High Band paraded out of the gym playing *Uptown Funk.* They were accompanied by a light show, performed by a singing Kwolek trio. With their appearance, the teens and younger adults took to the courtyard to show their moves.

Walter and Mrs. Golding were the couple to watch. He was Fred Astaire, and she was Xena, the warrior princess.

'An unlikely couple,' sneered Fitch.

Everyone watched as Principal Golding showcased her chops as a stunt performer with jumps and flips. I couldn't believe Wally had been in emergency first aid yesterday as he took center stage with a big smile and fancy footwork, though to be fair, his upper body was as stiff as an Irish dancer's.

The pulsating beats climaxed with a clash of cymbals. When the dancers jumped, Wally collapsed.

Mrs. Golding, Xena, ululated and held him to her breastplate.

The music stopped.

'Don't worry. The paramedics are here.' Fitch wore blue scrubs with a stethoscope hanging from his pocket.

Peggy sprinted from the EMT mobile response unit to Wally's prostrate body, carrying a green cylinder. She placed a clear plastic mask over his mouth and nose and turned on the oxygen. She observed him for a moment before shouting, "Anaphylaxis! Epinephrine!"

Another paramedic reminded her, "Sorry, Lieutenant Mutai. With the open house today, there are no prescription meds on board."

Peggy slammed her fist onto the ground before leaning close to Wally. "Do you have an epinephrine autoinjector?"

He gasped. "Always. In my jacket."

"Someone! Anyone! Get his jacket."

'No one will find it. Louis took it. Vicki has it in an evidence bag,' Fitch reminded me.

Puppies. That isn't good.

Peggy started chest compressions, but she looked worried.

Mrs. Golding sprinted through the crowd. "Hang in there, Wally. We have autoinjectors in the nurse's office."

Peggy continued with CPR and oxygen.

The principal returned, and Peggy administered the epinephrine. With that injection, I hoped the crisis was over. I watched her. She didn't sigh or relax her shoulders. She searched for a pulse and adjusted the oxygen.

An EMT handed her a naloxone nasal spray, the treatment for opioid overdose.

Fitch approved. *'Go for it. There's no harm in administering naloxone when it's not needed. If it's needed, it's lifesaving.'*

She fumbled with the package. Her fingers were shaking so hard she couldn't open it. Wally's arms suddenly relaxed, and the tension left his face. Peggy screamed and threw the nasal spray bottle across the courtyard. The epinephrine hadn't helped. Now, it was too late for naloxone. She curled up on herself and sobbed.

Tears ran down the principal's cheeks.

Stony Estancia Surfs posted: #MURDER AT STONY HIGH.

Coroner Persephone rushed to Wally. The news of his death spread, and the area around him cleared. The paramedics covered his corpse with a Mylar emergency blanket. Only his green and gold patent leather shoes remained visible.

'Those are Stony High colors. Do you think he had expensive shoes like those for every school he visited?' Fitch did a shim sham wearing suede tap shoes—also green and gold.

He's dead. His shoes are the last thing I care about.

An abandoned stretcher lay beside Wally, a sad picture of a failed rescue.

All eyes followed Persey, zipped up in her white protective suit and accompanied by two assistants sealed in white with Coroner in black letters on their backs. They parked their gurney and rolled out a body bag. Cerberus stayed out of the way while Persey raised the silver blanket and examined the body. "Who's this?"

"Walter Fisher, college recruiter," I replied.

Persey followed up with the question on everyone's mind. "What happened?"

Peggy answered, "He was dancing, and then he collapsed." She turned to Persey. "What do you think?"

Persey replaced the silver blanket. "I can't be sure until after the autopsy."

As a homicide detective, I'd learned to coax information from medical examiners. "We all watched him dancing. I think we can rule out trauma."

"That's reasonable. I'm guessing sudden cardiac death or, possibly, stroke." She looked at her phone. "Despite what *The Surf* says, not murder. They'll post anything for clicks."

'It has to be murder,' Fitch stamped his feet. *'This is a murder mystery, isn't it?'*

"Isn't he a bit young for a heart attack?" Vicki asked.

Persey explained, "Heart attacks can happen at any age, but I doubt this is one."

"You said, sudden cardiac death. Isn't that a heart attack?"

"SCD is something else, and it's more common with younger men."

'Potayto, potahto,' Fitch scoffed. *'Either way, Wally's dead.'*

Kwolek flew over to join the discussion. "I'm not a medical examiner, but have you considered exercise-induced anaphylaxis?"

Persey smiled at the quadcopter. "Good one, except that it's rare. If it's EIA, I'll see it in his medical history."

Kwolek wasn't discouraged. "How about polonium-210, the radioactive poison? Alexander Litvinenko was murdered with it in London in 2006."

Persey rolled her eyes. "Thanks, Kwolek. I'll check that out."

'She isn't going to waste time on that,' Fitch chortled.

Kwolek continued. "Okay, not polonium. What about a blow gun with a curare poison dart?"

"I doubt this is murder, but I won't know for sure until the post-mortem." Persey sighed. "I wish *The Surf* would check with me before they post those clickbait headlines."

Kwolek repeated, "I'm not a medical examiner, but—"

I shut down the flying video game. "Persey *is* the medical examiner. Let her do her job."

Kwolek returned to Dr. Telkes, landed, and her rotors stopped spinning. She was pouting like an offended teenager.

'I'm sure that AI could have spit out alternatives forever.' Fitch sat at a desk covered with thick books in dusty leather bindings and a few papyrus scrolls. He mimicked Kwolek's computer voice, *'I'm not a medical examiner, but let's see what Galen has to say.'*

Two assistants placed Wally in a body bag, loaded him onto a gurney, and wheeled him to the County Coroner's vehicle.

Persey called over to the quadcopter. "Hey, Kwolek. You can help."

The AI spun up her rotors and bounced into the air.

"What happened here?"

Kwolek began, "I'm not a medical examiner—"

Persey shouted. "I don't want your AI hallucinations. Just send me the video files."

Kwolek balked, "Privacy and data security are built into my design. I can't—"

Persey said, "I'm beaming you my search warrant."

Kwolek said, "Air dropping the MPEG files."

As each file transferred, Kwolek sounded *boop, beep, dum,* and Persey's phone acknowledged *dum, beep, boop.*

That was the end of the Halloween Dance. Persey drove away with Walter Fisher's body. Students and teachers disappeared. Mr. Mbacke arrived to put away the tables and chairs. Vicki and I hugged in the high school parking lot. "Say Vee, why don't you come to my condo for second dinner? I have leftovers from Four Rivers, and we can bake cookies."

She kissed my neck. "I'd love a quiet evening with just us, but let's wait for another day."

"Another day," I echoed.

We walked to our cars in companionable silence when her phone rang.

"Yes, Tsui, what do you have?... Really?... Again?... "I'm close. Meet me there."

She tapped her phone off and placed it in her black satchel.

"Let's go, Zee. Another graffiti incident, number five, is in progress. At the firehouse this time. Rush! We can catch the perpetrators."

"Perfect. We can have second dinner at the Firehouse Barbecue, better than leftovers."

Vicki jumped into her car. She spun her wheels and shouted out her window, "This is our chance to solve the graffiti case."

16. FIREHOUSE GRAFFITI

Vicki's unmarked police car fishtailed out of the high school parking lot. With her siren whoop-whooping and blue flashers spinning, she ran the red light at Blackett and Higgs, turning south to the firehouse. I followed.

'Hurry, you're losing her.' Fitch tightened his seat belt, put on a crash helmet, and stuck his tongue out the open window like Cerberus.

There was no reason to rush. *Calm down. We'll be there soon enough. It's only graffiti.*

Kwolek cleared the way for Vicki by weaving side-to-side with her flashing light show and blasting "Flight of the Bumblebee" by Rimsky-Korsakov. My phone beeped with *Surf SE* notifications as people uploaded Kwolek's antics.

Halfway there, Tsui appeared, speeding down the Desert Freeway exit ramp and drifting around the corner to join Vicki on Higgs. A short while later, they both disappeared.

With the police out of sight, I expected Fitch to shut up, but no such luck.

'They're gone. You drive like an old man.' Fitch banged on the dashboard like a toddler. *'We're missing the action.'*

I am an old man and don't have a Kwolek escort. I slowed down. *No worries. That graffiti isn't going away.*

When we arrived, Vicki and Tsui were nowhere to be seen. I parked in the Firehouse Barbecue lot in the flashing blue glow of Tsui's empty black-and-white cruiser.

The restaurant and the fire station were doppelgängers, red brick cubes with enormous garage doors, but only the firehouse's were functional.

"Hey, Kwolek, where did you learn to fly crazy like that?"

The flying cell phone looped around my car. "LOL. My codebase includes software for a self-driving car."

"Where'd everyone go?"

"All the action is out back. You're late." Kwolek chastised me.

'I told you to drive faster.' Fitch piled on.

Behind the firehouse, people were scattered across a vacant field of sagebrush with two neon-yellow quadcopters above them.

"Hey, Kwolek, are those your friends?"

"Don't insult me. Those are dumb flying cameras. Brainless. Remote-controlled. That trademarked color means they're *Stony Estancia Surfs* serfs." Kwolek made a gurgling sound that might have been a laugh.

The *Surf SE* app notified: CLICK FOR A LIVE #POLICECHASE.

I opened the *Surf SE* app for an overhead view of Vicki and Tsui in pursuit. Whenever they approached, their target disappeared into the sagebrush. They selected a new target and headed in a different direction. The *Surf* broadcast in sepia tones, accompanied by ragtime music, making the whole thing look like Keystone Kops slapstick.

From the bird's-eye view of the neon-yellow quadcopters, I recognized a tall blond girl, another in a headscarf, and my most certain identification was a barefoot boy moving through the brush with chassés and grand jetés.

Puppies. The graffiti artists were my grandkids. Puppets. What were they up to?

'Are you going to identify them for Vicki?' Fitch asked.

Maybe later. Maybe not.

Vicki and I went way back. I trained her as a rookie when we were both in the big city. When I retired, our roles reversed, and I followed her to Stony Estancia. I trusted my students, my honorary grandkids, and gave them my unconditional love, something every child needs and deserves. I wouldn't say anything until I knew the connection between the Sleuth Club and the graffiti.

17. FIREHOUSE BARBECUE

Vicki and Tsui were behind the fire station chasing my grandkids under the watchful cameras of the *Surf's* quadcopters. All the fire department vehicles, the ladder truck, both rescue trucks, the mobile first aid unit, and the electric pumper, paraded across the street to the church parking area. They had to be moved before Graffiti Abatement could get to work. When the huge roll-up doors closed, U B U. XX MARKS THE SPOT, spray-painted in ten-foot-high letters, was unveiled. Scaffolding was erected and pressure washers slowly erased the writing.

The *Surf's* live video of police versus students in the back field was collecting clicks, likes, and comments from everywhere except the firehouse. Peggy and her crew of paramedics were relaxing with an old movie about two musicians in black suits and dark glasses being chased by a long line of police cars somewhere in the Midwest, maybe Chicago.

Fitch kept time with the movie soundtrack on his double bass. *'I'm with the band.'*

Open pizza boxes holding discarded crusts, plates shiny with salad dressing, and empty two-liter soda bottles were scattered around the common room. The remains of that delicious feast made my stomach rumble. "Is everything okay?" I asked.

"Sure. They're on a mission from God," Peggy quoted from the movie.

"You have graffiti on your doors."

"No problem. Graffiti Abatement will wash it off before the paint sets."

Stony Estancia was graffiti-free. The rapid response squad erased vandalism before it could inspire other troublemakers. I wasn't going to learn anything from Peggy's crew. I headed next door to the Firehouse Barbecue to appease my rumbly stomach.

Inside, the dining room was spacious, like the firehouse, and saturated with the aromas of garlic, onion, and chili. The décor consisted of old-timey firefighting equipment—red pumps with red handles, along with red buckets, axes, and ladders. I took a table in the corner for privacy and raised the laminated menu to signal the server, who came over with water glasses and a hushpuppy basket with mild and spicy sauces.

Fitch admired the basket of fried cornmeal balls. *'Do you know why they're called hushpuppies?'*

I shrugged my shoulders. *Who cares?*

'Hunters tossed them to hungry dogs to "hush" them.'

Big whoop. I popped one into my mouth.

The server took out his tablet. "Mr. S, are you ready to order?"

Vicki and Tsui would tire of chasing teenagers. "Two others will be joining me. We'll have a small family feast with baby back ribs, smoked brisket, and a barbecue chicken, plus a pitcher of your on-tap beer."

"What sides would you like with that?"

"Cornbread, red beans with rice, and more hushpuppies."

"Any salads? We have locally grown, farm-to-table salads. Would you like Caesar, spinach, or taco salad?"

"My rule at the Firehouse is nothing green."

He frowned at this reply but quickly recovered. "Whatever works for you. Anything else?"

"Yes, Ice-Age ribs, to go."

"You know those are raw, don't you? Ice Age means before fire was discovered."

"They're for my cat."

Vicki and Tsui joined me. Tsui requested a large order of hushpuppies and ribs to go. "My kids love them." He explained, "My wife's writers' group is tonight. Dinner is my responsibility."

Vicki helped herself to a hushpuppy dipped in spicy sauce.

I poured three beers and took a sip of mine. "What's our next step?"

She washed down her hushpuppy and picked up her satchel. "Let's look at the big picture." She drew a horizontal blue line on a napkin. "This is the Desert Freeway." Below it, she drew another horizontal line, brown. "Here is the Pacific Electric jogging and bike trail to the south, and this vertical black line is your street, Higgs Road.'

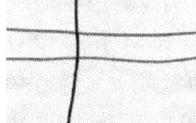

She turned the napkin to face me and dipped another hushpuppy in the spicy sauce.

"Okay, that's Stony Estancia." I pointed to a space above the blue freeway and right of the vertical Higgs Road. "That's where I live. Right?"

She nodded and moved the napkin out of the center of the table so the server could deliver our food.

"Let's start last Sunday night, Monday morning." She drew a star north of the freeway. "This is your high school. Someone graffitied the library with U DA BOMB. X MARKS THE SPOT."

"I recall. Kwolek suggested a horrific hate crime. I guessed a bomb threat. We were both wrong."

'Likely a student prank,' contributed Fitch, dressed as Björn, the Stony High mascot.

Vicki picked up a rib, examining it for the meatiest part. "Yes, we're beyond that initial hyperbole. The only hard evidence was when Kwolek scanned the scene with LiDAR and discovered shoe impressions in the dirt."

"I don't see why you rushed here with blues and twos, flashing lights and sirens."

She wiped her hands with her napkin and picked up a black marker. "Let's review. The first graffiti was at the high school library."

"I recall. Likely publicity for a party."

She made three more marks. "Three graffiti incidents in rapid succession." Then she drew a fifth mark southwest of the Higgs Road intersection and the Pacific Electric Trail. "Tonight we have graffiti at the firehouse."

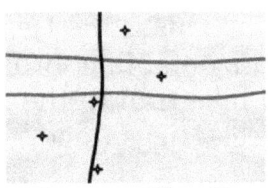

There it was, the big picture. The five sites formed a large "X" marking the firehouse in the center. "The target is the fire station, and something more ominous than publicity for a dance."

My *Surf SE* app notified me with: CAN YOU FIND THE PATTERN? CLICK HERE. When I clicked, my phone displayed a fancier rendition of Vicki's map.

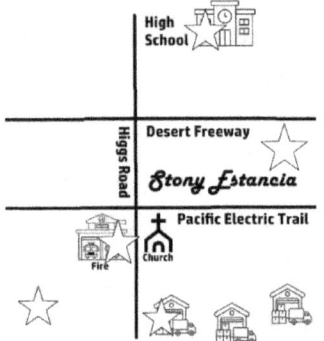

The server delivered the large Firehouse Barbecue bag holding the takeout containers Tsui had ordered for his five children. "Thank you. Please deliver those." He took out his phone and beamed his contact information to the server.

Vicki said, "We didn't catch them tonight, but now that we've decoded X marks the spot, we'll be waiting."

Tsui added, "Broadcasting the location over an open channel is an old spy craft technique. Everyone can see the message. Only the intended recipient can decrypt it and it's impossible to discover the intended recipient."

"This time it was XX marks the spot," I pointed out.

"Graffiti typo," Vicki dismissed my observation with a grin.

Tsui spoke to the server. "I'll have a large coffee and a couple of espresso brownies." When the server left, Tsui explained. "I'm on surveillance tonight. When they return to X marks the spot, I'll have them."

'XX marks the spot,' Fitch corrected.

The server handed me my leftover containers, and Tsui took his brownies and coffee. When he left for his all-night stakeout, Vicki stood to leave.

"Wait a minute." I held her hand. "What aren't you telling me?"

"Nothing." She furrowed her brow.

'Did you see that?' Fitch exclaimed, jumping up and down. Vicki furrowed her brow a second time. *'That's her tell.'*

I saw it.

I challenged her. "You wouldn't be keeping Tsui from his family for nothing." I reached into my bag of leftovers and swiped a hushpuppy."

"I don't understand how you keep your youthful figure," she said, changing the subject.

"Genetics. My teen metabolism." I answered her implied question and grabbed a rib to go with my hushpuppy. "Why are Tsui's five children going to bed without seeing their father?"

"You win. I'll explain after you give me a rib." Vicki held out her hand and sat down. "Gangs in San Amano have been using graffiti to set up drug deals."

'Graffiti and drugs?' Fitch waggled his fingers, making gang signs. *'Are your grandkids mixed up with San Amano troublemakers?'*

"What's the connection?"

She took a bite from her rib and chewed slowly. "Sophisticated dealers are operating in San Amano. They signal distribution locations and times with graffiti."

The pieces came together. "I get it. The low-level runners can't finger the bosses. They know the graffiti, not the people."

"Correct!" Vicki paused for another bite. "The San Amano police have foiled them. Their squads are hitting graffiti sites super-fast. Too fast. The messages don't get through."

"Do you suspect gangs are moving into Stony Estancia?"

"Exactly. Tonight, Tsui will be waiting for them."

Vicki paid for our food, Tsui's coffee, and Dahl's Ice-Age ribs.

I collected the leftovers. "Thank you for dinner."

Vicki gave me a side hug and said, "TANSTAAFL."

'There ain't no such thing as a free lunch,' Fitch translated. *'She wants something.'*

I snuggled her neck and whispered in her ear, "Vee, for you, anything. I have clean sheets at Higgs Haven—"

"Maybe another time." She broke the hug, reached into her satchel, and slid her tablet across the table. "Sign here."

I scrawled a signature with my finger. "What am I signing for?"

"Chain of custody." She pulled out a small plastic bag with a yellow warning label: CAUTION STATIC-SENSITIVE DEVICES. "After forensics reconstructed that beautiful parquet jewelry box and the USB sticks, they removed the sixteen data chips from the splinters and shards. Here they are." She handed the bag to me. "Can you get your friend Vinnie to find out what's on them? We need a tech miracle."

"No problem." I signaled the waiter.

He ran over, balancing water, napkins, and wet wipes. While he topped up our glasses, he asked, "Can I help you?"

"Yes, please. I need a small takeout cup."

He gave a questioning look at the empty table and my sack of leftovers, before he went to find a cup.

When he returned, I placed the computer chips in the cup, attached to cover, and slipped them in with my food. Ice Age ribs for Dahl, smoked brisket and red beans with rice for second dinner, and the rest to stock the freezer in my garage.

My phone beeped. I looked at the notification and placed it face down on the table.

"Are you two-timing me?" Vicki asked in a pretend-jealous voice. "Who's calling you this late?"

"Szilard's Sleuths. They can wait."

'They're the Sleuth Club, not Szilard's Sleuths.' Fitch puffed on his calabash pipe. *'You're asking for trouble by saying Szilard's Sleuths.'*

She moved away from me. "We talked about this. You agreed to disband your squad of teen busybodies."

"But Vee... They aren't mine..." Fitch was right. I'd backed myself into a corner. "Anyway, the Sleuth Club wants to find Goleta. After we find her, no more club."

Vicki pursed her lips and frowned.

"Goleta is missing, over twelve hours," I reminded her.

"We'll find her soon." She reached into my bag of leftovers, swiped a hushpuppy, and mopped up some sauce from her plate. "Make sure you shut down that club when we do."

"You sound confident about locating Goleta."

"Stony High kids aren't street smart. The police will find her electronically. We are monitoring her credit cards. Do you know how many credit cards she has?"

I had three. I guessed, "Six?"

'Don't underestimate Stony Estancia teens,' Fitch said, carrying shiny paper bags from the boutiques in the Bragg Vineyard Mall.

I guessed again, "Nine?"

Vicki laughed, "Eleven credit cards... plus four debit/ATM cards." She checked her phone and gave me a self-satisfied smile. "Homeland Security and the Highway Patrol have flagged her passport and driver's license."

I had to agree with Fitch. Vicki was underestimating Goleta, an honor student, top of her AP Physics class, and Astronomy Club president. Leeta might not be street smart, but she was smart smart. I challenged Vicki, "What if she has a new identity, like witness protection?"

"I doubt that. You overestimate these kids. You're too close to them. They aren't your grandkids, they're ordinary teenagers. She was abducted. She doesn't fit a runaway profile."

"Do you remember Pax Shelley? He was a runaway. He disappeared by walking over the hills, and you never found him."

'Pax Shelley was in The Library Club. This is a different book.' Fitch walked through the stacks of the Bodleian Library wearing a scholar's gown.

Vicki responded sharply, "Won't happen this time. The open space is patrolled by Kwoleks. No one will get past them."

'Kwoleks. Those AIs. I don't trust them.' Fitch frowned.

I retorted, "I'd rather give the case to my imaginary friend."

Fitch swelled with pride and floated up like a weather balloon.

My phone vibrated across the table. I picked it up and read the texts.

HAFSA: WE HAVEN'T FOUND LEETA [ANGUISHED FACE].

EMILY: SHE WAS ABDUCTED [ANGRY FACE].

'How does Emily know that?' Fitch pondered.

I reached across the table and took Vicki's hand. "Let's not fight about this. One way or another, we'll find Goleta. We always do."

She squeezed my hand. "We always do."

I picked up my sack of leftovers and computer chips. "Let's go back to my condo. I have Blu-rays, black cherry ice cream, and can bake cookies."

"Cookies and romcoms. Great idea. I'll race you."

We were stuck in the Firehouse Barbecue parking lot while Graffiti Abatement dismantled their scaffolding, and the fire department paraded their equipment back into the firehouse. When I saw Peggy and the EMTs moving the mobile first aid station, I remembered that Wally had died.

'Murdered,' corrected Fitch.

I'd never left a murder unsolved. "Wait, Vee. We're close to the Civic Center. Let's check in with Coroner Persey first."

"That's a plan. We haven't heard from her. Therefore, she's at the morgue. It'll be easier to relax knowing Mr. Fisher's cause of death."

I didn't want to show up at the morgue empty-handed. When Vicki turned left on Zeeman Way, I continued straight. Higgs Road darkened as I entered Warehouse-o-Rama. At Appleton Route, I went left and delivered the sixteen data chips to Purcell and Associates. A few blocks further, I parked in front of Stony Estancia's hidden treasure, la pâtisserie with no name, which offered the best confections outside of Paris. It was a beacon of light, glowing cases displaying a cornucopia of sweets.

Outside the bakery, the fragrances of butter and sugar embraced me. Once inside, the delicate aroma of vanilla contributed to the delightful blend. I ordered a liter of French roast coffee, mille-feuilles, tartes Tatins, Parisienne cream puffs, aka chouquettes, and crème brûlées in individual to-go ramekins. While waiting, I sat at a round bistro table, enjoying an espresso accompanied by three Tricolore macarons, blue, white, and red.

The shopgirl wearing a black T-shirt under a white apron carried the boxes to my car.

"Bonne soirée, Persey. I bear sweets and coffee, sugar and caffeine." I arranged the boxes in the staff room, opening them to allow the ambiance of la pâtisserie to drive off the odors of disinfectants and antiseptics with an undertone of decomp.

Cerberus looked at me with his sad puppy eyes. I returned to my car and swiped one of Dahl's Ice-Age ribs for the chocolate lab.

Fitch approved. *'What Dahl doesn't know won't upset her.'*

Vicki and Persey joined me. The coroner took a deep breath and said, "Delicious smells."

Vicki got right down to business. "Have you scheduled the coroner's inquest?"

Persey rambled. "In-house tox screen showed nothing." She bit into a Parisienne cream puff. "Stomach contents revealed muffins, plain; scones, with jam, but no clotted cream; and a lettuce and tomato sandwich, without bacon."

I took a spoonful of crème brûlée, reveling in the smooth custard and crunchy caramelized sugar. "Did that give you a cause of death?"

"No, but I contacted his wife. He'd been a vegetarian since long before she met him."

"That doesn't help, does it?" I sipped my coffee.

"Not really, this is a tough case. She's on her way here for a face-to-face discussion."

Vicki sipped her coffee. "I'd like to be part of that."

"Shouldn't be a problem."

Vicki broke through the puff pastry layers with her fork and took a bite of her mille-feuille. "I've never seen you stymied by cause of death."

"Not giving up. I've contacted the feds, posted the case on a coroners' forum, delayed the inquest a month, and hope to have an answer by then."

"Murder?" I asked.

"I'm leaving all options open. My only lead is anaphylaxis."

Leticia, the omniscient *Surf* reporter, wasn't as cautious. The *Surf SE* app posted: #MURDER AT STONY HIGH.

'This book is a murder mystery. We're in chapter nineteen. This better be a murder. I won't wait any longer.' It was ghoulish how Fitch danced around the room with cheerleader pom-poms. 'Give me an M. U. R. D. E. R. Mur-der. Mur-DER!"

Vicki sighed and shook her head. "That doesn't narrow it down much, does it?"

"I'm trying everything." Coroner Persey ran her fingers through her long black hair. "Kwolek gave me a list of 101 anaphylaxis causes from peanuts and bee stings to pollen and sunlight. The only one I could cross off the list was catamenial anaphylaxis caused by hormones during menstruation or pregnancy."

Cerberus barked, and we turned to the door.

"Evenin all," Mrs. Fisher greeted us. "I'm here to collect Wally. I have my funeral director waiting outside. I would like to complete the cremation as soon as possible."

Vicki, Persey, and I looked at each other, mouths agape and dumbfounded by her request.

'She isn't interested in the cause of death. She wants to incinerate the evidence.' Fitch held handcuffs, prepared to arrest Wally's wife.

Sandy must have picked up on our suspicious stares. "Stony Estancia is nice, but I'd like to take Wally's remains home before Thanksgiving."

Fitch put away his handcuffs, but that didn't appease my suspicions. She didn't sound like a grieving widow.

Vicki broke the awkward silence. "We're pushing forward as fast as we can. Can I offer you some coffee and pastries?"

Mrs. Fisher looked at Vicki as if she were an alien. "Excuse me? I'm here to pick up my husband's corpse, and you're offering me refreshments?"

"I'm Senior Detective Victoria Yukawa, Stony Estancia Police Department." Vicki took her badge from her satchel and displayed it to Mrs. Fisher.

"I know who you are. Why are you here?" Mrs. Fisher crossed her arms. "Should I call my lawyer?"

"You can, but why would you need one?"

That response forced Mrs. Fisher to reconsider her approach. "Let's settle this without lawyers. What do you need to know?"

I poured her a cup of coffee and introduced her to the pastry selection. "Perhaps you'd be more comfortable sitting."

She accepted my offer. Cerberus curled up at her feet, and she scritched his ears. "Good boy."

"I apologize, Mrs. Fisher. This is my fault." Persey took a chair next to her.

Mrs. Fisher speared a caramelized apple slice from her tarte Tatin and slowly chewed it. "You can call me Sandy."

"Okay, Sandy. I fear the police won't release your husband until I give them a cause of death."

Sandy took another apple slice with some coffee.

"I hope you can help me with some information."

'Clever that she hasn't disclosed that the inquest is delayed a month.' Fitch laughed.

Sandy relaxed. "Okay, if your questions go beyond Wally's cause of death…" She wiped a tear from her eye. "Excuse me." She took a deep breath. "If you go too far, I'm calling my lawyer."

Persey moved closer to her and spoke gently. "I understand. Shall we invite your funeral director to join us? He might appreciate something to eat while waiting."

Sandy turned red. "I exaggerated. He isn't here. I'm to call him when you release the body."

'Suspicious. *This lady isn't what she appears.*' Fitch took out his handcuffs.

Persey let that confession pass. "Can you give me the contact information for his doctor and release his medical history?"

Sandy smiled. "I'd love to. When I learned that he'd been having anaphylaxis episodes since childhood, I encouraged him to visit a doctor, but I haven't been able to convince him." She paused for coffee. "He is…was thirty-eight and believed in his macho immortality. My best efforts only got him to the dentist every couple of years." She drank some more coffee. "Even when he got sick, he didn't trust doctors."

That wasn't the whole story. I pressed for more. "I get that he didn't have a doctor. Where did he get that autoinjector he carried?"

She studied her tarte's apple slices.

Vicki jumped in. "We're only interested in your husband's death." She paused for emphasis. "Nothing else."

"I'm a nurse. My doctor wrote a prescription." When no one responded, she said, "As a favor."

"Let me see. Do I have this straight?" Persey leaned close to Sandy. "Your husband has been having anaphylaxis attacks since childhood, but he's never visited a doctor to find out the cause."

"Well, not exactly. As a child, his mother took him to several, but aside from prescribing epinephrine autoinjectors, no one helped." She wiped her eyes. "That was when he lost faith in the medical profession. He treated himself with a restrictive diet and homeopathic medications."

"How long have you been married?"

"Twenty years." She held out her left hand. "We gifted ourselves new platinum rings to celebrate."

'Wow. Look at those diamonds.' Fitch gave a low whistle. *'Four carats, flawless, colorless. Not cheap.'*

How did a nurse and a stand-up comedian afford that?

Persey continued. "You're a nurse and haven't been able to convince him to go to a doctor. Is that correct?"

Sandy countered with, "Tell me, Coroner, are you married?"

Persey shook her head no.

Mrs. Fisher looked at Vicki and me.

We admitted to being single.

"Well," she said. "You wouldn't understand, would you? In a marriage, you need to choose your battles."

I said, "Of course, I understand," thinking about withholding the full story about Szilard's Sleuths from Vicki.

"Thank you, Mr. S. If you explain this to the others, I can be on my way."

"Not yet. Please have another cup of coffee. Persey, Vicki, and I need a short conference."

Sandy refilled her coffee and took another tarte.

We left the buttery goodness of the staff room for the antiseptic cleanliness of the main morgue. I contemplated aloud, "Her rush to cremate her husband doesn't seem like a grieving widow."

Persey narrowed her lips. "Twenty years married to a medical professional, and he has no records. Hard to believe."

Vicki whispered. "I can understand why he hasn't been to a doctor in twenty years." She looked at me. "Men can be stubborn." With an air kiss, she added, "Just kidding." She paused before saying, "But she's a nurse. Why hasn't she figured out his need for an autoinjector?"

I concurred. "She knows, and she used that information to kill him. She had means and opportunity. I'm sure we'll find a motive with a little digging."

Persey counseled caution. "As coroner, I can't support any indictment without a cause of death."

"Relax, Persey. Zee and I have solved many homicides over the years. We have an intuition about these things. We just need a motive."

Vicki and I were on a roll. "Money is always a good motive. Has anyone checked for life insurance?"

Vicki took out her tablet. "Here it is. We must thank Tsui for his thoroughness. She has a large policy."

"Trifecta," I declared. "Means, opportunity, and motive." I squeezed Vicki. "We have time for second dinner at my place."

Vicki marched into the staff room.

Sandy looked up from her phone. "I was expecting you."

Vicki unhooked her handcuffs from her duty belt. "Mrs. Cassandra Fisher, I'm arresting you for your husband's, Mr. Walter Fisher's, murder. You might want to call your lawyer."

Sandy ran around Vicki, out of the staff room, and headed to the main morgue door before Cerberus blocked her way. "Call off your dog."

Vicki walked over to them, standing between Sandy and the door. She scritched Cerberus's ears. "Good boy."

Sandy addressed the closed door. "You'd better come in."

When the door opened, there was Ms. Burgess, the well-liked Stony attorney. "Welcome. Nice to see you again." I shook her hand. "Let me get you some coffee and pastries."

She smiled. "Thank you. I recognize those boxes from that wonderful pâtisserie in Warehouse-o-Rama."

She sat down and popped a chouquette into her mouth. "Since I'm here, I assume you're arresting my client."

Vicki smiled at her lawyer friend. "Correct."

'Wow! How could Mr. Fisher's wife appear more guilty?' Fitch banged his gavel, wearing judicial robes.

"No need for bail. I'll offer my surety for Mrs. Fisher."

"No problem, Burgess. In that case, I won't arrest her. We'll keep the District Attorney and the courts out of this."

Ms. Burgess and Sandy clinked their coffee cups.

Vicki said, "Just make sure she doesn't leave town."

"No problem. She'll be at the Stony Estancia Hotel for the duration."

'That's not the way I expected that to go.' Fitch said. *'How did we get this far without a cause of death?'*

While Vicki took a shower, Dahl sat in front of the TV cleaning her toes. I preheated the oven, lined two cookie sheets with parchment paper, retrieved my chocolate chip cookie dough from the fridge, and cut large cookies from the loaf.

Vicki called from the bedroom. "I love these linens. Where did you get them?"

The oven beeped. "Hold on a minute. Time to bake." I slid two pans into the warm oven, six large cookies each, and set the timer for twelve minutes. When I peeked into the room, Vicki was under the covers.

"These are lovely."

"Oh yes, those. I found them on the internet, a satin blend of silk and Egyptian cotton. I washed them, but haven't slept on them." I winked. "I bought them for you...for us."

"No time like the present."

"Agree." I didn't enter the bedroom. "Except, the cookies will be ready soon, and Dahl is waiting for us on the sofa."

"Okay. Shut the door, and I'll get dressed."

The cookies beeped, and I arranged them on cooling racks. "Vee, everything is ready. Time for a romcom and cookies."

Before she answered, the video doorbell app notified me. Mother Teresa, Sojourner Truth, and Sally Ride were at the door. "Trick or Treat," they shouted.

Vicki wore a silk Chinese robe embroidered with flying dragons.

"Wicked Halloween costume," said Sally Ride, performing a pirouette.

"Dope," said the white Sojourner Truth.

"Thank you." Vicki walked into the room with an expressionless face, performing a runway turn like a fashion model. "Welcome. Zee has baked fresh cookies."

'*Not welcome.*' Fitch held a broom and pantomimed sweeping the kids down the stairs.

I set the table with warm cookies, three kinds of cold milk, plates, glasses, and napkins.

Vicki sat with her arms crossed while my grandkids helped themselves to milk and cookies.

Emily, aka Sojourner Truth, looked at Vicki and said, "We're sorry to interrupt, but we're worried."

Vicki didn't respond.

I asked, "What's up?"

Louis, aka Sally Ride, said, "Goleta's location is linked to my phone. She must have been on a plane, because she disappeared before showing up in Miami."

Hafsa, aka Mother Teresa, nervously drummed her fingers on the table. After a bite of her cookie, she whispered, "She's a big girl. We didn't worry until I received a text from her saying she was in Boston."

Emily spilled her milk. She threw her glass and cookie into the trash and helped herself to a new glass and a fresh cookie. Dahl licked up the milk puddle. "We can't GPS-Find her phone. Something bad happened to her."

Vicki drank her milk and waited. When my grandkids didn't look up from their cookies, she said, "You can relax. Go home. The police have this under control. Homeland Security and the Highway Patrol have been notified. We'll have her found before morning."

The teens smiled. "Thank you." "Great." "Wonderful." They each took a cookie and left as quickly as they arrived.

'Why are they happy?' Fitch pondered.

"Zee, you can throw out that *'Silicon Valley is stealing Kwolek plans with Goleta as the mule to transport them up north'* theory. I don't know where Leeta is, but she's not in California."

"I agree. We have three crimes. Wally's murder. Goleta's abduction. Graffiti." I wasn't going to let them go unsolved, but there was no more police work to do on Halloween.

She untied the belt on her robe, and we walked hand-in-hand into the bedroom, leaving the dragons on the floor.

The next morning, Dahl was sleeping on a mountain of silk.

Tsui called. "No drug drop at the firehouse. It's my turn to get the kids ready for school. I'm heading home."

Vicki rubbed her eyes. "You can take the day off. Let's hope San Amano PD took care of the problem."

Fitch said, *'XX marks the spot.'*

THANKSGIVING

21. Coroner's Inquest

Thanksgiving, the fourth Thursday in November, was fast approaching, and our investigations were stalled. We didn't know the cause of Walter Fisher's death. Vicki and her high-tech investigators hadn't found Goleta Hardcastle. The good news was that there hadn't been another graffiti incident.

'No thanks to us.' Fitch made gang signs. *'San Amano shut down the drug traffic. Congrats to them.'*

And the data chips from Mr. Mbacke's flower beds—

'You haven't heard from Vinnie.' Fitch flipped through a picture book of Vinnie's granddaughter.

I was confident he would let me know as soon as he figured out the smashed USB sticks.

Stony Estancia Surfs posted: #CORONERSINQUEST MOVED TO CIVIC CENTER AUDITORIUM. I couldn't believe Walter Fisher warranted such a large venue. How could a coroner's inquest compare to the Women in STEM Symposium? Would it draw the same crowd as the mysterious Dr. Ruth Doyle or the brilliant Goleta Hardcastle's egg drop? Mr. Fisher wasn't from Stony Estancia. He was a college recruiter, stand-up comedian, and what else?

The *Surf* posted: #BOYCOTT BRUIN BISTRO. UNSAFE AND UNSANITARY. The internet story leading up to the coroner's inquest suggested that Wally died due to poor food handling. It was a clickbait headline. Bruin Bistro had never had a county health warning. Food poisoning was *Stony Estancia Surfs'* sensationalism, taking advantage of Persey's silence. I was surprised the community tolerated that fake news.

Fitch marched in front of the Civic Center with a placard reading #BOYCOTT STONY ESTANCIA SURFS, and Finch's sign read #SUE THEM FOR #LIBEL

The day of the inquest, Fitch woke me. *'Let's not repeat your late arrival for the Women in STEM Symposium.'*

That wasn't my fault, I protested while giving an accusing stare at Dahl, who was a purring loaf on the sunny windowsill. I had a traditional Swiss breakfast consisting of warm bread with butter and raspberry jam, accompanied by three varieties of cheese, muesli, and kaffee-crème. The meal was both efficient and satisfying.

I set off early enough to collect croissants from la pâtisserie on Higgs Road. However, the Civic Center surprised me with a traffic jam. Why had Wally's death drawn such a large crowd? After leaving my car in a distant space, I joined the others queuing for the X-ray scanners and metal detectors.

'I warned you. You shouldn't have stopped for croissants.' Fitch chastised me. *'By the time you get to the front of the line, there won't be any seats left.'*

Vicki led Tsui. A platoon of uniformed officers followed them like a brood of ducklings. I waved my croissants, and the security detail allowed me to join them in exchange for the flaky delectability of my freshly baked pastries.

I mocked Fitch. *Never doubt the power of la pâtisserie.*

Vicki enjoyed a warm croissant and gave me a peck on the cheek with her buttery lips. "No need to wait in that line. We need all the support we can get." Another kiss. "I deputize you."

'Who knew our gendarmes could be bought that cheaply?' Fitch wore a tall French képi.

Inside, the words DR. PERSEPHONE PATERSON, CERTIFIED FORENSIC PHYSICIAN, were projected on the big screen. The lectern adorned with the Stony Estancia seal stood at stage left. Opposite the lectern, sat the court reporter equipped with a stenotype machine and two laptops. Three empty witness chairs were in the center. In the back of the house, behind the audience, a glass-enclosed control room revealed a tech crew and our ubiquitous reporters, Tish and César.

Fitch cheered, *'The Surf is here.'* He crossed his fingers. *'I hope they post the truth this time.'*

Since the auditorium was full, I stood with Vicki and Tsui, confounded as to why the inquest had drawn a crowd. I asked, "Vee, did you expect a big group?"

"Sure did. I stationed uniformed officers in the aisles and the orchestra pit." Vicki pointed with her croissant. "I call those my prophylactic patrol. A visible presence prevents bad behavior."

Tsui added while brushing crumbs off his uniform, "The SWAT squad is on alert."

"Be prepared, but be cautious," Vicki said to herself. "Use of force is a last resort."

None of that answered my quandary. "Are you expecting a riot?"

"Tell me, Zee, has your phone been dead?" She reached into my la pâtisserie bag for a second croissant. "Parents are up in arms. The *Surf SE* app has been broadcasting alerts around the clock, insinuating that the Bruin Bistro poisoned Wally."

Tsui added, "Persey hasn't helped by her silence."

'Lunch Lady drama,' Fitch chortled, wearing a green apron, pushing a trolley holding the antique espresso machine that looked like a cross between a samovar and a calliope.

At precisely ten o'clock, the house lights dimmed, and a follow spot tracked Persey's entrance. She wore black judicial robes. Cerberus sat beside the lectern, mouth open and tail wagging in contrast to the coroner's somber appearance.

Persey spoke into her microphone. "Good morning."

That greeting grabbed the crowd's attention. They waited silently, like the best-behaved class ever. A pang of jealousy went through me. Teacher's Nirvana.

"Normally, we take witness testimony first and end with our findings. Today I will begin with the verdict." The only sound was Cerberus panting. "Walter Fisher, age thirty-eight, died October 31, at 8:07 PM, during the Halloween Dance at Stony Estancia High School. Something he ate killed him."

That was all it took.

The audience shouted, "Bruin Bistro unsafe," "Boycott Bruin Bistro," and "Protect our children." They chanted, "Shut it down. Shut it down," and "Make Stony High safe again."

I scanned the crowd until I spotted the Lunch Ladies. They looked like nervous dik-diks surrounded by lionesses patrolling for a first breakfast to feed their hungry cubs. The two young Hispanic women from the Lunch Ladies stood.

"¡Dios mío!" said the first Lunch Lady.

"¡Que Dios nos ayude!" said the second one.

The third Lunch Lady, an Asian man, tried to calm them by saying over and over, "Siéntate."

I pushed through the audience. After countless excuse-mes and thank-yous, I stood next to them in a posture I'd perfected during years of crowd control in the big city, my legs spread, my biceps flexed across my chest, and a no-nonsense expression on my face.

'In your dreams,' Fitch said, dressed as the Easter Bunny. *'That may have worked before you grew that salt-and-pepper, mostly salt, Santa Claus beard.'*

"Follow me," I said to the Lunch Ladies in my best Arnold Schwarzenegger voice. We moved to a sanctuary in the orchestra pit.

As the crowd ran out of steam, Mrs. Fisher riled them up by shouting, "The cops arrested me, but it was the Bruin Bistro that killed my husband." She approached the stage with tight fists and tears rolling down her cheeks. She bawled, "This is a free country, let me speak."

Persey controlled the room with her microphone. "I want to hear from the Lunch Ladies first."

The Lunch Ladies climbed out of the orchestra pit to the stage and sat in the witness chairs. The court reporter put on her headphones and booted up her equipment.

"Who's Dr. Macapagal?" Persey inquired.

The lady in the center raised her hand. "Yo soy. I have a PhD in Nutrition Science, but the Lunch Ladies have no hierarchy. We share the work and the responsibilities. You can call me Yasmine."

The Sleuth Club cheered with "You go, Yasmine," and "Bruin Bistro is the best." The Boycott-Bruin-Bistro crowd demanded, "Are you citizens?" and chanted, "Go home."

Cerberus stood and barked twice. His deep voice brought quiet to the room.

Persey scritched his ears, "Good boy," before continuing, "I find that the deceased only ingested your food on the day of his demise. Are you surprised to hear that his cause of death was from an allergic reaction to something he ate?"

'What?' exclaimed Fitch. *'She said she didn't know the cause of death.'*

'Calm down,' replied Finch. *'She doesn't know what caused the allergic reaction.'*

This question must have been on everyone's mind, for the crowd murmured among themselves while waiting for the answer.

"Si. Escandalizado." Yasmine took a deep breath. "This is serious. We follow all regulations. We track and label food allergens: milk, eggs, fish, shellfish, tree nuts, peanuts, wheat, soybeans, and sesame."

The Asian man added, "We didn't cause Mr. Fisher's demise."

The other Lunch Lady was wearing a headscarf. She whispered something to Yasmine, who nodded.

That lady said in a strong voice, "In addition to regulations, we follow cultural practices. We're certified for vegan, halal, and kosher."

The *Surf SE* app alerted: #BRUINBISTRO CLAIMS INNOCENCE. WHAT DO YOU THINK? TAKE OUR SURVEY.

"Fake news," shouted Mrs. Fisher. "You killed Wally and framed me!"

The crowd chanted, "Shut it down. Shut it down."

Szilard's Sleuths responded, "Shake it off. Shake it off."

SWAT dispersed a fight among standing-room-only attendees at the back of the auditorium.

'Where's the fire inspector? We're over the limit.' Fitch wore a helmet and a hi-vis fire suit.

The police escorted Mr. OOP from the swarm. His head hung, and his shoulders drooped as they led him down the center aisle. I couldn't imagine what he had to do with the inquest. Regardless, they held him in the orchestra pit, safe from the crowd.

Persey pleaded with the unruly audience. "Let's not rush to judgment." She walked over to the witness chairs and shook everyone's hands. "These folks are innocent. I called them for background. Now, we'll hear from Mrs. Fisher."

Sandy climbed the stairs, and a stagehand handed her a microphone. She gripped the mic tightly. Her fingers turned white. "Nuts. Eggs. Milk." After each word, she stamped her foot. She stood dangerously downstage, her face was red, and her body shook.

Officers stationed themselves in the orchestra pit, prepared to catch her in case she tripped.

'She was calm at the morgue. Do you think this excitement is an act?' Fitch asked, dressed as an Elizabethan actor at the Globe Theatre.

All faked for the audience. I concurred.

Sandy ranted, "Kosher, halal, vegan, blah, blah. Nonsense. Why don't they serve American food?" She tearfully sobbed, "He had no idea what he was allergic to. All those doctors his mother took him to were stumped. 'Idiopathic,' the idiots said."

Persey spoke calmly, "I need to clarify one thing. Your husband was thirty-eight. Did he have a doctor?"

'What's she doing?' Fitch tamped his calabash pipe. *'This repeats their discussion at the morgue...a month ago.'*

"No." Sandy gave Persey a quizzical look. When Persey didn't respond, Sandy continued. "As a child, he lost faith in the medical profession. As an adult, he treated himself with a restrictive diet. No doctors."

"Thank you, Mrs. Fisher. You've been helpful. I'm sorry for your loss."

Tsui came on stage and handed Sandy a croissant before escorting her into the wings.

The officers holding Mr. OOP released him.

Persey offered him a hand and led him to a witness chair. "Why the sad face, Mr. Drew?"

"This is my fault."

"How so?"

"Only Outstanding Picnics sent me an urgent message. When their vegan vitamin D flour-enrichment supply was interrupted, they used a non-vegan substitute." Mr. Robertson Drew hung his head and spoke to his feet. "With the Career Day excitement, I forgot to tell the Lunch Ladies that the vegan flour was contaminated." He covered his face and sobbed. "This is my fault."

Pandemonium broke loose.

The auditorium reverberated with chants of "Shut it down. Shut it down," and "Make Stony High safe again."

The Sleuth Club echoed back sarcastic teenage laughter, singing, "Shake it off. Shake it off."

Mrs. Fisher broke away from her escorts and pounded her fist on Mr. OOP's shoulders. "You killed my husband."

'Athena, save us. Plato is rolling over in his grave.' Fitch appeared as Aristotle. *'Why hasn't 21st-century forensic science solved this? Why isn't Persey clear? Does she know the cause of death or not? Why doesn't she finger the culprit?'*

The Lunch Ladies huddled together and moved deeper into the wings. Cerberus barked, and Persey picked up her microphone. "You should be ashamed of yourselves. Mr. Walter Fisher's death had nothing to do with food contamination or mislabeling." She waited for them to calm down. "The Lunch Ladies and Mr. Drew are blameless."

'How can she say that?' Fitch shook his head in disbelief.

"He admitted that the flour was contaminated!" someone shouted from the back of the room.

Persey took a deep breath. "Vegan flour is fortified from plant-based sources. Non-vegan flour uses animal-based sources. Parts per million in either case. Not enough to cause death."

'Why didn't she say that first?' Fitch shook his head and made tsk-tsk sounds with his tongue.

The room was silent. Persey had their attention. I was jealous. Never had such a large group hung on my every word.

"There was nothing sloppy..." Pause. "Accidental..." Longer pause. "Or negligent..." Longest dramatic pause. "About Wally's death."

Mrs. Fisher backed away from Mr. OOP.

"Walter Fisher was murdered. Premeditated. Deliberately poisoned. Exact forensic details await lab results."

Cerberus sat beside Persey with his tail sweeping the floor.

Fitch shook his head, wearing a white lab coat. *'How does she know that? Why are the lab results taking so long?'*

Tish and César came down from the control room. The crowd filed out of the auditorium, dodging César's stabilized camera rig and Leticia's microphone covered with a green dead cat.

'The correct term is wind muff or windscreen,' Fitch lectured me, *'Don't let Dahl hear you talking about dead cats.'*

Tish trapped Mr. OOP. "Chemist. CPA. How did you end up promoting Original Organic Products?"

Sweat stains marked Dr. Drew's shirt. He took a deep breath, and his eyes flicked left and right like he was searching for an escape. Air hissed between his closed lips. "Okay. You won't stop until I explain, will you?"

César focused the camera on his face.

"Robby Junior went to Stony High, and it was after Career Day that he disappeared. My wife and I grieved in different ways, and that was the end of our marriage. My accounting career was pointless. I transitioned to being the spokesperson for Out-of-this-world Oral Potions to stay at the school and honor his memory."

César panned his camera over the crowd while tears rolled down Dr. Drew's cheeks.

The *Surf* posted: MR. OOP'S SON ABDUCTED.

'That's old news and a rather large leap.' Fitch sat at his writing desk and dipped his goose quill into a bottle of iron gall ink. *'What happened to his son, and does it connect to Mr. Fisher's murder?*

Vicki and I met with Persey for a debrief in the parking lot. I distributed espressos and biscotti.

"Murder?" Vicki asked. "Have you found the cause of death?"

Persey shook her head. "No proof for murder, but the evidence disproves natural causes, accidents, or suicide. It's murder. Only the cause of death is a mystery."

'When you have eliminated all which is impossible, then whatever remains, however improbable, must be the truth.'

Fitch stood in front of 221B Baker Street smoking his calabash pipe.

Persey must have seen the puzzled look on my face. "I know the inquest was premature, but I'd already delayed a month, and I had to put down the rumors."

Vicki wanted more. "This is the 21st century. Don't you have a cause-of-death AI?"

Cerberus jumped into the coroner's van, and Persey followed him. Her parting statement was, "There's my problem. Folks expect instant answers. It isn't that easy. You must wait, just like everyone else. I'm not going to release some AI hallucination."

'You go, girl,' Fitch cheered with green and gold Stony High pom-poms.

Science had let us down. After a month, Persey needed more lab tests to find Walter Fisher's cause of death.

'Look on the bright side.' Fitch wore a comedy mask. *'Persey's quashed the accusations against the Lunch Ladies and Mr. OOP, shutting down the angry parents.'*

'Technology let us down.' Finch wore a tragedy mask. *'Vicki's high-tech investigators haven't found Goleta Hardcastle.'*

Fitch countered with, *'There hasn't been another graffiti incident.'*

'Our smart friends are stymied.' Finch added while painting tears drops on her mask. *'Vinnie hasn't decoded the smashed USB sticks.*

Nothing diminished Fitch's optimism. *'It's time to check with the Sleuth Club.'*

Following the inquest, Stony Estancia settled into autumn and the calm before the year-end holidays. Fall colors were a luxury of the northern states. In the Southern California desert, savvy trees lost their green leaves in preparation for the winter winds, and a few wet days heralded the approaching so-called rainy season. The joggers switched to long pants, and Dahl woke me before the delayed sunrises. I was frustrated by the lack of progress on my open cases, waiting for Wally's cause of death and Sleuth Club news of Goleta's whereabouts.

On the sleepy Wednesday morning before Thanksgiving recess, my phone sounded the ringtone for the substitute notification system, Chuck Berry's *School Days*. My fingers tap-tapped on autopilot. Before I was fully awake, I had a same-day assignment for Mr. Leaphorn's World Mythology classes, a favorite because he left interesting lesson plans. I always learned something.

The thought of a long school day made me hungry. I sautéed skirt steak, lamb chops, and boneless turkey breast, along with onions and garlic in Grandpa's cast-iron pan. I whisked a couple of eggs in a wooden bowl with heavy cream, salt, and pepper, and served myself the combined omelet, accompanied by sourdough toast.

Dahl pushed her dish against my shoes.

'She prefers your breakfast,' Fitch sat at the table with a fork in one hand, a knife in the other, and a green-and-gold checkered napkin tucked in at his neck.

I selected pieces of meat for Dahl and added a splash of her lactose-free cream to cool the hot dish. Like a true obligate carnivore, she dove into her treat, splattering cream over her face and whiskers. When the dish was empty, she jumped up on the windowsill for her postprandial grooming in the morning sun.

'Cheer up,' said Fitch, dressed as a Pilgrim. Thanksgiving is tomorrow. Today, school lets out early, a half-day.

I looked forward to a perfect day.

My expectation of order vanished when I was confronted with a forest of green Sleuth Club T-shirts. Classroom management depends on keeping an emotional distance between the teacher and the students. Too friendly, and the students ran amok. Too bossy, and their adolescent restiveness came out.

I hadn't helped my predicament when, back on Career Day, I taught the Sleuth Club lesson one: It's easier to ask forgiveness than permission. I expected that lesson to unleash their teenage independence on the school and the police, but now it turned back on me.

Can't you threaten them with detention or send them to the office?' Fitch went around the room slapping his ruler on the desks like some one-room schoolhouse tyrant.

Those remedies are offered to all subs. However, when they're used, the sub isn't invited to return.

I moved behind Mr. Leaphorn's desk to increase our physical separation and called roll as if I'd never met them.

The first name on my list was "Chee, Jaxon." He gave me a shaka wave with his thumb and pinky. I returned his gesture and went on to the next name. My roleplay established order.

For her response to, "Khattak, Hafsa," she adjusted her aqua hijab and said, "Allahu Akbar."

"Milhone, Emily," was met with silence. Clouseau sat on her desk in his Siamese cat glory, cleaning his paws. Emily lifted a single, well-manicured finger to acknowledge her name. I let that pass and continued with the list.

"Rawlins, Louis," popped out of his seat and performed a barefoot relevé with his arms extended over his head.

'Congrats. Distance established and order restored.' Fitch sat at his desk with his fingers interlaced like those of a model student in a one-room schoolhouse.

Mr. Leaphorn's lesson plan called for report presentations.

I started with Emily because she was the least likely to disturb the fragile classroom order.

'You hope.' Fitch wore a Sleuth Club shirt and a self-satisfied teenage grin.

Emily stood next to her desk in the middle of the room and had trouble deciding which way to face. Finally, she addressed Hafsa. "I chose Freya, the Norse goddess of love, beauty, youth, and—" She stammered. "—f-f-fertility."

The class laughed.

I jumped to her defense. "One more outburst and I'm writing your names on the board for Mr. Leaphorn."

That backfired. Emily sat down and hugged Clouseau. Hafsa ran over to hug Emily, and the rest of the class folded their arms in silent protest.

'Too much. Now you need to make friends again.' Fitch turned into a white rabbit puffing on a hookah, mixing up his *Alice's Adventures in Wonderland* images.

I moved from behind Mr. Leaphorn's desk to a student table in the back. I offered Louis my hand. When he shook it, the class relaxed. I spoke to him like we were the only ones in the room. "Wouldn't you like to hear the rest of Emily's report?"

"Sure would." He addressed her, "Sorry."

Emily stood up. "Freya wore a beautiful gold necklace called Brísingamen, and rode a glittering chariot pulled by two blue-gray cats, Bygul and Trjegul." With her mention of cats, her flame-point Siamese jumped to the floor and hid beneath her skirt.

I asked, "Why did you choose Freya?"

'D'oh. Cats obvs.' Fitch scrolled through cat memes. *'Cats rule the internet and Dahl rules Higgs Haven.'*

Emily teared up. "Freya was Leeta's choice. She loved Freya and talked about riding Freya's chariot to freedom." Emily rubbed her eyes with her fists. "Freya took her away."

My delicate order collapsed. The class chattered, voicing the same questions that ran through my mind.

"What happened to Goleta?" "Why haven't the police found her?" "What are her parents hiding?"

Order was every sub's top priority. Flexibility was the key to my success. Mr. Leaphorn's lesson plan had failed to hold their attention. I violated the number one substitute directive. I sacrificed the lesson plan at the altar of classroom management, worse than sending students to detention.

I surrendered to Szilard's Sleuths. "Has anyone learned anything about Leeta?"

Emily stood to her full height and told her surveillance story.

Hafsa and I waited outside Emily's house until her father came home. When he stepped out of his car, we addressed him with the patriarchal respect he demanded, "Good evening, Mr. Hardcastle. Has Goleta returned?"

He pursed his lips and shook his head. "No."

"Would you like us to search her room to find out where she went?"

He acted like that was something he never thought of, but I didn't believe him. He was concealing something. I remembered lesson one: It's easier to ask forgiveness than permission. I nodded to Hafsa, who gave me a half smile.

We held hands and ran into the house, leaving a polite Mr. Hardcastle shaking his head. We had been there before and had no difficulty going through the ballroom and by the library to the family staircase. We passed the Mr. and Mrs. bedroom suites and the guest rooms before entering Goleta's room with its view of the pool, tennis courts, and croquet lawn.

Emily sat down, placed Clouseau in her lap, and scratched the base of his tail. The kitten purred loudly enough to be heard by all.

I prompted. "What did you find?"

Hafsa walked to the front. "She had a pink, white, and blue flag hanging over her bed, which matched her bedspread that had a white stripe down the center, two pink stripes wide enough to cover her bed, and two blue stripes hanging down."

Emily commented, "That must be the biggest transgender pride flag ever."

Hafsa nodded, "I don't think her parents knew." After a pause, she continued, "Her desk had two computers, macOS and Windows. Above the desk was a Lynn Conway poster."

"Did you find anything to locate her?" I asked.

Emily began, "In the back of Leeta's closet, we discovered a wedding dress." She paused until Hafsa nodded to give her permission to keep going. "The lace-covered strapless bodice was intact, but the ball gown skirt and train of silk satin were cut up with only the seams and hems remaining."

'Who cuts up a wedding dress?' Fitch wore a mourning suit with a green waistcoat.

Leeta was too young to get married in Stony Estancia. She hadn't graduated from college, much less graduate school. "What was she doing with a wedding dress?" I queried.

Hafsa shrugged her shoulders. "No idea, most of it was missing. It was like a Thanksgiving turkey carcass. Only the bones remained."

Emily choked. "Leeta's father was an old-fashioned patriarch, demanding that she marry one of his business associates. That's why she wanted Freya to take her away. Her mother bought her that dress to bribe her to accept her father's choice. I recall that it was expensive."

'What does expensive mean in Stony Estancia? More than a computer? More than a car? More than a house?' Fitch transitioned to a dragon and sat on a mountain of gold coins.

Louis interjected, "I know what happened."

Everyone turned to him.

"Do you remember those weather balloons we used for meteorology experiments?" When the class nodded their heads, he said, "Now we know where she got the silk to make them."

The class erupted with, "You go, girl," and "Go, go, Goleta."

"What do you think happened to Leeta?" I asked, confident that the mythological Freya and a chariot drawn by cats weren't involved.

Hafsa shook her fist. "She was kidnapped. When her father discovered what she did to the dress, he had her abducted and forced into marriage."

Louis added, "She's probably barefoot..." He raised his bare feet. "...and pregnant in some foreign country."

'This is hearsay and getting out of hand. You've got to stop this.' Fitch wore a judge's black robes and banged his gavel.

I hear you.

"This is the 21st century, and we're in Stony Estancia. I doubt we're dealing with forced marriages. They're illegal in California. Does someone have a more credible theory?"

Emily crossed her arms, and Clouseau hissed. "I agree with them. Someone grabbed Goleta. It wasn't Freya. Bygul and Trjegul weren't pulling a golden chariot."

I didn't like the kidnapping scenario, but I let Emily continue. "What makes you say that?"

"When I searched her room, her closets and drawers were full. She would never have left without taking her stuff."

Hafsa added, "Her walk-in closet was packed with beautiful skirts, blouses, dresses, and cute shoes." She smiled. "Her dresser was packed with the best pretties—silky, lacey, every color of the rainbow—"

"That's enough," interrupted Emily. "It isn't proper to discuss her underwear. Besides, her mother bought that stuff. They weren't Leeta's style."

Hafsa changed the subject, "We didn't see her Russian Blue cats. She had two cats like Freya. She never let them out. They escaped when she was abducted."

'Stony Estancia kids don't travel light. Remember the luggage they had on that trip to Washington, D.C.?' Fitch ran through Dulles Airport with two suitcases, a backpack, a shoulder bag, and an umbrella.

Szilard's Sleuths presented a convincing scenario, though I knew Vicki believed Goleta was a runaway.

The omniscient *Surf SE* app posted: HONOR STUDENT FROM STONY HIGH KIDNAPPED #CHILDABUCTION.

'You were almost right.' Fitch wore a SWAT uniform. *'Those Silicon Valley venture capitalists wanted her to steal the Kwolek plans.'* Fitch moved to a district attorney's office with a big desk covered with legal briefs. *'She double-crossed them and agreed to testify against the vulture capitalists, and now she's in witness protection. She left everything behind when she assumed her new identity.'*

WITSEC. Good one, Fitch, but I doubt that's the answer.

Clouseau leaped from one desk to the next until he reached the front. Then, he did something only possible for a Siamese cat. His loud, low-pitched yowl silenced the class.

The buzzer signaled the end of the half-day before the Thanksgiving holiday.

On his way out, Louis handed me a note. ONLY DONUTS.

Fitch waved his green-and-gold checkered napkin like a flag. *'Only Donuts is my favorite restaurant, and it's within walking distance of the school.'*

I suspected Louis was interested in more than lunch, but what?

I entered the Bruin Bistro.

'Oh no,' said Fitch, wearing his green apron. *'You're not going to cut through here on your way to Only Donuts.'*

Only Donuts was a popular student hangout, across Blackett Street, south of the school.

Why not? It's *the shortest path.*

'It's like flying your private jet to a climate change conference.' Fitch scoffed. *'You can't be on both teams.'*

I entered the Bistro under a green and gold banner. THE BEST FOR YOUR HEALTH AND YOUR HUNGER. They cornered the market on wholesome, organic, and gourmet.

Mrs. Golding glared at me like she could tell that I was on my way to Donuts. The principal emphasized fitness and healthy eating. At the start of each school year, she unsuccessfully campaigned to have Only Donuts closed.

I couldn't face her. I backed out to the courtyard and walked around to the alley between the Bistro and the science building. Hafsa and Emily also chose to avoid Mrs. Golding.

"We should have cut through the Bistro." Emily picked up Clouseau and walked faster. "Now we're late, and Donuts will be packed. How are we going to find a table?" Together, we crossed Blackett Street, dodging student drivers heading home for Thanksgiving recess.

The Only Donuts' banner read: THE 4 FOOD GROUPS: SALT, SUGAR, FAT, AND MORE SALT. They claimed the other end of the food spectrum from the Bistro. Donuts as big as your head, fried in traditional lard or tallow. Despite their name, they also served funnel cakes, ginormous soft pretzels, triple-meat pizzas, and the best fries in Stony Estancia.

We entered together. Hafsa waved the long end of her scarf. "There they are."

Louis stood on a table in the center of the room, holding it by turning ballet fouettés. Mohamed crouched down to avoid Louis's kick turns while working on his laptop.

We ordered from the apps on our phones. I had fries with malt vinegar. The table offered four types of salt: kosher, sea, black, and pink. I sampled them all.

Louis ordered a chocolate éclair with Tahitian vanilla ice cream on the side. Hafsa had apple fritters generously sprinkled with powdered sugar. The menu tagged her fritters with a crescent moon icon, halal, which at Only Donuts meant they were fried in tallow instead of lard.

Emily settled for a pizza slice that was rolled up into a cone and filled with garlic knots. Moe was more interested in his laptop than in food. "I love their gigabit Wi-Fi."

In a nod to our health, we shared a pot of rooibos and peppermint tea—no sugar, no milk, no caffeine.

"What did you think of Persey's inquest?" I asked, sprinkling vinegar on my fries.

"It didn't look like murder." Hafsa took a bite into a fritter covered in powdered sugar. "We were at the dance and saw him collapse. No one was near him." She brushed the white powder off her hijab.

Emily nodded in agreement while nibbling on a garlic knot. She poured the remaining knots onto the table. "Help yourselves. One is enough for me. I wanted the pizza."

Moe typed on his laptop. "That inquest was the best diversion ever."

'What the puppies is he talking about?' Fitch raised his shoulders and held his palms up.

We looked at Moe with pinched faces and squinty eyes, body language for "What the puppets?"

He must have enjoyed the attention because he kept us waiting while he finished typing. "While Mrs. Fisher was proclaiming her innocence up on the stage, I borrowed her phone and installed a tracker."

'A tracker?' Fitch exclaimed. *'Mad Skillz. You've released a monster with the Sleuth Club.'*

"So what?" Emily took a bite of her pizza.

Hafsa completed Emily's thought. "Why do we need to track her? What does she have to do with Leeta?"

Moe leaned back from the table and whispered. "Patience, young grasshopper." He pulled an envelope from his backpack, held it upside down, and a piece of paper fluttered out.

Hafsa grabbed it mid-flight. "What's this?"

It had two stylized wings connected by a pair of interlocking M's.

Emily grabbed the paper. "That's Minerva's Mission. Where did you get this?"

Vicki had told me Minerva's Mission was a secret group that recovered missing children. I hadn't expected these teens to know about them.

'Szilard's Sleuths know more about Goleta Hardcastle's disappearance than they let on.' Fitch looked into his crystal ball.

Moe took the paper, now covered with grease stains, and placed it back in the envelope. "I found it when I borrowed Mrs. Fisher's phone to install the tracker."

"She had this?" Emily dropped her cone of pizza on the table. "How is she mixed up with Minerva's Mission?"

Moe returned the envelope to his backpack. "I hadn't thought of that."

Hafsa said, "Remember our first lesson: It's easier to ask forgiveness than permission. The *Surf* reported that Mrs. Fisher is under house arrest at the Stony Estancia Hotel. Let's break into her room." She paused before adding, "Tonight."

'First the tracker and now a break-in.' Fitch wore his judicial robes and banged his gavel. *'This is beyond lesson one.'*

Lesson five: If I can't control them, I might as well support them.

'Lesson five? I don't recall lesson five. Where did that come from?' Fitch tore off his robes and threw them on the floor.

I just made it up. Desperate times call for desperate measures.

Emily agreed with Hafsa. "Perfect, but not tonight. Tomorrow. Thanksgiving. We'll have more time to search."

I wondered aloud. "Do you know her room number? Do you have a key?"

A look passed between Hafsa, Louis, Moe, and Emily before Hafsa said, "Lesson four. Evidence is everywhere."

'I'd take that for a yes.' Fitch retrieved his judicial robes. *'Bailiff. Bailiff. Lock them up.'*

Their plan had too many holes in it. "Even when you can find her hotel room, how will you know when she's inside?" My grandkids had more enthusiasm than experience. "You know you can't search her room when she's there. Right?"

'They can drug her.' Fitch suggested.

I hope not. That's going too far.

"My tracker," said Moe with his arms crossed and a proud smile on his face.

Emily took a bite of her pizza and swallowed. "Perfect, we'll watch her on Thanksgiving and break in while she's eating Mr. S's turkey."

Hafsa tossed a fritter in my direction. "You won't forget to invite her, right?"

'Don't forget,' hooted Fitch. *'Lesson three: The lone investigator is a myth. You've been conscripted.'*

I caught the fritter, sprinkled it with powdered sugar, and took a bite. Since they included me on their team, I vowed not to let them down. "I'm texting an invite right now."

We fist-bumped.

'Lesson two: Good detectives don't attract attention. Be subtle.' Fitch hid under the table with Clouseau.

MR S: I ALWAYS HAVE PLENTY OF [TURKEY EMOJI]. I attached my contact deets.

Is that subtle enough?

We bussed our table, and Louis did a farewell fouetté. I checked my phone on the way out. Sandy hadn't responded.

'Maybe your text was too subtle.' Fitch flashed me a fingers-crossed emoji.

I didn't send a second text, not wanting to appear too eager. I had nothing else to do but prepare the feast and hope Sandy was hungry.

At midnight, Dahl and I stood on our balcony and surveyed the dark windows and empty parking lots. Higgs Haven housed young couples who were saving for a down payment on a starter home and singles. On holidays, they visited the larger dining rooms of family and friends. I hugged Dahl. We shared the warmth of my buffalo-plaid flannel shirt. "It's the two of us."

She purred.

Fitch went *Harumph*.

"The three of us," I corrected.

"Visitors," I announced, pointing to a short convoy of three vehicles turning into our parking lot. It was Thanksgiving Eve, and my sous chefs, Vicki, Coroner Persey, and Principal Golding, had arrived. I ran down the stairs and held the door as they filed in, arms full of mixing bowls and baking pans.

'Sous chefs? More like you're the junior to those three chefs de cuisine.' Fitch wore a green chef's toque and held a massive bowl under his arm, whisking so quickly that his hand disappeared. *'My Thanksgiving specialty, lighter-than-air meringue.'*

Spare me. Not only is your meringue light, it's colorless, odorless, and tasteless. I added one more. *And invisible.*

While the three ladies and I worked, little could be heard but the whir of mixers, the beep of timers, and the constantly repeated, "Behind." We did our best to avoid colliding with each other or Cerberus, who was alert to see what would hit the floor. Dahl sat on her shelf in Egyptian cat god posture, waiting for bowls to sniff and lick as her tribute for blessing our efforts. This was a traditional Thanksgiving, cooking and companionship.

The Sleuth Club's audacious plan depended on Mrs. Fisher joining us. Sandy hadn't responded to my subtle text, but I was confident Thanksgiving would draw her out. Nothing was sadder than being alone on this holiday.

Everyone contributed their personal favorites. Persey filled the goose with chopped portobello mushrooms, lentils, and chestnuts. Vicki shared those ingredients to prepare savory pies. Principal Golding stuffed pumpkins with wild rice pilaf, cranberries, and pecans.

By sunrise, home-cooking aromas of shallots, garlic, and caramel filled the apartment. The upper oven, halal and kosher, roasted the goose, and the middle one held the vegetarian pies. The lower one baked a glazed ham. My personal Thanksgiving favorite, whole stuffed pumpkins, were in the vegetarian oven. I slid open the balcony door to cool the kitchen and share our Thanksgiving warmth with the deserted neighborhood.

With the ovens going, we sat around the Thanksgiving table for the customary first breakfast. Vicki set the table, Persey made whipped cream, and Principal Golding took charge of the espresso machine. I served cranberry pear pie and apple chai-spice pie from la pâtisserie. Dahl received goose liver, and Persey served Cerberus a meaty knuckle bone.

I selected whipped cream for my cranberry-pear and cheddar cheese for my slice of apple chai-spice. Dahl rubbed against my legs. Thanksgiving morning filled me with gratitude and love. I fed Vicki apple pie, and she fed me whipped cream.

After the silence that inevitably follows food served to hungry people, I said, "I'm thankful that Vinnie Purcell accepted my dinner invitation. He copied these memory chips." I held up the Firehouse Barbecue take-out container. "I expect he'll have something to report. It will be good to tie up that loose end."

Vicki asked. "Has your teenage Sleuth Club made any progress finding Goleta Hardcastle? What have they been doing?"

'Go ahead, tell her you've been working with the Sleuth Club and their idea that Leeta was kidnapped.' Fitch chuckled.

Not now. Maybe later. I avoided Vicki's questions by asking Persey. "What are you thankful for?"

"I'm thankful for some high-powered help. I shipped Wally's blood and DNA samples to Maryland. The National Institute of Allergy and Infectious Diseases has agreed to take on Walter Fisher's cause-of-death mystery."

Vicki appeared frustrated. "I need that cause of death. Sandy Fisher's lawyer, my good friend Ms. Burgess, is pressing me to clear her client."

"Why not clear her?" I asked.

"My background investigation revealed that Mrs. Fisher has family in France. If I let her go, she'll disappear."

Vicki's problems were bringing the group down. I nudged her, "You must have something to be grateful for?"

She smiled and said, "I received good news in the latest Athena's Avengers newsletter."

Principal Golding said, "Who are they?"

Persey dropped her head into her hands. "California has too many extra-legal activists."

That's a euphemism for vigilante groups.' Fitch saddled up with Wyatt Earp and Bat Masterson, galloping out of Dodge City in pursuit of outlaws.

Vicki continued, "Athena's Avengers and Minerva's Mission are both secret groups that fight child abductions and trafficking."

Persey picked it up from there. "Minerva's Mission is more hands-on."

Vicki continued, "I was glad to read that they apprehended a group operating in the Gold Country, the mountains east of Sacramento." She ate another bite of pie. "I sent them a copy of the Goleta Hardcastle file and asked them to interrogate their captives."

I expect she said more than she planned, because she turned to Mrs. Golding. "How about you? What are you grateful for?"

"My gratitude list is nothing like returning abducted children or convicting murderers."

I put my arm around Principal Golding's shoulder. "You're among friends."

"Dr. Terez Telkes had been discouraged, but now she's expecting the Stony Estancia Makers Guild IPO by year's end.

I don't know what changed, but that's good news. It should mean a windfall for the school–" She lowered her voice. "And for me."

Dahl yowled a pitiful meow that felines have perfected over the millennia since they were gods in Egypt. She rubbed my legs, signifying: *Everything smells good, and my dish is empty.* She gave a pitiful meow and hissed at Cerberus. *I shared my food with that big dog.*

Cerberus sat politely, wagging his tail.

I said, "Patience, my fur babies."

The hour was too late to go to sleep. We had another round of pie and watched *Miracle on 34th Street*, while waiting for the ovens to do their magic. Both versions of the movie played simultaneously on side-by-side screens.

When the sun rose on our balmy Southern California Thanksgiving, the first guest to arrive was Officer Tsui. He carried garlic-parmesan carrots in his left hand and squash with poached cranberries in his right. His mouth opened wide. "Has the kitchen grown since my last visit?"

I followed his eyes. Three ovens. Two dishwashers. Two double sinks. A proofing cabinet, an espresso machine, and a food warmer from a restaurant bankruptcy sale. I never met a kitchen appliance I didn't need...mixers, bread makers, microwaves, toasters, blenders, air fryers, rice cookers...all lined up on what must have appeared to Tsui as miles of workspace.

Fitch walked around the kitchen, turning off unused devices. *'Your kitchen might be magically bigger than your apartment, but it uses real energy. Think of the planet.'*

No worries, mate. I have a wind turbine and solar panels on the roof.

I held the food warmer open for Tsui. "Just put your dishes here. There's always room for more."

After he placed them, he signaled his children, who had waited politely downstairs. "I take care of them for Thanksgiving." He smiled. "My wife is thankful to have a day's rest."

His oldest child carried two roast ducks, hanging by their necks from a shoulder pole. The next child placed bowls of pancakes in the warmer. The third one brought sweet bean sauce, while the fourth delivered julienned scallions and peeled cucumber sticks. The last one, barely three, announced, "Peking duck and all the dwimmings," a phrase that sounded rehearsed.

The ducks and pancakes went into the warmer—everything else was wedged into the fridge.

'You need another fridge,' Fitch joked.

Each child took a piece of pie and found an adult's lap. When the youngest snuggled with me, I resumed the DVD players.

As we watched the twin movies of Thanksgiving parades, my video doorbell app demanded attention. I tapped the unlock icon and shouted down the stairwell, "Come in."

With the agility of teenagers, Louis and Hafsa ran up the steps, each carrying two pies. He carried a purple sweet potato pie and a black-sesame pumpkin pie from Factory and Farm Foods. She juggled a pear and almond cream tart and a sour cherry tart with frangipane from la pâtisserie.

Hafsa dropped her pies on the table, collapsed into a chair, and cradled her head in her hands. She sobbed, "She's gone. She's gone."

Louis stood like a statue holding his pies.

I was baffled by Hafsa's distress. I looked to Vicki and mouthed, "Can you do something?"

Vicki rescued Louis's pies. Once freed of his burdens, he hugged Hafsa. "We'll find her. I'm sure we will."

Vicki and I looked at each other, puzzled by these distraught teens.

"First Leeta and now Emmy," cried Hafsa. "What's going on? Who's stealing Stony High girls?"

'Emily is missing? Where's she?' Fitch hoisted an orange distress flag with the internationally recognized black square and black ball.

Everyone stopped eating. Coroner Persey paused the movies, and Tsui's oldest took the children outside to the vacant playground.

I leaned over to Vicki. "When did this happen? I can't believe that two Stony Estancia girls would run away."

"Two abductions are harder to imagine," she rebutted.

'Runaways are more credible than abductions. These are Stony High women.' Fitch lined up in the first-class queue at the airport with plenty of luggage.

Principal Golding set a couple of places at the table. "I'm sure we can help. Thank you for the wonderful pies. Sit here."

Like two polite robots, the students dutifully let Mrs. Golding serve them. She removed the savory dishes from the ovens and placed them on the table. I served Louis a plate with baked ham and gave Hafsa one with roast goose, halal.

Hafsa helped herself to roasted squash, and Louis took carrots. They took small bites, and tears ran down Louis's cheeks. They calmed down as they ate.

Louis's phone beeped. He excused himself. "Mr. S, can you come out on the balcony?"

He showed me his phone. "We're going to leave soon. Mrs. Fisher is on the move. This is our opportunity."

"What?" He didn't respond. "Oh. The break-in." I said, realizing that he'd changed from Emily being missing to breaking into Mrs. Fisher's hotel room. Teenagers have short attention spans. I gave him a thumbs-up. "I hope she's on her way here."

Back in the dining room, Vicki was talking to Hafsa, "I'm sorry about your friend. Are you sure she's missing?"

'She was careful not to say runaway or kidnapped,' Fitch polished his magnifying glass. *'Not leading the witness.'*

Hafsa answered, "Like with Leeta, when we went to pick her up, she was nowhere to be found. We searched her room. She's gone." After a slice of roast goose and a drink of apple cider, she continued, "Unlike Leeta, she packed. There were empty hangers in her closet, open spaces in her drawers, and free slots in her shoe cabinets."

Louis showed Moe's tracking app to Hafsa. "Mrs. Fisher left her hotel. She's heading here. Time to go."

I went over to Principal Golding. "Please. No questions. Wally's wife will be here soon. Can you keep her here as long as possible?"

She gave me a questioning look but nodded in silent agreement.

Louis looked at his phone and showed it to Hafsa. "Problem. She stopped at the Firehouse Barbecue."

Hafsa laughed. "Not a problem. They're closed. Only upscale places open on Thanksgiving." She looked at me. "She needs a nudge."

'A subtle nudge,' Fitch bumped into me.

I 'liked' my text. **MR S:** I ALWAYS HAVE PLENTY OF [TURKEY EMOJI].

We huddled around Louis's tracker. Then the tracker refreshed, and we saw Cassandra Fisher continuing up Higgs Road. Hafsa said, "Thank you for the lovely food," and followed Louis down the stairs. They passed Tsui's children returning from the playground.

Someone resumed the DVDs.

The Thanksgiving parades from the *Miracle on 34th Street* movies were coming to an end when we heard someone storming up the stairs and shouting, "I'm going to sue."

Mrs. Fisher burst into my condo. "You're conspiring to frame me for Wally's murder."

I jumped up from the couch. "Over here, Sandy. I'll bring you a nice food plate. Would you prefer sweet or savory?"

That stopped her tirade. "Sweet," she said meekly.

"Coffee or tea? Or apple cider?"

"Cider, please."

While I prepared a plate with four kinds of pie, our four-legged squad smothered her in love. Cerberus lay at her feet, and Dahl cuddled into her lap.

The placated Mrs. Fisher enjoyed her pie with whipped cream and black cherry ice cream. We were out of vanilla.

I made my move. "We were remembering your husband. Can you tell us a bit about him?"

She collapsed back onto the sofa. "Where should I start?"

"At the beginning," Mrs. Golding replied, winking at me.

"We lived on the same street and met in pre-school..."

When she mentioned their first innocent kiss in second grade, I was confident this would be a long story. I slipped out to join the Sleuth Club at the Stony Estancia Hotel.

I turned left from Higgs Road onto Zeeman Way. The Stony Estancia Hotel parking lot was deserted. Leaving my Thanksgiving guests was above-and-beyond support for the Sleuth Club. But where were they?

My phone beeped for an incoming text. **JAX:** NOT THE HOTEL. COME TO THE BANK. [FACE PALM]

'How did he know where you were?' Fitch sat in front of a large monitor inside a surveillance van disguised as a delivery truck.

I turned back onto Zeeman, the way I came. I found everyone behind the Stony Estancia Community Bank. "Hey, Jax, how did you know where I was?" I gave him a big smile to show I wasn't upset. "Did someone install a tracker on my phone?" I couldn't hold the smile any longer. "Tracking Mrs. Fisher was a borderline problem, but hacking my phone was over the line."

"Chill, Mr. S." Louis laughed. "No one messed with your electronics. We saw your black-and-white electric car drive past the bank."

'Overreact, much?' Fitch abandoned his surveillance van for a lawn chair and a pair of binoculars. *'It's not like there's a lot of traffic on Zeeman in the middle of the night.'*

"My bad. Mea culpa." I opened my backpack to distribute drinks and energy bars as an apology. "Are you sure that Minerva's Mission is enough evidence to break into Mrs. Fisher's hotel room?"

Louis backed away. "Moe installed the tracker, but the break-in was Emily's idea."

When he mentioned Emily, Hafsa shivered.

I had doubts about this mission. Initiated with insufficient intelligence, and on scant evidence by Emily, now missing. They didn't know Sandy Fisher's room number, how to get in, or what they wanted once inside.

Fitch ridiculed my sleuths. *'What did you expect when you deputized a bunch of teenagers?'* He sat in the Dodge City Marshal's office cleaning his Colt single-action Army revolver.

Lesson five: If I can't control them, I might as well support them.

In my best upbeat voice, I said, "I'm with you. What's the plan?"

With Emily gone, Louis took charge. "Operation Pizza Delivery depends on Hafsa."

She replied, "Inshallah. If God wills it."

He handed her a name tag from C&NY Pizza, KIMBERLY.

"No way," protested Hafsa. "There has never been a hijab-wearing girl named Kimberly."

Louis went through the badges he'd "borrowed" from the pizza place. "Makayla, Stacey, Tracey, Barbie, Zara—"

"Zara," she repeated. "Give me that one." She took a bag of clothes from her car. "Everyone, turn around." While we watched the traffic on Zeeman Way, she hid her silk tunic under a baggy grey sweatshirt and exchanged her embroidered hijab for a pink polyester niqab that covered her face. "All set." She pinned the Zara badge on the sweatshirt and did a slow turn. "No more Hafsa. Call me Zara."

Louis took charge. "Your disguise looks great, Zara." Everyone laughed when he said Zara. "Next, we need communications and a pizza delivery car."

The student cars were too fancy for our clandestine op. "She can use mine," I volunteered. I tossed Hafsa my keys, and she handed over the fob for her metallic-blue German SUV.

"Everyone, join the group chat." Jaxon checked the phones. "Mr. S, hand me yours. I'll enter the private chat password."

'They don't trust you with the password.' Fitch was back in the surveillance van and laughing.

Hafsa led the way in my tiny electric car, as we caravanned down Zeeman Way to the Stony Estancia Hotel.

I parked in the guest parking lot, and Hafsa drove up to the main entrance. The doorman treated her as a guest, holding her car door and bowing. Hafsa wore wireless earbuds and bobbed her head like she was listening to music.

She carried two boxes in an insulated carrier. The thicker one, holding a Chicago-style all-meat pizza, was on the bottom, and the thinner New York-style cheese pizza was on top. Chicago and New York Pizza, called C&NY Pizza by the cool kids, offered both.

The doorman ran past her to hold the hotel door and directed her to the reception desk.

This was the first real-world test for the Sleuth Club, working under pressure and thinking on their feet.

'Bare feet in Louis's case.' Fitch stomped his snakeskin boots, dancing the *Boot Scootin' Boogie*.

We listened to Hafsa through group chat. "Soundcheck. Good news. Sleuth Mohamed Manuelito, Moe, is working the desk, but I don't expect him to recognize Zara."

I replied, "Can you hear us?"

She responded, "As clear as Mr. OOP selling organic foods."

"Operation Pizza, all systems go," Jaxon declared grandly.

The next thing to come over the group chat was Moe. "As-Salaam-Alaikum, Hafsa. Why are you delivering pizza, and Where's your car?"

The group chat went silent. Plan A was for Hafsa to pass as Zara, the pizza delivery girl. When Moe recognized her, she froze. Everyone in the parking lot looked at each other. That was when I realized that they had no Plan B.

'Time for lesson five. Support them.' Fitch rode in with his sword held high and playing a charge on his bugle.

I spoke in the group chat. "You can do this, Hafsa. Think. Smile. Speak slowly."

After a pause, we heard Hafsa, "Wa-Alaikum-Salaam, Moe. This is research for my AP Econ report: *Does the gig economy offer upward mobility?*"

Jaxon cheered. "Smart lady, Hafsa."

Moe didn't respond. Hafsa continued, "My car? They make me use that thing. It's electric and they recharge it from solar panels. You can thank the Ecology Club."

Finally, Moe said, "Cool. What can I do for you?"

Hafsa was a natural secret agent. Everyone outside the hotel applauded.

"I have a delivery for Mrs. Fisher."

"You're too late. She's gone."

"Let me check my phone." After a pause, Hafsa continued, "I have the right name and place. I can't afford to get fired. I need this job for my report. Let me leave the pizzas in her room."

Everyone froze when Moe said, "It's Thanksgiving. No one eats pizza on Thanksgiving."

I spoke slowly in group chat. "You can do this. We believe in you. Think. Speak slowly."

"Let me check the order." We could hear her tapping on her phone. "Look here. Special instructions."

Moe read, "If the customer is gone, leave the pizza. She'll have it for breakfast."

Hafsa said, "I love pizza for breakfast."

Moe said, "You can take the pizzas up." He paused as if reconsidering. "I wouldn't do this for anyone else."

Louis laughed. "He's sweet on her."

Moe continued. "I'll call housekeeping. Keith will let you in. Take the elevator up to room 413. You remember Keith Evans, don't you?"

"Of course, I know Kee. He was the student project manager for the new observatory."

"Hafsa passed that test like it was an AP exam, perfect score, all fives," Jaxon said with admiration.

"We have the room number. Now we need a key to get into the building. We can't march through the lobby." I reminded them.

"No problem," replied Louis. "We're set. Keith Evans is in the Sleuth Club." He sat on the ground to stretch his hamstrings. "Wait here, and I'll get a key."

"How are you going to get in? The doors require cards."

"Watch me, Mr. S." He went around the back and scaled the balconies as easily as a climbing wall in the gym, soon returning with a keycard. "Keith gave this to me. He had plenty of spares."

I took the card to the west entrance.

Outside the door, a rent-a-cop with an ill-fitting uniform was taking a break, sitting on one of those canes that doubled as a seat, and reading a thick book under the door light.

Confidence is the best cover. I walked past him like I was a hotel guest. "Evenin, sir." I tried the key six or seven times without the door opening. "I can never get these things right."

He snatched the keycard. "Haven't you taken modern algebra? This card is a simple Abelian group." He rotated it to the proper orientation and prepared to place it in the slot before he looked at me and stopped. "I don't recognize you. Are you sure you're a hotel guest? Are you looking for the Stony Estancia Motel? Hotel. Motel. People get confused."

I wasn't going to let this dilettante mathematician-cum-nightwatchman stop me. I grabbed the card from him and opened the door. "You're new," I said, feigning confidence. "I've been staying here for years," I added. "Thanks for helping me with the key. I'll put in a good word for you with the owners."

'Lucky he wasn't a long-time employee.' Fitch gamboled through a field of four-leaf clovers.

High turnover for the night shift is legendary.

Louis, Jaxon, and I went into the stairwell and headed to the fourth floor.

We met Hafsa and Keith eating pizza in the hall.

I reached into my pocket and handed everyone blue gloves. "Protect your fingers. Any forensic tech will tell you pizza fingers leave the best prints."

'Many a felon's been foiled by pizza.' Fitch served slices to inmates at the Stony Estancia jail.

Louis was all business. "Put that pizza down. We're on the clock. Search first. Eat later."

Keith opened the door. Jaxon turned on the lights. The Sleuth Club spread out, but what would they find?

I stood in the doorway. Mrs. Fisher had a suite. Straight ahead was a couch, and two easy chairs upholstered in cotton duck printed to resemble a Victorian brocade. The remains of a typical room service meal sat on the coffee table—Caesar salad, steak and fries, and blueberry cheesecake.

The left bedroom had an unmade bed and a flannel nightgown with a vintage floral print and eyelet lace trim. There was a copy of *Nineteen Minutes* by Jodi Picoult on the night table. That must have been Mrs. Fisher's room. On the right, the deceased Mr. Fisher's room was pristine. The bed was made, and the stripes on the carpet left by the housekeeper's vacuum cleaner were untrod upon.

My detective's eyes were drawn to a sparkle in Mr. Fisher's abandoned room. I went down on my hands and knees, reached under the bed, and grabbed a gold earring. "Look what I found! This is the kind of clue we're looking for." I held it up. It had an abstract design. "Any ideas?"

"That's Leeta's. It's her monogram," Louis said.

I unscrambled the intertwined G and H for Goleta Hardcastle.

Hafsa pulled back her niqab, uncovering her ears. Two earrings on the right and four on the left. "Leeta loved her earrings. She designed that monogram. She would never have left one unless it was an emergency," Hafsa fixed her niqab. "Pierced earrings don't fall off. She left it here for us to find."

Fitch posted on the scoreboard. *'Sleuth Club, one. Fishers zero.'* He wore a striped referee's shirt. *'The Fishers are involved with Leeta's abduction.'*

The night watchman burst into the suite. "What are you doing in Mrs. Cassandra Fisher's room?"

I slid the earring into my pocket.

"Don't lie." He pointed at me with his cane. "Especially you, Mr. S. Where's Senior Detective Yukawa?"

I held up my hands, palms forward.

He gave me a big smile. "You're not a hotel guest. I was here before you retired. I recall when you moved into Higgs Haven to be close to your girlfriend."

'He knows about you,' Fitch snickered, holding handcuffs.

Jaxon hugged the rent-a-cop. "Hey, Euclid. Nice to see you. I missed you at the last **S**tony **E**stancia **C**omputer and **R**adio **E**ncryption **T**ech meeting."

The rent-a-cop put away his cane. "I hate to miss a SECRET meeting, but I was back in Maryland. Vinnie Purcell and I were summoned to solve a national security problem."

'Stony is such a small town.' Fitch wore a plaid flannel shirt and chewed on a corn cob pipe. *'Everyone knows everyone. There are no secrets.'*

"Very cool, Euclid. Did you solve it?" Jaxon said with teenage hero worship.

"Sure did." Euclid's chest puffed out with pride.

"Goleta's been abducted." Hafsa joined the discussion. "You remember her? Leeta?"

"Sure do. Smart lady," Euclid answered.

"We're here to find clues."

I stared hard at Hafsa, willing her not to mention the earring in my pocket.

"I hope you found what you came for because you have to leave." He looked embarrassed. "Leticia from *Stony Estancia Surfs* called me, and they're on their way."

'Omniscient Tish knows everything.' Fitch dressed like The Pythia at the Oracle of Delphi in a white dress and a purple veil.

That was all he needed to say. Hafsa tossed my car key to me and shouted, "You can keep my fob. I have a spare," as she ran out the door. Louis disappeared over the balcony.

When César and Tish arrived, Mrs. Fisher's room was locked, and Euclid and I were in the hall sharing pizza.

"Greetings, Stony Estancia surfers." Euclid walked to the stairs with the reporters following. "Would you like to see our server farm?"

Tish said, "I didn't know the hotel had a server farm."

"Yes. You must see it. Thanks to the Makers Guild, Stony Estancia Hotel is AI-enabled."

César said, "Lead on. We love stories about AI, the Makers Guild, and billion-dollar markets."

Why were César and Tish promoting the Makers Guild?

'Dr. T has bought off everyone. Euclid and those reporters have friends-and-family stock options like Principal Golding.' Fitch sat before an accounting ledger. He wore green eyeshades, sharpened his goose quill pen, and dipped it into a bottle of iron gall ink.

Euclid escorted the *Surf* reporters to the basement, holding the banister with one hand and tapping the steps with his cane.

I silently thanked him for diverting the *Surf* from our break-in. Euclid's tour covered three underground levels.

I waited outside the hotel, eating deep-dish pizza. When Sandy returned from Thanksgiving at my apartment, I watched her park and collect plastic containers of leftovers. Vicki should have given her a bag because there were too many containers to carry easily.

I ran across the parking lot. "Let me help you."

"Thank you." She handed me a container of ham, along with two smaller ones with pie and whipped cream. Then, she stepped back. "Mr. Szilard! What are you doing here?"

"I was waiting for you." I walked towards the hotel. "Do you have a minute?"

"Sure. After your Thanksgiving hospitality, I can't refuse." She used her keycard to open the door. "Please make it quick. This has been a long day."

I took the earring from my pocket. "Do you recognize this?"

"No. Should I?"

"This is Goleta's earring. It was found under your husband's bed."

'Nice use of the passive voice.' Fitch wore the white collared shirt, string tie, and black waistcoat of a frontier schoolmaster. He completed his costume with a Holy Bible and reading glasses.

"What were you doing in my suite? Did you have a search warrant?"

I fabricated a quick lie. "Housekeeping found it and recognized Goleta's initials."

"Sorry. I have no idea how it got there." She grabbed the plastic containers out of my hands and headed to her room."

'Wow. That was close.' Fitch relaxed. *'Was that earring helpful enough for this subterfuge?'*

Maybe. I was disappointed we hadn't found any better clues to Goleta's disappearance. When Mrs. Fisher didn't question my flimsy excuse about housekeeping, she moved up on my list of suspects, clearly feeling too guilty to think clearly.

On my drive home, I returned to the coincidence of two missing girls. What happened to Emily?

The Friday following Thanksgiving should have been a time to wash dishes, pack away leftovers, and generally restore order. Instead, my apartment served as the command center for the missing students. Vicki commandeered my flat screens as bulletin boards. She taped the Goleta clues on the smaller TV and the Emily clues on the larger one.

Tsui staffed the espresso machine and served leftovers to the rotating crowd of searchers. The Sleuth Club, police, paramedics, and the Makers Guild were in and out, eating and posting clues. Dahl was an Egyptian god accepting worship and snacks.

At the end of the day, they vacated my apartment, no closer to finding Goleta or Emily. I ignored the chaos and fell asleep, dressed, on top of my covers. The last thing I recalled was Vicki covering me and saying, "I'll stop by tomorrow to help clean up."

Early Saturday morning, I stood with Dahl on our balcony, enjoying Higgs Haven's return to life after Thanksgiving. Joggers wearing neon shoes crunched the white gravel on the serpentine paths. Children splashed in the pool, while their parents sat in lounge chairs, bundled up and holding towels for when their progeny came to their senses, realizing that it was November, not July. Red-breasted nuthatches, annual winter visitors, introduced color and song variety to the year-round flock of house sparrows.

A loud noise, heralding the end of the world, interrupted the morning's tranquility. I slapped my hands over my ears, and Dahl retreated inside to hide under the covers. The racket was from a medevac helicopter that landed below the balcony.

'Scaredy cats.' Fitch mocked us.

Vicki opened the copter door and waved for me to join her. I read her lips. "Hurry. They found Emily Milhone in the mountains by Pauli Falls."

In addition to Vicki and the pilot, I saw Lieutenant Peggy Mutai and her paramedic crew. I didn't want them to go hungry. I grabbed what leftovers I could find: goose, ham, stuffed pumpkins, and pies, lots of pies.

Fitch wore his chef's toque and watched over my shoulder as I wrestled everything into my backpack.

I boarded the copter and mouthed, "You found Emily. Congratulations." After I buckled in and put on my headset, Vicki asked, "Would you like some more good news?"

I responded with two thumbs up.

"Remember those reconstructed fingerprints on the case buried behind the library?"

I nodded.

"We identified them. I don't know why it took so long."

The copter rose and flew north, passing over my condo, giving a spurt of power to my wind turbine.

Vicki revealed, "The fingerprints belonged to Wally."

Murdered Wally? Wally's prints were on the box of USB sticks buried behind the library. The library was graffitied with U DA BOMB. X MARKS THE SPOT. Wally's murder. Graffiti. USB sticks. How were they connected? I couldn't resist smiling. My favorite part of detective work was when multiple lines of inquiry crossed and joined.

'File that clue away. It's no help until we know what was stored on those USB sticks.' Fitch drove a forklift down a long aisle in a huge government warehouse until he found the place to raise his box and slide it between the Holy Grail and the aliens from Area 51.

The thought that any of my grandkids would spend days and nights in the hills concerned me. "I'm worried about Emily."

"You should be," said Peggy. "Stony kids aren't known for their wilderness survival skills. We hope she's okay, but we're prepared for the worst." She pointed to the rescue supplies stored behind her team: a transport litter, hoist, oxygen, helmets, other safety gear, splints, and first aid kits.

"Weren't the Kwoleks patrolling the hills? Why didn't they see her?" I wondered aloud.

'What was she doing at Pauli Falls in the first place?' Fitch added to the mystery.

When we landed, Pauli Falls was swarming with squabbling Kwoleks.

A red Kwolek berated the others, "How did we miss her? Who was responsible for infrared?"

A blue Kwolek whined, "My infrared couldn't find her. She hid in an insulated tent."

A green Kwolek flew in circles flashing her lights. "Malfunction. Excuses. I found her cat."

The red Kwolek wasn't satisfied. "Green is right. Malfunction. Your infrared sensors couldn't see her in her tent, but what about her latrine? Where were you, Blue, when she went to the latrine? She didn't put it inside that insulated tent."

The green Kwolek with flashing lights bragged, "I found the cat's sandbox behind that rock. A cat's sandbox is smaller than a human latrine."

The red Kwolek warned, "Silence! Here comes *Stony Estancia Surfs*. Don't tell them that Emily hid from us. It will hurt Dr. T's stock price."

Fitch fired surface-to-air missiles at the quadcopters. *'Leticia is omniscient. The Surf already knows.'*

César filmed us disembarking from the medevac copter.

Leticia broadcast our arrival. "Tish here, your *SE Surfs* reporter, live from Pauli Falls. The medevac helicopter has arrived to rescue Emily Milhone, the Stony Estancia High School student who has been lost in the mountains."

How did the Surf get here first? I wondered.

'Teleportation,' Fitch suggested. *'Or the delay while you packed food into your backpack.'*

Emily's blonde hair glowed in the morning sun. She wore a calico dress. Clouseau's pink nose and blue eyes peeked out from under her skirt. She waved her phone at us. "I called you an hour ago. What took you so long?"

'She looks more like a health spa guest than a wilderness survivor.' Fitch giggled, wearing a plush robe.

I'm just glad that she's okay.

Peggy signaled her team to return to the helicopter. "She doesn't need medical support."

Vicki ran to Emily. "Why didn't you call sooner? Everyone's been worried about you."

Emily reached into her pocket and pulled out a matching GH earring. "This is Goleta's. She loved her earrings. She designed that monogram herself. She would never have left one unless it was an emergency," Emily pulled back her hair, showing three earrings in each ear, and shook her head. "Earrings don't fall off. Goleta left it here for us to find." She pointed up the hill. "I've been frantically searching for her. Mea culpa. I forgot to call."

"Okay," Vicki said, but I could tell that she wasn't convinced. "You can get in the copter. Peggy will take you home."

Emily picked up Clouseau, who purred in her arms, and took the co-pilot's seat.

"Mr. S and I will continue to search for Miss Hardcastle."

I looked inside Emily's insulated tent. "Something isn't right."

Vicki joined my investigations. "You hallucinate as much as those Kwolek AIs. What makes you think something is wrong?"

"No hallucinations this time. She's been missing for days, and I don't see any signs of food. What has she been eating?"

Vicki crawled into the tent and retrieved Emily's sleeping bag and backpack. "You're right. Everything in her backpack is clean and folded."

I turned to question Emily, but the copter was gone.

"Emma Marple's passport cleared customs in the Charles de Gaulle Airport," the red Kwolek interjected.

After a pause, Green added, "Twice, arrivals and departures."

I turned to Vicki. "Is that the same Emma Marple as the driver's license you found when you brought Louis into Principal Golding's office last Halloween?"

"The passport and the driver's license match," the blue Kwolek asserted.

"Really?" I asked.

Blue hedged his pronouncement. "We can't be 100 percent positive. The Makers Guild has improved our facial recognition in preparation for the IPO, but female recognition doesn't match male accuracy."

Red flew over to César and Tish. "The Stony Estancia Makers Guild's proprietary algorithms underlie its billion-dollar applications. We expect a record-breaking IPO before year-end."

"Emma Marple. Emily Milhone. Same initials, like Currer Bell and Charlotte Brontë, like the Brontë sisters and the Bell brothers." Green repeated as she flew around us.

The blue Kwolek added, "Even in the 19th century, gender transition was common."

'Don't you get it? Emily wasn't in the mountains. She was in Paris. That's why the Kwoleks couldn't find her.' Fitch wore a navy-and-white striped shirt with a beret, red scarf, and a mustache. He carried a couple of baguettes and a bottle of red wine.

Vicki also put the evidence together. "But what was Emily doing in Paris?"

"Let's assume Emily was in Paris. Where did she get Goleta's earring?" I asked.

"Good point, Zee." Vicki shook my hand. "Emily isn't telling us the entire story."

'Winner, winner, chicken dinner.' Fitch tied his checkered napkin around his neck and opened a bucket of fried chicken. *The story of Goleta's earring in the mountains is fabricated. Why should we believe the story about the matching earring in Mrs. Wilson's hotel room?'*

I couldn't argue with Fitch and Vicki, but I didn't like the idea of my grandkids lying to me.

Stony Estancia Surfs posted: MURDER SUSPECT RELEASED. CASSANDRA WILSON'S CHARGES DISMISSED BY JUDGE.

"Oh no, Vicki. That's Ms. Burgess, your lawyer friend, isn't it?"

"I can't complain," sighed Vicki. "Burgess is a good lawyer, and we didn't have enough to hold Sandy."

Another *Surf SE* notification: WILL AI REPLACE HUMAN LAW ENFORCEMENT?

"Puppets!" I shouted. "Vicki, what does the *Surf* have against you?"

"I don't know." She seemed resigned. "I suspect this anti-police attitude can be traced back to the Stony Estancia's Makers Guild. They have a bigger internet ad budget than we do. Ads keep the *Surf* running, and I suspect law enforcement is another of Dr. T's targeted billion-dollar markets."

WINTER SOLSTICE

I was dressing for an early morning jog with Vicki when a gust of Santa Ana wind battered my garage. The door reverberated like the largest O-daiko taiko drum. Dahl hid under the covers. The National Weather Service warned high-profile vehicles to avoid the Cajon Pass, and *Stony Estancia Surfs* posted pictures of eighteen-wheelers blown off the road. When I contacted Vicki to cancel, my call went to voicemail.

'She can't hear her phone over the wind.' Fitch jogged in place. *'She's waiting for you at Heisenberg Park. Don't ghost her. Get going. You're late.'*

There was nothing I could do. In the winter, onshore winds brought rain from Pacific Ocean atmospheric rivers, and offshore ones, fondly called Santa Anas, brought clear skies and warm, dry Mojave Desert air. People surviving freezing temperatures, ice, and snow might wish for Santa Anas, but not Southern California natives.

When I opened the garage door, a gust blew me off my feet. Sitting on my buttocks, I wished for winter to be over. I placed my backpack and trekking poles into my car and drove slowly down Higgs Road, prepared to turn into strong gusts.

The hair on my arms stood up, my shoulders tensed, and my stomach ached. I cursed the low humidity and static electricity. A chill running down my spine suggested something else. *Stony Estancia Surfs* posted: UNSOLVED CRIMES MAR THE HOLIDAYS. MURDER. ABDUCTION. GRAFFITI. This was a morning of bad news. I stopped beside the only other car in Heisenberg Park, a Stony Estancia Police Department black-and-white.

'Whoooose car is that?' Fitch stretched out his words like the mournful sound of the wind. *'Sssomething's amisss.'* He shivered in sympathy with my feelings.

I stepped out of my car using my trekking poles to brace myself against the gusts. The police car was empty, except for a black satchel embossed with the Stony Estancia emblem sitting on the passenger seat. Vicki's satchel. Why was she driving a patrol car? Why had she arrived early?

I moved around the car, aided by my poles. When I reached the front, I found the hood to be cold. It had been parked for a while. The wind hissed like Fitch. *Sssomething's amisss.* We had a plan. Why hadn't she waited for me?

I held tight to my poles, turning like a lighthouse, searching for Vicki. Stony Estancia didn't need another abduction.

'You're overreacting.' Fitch flexed his muscles. *'She's too tough to be abducted.'*

I turned around two more times, willing her to appear, willing a Santa Ana gust to blow her into the park. Then, there she was, running towards me, the wind at her back. When she arrived, she checked her watch. "San Amano and back. My best time."

'Your record can't be official with that tailwind.' Fitch flew a kite high above the park.

She tapped my trekking poles. "Good idea. Too much of a breeze for you. That's why I went without you."

"You called that right." I leaned on my poles against the latest gust. "Can we get out of the wind?"

"Sure, we can sit in the black-and-white. My unmarked is in for service."

I grabbed my backpack from my car, moved her satchel to the back, and took the passenger seat beside her mobile data terminal. "You look cold. Something warm? How about first breakfast?"

She took off her fingerless running gloves and blew on her hands. "Sure."

I served coffee, tea, grilled cheese, soup, scones, and warm muffins. I enjoyed tomato soup with grilled cheese. Vicki had scones, jam atop clotted cream, accompanied by English breakfast tea. Outside the car, the sun rose, and the nighttime Santa Ana winds abated.

After breakfast, she asked, "Have you seen the *Surf's* latest post?"

Recalling the 'Unsolved crimes mar the holidays' notification, I said, "Old news. They've been posting about unsolved crimes since Thanksgiving."

"I can tell you didn't click." She pursed her lips and clenched her fists. "They added a contest." She left the car and took off into the wind.

'What did you do?' Fitch held his palms up. *'How did you upset her?'*

I had no idea. I didn't want to let her get out of sight. I sprinted after her. "Slow down. Pity the old guy," I gasped. When she paused, I rested my hands on my knees to catch my breath. "What contest?"

She jogged backwards. "The contest to guess today's excuse for police failures." She screamed against the wind, "Failures! That's the word they used. Someone's idea of humor at my expense." She stopped and stomped her feet.

I grabbed my phone from my waist pack, clicked on the *Surf SE* app, and read the most popular entries aloud. "Dog ate the evidence." "Aliens." "Crystal ball rolled away."

I forced a laugh. "Don't let those get to you. They're jokes."

She took a deep breath. "Keep reading."

Then I got to the most damning one, SENIOR DETECTIVE YUKAWA DISLOYAL. "Disloyal? That's nasty."

While that last one echoed between the fences that separated the trail from the surrounding homes, I asked, "Disloyal? What does that mean?"

She shouted, "This is President Roosevelt's Executive Order 9066! I'm Japanese. This is Pearl Harbor. They're going to send me to a concentration camp."

The way to break Vicki from her funk was to change the plan. She thrived on improvisations. "Okay. We've had our run. Let's go to my place for second breakfast."

'Is breakfast your solution for everything?' Fitch asked.

No. Sometimes the answer is lunch or dinner.

She beat me back to the parking lot, jumped into her car, and burned rubber, leaving with her lights flashing and my backpack on her front seat.

'Good thing your keys are in your waist pack.' Fitch put on his seat belt.

Back at my condo, Dahl snuck out from under the covers and cuddled on Vicki's lap. They shared a bowl of warm chicken soup. I opened the fridge searching for a second breakfast that didn't require cooking. I found thin-sliced cheeses, ham, veggies, and a bowl of hard-boiled eggs. I checked the cupboard...rye crackers, butter, and muesli.

'Skål! Swedish breakfast,' Fitch declared.

I enjoyed the smörgåsbord while Dahl feasted on hard cheese.

Vicki wasn't eating. She placed the chicken soup on the floor for Dahl and nursed a Swedish egg coffee, staring at her phone. "Listen to these 'Police excuses' contest entries. Everyone's laughing at us." She spoke in a squeaky voice, "Someone stole their Ouija board." She slammed her cup on the granite breakfast bar, splashing coffee onto the floor and frightening Dahl.

I couldn't bear to see her upset. She wasn't eating. She needed a change to break her out of her funk. "Let's visit Vinnie. Why hasn't he decrypted those USB memory chips?"

"Right." She perked up. "It's time for action." She unsnapped her holster and inspected her gun. "I won't let him brush us off."

'Now, she's overreacting.' Fitch put on his body armor.

Vicki skidded her black-and-white into the last space in a lot that was as much dirt as asphalt, driving over the weeds—shepherd's purse and buckhorn plantain—survivors and impervious to being run over. I had no doubt those plants would provide oxygen to whatever animal life survived global warming.

Purcell and Associates was the best-looking place in the rundown strip mall, with its new steel door, compliments of Stony Estancia City, after SWAT broke down the earlier one. Other stores included swimsuits, mixed martial arts, and surveillance electronics. The new door had an unwelcoming sign, PURCELL AND ASSOCIATES. BY APPOINTMENT ONLY. TEXT FOR ENTRY with no phone number provided.

"We need his help. Treat him with finesse," I warned Vicki.

She spat on the weeds, took out her badge, held it up to a CCTV camera, and the door promptly opened. Vinnie's assistant, Chad, had his spiky blonde hair tipped in red and green for the holidays.

Vicki rested her hand on her sidearm. "We're here to see Vinnie."

"Certainly. Please wait here." Chad pointed to plastic chairs beside the door. "I'll see if he's available."

Ignoring him, Vicki stomped past the cubicles of well-dressed agents and burst into Vinnie's office, leaving the door ajar. Chad and I followed.

Purcell's ego wall was covered with photos of himself shaking hands with military officers and politicians. These may have impressed his Stony Estancia clients, but they didn't affect Vicki—not today.

His granddaughter sat on his desk in digital photo frames.

'You and Vicki found that granddaughter he didn't know he had. He owes you, like, forever,' Fitch gloated.

Vinnie stood, wearing a bespoke suit tailored to his physique and showing off his hours in the gym. He offered his hand.

Vicki ignored the offer and stood barricaded behind her crossed arms. "You're supposed to be the smartest guy in the room. Why haven't you decrypted those memory chips?"

'Does she call that finesse? I'm glad she left her sidearm holstered,' Fitch murmured, holding an assault rifle with his bare chest displaying blackwork ink.

The chatter outside his office stopped. Everyone stared at their computers, ignoring the outburst in the boss's office. Chad backed out and closed the door behind him.

I expected Vinnie to refuse to speak to us, but he buried his face in his hands. Vicki's outburst transformed him from a Stony Estancia power player to a small child who was bullied in school. "Don't be mad at me. I'm sorry."

Vicki dialed it back. She put her hand on his shoulder. "It'll be okay."

I opened my backpack, set up the espresso machine on Vinnie's desk, and laid out a tray of croissants, cinnamon rolls, and cannolis. "Latte, cappuccino, or flat white?"

They didn't respond.

'This is going to take more than coffee and cakes,' Fitch advised with a smile.

I reached deep into my backpack. "I also have breakfast beer, oatmeal stout."

That did the trick. They smiled and each accepted a brown bottle with condensation rivulets running down its side.

"I'm a data guy," Vinnie sobbed. "Those broken USB sticks, data chips, bits, and bobs had me stymied. I need data files, not random pieces of electronic junk. I had to call on favors from the folks in Maryland. I couldn't rush them. I got the files back yesterday."

Vicki patted him on the back. "What's the good news?"

I could barely hear him. "Nothing yet. My decryption powers let me down. I handed off the file to Euclid Randolf and the Institute."

'The Institute? What kind of name is that? I've never heard of it,' scoffed Fitch.

Me neither. I wonder who he shared our data with.

I could see that Vicki was frustrated. She held her breath. She snapped and unsnapped her holster.

'Time for a carbohydrate intervention.' Fitch juggled three cinnamon rolls and licked the glaze from his fingers.

"Let's take a break." I passed around sweets.

Vicki had a cannoli with her flat white. Vinnie had another oatmeal stout with a cinnamon roll. I had almond croissants and a latte.

Once they calmed down, I took the opportunity to mediate. "Can you see why Vicki is unhappy? After we found your granddaughter, we thought we had a special connection, and now you're passing off our requests to the second team."

Vinnie finished his beer and took another cinnamon roll. "Euclid isn't the second team. I may be the smartest guy in the room, but he's the smartest one on the planet. Don't let his nighttime job at the Stony Estancia Hotel fool you."

"Are we talking about the security guard?" I asked.

"That same one." Vinnie took another bite from his cinnamon roll. "The smartest one alive. He reminds me of Srinivasa Ramanujan, the self-taught Indian mathematician."

A genius night watchman named Euclid. A mysterious Institute. A deceased Indian mathematician named Ramanujan. Vinnie spun a yarn that didn't bring us any closer to decrypting the smashed data chips. I was prepared to remind Vinnie that he owed us something better when Vicki spoke up. "Thank you, Vinnie."

Why had she accepted this non-resolution?

Vinnie walked us out of his office, past the cubicles, and to the front door.

I was taken by surprise when she said, "Our next stop is Coroner Persey and the mysterious cause of death."

Vicki spun her tires and fishtailed from the dirt parking lot, scattering gravel and vegetation in her wake. "On to another friend who has let us down."

I could hear those parking-lot weeds laughing. They'd be here long after people did themselves in with climate change.

Vicki turned on the flashing lights and siren, weaving around the eighteen-wheelers on Appleton Route. In Warehouse-o-Rama, the foundation of Stony Estancia's economy, these trucks ruled. When she cut in front of a red cab-over tractor lit up like a Christmas tree, the driver expressed her displeasure with her air horn. I jumped out of my seat. Vicki pulled off the road and killed her siren and lights. Neither could compete with the truck.

"Sorry, sorry. I'm frustrated. Why is this case so difficult?" She apologized to the truck as it disappeared down a long driveway. After several deep breaths, she pulled onto Appleton, drove slowly, and gave way to the warehouse deliveries.

I put a positive spin on our meeting at Purcell and Associates. "Vinnie said the nighttime security guy could decrypt those USB sticks. I believe him. We'll have answers soon enough."

"Not soon enough for me," she grumped while she waited for the intersection to clear at the left turn onto Millikan and headed north toward the Civic Center and the morgue. "I hope Coroner Persey has better news."

My phone signaled a notification from the *Surf SE* app. I muted it. I didn't want something else to upset Vicki.

That was a wise precaution, as Dr. T and the Makers Guild announced a plan to replace the Stony Estancia Police Department with AI, large language models, and Kwoleks.

'Augment or replace?' Fitch asked for clarification. *'Is Dr. T serious? Has she never seen 2001, Terminator, or Minority Report?'*

I shared my screen with Fitch. KWOLEK PATROLS. AI DETECTIVES.

'Vicki's not going to like that,' Fitch said while hiding his face behind his hands.

"What did the *Surf* post?" Vicki asked, waiting patiently at the left turn onto Zeeman Way.

I made up something. "Just more about that silly contest."
That only delayed the inevitable.

When she parked in the Civic Center parking garage, she took out her phone. "Kwolek patrols?" She groaned. "AI detectives? What's Dr. T thinking?"

'Isn't it obvious? Another billion-dollar market. She's hyping her stock for her initial public offering.' Fitch dressed in a top hat and a silk morning suit like that character from Monopoly. *'How many shares did Dr. T give César and Leticia to convince them to post this stuff?'*

Is hyping her stock legal? I wondered.

'No problem. They're not in a quiet period,' Fitch informed me.

"Dr. T's a crook and a swindler," Vicki exclaimed.

"Right." I agreed. "This has nothing to do with you or the police. It's about the stock."

That satisfied her. "Forget the *Surf*. On to the morgue."

I had to run to keep up with her as she marched off with determination.

Coroner Persey wore black satin scrubs. The stainless-steel autopsy tables were clear, and the refrigerated drawers closed. She looked up from a stack of reports, "I have good news. The National Institute of Allergy and Infectious Diseases came through." She waved a piece of paper. "I have the cause of death."

I opened my backpack. "This calls for a celebration."

Fitch looked at his phone. *'Time for first lunch. I'm famished.'* He tied a green-and-gold checkered napkin around his neck.

I took a long table from my backpack and prepared a Cape Town Braai with grilled sausage and chicken, accompanied by chakalaka veggie stew and pap maize porridge. I opened a nice bottle of South African merlot from Stellenbosch. For afters, I served up malva pudding with lactose-free vegan ice cream made from coconut milk and flavored with Madagascar vanilla. When everyone had full plates, I said, "Give us your good news."

Persey's face lit up. "Galactose-alpha-1,3-galactose, known to her friends as alpha-gal."

"Is that the red meat allergy?" Vicki asked, dipping a slice of sausage into her chakalaka.

"You got it in one." Persey tapped on her phone. "Here she is in her full glory."

"She sure is cute, but that doesn't mean anything to me," I responded with a fake smile.

Persey swallowed her chicken and continued, "Zarand, don't feel bad. Alpha-gal Syndrome or AGS is not common in California."

"How did Wally get AGS?" Vicki asked.

"He most likely caught it from a Lone Star tick bite. Most cases are in the Southeast."

"Allergy?" I wondered. "How much alpha-gal would it take to kill him?"

"Not much." Persey leafed through the reports on her desk. "The interesting thing is that the reaction takes hours to appear."

"Gosh, I don't get it." Vicki shook her head. "Alpha-gal is found in red meat. Mr. Fisher was a vegan."

'Not only a vegan, but also iatrophobic, afraid of doctors. Recall he had no medical records. He'd never been to a doctor.' Fitch wore a white coat and had a stethoscope hanging from his pocket.

"Being a vegan is a minor obstacle." Persey grinned. "Pure alpha-gal is available on the internet."

"Why?" said Vicki.

"Scientific research," the coroner replied.

"I hope you've been tracking his wife." I served myself ice cream while stating the obvious. "She's the only one who could have known about his condition. She's a flight risk."

"Gosh. No problem." Vicki tapped on her phone before turning to us. "TSA law enforcement hotline."

"Hello. TSA?" Vicki smiled. "Stony Estancia Senior Detective Victoria Yukawa here. I'm looking for Mrs.

Cassandra Fisher." She paused. "Yes, that's her." She gave us a thumbs up."

'Lucky guess,' said Fitch.

She circled her hand impatiently. "Yes, Stony Estancia. We're east of LA on the Desert Freeway." Then her smile disappeared, and her brow furrowed. "No, we're not in the desert. Lots of people live here. We have an international airport."

That explanation helped. Her smile returned. "Right. That's us. Can you pick up our suspect?" Back to her furrowed brow. "Warrant? Of course, we have one. We may be in the burbs, but we have judges and know about warrants." Back to smiling, "Thank you. I'll text you the details, and our helicopter will collect her."

I gave Vicki a questioning look. "When did you get a warrant?"

"No warrant." She blew me a kiss. "Don't you always say, it's easier to ask forgiveness than permission?"

"I can't say it's nice to see you." Ms. Burgess sat next to Mrs. Fisher in the Stony Estancia Police interview room. "Let the record show that my client isn't under arrest, and she's here voluntarily."

'Voluntarily after the TSA picked her up.' Fitch locked and unlocked a pair of handcuffs.

Vicki sat opposite them. Tsui and I watched the video feed from the observation room.

"Agreed," said Vicki. "We thank her for her cooperation, and since she missed lunch, we had some brought in."

"Thank you," replied Mrs. Fisher. She mixed wasabi and ginger to go with her crunch roll.

"Mrs. Fisher, can you tell me when you learned that your husband had alpha-gal syndrome?" Vicki asked casually, leaning back and sipping her green tea.

Ms. Burgess refilled everyone's cup from the cast-iron teapot. "You don't have to answer that."

"No problem." Mrs. Fisher picked up a crunch-roll slice with her chopsticks. "We're friends here. Please call me

Sandy." She discarded the tempura shrimp tail on the edge of her plate. "I learned about that syndrome today, from you. I had to search for it on the internet. I've never heard of it and had no idea that Wally had it." She took another slice of crunch roll. "He was a vegan. It never came up. He must have caught it as a child. He grew up in Tennessee."

Vicki's phone beeped. She looked at it and placed it face down on the table.

Ms. Burgess ate a slice of bluefin tuna sashimi. "My client has missed her flight. Can you show me your warrant?"

Vicki's phone beeped.

I checked my phone. The *Surf* was silent. I had no notifications. Who was texting Vicki?

Vicki came clean. "No warrant. I couldn't allow your client to leave. Her husband has been murdered, and she's the prime suspect."

The lawyer spoke slowly. "This. Interview. Is. Over. We'll be filing harassment charges." She took Sandy's arm. "Stand up. Let's go."

Vicki's phone beeped a third time. She silenced it and spoke to Ms. Burgess. "You're free to go. Please ask your client to stay in town. We'll pay for the missed flight and her usual suite at Stony Estancia Hotel."

"Three more graffiti attacks." Vicki ran down the hall with Tsui and me following. "Tsui, you go to the hospital. Zarand, the Bragg Vineyard Arena. I'll take the helicopter up to Pauli Falls."

"I'm on my way." My car was in the parking structure at a public charging station. "Would it be faster to dispatch Kwolek for video surveillance?"

"Bite your tongue." Vicki stopped. "The last thing I want to do is encourage Dr. T to get mixed up in police business."

We debriefed that evening at Four Rivers restaurant.

Vicki drew her rough Stony Estancia map on a paper napkin with the Desert Freeway and Pacific Electric Trail east-west, and Higgs Road north-south. The latest map recorded eight graffiti incidents.

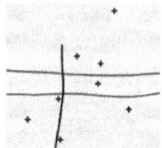

"I'm tired of everyone laughing at me. With the first five graffiti, X marked the fire station, but with three more attacks, that theory is shot. This is a mess."

"I've got nothing," Tsui said as he ate a spring roll. "When I arrived at the hospital, forensics were complete, and graffiti abatement were preparing to clean up. The message was slightly different this time." He showed us a picture on his phone. XY MARKS THE SPOT. GOT UR BACK.

'Last time was XX. Now XY. Chromosomes.' Fitch wore a white lab coat. 'XX and XY represent genetic sex. There's more to come. Genetic sex isn't binary.'

Vicki asked, "Any fingerprints?"

"Nothing."

"The scene at the arena was similar." I felt awful. Vicki needed some positive news. I snitched on my grandkids. "Remember when I showed up late at the firehouse graffiti? Well, puppies, I recognized the vandals. It was the Sleuth Club."

'The Sleuth Club is all about Goleta.' Fitch wore a deerstalker hat and looked through a magnifying glass. 'What do graffiti have to do with the missing Miss Hardcastle?'

Vicki threw her spare rib bones into an empty rice bowl. "Zee, you've got to choose your team. You can't be both a teen and an adult. Are you with the Sleuth Club or the police?"

"I'm an adult. I'm with you."

"Well, I need you to find out what they're up to."

I reflected that, no matter how much I supported my grandkids, I would never be their peers. They didn't share the group chat password with me. At the end of the day, my allegiance was with the adults, with Vicki. I paid the check and collected the leftover boxes. "I won't let you down."

I stared at my phone. On one hand, I didn't want to spy on my grandkids. On the other hand, I'd promised Vicki, "I won't let you down." What could I do?

'No problem. Tomorrow is the last day before winter break.' Fitch wore a green and gold snowsuit, with skis and poles resting on his shoulder.

I practiced what to say to Vicki while her phone rang. "I can't figure out what the kids are up to. There's no time. It's too late."

"Hey, Zee, what's the good word?"

She sounded cheerful. After Vinnie handed us off to the night security guy and the graffiti mystery remained unsolved, I had to do something. "Vicki?"

"What do you want, Zarand?" Some anxiety crept into her voice.

'Quit stalling. Just rip the bandage off. Tell her you're not going to spy.' Fitch was schussing down a slope, spraying white powder in his wake.

"My bad. I butt dialed you. Sorry." I ended the call.

"Mr. Leaphorn here. Who am I speaking to?"

"This is Mr. Szilard. I'm a Stony High substitute teacher."

"Oh yes, Mr. S. You've subbed for my World Mythology classes. What can I do for you?"

"Mr. Leaphorn, I need a favor."

"Sure, Mr. S. Anything."

"Can I teach your World Mythology class tomorrow?"

"I don't know about that." Mr. Leaphorn spoke softly, like he was talking to himself, then the line went silent.

'I hope you have a plan B.' Fitch smiled, enjoying my predicament. *'You shouldn't have promised Vicki you would spy on your grandkids.'*

"Hello? Hello? Are you there?" I feared that Leaphorn had disconnected, but the call timer kept ticking.

No response. No backup plan. Tomorrow was the last day before winter vacation. When school let out, my grandkids would scatter to the mountains or beaches. I needed to act.

"Mr. Leaphorn?"

"I'm here. I can't abandon my classes."

I explained how I misled Vicki to protect the Sleuth Club. "She was mad when she discovered my betrayal. I need to make amends."

"Well, you've got yourself into a fix." He didn't sound sympathetic, but after another silence, he said, "I can imagine how my wife would react. You messed up." A short pause. "Why my classes?"

I thought fast and impressed myself with my response. "The Sleuth Club started there."

"Aren't you the club advisor?" he asked.

'This wasn't your idea. They printed T-shirts before they spoke to you. The inmates are running the asylum,' Fitch played Whack-a-Mole, hammering down a never-ending sequence of heads popping up.

I didn't want to admit how much Szilard's Sleuths were out of control, not to Leaphorn, not to myself. "I'm being a responsible advisor and checking on my charges."

"You want to use my classroom to spy on them?"

I couldn't tell whether he approved or not. I crossed my fingers and presented my best case. "Not spy on them. Touch base before they go on vacation."

"Okay. It's the last day before recess, and half the class will have taken off for skiing or surfing. Let them present their plans for the holiday assignment."

"Thank you. I owe you one. What's the assignment?"

"You'll find out." He disconnected.

Armed with Mr. Leaphorn's vague lesson plan, I jumped in and hoped for the best. "Today you're going to present your plans for the holiday assignment."

'You're in trouble. They can smell fear.' Fitch was a cheetah stalking a dik-dik on the Serengeti. I laughed when he performed the cat-butt wiggle.

"What a colossal waste of time." Emily protested. "Why should we present our holiday plans? We'll only have to do it next year for Mr. Leaphorn."

"You're only the sub." Louis did a pirouette, sat down, and crossed his arms. Just like that, I had seventeen grim-faced teens glaring at me.

'They sussed out that you're here to spy on them.' Fitch mirrored their posture, leaning back, arms crossed, chin out.

I didn't let Fitch discourage me. *Wipe that silly grin off your face. I have a plan.* I didn't have a plan, but I'd think of something.

A knock at the door broke the impasse.

I welcomed César with his camera and Leticia with her boom microphone. I'd never been so happy to see the *Stony Estancia Surfs* news team. I winked at Tish and addressed the class, "No problem. The *Surf* will record your presentations."

'Whoa. What about student privacy?' Fitch always found something to object to.

Lesson one. Ask for forgiveness after. Students post everything on social media anyway.

I walked over to Emily's seat. "You won't have to repeat anything. Mr. Leaphorn will see you on *Stony Estancia Surfs.*" I pointed to her phone. "You can link to the *Surf* from your socials."

After César set up his stabilized camera rig, Tish began, "I'm in Mr. Leaphorn's World Mythology class. Learning never stops at Stony High. These students have anthropology projects for the winter break." Tish energized the room. The students leaned forward. She turned to the class, "Who's first?"

Jaxon stood up. "My family is driving to Arizona to visit Canyon de SHAY." He wrote CANYON DE CHELLY on the whiteboard. "My mother is one-quarter Native American, and we visit the Navajo Nation every year." He raised his fist and shouted, "Diné pride!"

After several other presentations, Keith Evans said, "I'm next."

César moved in to record him.

"I'm visiting Skara Brae in the Orkney Islands. My Scottish ancestors lived in Neolithic homes long before the English built Stonehenge." Keith pulled something from his backpack, a Scottish flag, a white X on a blue field, St. Andrew's Cross. "End London Rule!" he shouted.

'How is this going to help you with Vicki?' Fitch asked.

Patience. A good detective has patience.

We were five minutes from the buzzer, and I hadn't heard anything useful for Vicki's investigations.

Then Emily waggled her fingers at Tish. "I'm next," she demanded.

Tish stepped in front of the camera. "For our last presenter, we have Emily Milhone and her adorable cat, Clouseau."

Emily snuggled her flame-point Siamese against her cheek. Clouseau swatted at Emily's straight blonde hair. "I'm off to pahREE."

'Wake up, sleepy head.' Fitch banged a sauté pan with a wooden spoon.

I got it, Fitch. Over Thanksgiving, Emily went to Paris using the alias Emma Marple. When she returned, she pretended to be lost in the mountain by Pauli Falls. Now, a month later, she was returning. Suspicious. This was the lead I'd been waiting for. I had something to report to Vicki.

While the *Surf* packed up, Hafsa said, "Come weeth me to ze kasbah." This made no sense. The Kasbah was in Morocco, not France.

'Morocco was once part of France,' Fitch said, wearing a navy-and-white striped shirt with a beret, red scarf, and a mustache.

When I told Vicki we were going to France, she said, "Fun! I love impromptu trips. My suitcase is always packed." After a moment, she added, "I expect Emily is on a shopping trip to buy a gown for the New Year's Ball. Following her may not help our investigations, but that's not a reason to pass up the opportunity."

"You may be right."

'Or she may be wrong,' Fitch packed for the trip.

Fitch walked the wings of our Boeing 777 like an old-time barnstormer. 'Hooray! Back to Europe and international crime fighting,' he cheered.

Vicki and I ate our airline microwave dinner while Atlantic Ocean whitecaps passed beneath us. After the cabin stewards removed our trays, Vicki slept, and I made a phone call.

"Gendarmerie Nationale Capitaine Valery Renoir, bonjour."

I quickly responded, "Hello, Valery, hello," to cut off any more conversation in French.

"You're not in my contacts. How did you get my private number? Who's this?" he asked in his accented English.

"Valery, it's me, Zarand Szilard. It's been a long time."

"Ah, mais oui! Zarand! Comment vas-tu?"

"Fine. Fine. I need a favor."

"Anything, mon frère, anything."

"I'm tracking someone headed for Paris. Can you tell me where they go after they land?"

"Pas de problème."

"Emily Milhone," I recalled that she'd used an alias over Thanksgiving. "Or Emma Marple."

A pause, then, "I'd love to help, but I don't see those names in my air passenger database."

"I'll find another alias."

The Kwoleks jumped to mind. They'd easily track down Emily's newest forged passport.

'*Are you crazy?*' Fitch threw his deerstalker hat into the airplane aisle. '*Not the Kwoleks. Dr. T is already out of hand. Her and her crazy IPO.*'

This time, I had a backup plan. I called Vinnie, who had access to many databases. "Vinnie?"

"What can I do for you?" he replied.

After our difficult discussion last time, I started with some small talk. "Tell me about your darling granddaughter."

"Alex." His voice changed to a squeaky soprano that grandparents used to talk to small children. "She's walking. She calls me Pawpaw. She's the smartest."

"That's cute." I let him bask in his grandpa's glory before I got down to business. "I need to find an alias. Emily Milhone used Emma Marple the last time she flew to France. Now, she's returning, but not with either of those names."

I could hear his super-human rapid keystrokes buzzing in the background.

I continued, "Let's assume she sticks with those EM initials. Can you find all the matching US passports cross-referenced by facial recognition, age, and height?"

"No problem."

I'd never heard anyone type with his speed. The keyboard buzzed until he said, "Yes. Here it is. Elizabeth Macbeth. Bonne chance."

"Thank you. Thank you."

Before disconnecting, he added, "Not so fast. My search turned up another hit. Edward Murdoch, but Edward is male."

"Male. Female. Whatever. Gender is a social construct."

Vinnie laughed. "I hear you. Both Edward and Elizabeth match Emily and Emma for facial recognition and height."

After a nap, I checked the time in California. It was morning. I called Coroner Persey. "How's Dahl doing?"

Before she could answer, Cerberus barked. "Did you hear that?"

"Yes. Can you translate?"

"Cerberus says he's happy that his best friend is staying with us."

Vicki and I were approaching Charles de Gaulle Aéroport when Valery called back. "I found Edward Murdoch flying from Los Angeles."

I suggested, "Can you send an agent to tail this Edward?"

He replied, "Too late. He landed, cleared customs, and disappeared."

"Puppets." I declared. "Do you think you can find him?"

Valery replied, "Not necessary. Elizabeth Macbeth booked a transfer to Orly. She's going to Tangier."

"Merci, Valery, Merci."

I was proud of Emily. She did an excellent job of covering her tracks. Alias Edward landed in Paris and disappeared.

Alias Elizabeth never arrived in France but transferred to Tangier. Still, not enough. I'd see her in Morocco.

The plane hit the runway hard, and my phone bounced from my hand.

"Now what?" Vicki asked while I retrieved the device from under my seat.

"Emily isn't staying in Paris. What could she be doing in Tangier?"

"No idea," Vicki replied. "That shoots down my idea that she'd planned a Paris shopping spree."

I told Vicki my plan. "I booked a great hotel in the premier arrondissement. Let's rest there before we go to Morocco."

Vicki objected. "Plans are made to be changed. Best to cancel."

"Okay, but where will we stay?"

"I'm not worried. You'll find something."

'Where will we eat?' wondered Fitch.

For someone imaginary, how can you be concerned about meals?

'I'm being supportive.' Fitch carried a baguette and a bottle of wine.

I scrolled through my old contacts from my international crime-fighting days in Los Angeles. "Problem solved. I found someone. He'll know what to do."

"Good." Vicki took out her phone. "I'll have Tsui book us a transfer from De Gaulle Airport."

I called my friend in Tangier.

"Inspecteur en chef Chafik Marleau à l'appareil, comment puis-je vous aider?"

I responded, "Hello, Chaffey, hello," to cut off more French conversation.

I explained our predicament, and he agreed to help.

"Chaffey will meet us at Tangier-Ibn Battouta airport. He's booked rooms at Dar Sultan in the Kasbah of Tangier."

"Will he detain Emily?"

"No. He'll put a tail on her. We want to see what she's up to in Morocco."

Chaffey met us when we disembarked from the Royal Air Maroc plane. I recognized him at once, short with a goatee, now gray, and wearing a djellaba, the same white cotton shirt with a hood and pale purple stripes as last time. His kufi cap was sparkling white with crocheted roses. We hugged, and I tapped his head with my chin. "My brother. My Moroccan djinn."

"Mon frère. My American teddy bear."

I introduced him to Vicki. "Chief Inspector Chafik Marleau, this is Senior Detective Victoria Yukawa from Stony Estancia."

"Nice to make your acquaintance." He kissed her hand.

"Thank you for meeting us," Vicki said.

"Pas de problème, Mademoiselle Yukawa," he replied.

"You can call me Vicki."

"You can call me Chaffey. Please follow me, we'll be on our way to your rooms."

He escorted us through customs. We felt like royalty as every Sûreté Nationale officer saluted us.

"What about our luggage?" I asked. I didn't like to be separated from my bags.

Chaffey tapped his nose and gave us a djinn smile. "Vos bagages? Already in the car."

Vicki returned his smile. "Gosh, you're efficient."

Having finished the pleasantries, I returned to business. "Are you tracking Emily Milhone...I mean Elizabeth Macbeth?"

He didn't answer. We had no more discussion until we were settled in the black SUV festooned with small Moroccan flags, a green star on a red field.

'I love seeing Christmas colors in an Islamic country.' Fitch ho ho ho'd dressed as Santa Claus.

Silly Fitch. Red is bravery, and green is the color of Islam.

As the driver pulled away, I said, "Elizabeth Macbeth?"

Chaffey ignored me. He opened a small refrigerator. "Can I get you a cold drink? I have US soft drinks, Casablanca Lager,

French wine, Ain Soltane mineral water, and Moroccan mint tea."

"Mint tea, please," said Vicki, and I stuck with the local mineral water.

I opened my backpack and served Moroccan orange cake.

Chaffey accepted a slice. "That's excellent meskouta."

Once everyone was refreshed, I pressed Chaffey a third time. "Where's Elizabeth Macbeth. You have her under surveillance, right?"

He frowned. "We were ready for her. We distributed her picture. That blonde hair was easy to follow. We captured her on video as she disembarked from her plane. Women were stationed at customs. They attached trackers to her luggage. Can you believe she had two large suitcases?"

"Easy." Vicki laughed. "Stony High women aren't known for traveling light. I expect she'll have three suitcases when she returns."

Chaffey continued. "We alerted the rental car agencies, taxis, and car services. Hotels and guest houses were warned to expect her. We flagged her passport and her credit cards."

'This doesn't sound good.' Fitch shook his head. 'He hasn't answered your question. You always say that the longer a suspect rambles, the more chance they're prevaricating.'

"Where's she now?" I repeated.

Chaffey took a deep breath. "No blonde women passed through customs."

"She must have put on a hijab on her way there," Vicki conjectured.

"Oui, oui," he agreed.

"What about those two suitcases?"

"Oui, mademoiselle. Her suitcases? Les valises?" He took another slice of meskouta. "When we opened them, we found a form to donate everything to the Red Crescent."

"You lost her?" I asked Chaffey to confirm Emily's incredible disappearance act.

'This Sleuth Club knows a lot of spy craft,' Fitch wore Elizabethan ruffs at his collar and cuffs. 'There are more things in heaven and Earth, Zarand, than are dreamt of in your philosophy.'

Agreed.

The car stopped, and Chaffey eagerly changed the subject. "We're at the Kasbah district, Tangier's military and political center since the Roman era."

The roads were too narrow for our car, but several men appeared to carry our luggage, and Chaffey guided us through the maze of narrow streets to Maisons d'hôtes Dar Sultan.

"I've booked you two rooms. You'll be well taken care of here. This house boasts a 300-year tradition of hospitality excellence."

We entered the reception area packed with eclectic treasures like brass platters, ceramic tiles, and old photographs.

"Cute! This is wonderful," Vicki exclaimed.

"I've booked the lady in the best of the seven rooms—on the third level with a panoramic ocean view," Chaffey proudly announced.

When Vicki reached the first landing, she asked, "What about Elizabeth?"

"Tangier isn't big. We'll search for her tomorrow when you've recovered from your travels." He climbed the next flight of stairs. "I recommend a light dinner. Their seafood tagine with shellfish and the catch of the day is the best."

Vicki wasn't going to forget Emily, alias Elizabeth Macbeth. "Where will we search?"

Chaffey was stymied.

Fitch was back in Stony High. *'Do you remember Hafsa saying, Come weeth me to ze kasbah?'* He held up four fingers.

I get it, Fitch. Lesson four. Evidence is everywhere.

I broke the uncomfortable silence. "She's in the Kasbah."

"Really?" asked Vicki suspiciously.

"Intuition," I said.

"Pas de problème finding her in the Kasbah," Chaffey said with his first smile since he confessed that he'd lost the blond Elizabeth Macbeth in the airport.

'And that airport is smaller than the Kasbah,' Fitch muttered with teenage sarcasm.

31. THE KASBAH

At dawn, I was awakened by the muezzin at the Kasbah Mosque calling the faithful to Fajr prayers. I searched for Dahl in the blank space beside me before my sleepy consciousness realized that I wasn't home. I checked my phone. *Is ten in the evening too late to call Coroner Persey?*

'Leave her alone. She promised to take care of Dahl. Don't be a pest.' Fitch pulled the covers over his head.

I would've followed Fitch's example, but I worried about Chaffey's optimism. *Why should I follow him when Emily evaded his carefully constructed net? He had her arrival on video, and then she disappeared.*

'You have no choice. You have no plan B.' Fitch returned to his sanctuary under the covers.

I refused to let him curdle my custard. Vicki and I had traveled for over twenty-four hours and tracked Emily to Tangier. This was no time to quit. The first rule of surveillance was to blend in with the crowd. I pulled on my jeans and a Tangier T-shirt with a picture of a mosque.

The weather was cool and wet. I put on a light jacket, green and gold Stony High colors, and a San Diego Zoo hat before I climbed the open-air stairs to Vicki's penthouse.

'Do you call that blending in?' Fitch wore an inflatable T. rex costume.

Would you have me wear a burqa? I plan to blend in with the tourists.

Vicki and I enjoyed a private breakfast set up in her room, small round khobz loaves, ubiquitous in Morocco; sliced baguettes, a legacy of Morocco's French colonial past; and semolina pancakes, served with butter, honey, and apricot preserves. These were accompanied by mint tea, orange juice, olives, soft, creamy Jben goat cheese, and Amlou, a classic Moroccan dip made with almonds, olive oil, and honey.

Vicki carried her plate onto her balcony. I stood behind her and put my arms around her waist. "What do you see?"

"Beauty. So much beauty." She turned to the sea. "Listen to the fisherfolk and the gulls. Can you smell the fish market? Doesn't the morning fog make you hungry?"

'Everything makes you hungry. You have a teenager's metabolism.'

I looked down. "Yes, and someone else is hungry." A calico cat stared up at us from the alley behind the hotel. I tossed some cheese to the grateful kitty.

"How will we find Emily?" I asked no one in particular.

Fitch looked down. *'Maybe the kitty has seen Emily.'*

Maybe. I tossed more cheese. "Have you seen Emily? She's eluded us."

"You worry too much. Chaffey, the Moroccan djinn, promised to track her down." Vicki held my arms tight around her. "You're warm."

I hugged her. "My friend promised to follow her from the airport. He lost her."

Vicki walked to the other side of the penthouse. "Look at the Kasbah. It's small, a few streets. Just pathways. How hard can she be to find?"

Something distracted me. "I smell fresh bread."

She smiled at me. "I've been on the internet. Can you see those chimneys? Those are community ovens. People bring their dough and bake their bread together."

I relaxed. Any place where people baked bread together had to be good.

Chaffey joined us. "Bonjour, mes amis," He went straight to the food table set up in the sitting area. "After breakfast, we'll find your blonde friend."

We all sat on pillows around the low table.

"First stop, the medina. All good visitors must support the local economy." Chaffey examined my San Diego Zoo cap. "We can't have you looking like tourists."

Fitch giggled. *'I told you.'*

Vicki stood up. "Allons-y." She was wearing a burgundy tunic and sandals.

Chaffey smiled. "You need a headscarf."

She opened her suitcase and pulled out a teal one.

'*Stunning,*' exclaimed Fitch atop his camel with his head wrapped in a keffiyeh.

In the medina, Chaffey bought me a djellaba and traded my San Diego Zoo hat for a white kufi cap.

Fitch approved, '*You look like a local.*'

Since it was getting warm and time for second breakfast, I stopped at a fruit stall and bartered my Stony High jacket for three bags, almonds, blueberries, and tangerines.

My calico cat friend rubbed against my ankles. I petted the cat. "Would you like second breakfast?"

The cat wrapped her tail around my ankle and purred.

I convinced the vendor to throw in some lamb scraps.

'*Tangerines.*' Fitch juggled five small orange fruits. '*Tangier. This is where they come from.*'

Everyone shared second breakfast as we wandered through the Kasbah. Chaffey stopped an officer wearing a headscarf and a red shirt with an embroidered green Moroccan star. I offered her some fruit, which she accepted. Chaffey interrogated her in Arabic and summarized their talk with, "She *might* have seen a blonde lady who *might* have been Elizabeth."

We continued through the Kasbah, stopping at a snake charmer who called his snake Bāythūn and fed it blueberries. Chaffey joked with him about the name and the diet before asking about Elizabeth. He touched his head and said, "Blonde." The result was the same as his interrogation with the police officer. Maybe. Might have. Maybe not.

Here on ground level, the Kasbah seemed larger and harder to navigate than from Vicki's Dar Sultan penthouse. I lost confidence in my Moroccan djinn. He spoke to many people, and no one had seen Emily. Emily proved herself superior to his detective skills. I was torn between Sleuth Club pride and disappointment at not finding her.

'*First lunch?*' Fitch took off his keffiyeh scarf and tied it around his neck.

Chaffey led us into a mosque. "Shortcut," he said.

I looked around. "I don't see any pictures of people."

"That's our way," said Chaffey. He pointed to circles of chaotic scribbles. "Those are quotations from the Quran."

"Don't you love the flowing Arabic calligraphy?" Vicki asked.

My re-examination did not find any patterns, Still, I said, "Yes. Exquisite," and squeezed her hand. I was chagrined that I couldn't speak the language or read the script. I wasn't much of a detective in Morocco. We exited the mosque into a narrow alley.

GREEN DOOR CUISINE.

The small English sign grabbed my attention as much as an animated electric billboard in Times Square. In a smaller font, it offered, MAKE AND BAKE MOROCCAN BREAD.

I couldn't pass this up. I walked in, and the others followed. We drank mint tea poured from high above the glass, learned about spices, and kneaded flour, salt, water, and yeast into round khobz loaves like the ones we had for breakfast.

"Enjoy your tea, and I will take the bread to the community oven." Our host refilled our cups.

'Go. Go.' An excited Fitch put on his chef's toque.

"Can we go with you?" I asked. There was no way I was going to miss those ovens. Tangier boasted a palace, a mosque, a beach, and ancient archeological sites. I wanted to see the ovens.

'Bread made in communal ovens doesn't heat the house in the summer, nor does it waste fuel warming up for a single family's baking. The ovens are an ancient practice.' Fitch lectured in his doctoral robes and his eight-sided tam.

The oven was down a narrow alley. The room held trays of khobz waiting and trays of warm baked khobz. I didn't mind the heat because the room smelled heavenly.

While I watched the loaves move in and out of the oven, Chaffey questioned the waiting women until he tugged on my djellaba. "Forget the bread. Follow me."

I wasn't going to leave our bread. I grabbed the hot loaves, juggling them to avoid burning my fingers, and followed Vicki and Chaffey. "Where are we going?"

"We're almost there," Chaffey signaled us to halt. We peeked around a corner into a pleasant piazza bordered by planters overgrown with greenery and filling the air with a minty aroma. A white façade faced us across the space with an Arabic sign in gold...

المعهد

...over a huge Moorish arch.

"Al Mahad," Chaffey read to us.

He hid behind a planter overgrown with oleander and signaled us to join him. "Over there. Do you see her?" He pointed to a tall woman with a few stray blonde hairs poking out from her headscarf. She carried a basket of bread. "Blonde hair. Is that her?" he asked hopefully.

I didn't need to see the hair because that was Emily's face. I'd know it anywhere, and peeking out from under her skirts was the calico kitty from breakfast at the hotel.

"What's al Mahad?" I asked.

"The Institute."

The Institute? Like the place where Vinnie sent the data file for decryption? That Institute?' Fitch sat in his favorite armchair in the sitting room at 221B Baker Street.

Vicki and I joined Chaffey behind a large oleander.
Pink blooms in blue ceramic pots bordered the piazza, giving
off a delicate vanilla aroma and reminding me of home. The
same hardy, poisonous plants lined the Desert Freeway in
Stony Estancia.

Emily approached the white marble façade across the
piazza. The magnificence of al Mahad grew. The wooden door
carved with Islamic calligraphy, like the Quran quotes in the
mosque, opened. Emily, the calico cat, and the bread slipped
beneath the Moorish arch that extended far above her six-foot
frame.

Vicki found a café table near one of the blue planters. No
sooner had we sat down than a waiter appeared. He wore a
white djellaba, a red silk vest, and a matching fez with a black
tassel. "Mint tea?" he asked.

We all nodded, and he disappeared.

"Al Mahad? The Institute?" Vicki asked. "What do they
do?"

"The Institute has foreign visitors. We can't trace the funds
it receives." Chaffey tapped his nose and gave us a djinn smile.
"They're under surveillance. Our anti-terrorism AI has placed
them on the watch list."

"Artificial Intelligence?" Vicki asked. "Where did you
acquire that technology?"

Chaffey leaned across the table and lowered his voice. "The
AI is from your friends at the Stony Estancia Makers Guild."
He sat up. "Dr. Terez Telkes herself visited us."

'Oh, no.' Fitch rested his face in his hands.

"Terrorists?" I asked. "What kinds of terrorists? Religious?
Political? Criminal? Domestic? International?"

"For sure, international," Chaffey answered. "We don't
know about the rest," he admitted.

The waiter reappeared with three mint teas and a tray of
croissants, butter, and soft Jben goat cheese.

I picked up a flaky croissant and unrolled it like a papyrus scroll, searching for answers to unknowable questions, covering myself with crumbs. "Is Emily...Elizabeth in danger?"

Vicki squeezed my hand.

'Chaffey's AI hallucinates like the Kwoleks,' Fitch laughed, flying his own quadcopter over the piazza.

Vicki sipped on her mint tea. "Can't you place someone undercover in al Mahad?"

Chaffey took a deep breath and exhaled. "Our best agents applied to work there. They didn't get past the interviews."

"Those interviews must reveal something." Vicki wrote al Mahad in Arabic with a wet finger on the table.

"Ah, those interviews." Chaffey chuckled. "Our people never get normal questions. They're asked riddles, math problems, and cryptic crossword puzzles." He took a bite of croissant and cheese.

"Have you considered a direct approach?" Vicki asked. "How about a search?"

"We have repeatedly applied for a warrant, always refused."

"The Kasbah is old," I observed. "Surely there are smuggling tunnels."

"We used ground-penetrating radar. The tunnels have been barricaded with cement and rebar."

"Have you considered breaking in?" I said with a smile. "Sometimes it's easier to ask forgiveness afterward rather than permission before."

Fitch held up his index finger. *'Lesson one for sleuths.'*

Vicki added, "Emily...Elizabeth is an American citizen. We can't leave her with those terrorists."

Chaffey tapped on his phone. "Attention, special teams: the American girl is in the Institute. Prepare for breach and extraction."

Fitch wore a tactical vest and a ballistic helmet, both patterned with desert camouflage.

Two armored personnel carriers, intimidating vehicles with eight wheels and a capacity for a dozen fighters, lined up behind Chaffey. I recognized these as the same US Marine surplus APCs sold to Stony Estancia SWAT.

'*How did they get those things through the narrow Kasbah alleys?*' Fitch defended the laws of physics while wearing a long wig like Sir Isaac Newton's.

"Aren't those soldiers overkill?" Vicki buttered a croissant. "Emily delivered bread."

'*Stockholm syndrome,*' said Fitch, waving a Symbionese Liberation Army flag. '*She's been brainwashed.*'

"Potayto, potahto. Call it what you like." Chaffey stood up and took Vicki's hand with his left and mine with his right. "They've been under surveillance long enough. It's time for action."

With my other hand, I rescued the croissant Vicki had abandoned on the table. We approached the gold al Mahad sign. The APCs followed us, and foot soldiers followed them.

'*Armageddon, here we come.*' Fitch wore a bandolier of grenades over his tactical vest.

We were in the center of the piazza when Emily stepped out of the al Mahad door wearing a big smile. "Senior Detective Yukawa and Mr. S, it's nice to see you."

The battalion stopped. Chief Inspector Chafik Marleau let go of our hands, unholstered his sidearm, and advanced.

I handed Vicki her rescued croissant. She took a bite and waggled her fingers at Emily.

Emily smiled back and winked.

Chaffey kept moving forward until he was toe-to-toe with Emily.

She didn't retreat.

'*Go, Bruins.*' Fitch wore his green-plush Stony High mascot costume and made bear claws with his hands.

My phone beeped. The omniscient *Surf SE* app had posted: STONY HIGH OUTSTARES MOROCCAN ARMY. #GIRLPOWER.

The piazza was silent except for the calico cat that meowed while strutting between Emily and Chaffey with its tail high. It stopped before Vicki and me for scritches. We looked at each other, and I squeezed Vicki's hand.

Throughout this, Chaffey stood at attention.

Emily brought both hands to her headscarf and pulled it back, revealing her radiant, blonde hair, which shone brighter than the morning sun.

At this dazzling unveiling, Chaffey and his troops backed away.

'That gives a new meaning to blonde bombshell.' Fitch combed his pompadour.

The Mediterranean sunshine, outdone by Emily's glowing tresses, hid behind dark clouds. An angry thunderclap, sounding like a challenge from the gods, preceded a lightning flash that outshone Emily, and another thunderclap. She looked up and nodded as if to say, "Nice one."

She spoke to Chaffey, "You're welcome to come in before the downpour."

Chaffey, Vicki, and I entered the Institute.

"Help yourselves to tea and crumpets," Emily invited us with a posh British accent, pointing to the tables inside the intricately carved Moorish door.

The large room resembled a university lecture hall. Ahead were tiers of students with the stage below us. Each student had a small desk and an electrical outlet. The side walls were painted with flamboyant Arabic calligraphy. I marveled at the beauty and symmetry.

From their attire, I deduced that the men and women represented students from around the globe. One couple sitting in the center caught my eye. They were an older woman with fine gray hair wearing a red embroidered silk jacket and a boy in lederhosen who couldn't have been older than eighteen or nineteen. Everyone had at least two devices. A woman in an Indian sari had a small laptop and three phones. Whiteboards, each ten meters wide, flanked the screen in the center of the stage.

The boards were covered with what I assumed to be advanced mathematics. I recognized some Greek letters. There wasn't an Arabic numeral in sight. The screen displayed Tsui's photographs of the smashed USB sticks.

'I told you this was the Institute, where Vinnie sent our data chips for decryption.' Fitch gloated.

You're a genius in hindsight, I taunted him.

The lecturer was dressed the same as Chaffey and me, a djellaba and a kufi cap. When I looked carefully, I realized he was Euclid Randolf, the night watchman cum mathematician and cryptographer.

"Congratulations, students," Euclid said. "Al Mahad has broken an unbreakable code. We've shown how our people can solve problems where AI and deep learning fail."

The audience cheered Euclid's announcement.

He held a black box printed with gold Arabic script. "Here are the results of your brilliant work." Euclid welcomed Vicki and me with a sweeping gesture. "Please give an Institute welcome to Senior Detective Victoria Yukawa."

The room was silent as we joined Euclid on the stage.

"And Teacher Zarand Szilard," he added.

They burst out with applause.

'Seems like teachers are more important than police at the Institute.' Fitch wore his doctoral robes and eight-sided tam.

I looked at Vicki. "Did you expect this?"

She shook her head. "I'm glad your Moroccan friend didn't rush in with guns blazing."

Euclid Randolf handed the black box to Vicki.

She accepted it with a puzzled look.

I shrugged and held my palms up.

Mr. Randolf spoke to the students, "They've come from Stony Estancia."

Everyone jumped to their feet, whooping and hollering.

'They love Stony Estancia.' Fitch did cartwheels in his Björn, Stony High mascot, costume.

Euclid tapped the golden calligraphy on the box.

"Al Mafatih. The keys. The answer to your questions." He smiled. "This is an al Mahad Geo*Vault, US patent number 7657076." He displayed multiple patent certificates on the large screen. "This is the next generation in data security, invented at the Institute and a billion-dollar market."

I examined the box. On one side, al Mafatih was printed in gold. The opposite side had ten buttons.

"What does it do?" Vicki asked.

Euclid explained, "The data is encrypted and password-protected." With a flourish, he pointed to the ten numeric buttons. "You enter the secret code here and..."

"Yes. Yes." Vicki interrupted him. "Don't you have internet here? What fool gave you a patent for that?"

Euclid smiled. "Let me demonstrate. Write this down: seven-six-five-seven-zero-seven-six."

"But—"

He interrupted Vicki. "Just give me a moment." He tapped the numbers, and a small light blinked red.

Vicki smiled. "Is your toy broken?"

"No. It worked perfectly. Had it been in the right place, the light would've been green, and your data would've been available. That's the crux of our invention."

"Huh?" Vicki waited for him to continue.

"Our clients were concerned that bad actors would take a device back to their lab and discover the password."

"I see," said Vicki. "How does your device protect against that threat?"

"The al Mahad Geo*Vault can only be decrypted when it's in the proper location."

'I get it,' Vicki exclaimed. "A device coded for an embassy would be safe from bad actors getting the device and the password. They won't be able to access the data from their lair. Wrong geolocation."

"Exactly."

"Where's this one located?" I asked.

"This one can only be decrypted when it's in Vincent Purcell's office."

'Super clever.' Fitch threw his deerstalker hat and calabash pipe into the air. 'Except...how did they get his office's GPS coordinates?'

"Did you decrypt our data chips?" I asked to confirm.

"Did we decrypt those data chips?" he shouted to the lecture hall. "We sure did."

They chanted back. "Sure did!"

'Go ahead, ask him,' Fitch nudged me.

I turned my back to the students and addressed Euclid. "You decrypted these files when Vinnie Purcell couldn't. How?"

"Do you want our secret?" Euclid gave me a smug smile.

"Yes, please," I humored him.

"Teamwork and diversity." He pointed to the woman in the Indian sari. "Her family wanted her to marry, but she wanted to do math. She applied to universities at home and abroad. None, except us, accepted her. Their loss. Our gain."

"All those students you see in front of us contributed." Euclid walked over to the old woman with gray hair and the teen in lederhosen. "Another example. Our transgender twins. We are their sanctuary."

Vicki whispered, "Is she really a male and is he really female?"

"No," I explained. "She's female, and he's male."

Fitch waved a pink, blue, and white transgender pride flag.

Emily stood in the back of the hall by the refreshments. She gave Euclid a slow clap until all the students broke out in a crescendo of applause and cheering.

"It looks like we'll be back in time for the New Year's Eve Ball," I said, looking forward to catering by Four Rivers, Firehouse Barbecue, and that pâtisserie on Higgs Road.

Vicki frowned. "Not so fast." She pointed to the back, where Chief Inspector Chafik Marleau and his army were leading Elizabeth away in handcuffs.

'Puppets! Puppies!' Fitch shouted. *'Why did they arrest Elizabeth...Emily?'*

'From the halls of Montezuma to the shores of Tripoli.' Fitch sang while carrying a large American flag. *'Chief Inspector Chafik Marleau isn't your friend. Call the Marines. Free Emily.'*

Vicki said, "I'm calling the American Embassy."

Euclid shook his head. "Don't bother. They're three hours away, and they won't send the Marines for a high school student from California."

The *Surf SE* app on my phone sent a notification. I showed it to Vicki. DETECTIVE YUKAWA AND MR. SZILARD ESCAPE MOROCCO.

'Wow,' said Fitch, dressed as The Pythia, Oracle of Delphi, and examining his crystal ball. *'The Surf has gone beyond omniscience to clairvoyance.'*

"What are we escaping from?" said Vicki.

Before I could admit that I had no idea, I received a call from Gendarmerie Nationale Capitaine Valery Renoir. "Zarand, you need to leave Tangier. They're planning to use you in court, against that high school student."

"How can they do that?"

"No time to explain. I've booked you a flight to Paris." He sent me the details in a text. "Get to the airport. Vite. Au plus vite. Tout de suite."

'Panic time!' Fitch ran in circles, without his head, clucking like a chicken.

Valery disconnected, and Vicki gave me a questioning look.

"Allons-y. We're going to the airport." I said with urgency.

"Now?"

"Now!"

I put my suitcase on the scale at the Tangier-Ibn Battouta airport.

A young man in a Royal Air Maroc uniform took my passport and asked, "Shall I check your bags to your final destination?"

I turned to Vicki. "That's the plan."

Vicki wasn't a believer in plans. "Best not. We have a long layover before our LAX flight."

The young man said, "In that case, you'll have to clear customs and check through security in Paris."

"No problem." I held out my hand for my passport, boarding pass, and luggage receipt.

As we walked to our gate, a flashing neon sign, BEST TAGINE, grabbed my attention. "We have time. Let's stop here."

'Don't you think about anything beyond meals?' Fitch took a superior tone while watching the TV screen. *'Is this first or second lunch?'*

Second. Did you forget the lamb skewers and communal oven bread that the hotel prepared for us to eat on the way to the airport? That was first lunch. I'm going to miss that bread.

The waiter brought Vicki and me chicken tagine in a traditional clay pot. When he removed the conical ceramic lid, a cloud of steam enveloped us. Paprika. Ginger. Cinnamon. Garlic. And other spices I couldn't place. When I bit into the tender chicken, it was the finest tagine I'd ever had. My taste buds shouted, "Puppets! Puppies! The best, putting airport food everywhere to shame."

'Listen to this.' Fitch floated up to the TV and turned up the volume. The broadcast pulled me away from my epicurean enjoyment. The crowd in the departure terminal stopped talking.

"Not guilty."

I recognized that voice, the sound of home. The news crawl said, AMERICAN TERRORIST ON TRIAL IN TANGIER. The voice belonged to Emily, my honorary grandchild.

She wore a pink headscarf with loose, matching slacks and a tunic embroidered with an intricate design at the hems. Beside her were two lawyers in black robes with white jabots.

'*I told you. Stony High students have lawyers, accountants, and agents.*' Fitch stuck out his tongue.

I felt bad panicking when Capitaine Valery Renoir told me to leave Tangier. My guilt faded when I saw how well Emily was represented and defended.

'*You've underestimated the Sleuth Club.*' Fitch relaxed on the Tangier beach. '*Emily doesn't need those lawyers.*'

Above her sat a three-judge panel dressed in black.

Vicki nudged me. "That embroidery. How bold of her."

I studied the stitching. It was the same color as the tunic and looked like the other geometric designs we'd seen in Tangier. Designs that every guide was quick to explain followed the Islamic tradition against the depiction of people. I gave Vicki a questioning look.

"Look again."

'*I know,*' gloated Fitch, dancing with bikini-clad women at the Tangier beach.

The subtle, cryptic pattern depicted women in bikinis carrying protest signs. Bold, indeed.

The judge in the center wore a niqab with only her exquisitely made-up eyes visible. She questioned Emily. "Elizabeth Macbeth, do you deny that you support al Mahad, a terrorist organization?"

The judge on the left, a man with a gray beard and black hair, said, "Perhaps you'd like to hear the evidence before entering your plea."

'*I heard her plead not guilty. Is he deaf?*' Fitch chortled, holding a brass ear trumpet.

The judge turned to Chaffey. "Chief Inspector Chafik Marleau, would you refresh the defendant on the facts of this case?"

"Al Mahad came to our attention when AI surveillance uncovered the transfer of foreign funds without the required paperwork. Significant amounts, over the legal limits."

Emily stood motionless.

"Our follow-up discovered many foreign nationals housed at the barracks within the Institute compound. Their communications mentioned training and fighters." He pointed at Emily. "The defendant, Elizabeth Macbeth, regularly visits al Mahad using different aliases. She also has connections with Purcell and Associates in Stony Estancia, California, a secretive group affiliated with US intelligence organizations."

On the TV, Emily smiled, brought both hands to her headscarf, and paused until everyone was watching. She pulled the scarf back, revealing her blonde hair. I looked around the airport terminal. All the women covered their hair. On the TV, the judges gasped. The people in the departure terminal froze.

Emily repeated, "Not guilty."

Vicki whispered, "How bold."

Emily called the boy we'd seen in the lecture hall. "Here's a fighter trained in the Institute's barracks," she said with the sarcasm of an American teenager.

He wore a djellaba and a kufi cap, not the Tyrolean attire we'd seen earlier. "When they found me, I was bullied because I preferred maths over etiquette. The teachers laughed at me." Tears pooled in his eyes as he recalled, "My maths teacher didn't understand the difference between undefined and imaginary. My mother told me to be polite, and my father was embarrassed." The old lady from al Mahad put her arms around him. He continued, "At al Mahad, I learned number theory and abstract algebra. No one bullies me here." He sat down.

The judge in the niqab with exquisitely made-up eyes wasn't listening. She said, "Your passport says you're a girl."

The courtroom and the airport were silent. People covered their mouths and looked at each other, too shocked to respond. Finally, Emily spoke, "He doesn't sound like a terrorist to me. Number theory isn't terrorist training. The only thing he learned to fight was encryption."

Before the judges could respond, Emily called the old lady, who wore a local costume, including a headscarf covering her gray hair.

The woman stood with her hands clasped and her head bowed until a judge said, "You may proceed."

"I missed going to school due to Mao's Cultural Revolution. My children and grandchildren treated me like an ignorant, useless old man, only fit to work in the fields. Like my young friend, I was miserable. I'm not a terrorist." Her voice was strong. "At al Mahad, I program in C++, SQL, R, and Bāythūn."

"What did she say?" Vicki asked.

I answered, "She said, Bāythūn. Remember the snake charmer we saw in the Kasbah? That was the name of his snake."

Fitch explained, *'Bāythūn is an Arabic transliteration for Python, the computer language, not the snake.'*

I corrected myself, "Bāythūn is another computer language."

Emily thanked the gray-haired old woman. "The Institute searches for gifted people and brings them here for the education they deserve."

The judge on the right was the youngest with neatly trimmed black hair. He dismissed the witnesses from the Institute and addressed Emily. "Tell me, Elizabeth Macbeth, why Tangier? You're from California. Why not there?"

Emily put her headscarf back on, faced the judges, and said, "Je suis vraiment désolée. Let me explain." She walked up to a large pad, picked up a marker, and wrote:

"House of wisdom. Algebra was invented there. Al Mahad is modeled on the Baghdad House of Wisdom, which was an international place of learning over a thousand years ago. In the 21st century, Baghdad wasn't a possibility. We chose Tangier."

The judges nodded in agreement.

'Emily's Arabic script convinced the judges,' Fitch concluded, wearing a djellaba and a kufi cap.

Emily turned to Chaffey, sitting on the prosecution bench. "Why is the Sûreté Nationale harassing the Institute?"

The youngest judge questioned Chaffey, "Are you harassing al Mahad?"

Chaffey jumped, "Zut alors. My next witnesses will show that al Mahad is an enemy agent from Stony Estancia."

My photo and Vicki's were shown on the screen with the caption, MISSING WITNESSES.

Vicki pulled her teal headscarf from her carry-on.

The judge with the exquisite eyes asks, "Where are they?"

Chaffey held his hands together, begging the judges, "At the airport with French diplomatic tickets."

'Diplomatic tickets? Is that even a thing?' Fitch asked, dressed as Pooh-Bah, Lord High Everything Else.

The judges conferred, and the one with the gray beard said. "Before violating diplomatic protection, tell us where you acquired this intelligence."

"Confidential sources," said Chaffey with a smile.

"Pas de problème," the head judge said, "Case dismiss–"

"Zut alors. I'll tell you," interjected Chaffey. "We have an anti-terrorism AI."

"Is it from the Stony Estancia Makers Guild?" the older male judge asked.

"Oui," Chaffey replied in a subdued voice.

"Did Dr. Terez Telkes award you stock options?" the younger male judge asked.

Chaffey didn't answer.

The judges conferred, and the woman in the center announced, "Case dismissed."

The audience at the airport applauded.

Vicki and I flew back to Paris, where we had a three-star dinner overlooking the Rive Droite and a night at the hotel in the premier arrondissement. Before our flight home, we made time for a tour of the Louvre, during which we met several splendid ladies: Mona Lisa, Venus de Milo, and Athena of Velletri. We landed at LAX in time for the New Year's Eve Ball, meeting Emily at the luggage carousels. She had arrived on a different flight.

Vicki ran up to her and shouted, "Elizabeth Macbeth. I'm surprised to see you."

The blonde student pulled a suitcase from the carousel and showed Vicki the luggage tag.

Vicki held her hands up, palms forward. "Mea culpa, Emily Milhone. It's hard to keep track of your aliases."

'Sure enough, she had three suitcases for her return trip, just as Vicki foretold,' Fitch snickered, pushing a cart with four suitcases.

I cradled the al Mahad Geo*Vault like a baby all the way from Paris to Los Angeles. "We have it, Vee. It's been a long journey."

She touched the shiny black rectangle. "When Kwolek identified shallow graves behind the library, I feared evil in Stony Estancia."

"Fortunately, the only thing buried in Mr. Mbacke's garden was smashed USB sticks." I took a napkin from my untouched airline meal and polished the Geo*Vault.

Vee picked at her mystery chocolate dessert. "That led us on a quest. First, Vinnie, then his friends in Maryland, and ultimately to al Mahad in Tangier."

I raised the black rectangle over my head and shook it in victory. "What secrets will this reveal?"

Vicki covered her unfinished dessert with her napkin. "I hope it reveals Wally's murderer."

When the steward cleared away our trays, I placed the Geo*Vault on my table and spun it. "Round and round, she goes. Where she stops, nobody knows." I kissed Vicki. "I'm hoping this brings Goleta home."

'Looks like a scam to me.' Fitch wore a black hoodie pulled over his forehead. *'Good luck finding anything useful.'*

We landed in Los Angeles mid-afternoon and took a limo to Purcell and Associates. Chad stored our luggage on the plastic chairs. "He's expecting you."

Vinnie stood when we entered his office. "Welcome home. Euclid called early this morning to inform me that they decrypted the data files and sent them back with you, though I have no idea why they didn't email them."

I handed him the Geo*Vault. "Here's why. This invention is their pride and joy. They want to show it off."

Vinnie turned the box over and pressed the number buttons. The light blinked red.

"This deserves a celebration." My backpack provided champagne, chilled flutes, and an ice bucket, along with fresh oysters and caviar with toast points.

Vicki uncorked the champagne and poured.

Vinnie held up the black rectangle. "I give up. What's this? Why are they proud of it?"

"That's an al Mahad Geo*Vault," I said. "It's been awarded US patent 7657076, their first one. They have high hopes. They also have protection with the European Patent Office."

He traced the Arabic script. "What does it say?"

"Al Mafatih. The keys." I let this mystical label sink in. "Euclid promised that these files would answer our questions."

Fitch shrugged and held his palms up. *'We have lots of questions. Which ones?'*

Vinnie pushed the number buttons, and the light flashed red. "Al Mahad Geo*Vault? What does it do? How did they get a patent for this?"

"The Geo*Vault uses two-factor authentication. You can't access the vault without the proper passcode and–"

Vinnie jumped ahead. "The second factor is special. That's how they received a patent."

Vicki responded. "Right. The second factor is the device's GPS location. This one only opens when it's in your office, no place else."

He looked up the patent on his computer. "Method and apparatus for data security. I get it." He smiled. "Clever. Let's not delay any longer. What's the code?"

"Seven-six-five-seven-zero-seven-six," Vicki said.

'The secret code is the same as the patent number,' Fitch chortled. *'Not much of a secret.'*

Vinnie typed in the numbers, and the device blinked red as it had in Morocco.

'We're in Vinnie's office. That's the correct second factor.' Fitch crossed his arms. *'I told you this was a scam.'*

"Not good. That light is supposed to be green," Vicki said.

"Just kidding." Vinnie headed outside. "My building is a Faraday cage. It can't work in here."

Fitch was trapped in a cage. He shook the door. *'I'm Faraday and I can't escape my cage.'*

Don't do that, Fitch. You're confusing everyone. A Faraday cage doesn't trap anything inside. It keeps signals out.

'What about GPS?' Fitch asked while rattling his cage.

No GPS. The Faraday cage blocks the signals from the GPS satellites.

Vinnie said, "We have to get out of the building." He tried the vault in the front parking lot. The light flashed red. "Now we need to be closer to my office. Let's move to the back."

The Geo*Vault blinked red.

"Are you sure of the number?" Vinnie asked.

I had the code on my phone. "7657076 is correct."

'How could they know his office's GPS coordinates?' Fitch continued to rattle his cage.

I suggested the roof. "We can position ourselves above your desk."

"Good plan." Vinnie leaned a ladder against the wall. "GPS is no good for altitude. The Geo*Vault won't realize that we're on the roof." We climbed up. That didn't help. He tried different places. All red lights.

Fitch shook his head and said, *'It's a scam. It's never going to work.'*

Do you have a better idea? I snapped at him.

Vinnie slid down the ladder. "Intuitively obvious to the most casual observer. There's an eight-hour time difference. I never call them from here."

He jumped into his car and sped away.

'His home office,' Fitch explained, wearing his jammies.

"Obviously, his home office," I said to Vicki.

She followed Vinnie's car up Van Vleck Avenue and through the gate to the Stony Estancia Haciendas.

***

In honor of the al Mahad mathematicians, I served lamb tagine and Moroccan bread circles fresh from Vinnie's stone oven. The tagine wasn't as good as what was on offer at Tangier-Ibn Battouta Airport. Ginger and garlic were there.

191

Paprika and cinnamon were missing, as were the spices I hadn't been able to name. We dipped our bread in tagine and drank mint tea.

Vinnie held the Geo*Vault over his head and whooped, "I found eight files decrypted by the Institute. They called them the keys, al Mafatih. I sent you the cleartext links."

Stony Estancia Surfs posted, THE KEYS OR THE HOAX?

"Are these files just numbers?" Vicki scrolled through them on her phone. "No text? Nothing else?"

Vinnie frowned. "Just numbers. An AI analysis shows the small files have two columns, and the large ones have four. I've sent spreadsheets to you and *Stony Estancia Surfs*. One of their readers might notice a pattern."

I reviewed the four-column files on my phone.

'Easy-peasy,' Fitch laughed. *'The numbers in the first column are sorted, smallest to largest, starting in the forty-thousands. Those are spreadsheet dates.'*

"I solved one part," I announced. "The first column holds dates. Recent ones that ended last October."

'Last October?' Fitch flipped through his calendar. *'The data stops when Wally was murdered.'*

Vicki gave me a peck on the cheek. "Gosh. Dates. Good one."

Vinnie sighed. "I considered climate change. I tested the other numbers as latitudes, longitudes, and temperatures, both Fahrenheit and Celsius. Nothing."

Vicki whistled. "I tried daytimes to go with the calendar dates. Nothing made sense."

I was disappointed. After reconstructing the smashed USB sticks, we had nothing. "This is frustrating. We solved one mystery and uncovered another."

Fitch made a raspberry sound. *'Like I said, scam. Good luck finding anything useful.'*

My phone beeped. *Stony Estancia Surfs* posted, CRACK THE CODE CONTEST. WISDOM OF CROWDS. They posted links to the spreadsheets and challenged Stony Estancia to interpret the numbers.

The comments piled up rapidly without any progress.

'*No surprise. Show most folks a screen full of numbers and their minds go blank. You might as well ask them to find a pattern in the dust motes sparkling in a sunbeam.*' Fitch held up a prism to make a rainbow on the wall. '*Gay pride.*'

The steady comment stream was interrupted by another post. STONY ESTANCIA MAKERS GUILD IPO POSTPONED INDEFINITELY.

Vicki and I arranged to carpool on New Year's Eve. I surrendered my room for her preparations and dressed in front of my two flat-screen TVs.

"Kawaii!" I exclaimed when she appeared. Her hair was up in the classic nihongami style, adorned with a cherry blossom kanzashi hair ornament.

"Arigatō," she replied. "This is my mother's wedding kimono, red and gold for good fortune." She ran her hands across the wide belt that held her kimono in place. "I'm glad you found a champagne-colored cummerbund and bow tie to match my grandmother's obi."

"We should get going. I'm worried about the traffic." I went down the stairs to the garage.

She followed, stepping carefully in her wooden kimono sandals.

As soon as I pulled out of Higgs Haven, I was stuck in traffic.

'The whole city comes out for inclusive holidays like Thanksgiving and New Year's Eve.' Fitch shifted to an androgynous persona with indeterminate racial characteristics. *'You can call me Finch.'*

I drove around Heisenberg Park twice before finding a spot to squeeze my car into.

"Yo, Vicki. Over here, Mr. Szilard." Coroner Persey waved. "Pile into my coroner's van. It's not a fancy limo, but it'll reduce the traffic and air pollution."

We followed Cerberus's bark to the back door.

'I can't believe they built the BV Arena without considering the traffic. Did they expect people to take our non-existent mass transit?' Fitch held a portable printer that spewed out parking tickets.

They planned on using the BV Mall car park, I hypothesized.

'How's that working for them?' Fitch chuckled, carrying shiny paper bags from the boutiques. *'The mall never closes nor relinquishes their parking spaces.'*

Vicki, Tsui with his five children, Vinnie with his granddaughter Alex in a stroller, and Principal Golding piled into the back of the van. Cerberus sat in the front with Persey.

Hafsa chauffeured the Sleuth Club in her SUV.

"Buckle your seat belts," Persey said in jest. We stood in the space where the gurney usually went. As we approached the arena, Persey slowed to a halt. "Happy New Year," she muttered in preference to a stronger expletive. She flipped on her flashing light and pulled into the emergency lane. Hafsa's SUV followed.

When Persey parked in a red zone, Hafsa pulled onto the sidewalk beside us. Her SUV was like a clown car. Sleuth Club members continued to climb out, long after it should have been empty.

"Dance or dinner?" asked Louis, turning fouettés.

'Time for second dinner.' Fitch tied on his green-and-gold checkered bib.

Emily took the lead. "The mall restaurants close at midnight. Dancing in the BV Arena will continue until sunup. Therefore, dinner first."

Hafsa said, "In memory of Walter Fisher, we should have vegetarian for our final meal of the year." She walked away from the arena and turned into the mall. "I know just the place."

Tsui's children ran off shouting. "Crepes," "Chocolate crepes," and "Yummy crepes."

I shrugged and looked to Vicki. "Do we follow the little kids or the big kids?" Cerberus tilted his head and stared at Persey.

Principal Golding said, "The Stony High teens have never led me astray." With an assist from Cerberus, Tsui rounded up his crew. "No chocolate tonight," he said to their disappointment.

The teens led the way. We were an unruly mob, in fancy dress, fighting our way through the outdoor mall against the crowd heading to the arena.

Each time one of Tsui's progeny wandered away, Cerberus jumped in front of them, barking, panting, and wagging his tail. The child hugged the chocolate lab and returned to the group. In this way, Cerberus herded the children through the crowded mall.

'They got the chocolate they were shouting for,' Fitch laughed. *'Chocolate Labrador retriever.'*

Outside the restaurant, a vendor wearing a turban, a long cotton shirt, and loose trousers sold Stony Estancia New Year's Eve head scarves.

'He's a Sikh,' Fitch declared, pointing to the small ceremonial dagger he wore. *'His kirpan.'* Fitch wore a turban and a full-size kirpan.

I counted out a headscarf for everyone in our party and left a generous donation in the basket. Curry, chili, and garlic aromas drew us into the restaurant.

"That smells delicious," Persey said while putting on her scarf.

I removed my shoes and rinsed my hands before wading through a shallow moat to clean my feet.

"This is like a Theravāda Buddhist temple," Vicki said, scrubbing her hands.

"Welcome to the Golden Temple." The hostess wore a jeweled kirpan. "All the tables are occupied. I'll invite you to enjoy our Roti Experience while you wait."

'Bread,' Fitch cheered, wearing a black apron and toque.

I joined the line, and when it was my turn, I accepted two dough balls and a roti belan, a small rolling pin. Kneeling on the floor at a low wooden table generously dusted with flour, I rolled my dough into thin rounds.

Vicki's roti was a perfect circle. Mine looked more like an oyster that had lost its shell and been run over. Tsui's children traced happy faces on theirs, and Cerberus ate his.

We cooked our circles on a huge rotating griddle with long-handled spatulas.

"Party of twenty." The hostess led us into a large room. We sat on the floor, ate roti, and drank chai.

'Bread. I love bread.' Fitch jumped up and down as we were offered one breadbasket after another. *'Roti, plain naan,*

paratha, garlic naan, poori, goat cheese naan, and another roti.'

The table held large bowls of dhal, lentil curry, and smaller dishes of aloo gobi, literally potato and cauliflower. I spooned the tasty food onto my plate and scooped it up with bread. When Tsui's kids found this challenging, they ate with their fingers.

'Did you notice that Dr. T canceled the IPO?' Fitch asked while juggling three rotis.

"Does anyone know what happened to the Makers Guild IPO?" I asked.

"I have no idea," said Mrs. Golding. "I was counting on the money. No selling the naming rights to the Bruin Bistro. No Makers Guild Gourmet Grill animated on a digital display." She assuaged her disappointment with aloo gobi.

Vinnie fed granddaughter Alex soft curried potatoes. "I could see an online retailer, a social media company, or even a search company, acquiring Stony Estancia Makers Guild. AI is hot. No IPO, but good news for the company and the city."

Emily said, "We'd better hurry. We want to be in the arena before midnight."

The teens cleared the table and handed out bowls and wooden spoons in time for the kheer rice pudding. Tsui's children made up for their small dinners with large desserts.

I paid the check, and our parade headed to the arena.

'I don't think any big tech company is going to acquire the Makers Guild.' Fitch cross-dressed as The Pythia, Oracle of Delphi, wearing white robes and a veil.

Oh, clairvoyant one, what do you see?

'Evil. I see evil.'

Fitch's pronouncement sent a shiver down my spine.

After dinner, we joined the flow of people heading for the arena. Principal Golding asked her students, "Have you made New Year's resolutions?"

Emily replied, "You can't be serious. No one does that anymore."

Louis performed a barefoot relevé with his arms extended over his head. "Resolutions emphasize deficiencies and disabilities. We celebrate abilities and accomplishments."

Hafsa added, "I'm fine the way I am."

'My admiration for this generation has gone up 100%.' Fitch moved away from the adults and joined the Sleuth Club.

Mrs. Golding accepted their rebuke and returned to the grown-ups. "What about the older generations?"

Persey rushed to respond like she'd been waiting for someone to ask. "When the NIAID named alpha-gal syndrome as the cause of death, we were one step closer to finding Mr. Fisher's killer. For the next step, we needed the murder weapon."

"Did you find a smoking gun in his stomach?" I joked.

'Yuck. That's an awful image.' Fitch made a disgusted face.

My silly question allowed Persey to show off her brilliance. She gave us an animated explanation. "Absolutely. I found the murder weapon by elimination." Persey waited until everyone was listening. "The autopsy didn't turn up any alpha-gal sources. No red meat. No dairy. No gelatin. Wally hadn't eaten anything containing alpha-gal."

Cerberus wagged his tail, enjoying Persey's conundrum.

Vicki, ever the detective, asked, "Are you certain alpha-gal was the cause of death?"

Persey crossed her arms. "Absolutely."

"I'll bite," Mrs. Golding said. "Where did it come from?"

"Where does everything come from?" Persey paused. "The internet."

"The internet?" Vicki asked.

"Yes. For a few thousand dollars, alpha-gal is available in sufficient microgram quantities to have induced Mr. Fisher's delayed, but fatal, anaphylaxis."

'That doesn't narrow the suspect list. A few thousand dollars is no big deal in Stony Estancia,' Fitch scoffed, wearing his Björn costume, the plush, green, Stony High bear.

Persey punched the air. "I have the murder weapon." The adults, the Sleuth Club, and Tsui's children gathered close to hear what she'd say next.

I was jealous. Teacher's Nirvana. All eyes were on her.

"Alpha-gal is easy enough to get." She drew her audience in, pausing between revelations. "It ships with dry ice. Unfortunately for our murderer, storage is an issue. It needs to be kept at -20° C."

I knew the next part of the story. "That would have been helpful before COVID-19."

"Correct. Before COVID-19, such cold storage was rare, but the vaccine cold chain required hospitals, clinics, and pharmacies to be -20° C capable. The list is long but finite." She took a deep breath. "I will track down the killer soon enough. That's my New Year's resolution."

The Sleuth Club applauded. Hafsa said, "Correction. We have a New Year's resolution."

Louis performed a saut de chat landing beside Coroner Persey. He shook her hand. "You are our inspiration."

Emily continued. "Our New Year's resolution is to locate and rescue our missing classmate, Goleta Hardcastle."

Vicki whispered to me, "If I can't control them, I may as well support them."

'Lesson five,' said Fitch.

Vicki spoke to the Sleuth Club, "If you're going to solve Goleta's disappearance, you should investigate Athena's Avengers and Minerva's Mission. The police are sure they're involved."

Hafsa said, "We've heard of them. Nothing good. We'll find Leeta without their questionable tactics."

Vicki continued. "Do you know the history of missing students at Stony High?" The Sleuth Club didn't respond. "Before Goleta, Robert Drew disappeared. Don't forget Xanthia Kaldis."

Emily asked, "Who's Robert Drew?"

"Robert was before my time," said Principal Golding, "but he vanished from Stony High without a trace. The school board warned me about him when I was hired."

Fitch informed me, *'His father is Mr. OOP, Robertson Drew, Senior.'*

How did you know that? I asked Fitch.

'Everyone knows the story.' Fitch took out a laser pointer, put up a screen, and displayed his slides, starting with a

corporate picture of a young Mr. OOP in a white lab jacket. *'Bobby, Senior, was a research chemist.'*

The next slide was Los Angeles Skid Row. *'After his son disappeared, he lost his home and lived on the streets.'*

Successive slides followed Mr. OOP's saga. *'When he got sober with Alcoholics Anonymous, he became a CPA but went back to drinking and lost his license. After that slip, his AA sponsor got him the job as Mr. OOP with the Bruin Bistro, where they didn't serve alcohol.'*

Emily conferred with the Sleuth Club before her pronouncement. "Minerva's Mission, Athena's Avengers, Robert Drew, and Xanthia Kaldis are all interesting. However, as high school students with limited resources and experience, we will focus on Leeta.

'The lady doth protest too much, methinks.' Fitch wore an oversized Elizabethan ruff collar.

For sure. Whenever someone from Stony High pleads lack of resources, they're hiding something.

Phone notifications interrupted this Sleuth Club chicanery. My phone beeped. The *Surf SE* app posted, CRACK THE CODE CONTEST. UPDATE.

I read aloud from the story. "The *Surf* has received a partial decryption from the Kwoleks. They have deciphered the words Goleta, China, and Institute."

Hafsa blew a long puff of air between her lips. "The Makers Guild is wasting everyone's time."

I read on, "This may seem like an insignificant start. Difficult decryptions start small. The names of pharaohs led to deciphering the Rosetta Stone."

Emily said, "Not relevant. Apples and hand grenades."

'Make a note,' Fitch wrote in his casebook with a fountain pen. *'Find out why Emily and the Sleuth Club have a problem with the Makers Guild.'*

Competing detectives, I opined.

'Too many fingers and not enough pie,' Fitch giggled.

Vinnie spoke up. "My friends in Maryland report that the Chinese have technology to overlay coded messages with decoy decryptions. I suspect the Makers Guild is reporting a decoy coding. This is a step beyond steganography."

Vicki stood up. "Let's join the crowd in the arena. It's almost midnight."

I said. "There's nothing left for us to do. We have to delegate deciphering those coded messages to the mathematicians. Persey will find Wally's killer. The Sleuth Club will find Leeta."

She bumped me with her hip. "We can solve the graffiti mystery."

I kissed her forehead. "Never a dull moment."

'We aren't at the end. There are a few twists and turns left.' Fitch searched the night sky through his Galilean telescope.

VALENTINE'S DAY

For Valentine's Day, Vicki and I slept at my place on Valentine's Eve and at hers on Valentine's Night. We shared meals, starting with Valentine's Eve's second dinner. I prepped all week for my midnight extravaganza–five pink courses.

'You have three ovens and two dishwashers. Why not another refrigerator?' Fitch asked, opening the double doors and pointing to the packed shelves.

Where would I put it?

Fitch closed the fridge and clasped his hands together, flexing his biceps and perfect pecs. He signaled something important, celebrating his Polynesian heritage, showing off his lavalava and his geometric blackwork ink.

I'm listening. How do you suggest I make space in the jam-packed kitchenette of my one-bedroom apartment?

He pointed with his Valentine's apron, the one embroidered with pink cherubs and hearts. *'Right here should work.'*

You're kidding, right? There's no space between my old refrigerator and that triple oven.

He smiled. *'Did you forget this kitchen is multi-dimensional, like your backpack. When they deliver the new appliance, the space will be there.'*

I ordered a second fridge from an online AI—the latest Fahrenheit-451 model, Wi-Fi enabled, with a hands-free auto-opening glass door. They promised a twelve-hour delivery, Valentine's Day morning. I entered delivery comments and a code for the electronic lock. THE INSTALLATION LOCATION WILL BE OBVIOUS.

'Obvious. Clever.' Fitch pointed to the expanding spacetime between the old fridge and the oven. *'Better living through dark energy.'*

The AI responded, "Your new appliance will text you."

As the gap grew, Dahl's nose explored the expanding space.

I scritched her ears, gave her a teeth-cleaning treat, and said, "Perfect. You show them where to put it. I'll be teaching Ms. Dupin's math class."

The dough for the appetizer pizzas was on the counter along with San Marzano tomato sauce and my Valentine's Day toppings—Pink Queen cheese, cherry tomatoes, smoked salmon, and my secret ingredient: flying-fish roe, tobiko in Japanese.

Under normal circumstances, toppings would be added when the pizzas were ready to enter the oven, but pink banquet logistics required some compromises. I scattered the tobiko last. The translucent orange dots looked like the pattern of graffiti across the map of Stony Estancia.

'As they should,' Fitch commented with a sarcastic tone. *'Fish eggs and graffiti sites, meaningless distractions.'*

Not really. I'm certain those graffiti locations are sending a message. The pattern is a one-way communication to someone. The Surf's reporting is available everywhere. We'll never know the purpose or whether Stony Estancia Surfs was complicit.

'Fantasy. Total fantasy. The graffiti sites have no more meaning than those fish eggs,' Fitch declared with his head buried in an old grimoire.

I regretted that the new fridge hadn't been delivered as I rearranged everything to make room for the pizzas.

Dahl interrupted me with a plaintive meow.

"What's your problem?" I pointed to her dish. "Your second dinner is right there." I read "a delicious poultry medley" from the label.

She wasn't impressed and made a covering-up-bad-smells motion with her paw before rubbing against my legs.

I put some of the grated Pink Queen cheese in a bowl. "You can have this. It's kitty-friendly, lactose-free."

She smelled it, walked around the dish twice, and ate with gusto.

The banquet's second course epitomized simplicity. Maine lobster tails and red corn on the cob, drawn butter colored with rhubarb, and red cabbage slaw—a regular, pink Downeast lobster bake. The lobster tails thawed in the fridge, wherever they fit. My sixteen-quart stockpot waited on the stove, filled with water and a cup of sea salt.

Fitch played a sea shanty on his fiddle. *'Nothing's more relaxing than a simple pot of boiling salt water.'*

I had to agree, lobster is lobster, and corn is corn. Am I overthinking everything? Is there a simple explanation for Goleta Hardcastle's absence? What about the keys our friends at al Mahad extracted from the smashed USB sticks? Why do they have to be some secret code? KISS, keep it simple, stupid. Perhaps the numbers were just numbers.

With that calming thought, I moved on to the third course, an amuse-bouche, watermelon panna cotta, but where were the shooters holding the delicate palate cleansers? I examined every shelf in my packed fridge, but no panna cotta. I was frantic. They were a small thing, but they set the tone for the banquet.

I had no choice but to empty my five-year-old refrigerator, ancient compared to the new one with internal AI cameras. The new one would find the shot glasses at once, but it hadn't been delivered.

'Where's AI when you need it?' Fitch asked, mocking my faith in the new tech.

With everything arrayed on the counters, I hadn't found the shot glasses. I had no choice but to start anew. I mixed milk, cream, and watermelon with Hawaiian cane sugar and Tahitian vanilla from the pantry.

Fitch wore his lavalava and displayed his blackwork ink. *'Tahiti, Polynesia. Home, sweet home.'*

After combining the ingredients in a saucepan, I made small tastes in shooter glasses. I poured the leftover cream on Dahl's wet food. She rubbed her head against my leg in appreciation.

I didn't have time for the panna cotta to set in the refrigerator. I ran them downstairs to the deep freezer in the garage, starting a timer so I could rescue them before they formed ice crystals.

The fourth course was prime sirloin carpaccio and roast veggies. The meat was tucked safely in the fridge, and the red potatoes and baby beets were roasting in the top oven. I placed heart-shaped salt cellars with rosewood spoons on the table and filled them with Himalayan pink salt. This was one pink course with no problems.

I checked the veggies and drizzled them with EVOO. There can never be too much extra virgin olive oil. A quick trip to the balcony yielded fresh rosemary, which I washed, chopped, and sprinkled on the glistening veggies. It was hard to distinguish the potatoes from the beets.

'Not difficult. Just bite into them.' Fitch returned from the pantry, juggling different colored espresso pods. *'Sometimes differences don't matter. These have different names, but they're all espresso.'*

This made me think about Athena's Avengers and Minerva's Mission. Could those be two names for the same group? After all, Athena and Minerva were the same goddess, Greek and Roman.

Fitch chuckled. *'Potayto, potahto.'*

For dessert, strawberry shortcake and pink lemonade tarts waited in the packed refrigerator. Four of each took up an entire shelf. I had rooibos red tea to go with the sweets.

'You're not going to serve that South African apartheid tea.' Fitch stood in Nobel Square beside the bronze statues Cape Town had erected to recognize their four Nobel Peace Laureates.

I challenged Fitch. *What history books are you reading? Khoisan pastoralists and San hunter-gatherers drank that tea long before the Europeans arrived.*

'That's one theory,' Fitch conceded.

Is the tea like Walter Fisher's murder?

Fitch gave me a high five. *'You've got it. Too many fingers and not enough pie.'*

I didn't let this confuse me. Once I figured out the motive for Wally's murder, everything else would fall into place.

My phone beeped, reminding me to remove the panna cotta from the freezer. I ran downstairs. They set perfectly.

Another beep marked midnight. When I checked Vicki's location from my phone, she was on Blackett Street, crossing the Millikan intersection, en route to my place. I kissed the phone. "See you soon."

Second dinner was ready. I checked the bedroom. My queen-sized bed was made with my best sheets and the quilt we bought in Saskatchewan. I brushed my teeth for the third time and returned to the kitchen to pour the gazpacho into heart-shaped bowls, arrange a dozen pink roses as a centerpiece, and pop the small pizzas into the lower oven.

I opened the rosé wine and placed it in the ice bucket to breathe.

Surprise!

The original panna cottas sat primly among the ice cubes. I had tucked them there to conserve space in the overloaded fridge.

'*You outsmarted yourself,*' mocked Fitch.

This made me wonder about the alpha-gal reagent. Persey was confident that a small bottle stored at -20° C had murdered Wally, but she hadn't found it. Had she outsmarted herself? Was she looking in a refrigerator when she should have been checking dry ice buckets?

'*Could be. Could be,*' Fitch refilled his calabash pipe with tobacco from a Persian slipper.

I put the shooter glasses in the fridge with the others and checked my phone to see when Vicki would arrive.

But there was no Vicki. She had disappeared. Minutes ago, her dot was near, but now the tracking app displayed North America. No Vicki. Not in Stony Estancia. Not in California. Not in Saskatchewan.

I ran to the balcony, expecting her to be in the parking lot. Nothing.

From there, I called Tsui and asked between deep breaths, "Vicki has disappeared. Do you know where she is?"

"Calm down. I'm sure there's nothing to worry about. Let me check." After a delay, during which I could hear him calling the dispatcher, he said, "I can't locate her either."

He didn't sound concerned, but I was concerned enough for us both.

I turned off the ovens, grabbed my 5,000-lumen searchlight, and leaped down the stairs three at a time. I drove to the Millikan and Blackett intersection, the last location I had for her. After driving up and down the streets, I parked my car on the sidewalk and searched on foot.

I was ignoring my detective lessons. Lesson two: Good detectives don't attract attention. Lesson three: The lone investigator is a myth. I was running around the intersection, waving my searchlight, and crawling through the bushes.

I checked my phone. No location signal for Vicki. Where was she?

'Have you checked her home?' Fitch sat in the car.

I might have stayed on that corner, but the sprinklers came on, ending my indecision. I drove to Vicki's house. It was locked. I knew the code. Lesson four: Evidence is everywhere. That lesson let me down. I left without a clue and returned to Higgs Haven.

Between cat naps and frantic location queries, no Vicki. I nibbled at the pink banquet all night. The table was covered with half-eaten plates and soiled cutlery. First breakfast was a desultory affair—my second Valentine's meal without Vicki. My body struggled between up-all-night exhaustion and adrenaline. The nervous energy from fear that something bad had happened won the battle. It was time for a morning jog.

Fitch wasn't sympathetic. Costumed as Björn, the Stony High mascot, he sang, *Oh, What a Beautiful Mornin.*

"Oh, shut up!" I said. My hands trembled. It took three attempts to tie my shoes. I stood in the dark parking lot ready to run off my anxiety. Higgs Haven was a serene oasis, lit by fairy lights wrapped around the palm trees. The only sounds were my shoes on the serpentine gravel paths.

Stony Estancia was my twenty-four-hour gym. With solar-powered streetlights, I could jog around the clock. I scrutinized every shadow and car for signs of Vicki. I didn't find her. Two glowing eyes on the Blackett Street bridle path warned me I wasn't alone. I stopped running and cautiously entered the haze that surrounded Stony High.

Stony Estancia Surfs had posted FAUNA RETURNS TO STONY HIGH. The new state-of-the-art observatory required dark-sky protocols. The Ecology Club placed camera traps around the school as part of their senior project. They confirmed that, like the astronomers, the local fauna preferred the darkness. Predators and prey took advantage of the wide circle of shadow surrounding the observatory.

Those yellow eyes didn't move, staring at me, and enlarging as I approached. They likely belonged to a coyote, but the open space to the north provided habitat for bobcats, mountain lions, and bears. None of these were welcome as early-morning jogging partners.

'Whatever wild species she is, she fears you more than you fear her.' Fitch bumped into me when I stopped.

I didn't run away. The experts warned that she would chase me. I moved forward slowly until a sharp chirping made me freeze. In a twisted eucalyptus shadow was a mountain lion, the most frightening local fauna. I stood tall, waved my arms, and spoke calmly, "You have long legs and plenty of room to escape."

I was emboldened by her chirping, without growling or hissing.

"You're not threatened," I repeated, in what I hoped was a cougar whisperer's voice. I took out my cell and turned on the flashlight. She was exquisite, tawny, soft, and round. Round face. Round muzzle. Round ears. I wanted to pet her and bring her and her pink heart-shaped nose home for Valentine's Day, but her ears were flat against her head, and her tail was twitching. I waved my phone's LED flash.

In an instant, she leaped over a fence, bounded across the empty street, and disappeared. When she was out of sight, I regretted not taking a picture.

'Pics or it didn't happen.' Fitch chortled.

I resumed jogging along Blackett Street, checking for Vicki in every shadow and empty field. Millikan Road required a decision. Straight for a long run or right to return home.

'Better cut this short. You're expected in Ms. Dupin's math class.' Fitch's green electric scooter with gold flashes turned south.

I followed. When I reached Stony Estancia Regional Hospital, I was greeted by a familiar bark. I sprinted across the street to join Coroner Persey and Cerberus.

"Did someone die?" I asked.

"Fortunately, not."

"Have you seen Vicki?"

"No. Isn't she with you? It's Valentine's Day." Persey replied.

"No. I'm worried about her. She's missed two Valentine's meals, and I can't find her." We didn't have a clinging relationship, but she was always within a few miles. Cerberus must have sensed my worry. He licked my hand. I followed Persey to the hospital staff entrance like a second puppy.

A security guard with curly blue hair waved Persey and Cerberus through with a smile, but blocked me, arms crossed, legs spread, and her hand on her sidearm, a serious Glock. "Are you lost?" All traces of that smile had vanished. She wasn't letting me pass.

'Careful, buddy,' Fitch warned me. *'That's a sharpshooter award below her name badge.'*

I looked at my reflection in her glasses. How was I going to explain my black tights with high-viz orange stripes, green Stony High gym shorts, and a white technical running shirt? I wasn't dressed like someone who worked at the hospital. Perhaps I could pass as a dog walker for Cerberus?

Before our confrontation escalated, Persey interceded, "I'm bringing him in for a cardiac stress test."

"Nice try, Mom." The guard didn't move. "The patients' entrance is at the front."

The guard's badge read, Ms. Dalgliesh. Why did she call Persey Paterson, Mom?

'D'oh. Dalgliesh is her married name,' declared Fitch.

I don't think so. Look how young she is—barely older than my honorary grandkids at the high school.

I turned around and headed for the exit. There wasn't any reason for me to be at the hospital. I needed to finish my run in time to feed Dahl and teach Ms. Dupin's math class. I didn't want to miss Vicki when she arrived for second breakfast.

'If she does,' taunted Fitch.

Persey grabbed my arm. "Not so fast." She moved close to the guard, their cheeks touching. "Dally, you know why I'm here, don't you?"

The guard relaxed. "Sure, you want to find Wally's killer."

"Right." Persey pulled me past the checkpoint. "This is Zarand Szilard, retired homicide detective extraordinaire."

"I know who he is," she replied with that familiar teen sarcasm. "He's also a sub and solved Ms. Salas's murder during my senior year at Stony High. Go, Bruins." She returned her hand to her sidearm. "I'm not letting him pass."

"Right. Well, I need his help."

'What does she need?' pondered Fitch.

No idea.

"Okay, Mom, but he can't wander around the hospital like a lost jogger." She pointed to the employee locker room. "Go to locker 67. Dr. Mbacke took Valentine's Day off to spend time with his wife and newborn baby. I'm sure he won't mind you borrowing his white coat and stethoscope."

Dr. Mbacke? I was puzzled. Euclid, the nighttime security guard at the hotel, was a PhD mathematician. Was the Stony High maintenance guy, Mr. Mbacke, the same as the medical doctor, Dr. Mbacke?

'Don't be fooled. Same name. Two different people.' Fitch laughed. He wore a white coat and carried a stethoscope. *'However, I'm a PhD mathematician and a medical doctor, among other things.'*

Sure, you are, Fitch. Imaginary. Invisible. Anything you want.

None of this distracted me from Vicki. I checked her location, expecting my phone to report that she was waiting for me at Higgs Haven. Nothing.

I regretted greeting Persey and Cerberus. Beyond missing second breakfast and being late for Ms. Dupin's class, Persey wanted me to impersonate a doctor. I turned to leave.

The guard blocked my way, this time, preventing my departure. "Mom needs your help."

I knew better than to argue with two women—one with a dog and the other with a gun. I followed Persey into the locker room. "Mom? I didn't know you were married."

"You're old-fashioned. Plenty of people are parents without being married." Persey wiped Dr. Mbacke's stethoscope earbuds with alcohol. "No one likes to share earwax." She thought for a moment. "Better drape it around your neck. If you use it, you'll give yourself away."

'Even better—keep your mouth shut.' Fitch giggled.

When I was disguised as a doc, she said, "Dally isn't my biological daughter. You're out of touch. There are many ways to be a parent."

'Birth parent, stepparent, adoptive parent, foster parent, godparent, and you, an honorary grandparent,' Fitch ribbed me before saying, *'Okay Boomer,'* with a smirk.

Persey explained, "Isla Dalgliesh ran away from home at eleven. She lived at Stony Estancia Family Shelter until she turned eighteen. Formally, I'm her mentor, but she prefers to call me Mom."

"I understand." I winked at Fitch, feeling I was up with the latest trends.

Persey swiped her hospital ID and led us through a door labeled No Unauthorized Access. The room had long rows of shiny white machines with blue accents, computers, vented workstations, and tables with microscopes.

Warning placards were everywhere. I recognized the symbols for eye wash stations, laser beam hazards, and gloves required, but the other yellow triangles and white diamonds were a mystery. My biggest surprise was how many people were working before sunrise.

Several looked up and waved to Persey. She handed me blue gloves, an N95 mask, and safety goggles. We walked down a long aisle. The lab was fascinating, but my phone alarm told me I needed to feed Dahl, have second breakfast, and be in Ms. Dupin's math class. "Why am I here?"

"I've searched all over town—clinics, doctors' offices, pharmacies. Those were small operations. I'm confident I didn't miss any clues. I didn't find and trace of the alpha-gal reagent used to murder Walter Fisher."

She pointed to freezers along the back wall. "As Sherlock Holmes observed, 'When you have eliminated all which is impossible, then whatever remains, however improbable, must be the truth.' That leads us here."

As much as I loved Sherlock Holmes, I couldn't shake the thought of those panna cotta shooters hidden in the ice bucket. Was the flaw in Persey's reasoning her limited idea of 'whatever remains?'

I could cut my run short, get someone to drive me home, and skip second breakfast. I was running out of time. I needed a shower and clean clothes.

'Don't forget feeding Dahl,' Fitch reminded me.

The long wall of freezers was daunting. I'd never be home in time. They went on forever. I asked, "How many are there?"

Persey said, "I counted them twice. Twenty-seven."

'Three cubed,' Fitch said.

I surveyed them. Some had glass doors, others were chest freezers, but most had solid double doors. I admired the glass doors, thinking about my recent purchase. I checked my phone. Zero bars, no cell signal, but a strong Wi-Fi. That connection brought no satisfaction. No Vicki. No new refrigerator. I was wearing Stony High gear. I considered going to school without changing.

I turned towards the exit. "It's too late, I have to head home."

"Can't you cancel your sub assignment?" Persey pleaded. "This is my third visit to this lab, and I don't want to delay again."

"How can there be a rush?" I held my palms up. "Wally was murdered on Halloween, and today is Valentine's Day. There won't be any clues left."

Persey looked sad as we retreated. When we reached the lab door, I could hear Cerberus whimpering outside in the corridor. I took one last look around. "There may be a way."

Persey perked up. "Yes?"

I pointed to the CCTV cameras.

Persey found the lab supervisor. "How long do you keep the CCTV videos?"

"A week or ten days," the short man replied.

Persey looked dejected, but I had a thought. "Then what happens to them?" I asked.

He spoke softly. "Not sure. I send them to Purcell and Associates."

"I know Vinnie. He says it's cheaper to warehouse data than to summarize and index it. I bet he has them."

Persey hugged me. "I knew you'd be helpful. Let's go. I'll get you home in time to feed Dahl, but let's see Vinnie first."

Persey burned rubber, leaving the hospital parking lot with lights flashing and her siren whoop-whooping. The polite Stony Estancia drivers pulled over as the coroner's van sped south on Millikan Road to Warehouse-o-Rama.

I phoned Vinnie. "How's little Alex?"

"What do you want?"

I could tell he was trying to sound stern, but he never passed up an opportunity to brag about his granddaughter.

"I know you, Zarand. You always mention her when you want a favor."

"Guilty as charged. Tell me about her anyway."

His voice changed to a squeaky soprano. I called that his proud-grandpa voice. "She's the smartest. She's putting words together. She says, 'Pretty flower,' and 'Read book.'"

"I'm sure 'Read book' is your favorite."

"Absolutely. What do you need?"

"The hospital CCTV records."

"You're in luck. I keep them. Some are onsite, and the rest are in remote storage."

I turned to Persey. "I told you. He has the discs."

She gave me a thumbs up as she drifted around the corner onto Appleton Route.

"I need October."

"I have those here. When do you want to pick them up?"

"Soon. We're coming down Appleton. You should be able to hear Persey's siren."

"I'll meet you in the parking lot."

"Wait a moment, Vinnie. One more thing."

He was in a good mood. "Sure. Anything."

"Vicki, Senior Detective Victoria Yukawa—"

"Yes. Yes. I know Vicki."

"She's missing. Can you find her?

"I'll give it a shot."

"A thousand thanks."

The coroner's van skidded to a stop in the strip mall parking lot in front of Purcell and Associates.

A sad-looking Vinnie Purcell met us. "I'm sorry. October is already in deep storage."

"This is important. How soon can you retrieve them?"

"A week."

"And—" I prompted him.

"I hated to bring more bad news." He hugged me. "Nothing on Vicki, either."

"Thanks. Hug Alex for me."

Persey spun around and headed to Higgs Haven. "Sorry about Vicki. Nothing is ever easy."

True to her word, Coroner Persey delivered me to Higgs Haven in time to feed Dahl and teach Ms. Dupin's math class. Cerberus and Dahl played in the kitchen while I showered and dressed. No second breakfast. Without Vicki, I wasn't hungry. I shuffled down the stairs muttering, "What happened? Where could she be?"

'Anywhere,' answered Fitch, surfing Teahupo'o in Tahiti. *'Plans are sacred to you, but she is a free spirit.'*

Persey followed me into the garage. "I'm sure she'll show up."

"I hope so. It's not like her to miss Valentine's Day." I handed Persey my backpack. "Here. You can help."

She held the sack open, and I stocked it with leftovers, Firehouse Barbeque ribs, a takeaway box assortment from Four Rivers, and Cocina de Cetto enchiladas.

"Are you expecting a big crowd?"

"Just Vicki. She missed breakfast. She'll be hungry." Some pastel-colored macarons from that wonderful pâtisserie around the corner from Purcell and Associates caught my eye. I tossed them in. "I want to be prepared."

'I don't expect her,' Fitch cautioned.

That set me worrying. Had I done something wrong? Did she meet someone else?

'You're being foolish,' Fitch mocked me, *'She probably drove off the road and is lying unconscious at the bottom of a ravine.'*

Don't joke like that.

What if Fitch was right? I called Tsui and then Peggy, but neither the police nor the fire department had any news. Worse, they didn't take my concerns seriously. I heard laughter when Peggy checked with the EMTs.

'Calm down. Now you're late for school.'

Fitch was right. To make matters worse, when I jumped in my car, I discovered I'd forgotten to plug it in. Dead battery. I took my electric scooter. That turned out to be a good choice because the school parking lot was full.

I ignored the rules, neglecting to sign in with Mr. Sendak or get a visitor's badge. I rode my e-scooter across the courtyard, zigzagging around the students. My first-period students applauded as I coasted my e-scooter into Ms. Dupin's room.

"**Ms. Dupin** assigned you to collect real-world data for today's lesson—mean, median, mode, and standard deviation." I dimmed the lights and projected Ms. Dupin's first slide. MATH SYNONYMS: MEAN AND AVERAGE.

Fitch yawned.

This day wasn't going well. Agile teen fingers were tap-tapping on their phones. This was the opposite of teacher's Nirvana.

Fitch sat in a meditative posture. *The best antonym for Nirvana is found in Sanskrit, Samsara.'*

Yes. Samsara. The endless cycle of suffering.

Phones glowed in the darkened room, games or social media. Ms. Dupin's lesson was a sub's nightmare, busy work that didn't count for their grades. I made a spontaneous decision to disregard it. "Put away your phones. Close your laptops. Tell me how you got your data."

That got their attention.

Emily stood and pointed to the agenda Ms. Dupin had left on the whiteboard. "That's not in the lesson plan. Why do we need to talk about it?"

Clouseau poked his head out from Emily's skirt. *Meow.*

'Now you have a rebellion on your hands.' Fitch sang *La Marseillaise. 'Let's go, children of the fatherland. The day of glory has arrived!'*

I changed directions. My substitute superpower was the ability to think on my feet. I couldn't find Vicki, but I could rescue this class. "You're right, Emily. Let me ask you something else. When did you notice that I wasn't Ms. Dupin?"

She couldn't resist. "As soon as I walked in."

"What was your clue?"

She looked at the class with a big smile. "It was the beard. Ms. Dupin doesn't have a beard."

Louis added, "Old graybeard. Ms. Dupin is young."

The room went silent, waiting. Had Louis crossed some line?

I bent over, put one hand on my back, and grabbed a meter stick for an impromptu cane. I hobbled around the room. All eyes were on me. I had them. Teacher's Nirvana. In a thin, creaky voice, I said, "Ancient. That's me. I remember landline phones, VHS tapes, and CDs." They laughed.

I didn't care that Louis's answer was disrespectful. He'd made my point. "I'm not Ms. Dupin. Expect something different."

'They're pleased you abandoned that tedious assignment.' Fitch wandered around the room and assured me they were ready. *'If not Ms. Dupin's plan, what are you doing?'*

I always have a backup. Every good sub does.

Mohamed raised his hand. "My numbers are from Stony Estancia Hotel. They're final balances for the week's guests."

I jumped up on an empty seat. "Excellent."

Keith high-fived Moe. "Go, Stony Estancia Hotel. I copied the room numbers."

Several students groaned at Moe's choice, but he gave them a big grin.

I kept up the momentum. "Anyone else?"

Hafsa spoke with a calm voice that held everyone's attention. "I went to the Stony Estancia Mosque—five times a day, every day. I counted the faithful."

Louis responded next. "There are over ten thousand dance studios in the US. I downloaded student enrollment stats."

Fitch marched around the room waving the French flag, le Tricolore. *'The crowd is yours. Storm the Bastille.'*

I had engaged students and couldn't resist smiling.

Emily, holding Clouseau, contributed, "I went to the local supermarket and watched the cash registers. I copied the total for each shopper."

Jaxon said, "I was with her. I collected the shelf prices."

I strutted back and forth like a rock star on an arena stage. I had everyone's attention, except Emily, who was engaged with Clouseau.

"Now you need to count the leading digits from your numbers." I wrote some arbitrary numbers on the whiteboard. "11, 1,870, 163, and 1,000,000," and circled the one at the start of each. "These all count as a one. Count the 1s, 2s, and so on."

Louis moaned. "You can't be serious. I have thousands of dance studios."

'He has a good point,' Fitch agreed. He sat with the women computers who cataloged stars at the Harvard Observatory in the 19th century.

I hadn't thought of that.

Moe jumped up. "No problem."

Along with the rest of the class, I looked to Moe. Like an experienced teacher, he stood silent until he had everyone's attention. Teacher's Nirvana. I was jealous.

"I released an app to do this. You can download the 'MOE'S BIN IT' app using your Stony High ID and password."

With Moe's app, they completed the first step quickly. Everyone was engaged. Ms. Dupin's lesson plan was boring because they'd calculated mean and mode in primary school and in middle school, but my lesson was something they'd never done.

Fitch high-fived me. *'Super teacher.'*

"Now make a graph for the totals for one through nine."

"No zero?" asked Mohamed, standing up for the Asian mathematicians who discovered zero.

"Good observation."

He smiled.

"Numbers never start with a zero."

He smacked his forehead. "D'oh."

"Let's look at your graphs. You might have a downhill ski slope, starting high and descending." I projected an example.

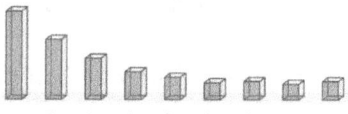

"This is the area of all countries from Russia to Vatican City. You can imagine shussing down this slope."

Emily interrupted, "Is that the area in square kilometers or acres?"

Louis laughed, "Or, perhaps, square feet."

"Great questions." This was my teachable moment. "I don't recall, but it wouldn't make any difference. You'll find a ski slope to shuss down regardless."

Moe asked, "Will everyone get a slope like this?"

"No. Sometimes you get a cross-country ski trail like these random numbers."

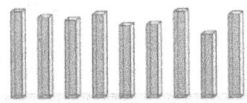

You can stride across this trail.

'Congrats. You rescued the class.' Fitch couldn't resist ridiculing my success, *'Great entertainment, but are you teaching anything?'*

Patience, young grasshopper. Watch and learn.

Louis did a grand jeté across the room. "My graph is a black diamond slope. During winter break, I'll be shussing down Whistler Mountain in British Columbia for spring skiing."

Not to be outdone, Jaxon said, "My flight leaves tonight. Double black diamonds. Europe for me. Kitzbühel, Österreich." He spoke with an impressive Austrian accent.

Keith, who had copied hotel room numbers, said, "Uff da. The best cross-country trails for me. I'll be striding at Giants Ridge in Minnesota."

Emily, who had recorded the grocery totals, held up her flat graph. "Cross-country. Davos, Switzerland."

I turned to Fitch. *Are you paying attention? I know why Emily isn't engaged.*

"Thank you, Emily. Please tell us what you were doing while Jaxon was walking the aisles to record shelf prices."

"I sat in the front of the store recording checkout totals."

"I don't think so."

Emily crossed her arms. She was silent, as was the rest of the class.

Stony High rarely experienced teacher-student confrontations. They looked at each other and shrugged their shoulders.

This was it, another teachable moment.

"Frank Benford published *The Law of Anomalous Numbers* in 1938. After extensive research and data collection, much like Ms. Dupin's assignment, he discovered that your graph should have been a downhill ski slope, not a cross-country trail. You didn't record the grocery totals. You made up those numbers."

The class turned to Emily, waiting for her response. She looked down at Clouseau. After a while, they returned their attention to me.

"Don't feel bad, Emily. Benford's Law has been used to uncover financial fraud from expense accounts to stock market manipulations."

I held up Emily's cross-country graph. Graphs like this indicate sequential numbers like Keith's room numbers or random numbers."

Emily spoke softly. "Mea Culpa. My numbers were made up. I read those awful gossip magazines while Jaxon was working."

The class was intent on discovering data sets on the internet and testing them. Louis did a fouetté. "The student enrollments in dance schools are a downhill slope. Also, the dance company sizes."

Hafsa announced. "I checked the data for the thousands of US mosques. A downhill slope."

Emily said, "I checked those datasets from the keys reconstructed by the Institute in Morocco. Half were downhill slopes, and the other half were cross-country trails."

She sandbagged Ms. Dupin's original assignment by making up numbers. Benford caught her. Now she redeemed herself. "You caught me. Now, I've caught someone else. Half the keys are legit, downhill slopes, and half are bogus, cross-country trails."

The class shook index fingers at the absent cheater. "Naughty. Naughty."

The *Surf* posted, THE KEYS ARE FRAUDULENT.

Emily had uncovered something important. I was sure, but the buzzer sounded before I could figure out what.

I sat alone in the Bruin Bistro—doom-scrolling and picking at my Cobb Salad–an avocado slice from the left, a cucumber piece from the right. I stabbed a currant tomato with my fork before returning it to the bowl. No word from Vicki. I picked up a crisp bacon rasher with my fingers.

A text interrupted my missing-Vicki funk. **F-451:** YOUR FAHRENHEIT-451 IS ONLINE AND CHILLING.

That was my new Wi-Fi-enabled, hands-free, auto-opening refrigerator. Every minute, it sent another notice. **F-451:** ENERGY SAVING MODE. DOOR AUTOMATICALLY CLOSED.

I texted a message to the customer service AI reporting the defective door that kept popping open.

The AI responded with pictures of Dahl activating the hands-free, auto-opening door.

I responded, **MR S:** CRAZY HALLUCINATING AI. THAT'S A CAT. FROM NOW ON, YOUR NAME IS CRAZY AI.

CRAZY AI: LEARNED CAT. CRAZY AI WILL NOT OPEN FOR CAT.

Valentine's Day must have been slow news. *Stony Estancia Surfs* ran a story about importing long-stem roses from Ecuador, logistics, and tariffs. They repeated the rumor that Stony Estancia Makers Guild's initial public offering was on hold. IPO IS PUT OFF.

'Clever. IPO. *Is. Put. Off.*' Fitch giggled.

The lead story was a retrospective on Goleta Hardcastle, the brilliant student missing for over a hundred days.

In an advertising banner, animated Kwoleks announced progress in decrypting the recovered USB data—three more words: balloon, giraffe, and fool. Worst of all, there was no news of Vicki. My half-day teaching for Ms. Dupin was over, and my big Valentine's Day plans had degenerated into riding my e-scooter home to take a nap with Dahl.

I stared across the empty Bruin Bistro dining room, willing Vicki to join me for second lunch. The Bistro door came to life. My heart raced, and I closed my eyes. When I opened my eyes,

Dr. Telkes's auburn curls sat across from me, not Vicki's straight black hair.

She picked up my fork and ate the tomato. "Delicious. I missed lunch. Are you going to finish that salad?"

I pushed the bowl across the table.

"Kwolek is going to eat your lunch," Dr. Telkes boasted. "Two more words today. Bacon and hoax. Those eight data files decrypted by The Institute hide a secret message. The Kwoleks will find it."

'She's in for a rude awakening.' Fitch basted a suckling pig as it turned on a roasting spit over maple coals. *'Nobody eats your lunch.'*

I taunted Dr. T. "Your AIs are hallucinating patterns where none exist, like when our ancestors gave names to groups of stars that appeared close, but were light-years apart."

I dug into my pocket and retrieved Vicki's napkin with the graffiti incidents. I paused. It scented the air with the fresh aroma of her green tea shampoo. "Have your pattern-matching idiot savants found anything in these graffiti locations?"

Dr. T took out her phone. "Thanks for asking." She opened *Stony Estancia Surfs* and rotated the graffiti incident map. "The place you should be looking is that fancy observatory behind the football field."

"How do you figure?"

"Kwolek connected the dots." She drew on the map with her finger.

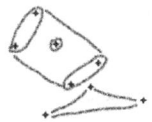

"See. It's a fourteen-inch Newtonian telescope. It's obvious once you see it." Dr. T announced proudly.

'She can't be serious. Tsui's kids could have done better.' Fitch dropped a crayon box on the floor.

"Your IPO is delayed." I felt bad raising this issue, but I was frustrated that she couldn't see the foolishness of Kwolek's hallucinations. "How are you going to take your company public when those Kwoleks keep hallucinating words from random numbers and telescopes from scattered dots?"

She froze when I mentioned her delayed stock offering.

While I was trading insults with the Kwoleks' inventor, Officer Tsui called, "We have another graffiti incident, and Senior Detective Yukawa is off duty."

'Just off-duty. You worry too much. She's not missing. She took the day off,' Fitch relaxed in a hammock strung between two palm trees, drinking something blue, garnished with a paper parasol and maraschino cherries.

She can take care of herself. I'm going to solve the graffiti mystery without her.

I replied, "Okay, Officer Tsui. I'll meet you. Where are you?"

"At the Civic Center, but the graffiti is at the Community Church, in the back, by the loading docks."

"On my way."

Oh no. I didn't have my car. It was home with a dead battery. "Wait! Can you pick me up from the Bruin Bistro? I only have my e-scooter."

"On my way," he echoed before adding, "You're on an e-scooter like a teenager? Cute."

Tsui drove to the back of our local megachurch, housed in a repurposed supermarket. The large red letters, Luv U. XXY MARKS THE SPOT, brightened the dismal alley. When they remodeled the church's façade, they didn't touch the back.

'XXY this time. I'm betting on chromosomes,' Fitch wore Dr. Mbacke's stethoscope and white coat.

Tsui collected paint samples. "This is the ninth event. I doubt we'll find any new evidence." He released the site to Graffiti Abatement, who were being interviewed by Leticia and César.

I offered Tsui second lunch. He opened a chopstick packet to sample a whole steamed bass swimming in a sweet sauce on a Ming-style blue serving dish while I enjoyed one spare rib after another, collecting the small bones in an empty carton.

"Thanks for the fish." Tsui wrapped a piece of skin around his chopstick before placing it in his mouth. "Look how the spray-chalk washes down the walls into the gutters. No evidence. No damage. Why do we respond anymore?"

I pulled Vicki's napkin from my pocket and smoothed it atop the center console of Tsui's black-and-white. I added the latest scene across from the firehouse, two spots opposite each other on Higgs Road.

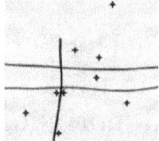

I showed it to Tsui. "I think there's a pattern to these incidents. Kwolek rotated the map and suggested the observatory telescope."

He shook his head. "I don't see that."

"You shouldn't. With this new spot, the telescope disappears. Your children could do better."

Tsui took a picture. "Let's test your assertion. I'll text it to my kids."

I reached into my backpack and found stir-fried snow peas to go with Tsui's steamed fish. "I know you like these."

"Perfection. Thank you."

After putting away the napkin map, I served dessert—moon cakes, fa gao, and sesame balls. "I'm worried about Vicki. Do you know where she is?"

Tsui popped a sesame ball into his mouth.

I waited.

"I'm not supposed to say."

Like an experienced inquisitor, I was silent.

"I can tell you she's not in any danger."

I took a small bite from a fa gao fortune cake, and then another.

"That's all I know."

Vicki was off on some secret mission. What could it be, and why didn't she delay until after Valentine's Day?

'She's meeting with a confidential informant,' Fitch said, dressed in a white spy-vs-spy outfit.

Our heart-to-heart ended with a notification on Tsui's phone.

He held it out to me. "It's good. Isn't it?"

I admired the artwork. "Do you think that's me on my e-scooter?"

"Could be?" Tsui opened his patrol car's trunk. "Here's your wheels. I must get back to work." He drove south toward the Civic Center. I pointed north on Higgs Road, where my afternoon nap awaited.

A police van passed me going south. When it signaled right to change lanes, the traffic slowed to let her in. The driver was a woman with straight black hair.

All my attention was on the police van and the woman with straight black hair. I didn't notice my e-scooter veering into traffic until a golden-brown sedan honked. I overcorrected, jumped the curb, and crashed into a palm tree. The e-scooter fell to the ground with its wheels spinning. Then everything went black.

'Get up. You look like an old drunk,' shouted Fitch, shaking me. He freed my trapped right foot.

This has been an awful Valentine's Day. I'm going to take my nap right here. Black again.

Someone shook me. "Excuse me, sir. Shall I call nine-one-one? The Higgs Road firehouse and the paramedics are close."

"Yes, yes, I know. Did you see where that police van went?"

"Are you okay? I think you have a concussion. That car almost hit you."

I opened one eye and saw the Athena of Velletri from the Louvre leaning over me. I'll never forget the perfect symmetry of that face. "I'm fine." I blinked. "Are you the Goddess Athena? Am I dead?"

The woman gave a hearty laugh. "I recognize you. You're Mr. Szilard. Where's your friend Detective Yukawa?"

I blinked my eyes to clear my mind. "Who are you?"

"Me? I'm not Pallas Athena, but I am Greek." She tossed her waves of long, dark hair. "I'm Athena Kaldis, owner of Epicurean Eats."

I sat up. "Yes, I recall. I love your roast goat."

"Are you looking for a police van? There's one parked in front of the Firehouse Barbecue."

'That's her!' Fitch exclaimed, bouncing up and down and throwing pink Valentine confetti in the air.

No. No. It's not her. She would have stopped when she saw me. You're as bad as the Kwoleks. All hallucinations.

'Nonsense,' Fitch countered. *'She didn't see you. Who notices someone on an e-scooter? Only kids ride e-scooters.'*

I wanted Fitch to be right. I wanted it to be her. My last night with Vicki flashed back to me...

We sat in her *living room watching a rodent that aspired to be a French chef. She murmured, "Let's go back to Paris."*

I put my arm around her shoulders. "We will, but first is Valentine's Eve and the traditional pink feast."

"Wouldn't miss it." She touched my lips with her salty buttered-popcorn fingers.

I turned and hugged her.

She paused the movie. "Just to be clear. I'm not having seven meals at your place. This is the 21ˢᵗ century, and there must be some balance."

I removed my arm from her shoulders. "You won't miss the Valentine's Eve pink banquet, will you?"

"Of course, not." She ate some more popcorn. "Unless we do something different this year. We've been in a rut."

"I planned something different. I'm teaching. We can have first lunch at Bruin Bistro. That's not my condo."

"Teaching?" She pouted. "You're teaching on Valentine's Day? Isn't that our day?"

"I'm only at school in the morning. After that, I'm yours." I leaned in to give her another hug, but she pushed back. "Valentine's Day dinner at Epicurean Eats."

"Okay." I kissed her salty fingers. "It's a date."

She resumed the video. The rat explored the kitchen.

Ms. Kaldis delivered me and my e-scooter to the Firehouse Barbecue. As she returned to her car, she said, "I'll see you tonight."

'How did she know you were having dinner at her restaurant?' Fitch wondered.

I locked my e-scooter to the bike rack and rushed into the restaurant. The place seemed bigger as I searched for Vicki. I didn't see her. I burst into the kitchen.

"Out, Zarand," the cook demanded while loading mesquite logs into the huge smoker.

My phone beeped with a text from my new fridge. **CRAZY AI:** ENERGY SAVING MODE. DOOR AUTOMATICALLY CLOSED.

I shouted, "What now, Crazy AI?"

CRAZY AI: RESPONSE REDACTED. PLEASE READ MY PRIVACY POLICY.

I murmured, "What response, Crazy AI? Whatever." I barged out of the kitchen. The door flapped closed, open, closed, open, and finally closed.

I gritted my teeth. "Crazy AI. No. Time. For. Privacy Policies. Lock the puppet door."

CRAZY AI: PUPPET DOOR LOCKED.

Finally, there was Vicki, her back to me. I'd recognize her straight black hair anywhere. She sat with Lieutenant Mutai and her EMT team. I shouted, "Vicki!"

Peggy turned around. "Sorry, Zarand. She isn't here."

The straight black hair turned around. He was a Stony cop. Not Vicki.

My cheeks got hot as I backed out.

I didn't go home. I went down Higgs Road, then turned left onto Zeeman Way. When I pulled into the police parking garage, the guard raised the gate and waved me in. "Good afternoon, Mr. Szilard. Nice e-scooter. Cute."

"Have you seen Senior Detective Yukawa?"

He fumbled his tablet, and it clattered onto his desk. "No. She hasn't been in today," he stammered. After a pause, he asked, "Should I notify Officer Tsui that you're looking for her?"

"No. No problem." I backed out and continued down Zeeman Way. I didn't want to return to my empty condo.

'I won't tell Dahl you said the condo was empty,' Fitch scolded me.

I gave him a forced smile while disaster scenarios flooded my mind–Vicki's car in a ditch, kidnapped, amnesia... I scootered farther from home, checking for Vicki at Four Rivers, Cocina de Cetto, and Epicurean Eats.

Nothing.

It was late afternoon when I stopped at la pâtisserie around the corner from Purcell and Associates. "I'll have a mocha, mille-feuille, and macarons. S'il vous plaît."

I sat at a small wrought iron table, recalling that magical day in the premier arrondissement during the layover between our diplomatic flight to Paris and the commercial flight back to Los Angeles. I took small mille-feuille bites and waited for my coffee. When my mocha arrived, I threw away my manners and dunked the macarons, dripping soggy cookies over my shirt.

I checked *Stony Estancia Surfs* and my GPS. There was no trace of Vicki. Nothing to erase my fears. Abandoning the flaky pastry, soggy cookies, and cold coffee, I headed for the door.

'*Dessert,*' Fitch whispered.

In a daze, I returned to the refrigerated display case and said, "Mademoiselle, s'il vous plaît." I pointed at random, and she placed pastries in a box. When I left the shop, I had pain au chocolat, pistachio croissants, and madeleines tucked away in my backpack. Whether Vicki appeared or not, dinner would need dessert.

The sun sets early in February. When I arrived home, the LED headlight on my e-scooter swept across the parking lot. There was Dahl! I stomped on my brakes, dropped the e-scooter, and sprinted to her. She looked dejected, sitting on the doormat that proclaimed, KEEP DOOR CLOSED. DON'T LET THE CAT OUT.

'*A lot of good that doormat did,*' Fitch commented sarcastically.

41.SLEUTH CLUB

I held out my hand and approached Dahl slowly. I said, "Puppets. Poor kitty. Pobre gatita." Her tail stopped swishing, and her head moved forward to smell my hand. I lifted her and cuddled her cold fur against my chest. "You must be cold and hungry." She head-butted my chin. I scritched her ears and asked, "What are you doing outside?"

She meowed twice and hissed.

'Bad people,' Fitch translated, shaking his finger at the door.

I looked up at my apartment. The lights were on, and I could make out silhouettes against the curtains. Stony Estancia was no longer an idyllic suburb. Walter Fisher had been murdered, Goleta and Vicki disappeared, and now my condo had been broken into. My instincts told me not to rush in until I knew what was going on.

I returned to my car and sat in the front seat. I stroked Dahl. "You're safe now."

She purred, snuggled against me, and closed her eyes.

I rested my phone on her belly and opened the app for my video doorbell. It reported an unprecedented, incredible seventeen videos.

I couldn't believe my eyes...

My sleuths—Louis, Hafsa, and Emily gathered around the keypad that controlled my front door. Others could be heard beyond camera range.

"We need the code to open his door." "His birthday?" "What about Detective Yukawa's? He's sweet on her." "What's our lat-long?"

Clever. I never considered latitude or longitude for my electronic door lock. Al Mahad had patented location-based PINs, but that was different.

"Apartment address?"

"ZIP code?"

The door opened with a whir and a beep.

The Sleuth Club rushed upstairs, and a curious Dahl got locked out.

The remaining videos captured Dahl yowling and pacing.

'You should have chosen something harder to guess than your ZIP code,' Fitch threw darts at a keyboard and recorded the random letters.

What's worse, a guessable code or getting locked out? I countered.

I opened the door. Dahl rushed upstairs, and I followed her. Together, we confronted the interlopers. "What are you doing here?" I tried to look stern, but I kept breaking into a smile. "You know you can be arrested for breaking and entering? How would that look on your college applications?"

Dahl was better at being offended. She walked to her bowl with her tail twitching. The only sound was the crunch of kibbles.

'Crazy AI,' Fitch exclaimed. *'Its privacy policy suppressed your apartment full of students. You should have subscribed to the intruder option—another billion-dollar market.'*

The detritus of hungry teens covered the apartment. Burnt chocolate chips stuck to dirty baking pans. Melted black cherry ice cream puddled in bowls. My best gourmet kernels, raw and popped, besieged my popcorn popper. An oil patina surrounded the deep fryer. Smashed kettle-cooked potato chips. A mountain of used pods beside the still-warm espresso machine.

'It's good to have food on hand when visitors drop in.' Fitch prepared himself a sandwich.

Hafsa broke the silence. "Lesson one: It's easier to ask forgiveness than permission."

'Fast learners.' Fitch chuckled.

I mumbled, "Puppies. If I can't control you, I might as well support you." I made myself a double latte and served the madeleines from my backpack. "Why are you here?"

They spoke all at once. I picked up fragments.

"Senior Detective Yukawa..." "Forensics report..." "DNA evidence..."

I rapped on the granite counter with a wooden spoon. I didn't care about forensics or DNA. "What do you know about Detective Yukawa?"

They all spoke. Dahl yowled. Emily brushed potato chips from a chair and stood on it. "Let me explain."

Louis performed three quick fouettés, knocking over a popcorn bowl with the last one. "Quiet, everyone. Listen."

Emily sat. "Senior Detective Yukawa sent me a text to collect the Sleuth Club." She proudly pointed to the room full of students. "Lesson three: The lone investigator is a myth. We're all here." She paused. "Most of us."

"No one saw us," Hafsa interjected. "Lesson two: Good detectives don't attract attention."

I didn't care about the detective lessons. I wanted to know about Vicki. "Did Vicki say where she was? Why is her phone off? Is she in danger?"

'Panic time!' Fitch ran in circles, without his head, clucking like a chicken.

"Nothing like that." Emily showed me the text from the official Stony Estancia Police Department account.

SEPD OFFICIAL: IMPORTANT MEETING.

The message included my contact details.

"We found this on your dining table," Louis said, handing me an official Stony Estancia PD envelope. "It's a forensic report."

I read aloud from the report. "The DNA from the shooting site atop the library came from 67 unknown individuals. No fingerprints."

"The report states—" Hafsa laughed. "It's like someone had swabbed a children's playground."

'Brilliant,' cackled Fitch, tearing off his gloves. *'Overwhelm the scientists with useless evidence.'*

I recalled Locard's Exchange Principle—the perpetrator will bring something to the scene and leave with something from it. After a long delay, tonight, we'd solve the shooting. "Forget DNA and high-tech forensics. We're going old school. We need drones and double-stick tape. Meet me at Stony High."

We assembled at the locked gate and didn't need to wait long for Mr. Mbacke, wearing his official gray twill shirt with an embroidered district patch above the right pocket and his name over the left. "Evenin folks. School is closed."

I explained our mission, and he let us in. Jaxon led the drone pilots into the courtyard, and the rest of us met in the biology lab.

"The drones will collect fibers with the double-stick tape. While we're waiting for them, familiarize yourself with the differences between synthetic ones like polyester and nylon, and natural ones like cotton, silk, linen, and wool."

Moe stood in front of the bio lab, projecting images from his phone. "These are synthetics—smooth and translucent. Nylon, polyester, polypropylene. They're the same." He flipped through dozens of similar images.

He touched his pants. "Cotton, Egyptian." He displayed a twisted ribbon. His shirt. "Silk, Mulberry." A shiny triangular fiber. His sweater, "Wool, Merino." Curly with scales. He reached for his belt. "Trust me, my boxers are linen from Flanders." Sticks with joints like microscopic bamboo. "You'll never mistake these for polyester," he concluded with a laugh.

When the drone pilots delivered the sticky tape, the lab came to life. Students picked fibers off the tape with tweezers and examined them under microscopes.

"Polyester." "Nylon." "So many polyesters died up there." "More nylon." "Has anyone seen a natural fiber?"

A chorus of "No," "no," "no way," and "never."

My privileged grandkids turned to me incredulously. "Who wears polyester?"

"Lots of people."

Dressed in their natural fibers, they gave me puzzled looks.

"Synthetic fibers are durable and lightweight, wrinkle- and stain-resistant, perfect for uniforms." I let that sink in for these teens who wouldn't learn about laundry until they went off to college.

"Mr. Mbacke's work shirt was polyester. The police and military use synthetics, as do baseball and football players."

That opened their eyes.

'Second lunch, first dinner, high tea. I'm hungry.' Fitch tucked in his gold-and-green checkered bib.

"Reconvene at my apartment for refreshments."

I didn't have to ask them twice. They were growing children. A caravan of fancy cars followed me to Higgs Haven.

Hafsa stood in front of my new refrigerator. "I gave the forensic report to Kwolek for analysis." When she touched the door, the electronic bulletin board lit up. "Very up to date, Mr. S." She tapped her phone. "Here's the AI findings." A video of children climbing a play structure appeared on the display.

'That's the best hallucination.' Fitch rolled on the floor with glee.

Louis did a jeté. "We're going to follow the evidence..." He tapped the electronic bulletin board twice to show the Stony Estancia SWAT team and the Marine recruiters with their helicopter. "Polyester and nylon. Better living through chemistry." He held his arm out to Hafsa. "Our fiber evidence points to people in uniforms."

Fitch marched, beating on a bass drum to a John Philip Sousa soundtrack.

Not to be outdone by Louis and Hafsa, Emily posted a picture of smooth green aliens. "These guys have no fingerprints. They sprayed the site with DNA from abducted humans."

Someone shouted out, "DNA harvested from anal probes."

This was met with sarcastic laughter.

I ended the foolishness with, "The fibers were deposited by SWAT and the Marines when they secured the location."

Moe waited until they settled down. "I took a course on bullet trajectories." They all listened. "The shooter wasn't atop the library building." He posted a picture of a sniper rifle, accompanied by labels naming a spotting scope, a laser rangefinder, and a bipod, along with a map. He pointed to the hills that surrounded the campus. "The shooter was there—a quarter mile from the target."

I stood beside Moe. "I like the sniper theory, but a trained sniper wouldn't miss from a distance as short as a quarter mile. A sniper would have killed Wally. Therefore, no sniper."

'Besides, you saw the rifle on the library roof.' Fitch reminded me.

Jaxon raised his hand.

"Yes, Jaxon?"

"Emily was closest when she proposed aliens. The shooter wasn't human. Intuitively obvious to the most casual observer." He paused. "A drone."

'Smart kids. Why didn't you think of that?' Fitch mocked me.

My phone chimed with *A Bicycle Built for Two*—the ringtone for Vicki. I left it on speaker. "Evenin, Zee. It's Valentine's Day. We agreed to second dinner at Epicurean Eats. Where are you?"

The Sleuth Club shouted, "Surprise! We surprised you, didn't we?"

Every muscle in my body relaxed. I took a deep breath and did my best to remain calm. "On my way."

My grandkids ran down the stairs and headed for the restaurant while I held Dahl.

I opened a can of tuna. "Don't wait up for me."

I rehashed the last twenty-four hours while driving down Higgs Road.

'I can't believe she missed the pink banquet.' Fitch sprouted ten arms to prepare pizza, lobster, panna cotta, prime sirloin, and pink lemonade tarts.

I shouted, "You disrespected my planning!" I wanted to step on the gas, blast my horn, and speed around the corner onto Zeeman Way, but it was impossible to stay mad. Vicki was safe. Valentine's Day wasn't over. We were having second dinner together. While I followed the agenda, she was full of impromptu surprises. Her free spirit balanced my caution, and I loved her.

My relief ended when I turned into the packed parking lot. There were no lights in the dining room or the kitchen, which was strange for a place open around the clock. The Epicurean Eats landmark, normally visible for miles, was dark. The three-story-tall, blue, neon Acropolis with Epicurean Eats spelled out in Greek letters blended into the night sky.

'I love how they used a rho for the letter P,' Fitch joked.

And a Latin S, I added. *Why are the lights out?*

Fitch wore an orange safety vest. *'Many possibilities, a bomb, a power outage, or an earthquake.'*

Not an earthquake. I would have felt it. I took a deep breath to check for smoke. Comforting garlic, lemon, and basil aromas filled the air.

'Something's not right,' Fitch asserted. *'Their late-night business is takeaway and delivery. Why so many cars?'*

Two streetlamps, with dark-sky shields above, lit the lot. I zigzagged around the parked vehicles. A red and gold ambulance flanked by two Stony Estancia black-and-whites made me wonder what could have happened.

I parked by the front door. With my phone set to nine-one-one and my thumb hovering over the green call button, I pressed my face close to a window, wishing I had my gun.

The blue neon lights outlining the Acropolis flashed on, as did the mixed-font EPICUREAN EATS. The door swung open, and people streamed out.

The crowd shouted, "Surprise!"

Vicki hugged me and whispered in my ear, "Happy Valentine's Day."

I looked around. Everyone was there: Coroner Persey with Cerberus and Dally, her daughter. César and Tish from *Stony Estancia Surfs*. Principal Golding. The Sleuth Club. Mr. Mbacke from Stony High. Dr. Mbacke with his wife and new baby. Dr. T and a Kwolek swarm. Everyone. Even the guard from the police parking garage and Euclid from the Stony Estancia Hotel.

Vicki wrapped her arm around my waist and, with a gentle squeeze, guided me past a buffet with roast goat, moussaka, spanakopita, dolmades, Greek salad, and fresh pita. Everyone applauded as we made our way through the crowd to a table decorated with silver hearts and white irises. On the wall behind us was a Mylar banner: HAPPY SILVER ANNIVERSARY, VEE AND ZEE.

'You missed that, didn't you?' Fitch wore a silver tux.

What silver anniversary? I asked.

The wait staff appeared with mezé platters—cherry peppers stuffed with goat cheese, assorted cured meats featuring Aegean prosciutto or louza, marinated olives and feta cheese, hummus, and more fresh pitas. The louza was my favorite, pork loin baked in wine and secret spices.

I inserted a louza slice into a split pita, rolled it, and offered it to Vicki. While she chewed, I asked, "Twenty-five years?"

She picked up a spoon and chimed her water glass.

Like magic, the waitstaff, wearing short blue jackets, filled the room with trays of blue shot glasses of ouzo.

'They're asking for trouble serving alcohol to these late-night drivers and underage teens,' Fitch tore up the restaurant's liquor license.

"What are you pouring?" I asked the closest blue jacket.

"Non-alcoholic ouzo, the best, imported from Mytilene, Lesbos. Kosher. Halal," was her proud reply. "This younger generation likes to be inclusive." She pointed to the rainbow and blue-pink-white flags that flanked the blue and white Greek flag. "...and they aren't interested in getting drunk."

The clear shot became cloudy when water was added, releasing a distinctive anise scent.

Vicki stood and raised her glass. "Twenty-five years ago today, I graduated from the police academy. I spent hours ironing my uniform and making a straight part in my hair." She pointed to the white line that ran back from the center of her forehead. "All of us probies lined up and hoped for good assignments."

Fitch poked me in the ribs. *'You should say something now.'*

Should I chastise her for missing the pink banquet and frightening me?

'No. No. Tell your story.'

I stood up. "I was late for the draft of probationary officers. I ran into the room after having been up all night on a stakeout." I messed up my hair and untucked my shirt to give them the idea.

Vicki smiled and continued the story. "The ceremony had been halted. Everyone was waiting for Zarand. He had the first draft choice." She hugged me. "I was attracted to your energy."

I kissed her on the mouth. "There she was. Her uniform had military creases, and she had that laser-straight part down the center of her skull without a single hair crossing to the wrong side. Her black eyes sparkled with intelligence. If she wore makeup, I couldn't tell. I thought: This lady has strong attention to detail and will make an excellent detective." I hugged Vicki and kissed her forehead. "I had the first draft pick. I pointed and said, 'That one.' The rest was history."

Everyone applauded.

Across the room, the Sleuth Club laughed and clinked glasses of cloudy ouzo. The only words I could make out were "Minerva's Mission."

I leaned closer to Vicki, "The Sleuth Club is talking about Minerva's Mission. You know about them, right?"

"Sure. They're your amateur detectives from the high school."

I played the straight man. "What about Minerva's Mission?"

"Oh no. How did your sweet grandkids get mixed up with those thugs?"

"Why do you say that?"

Vicki emptied her ouzo and held her glass up. A new one was placed in her hand. "They're an extra-legal vigilante group that goes after human traffickers in California. Their violent interventions are in the news." She emptied her ouzo. "They always leave their calling cards with Minerva's Mission's winged-M logo."

"They sound nasty."

"That's why I don't want your suburban naïfs mixed up with them."

I had retired to Stony Estancia to avoid such unpleasantness. I picked up a handful of olives and changed the topic. "Why the funny name? Isn't Minerva a Greek God?" I popped a couple of olives into my mouth.

'How can you teach that World Mythology class?' Fitch sneered. *'Minerva is Roman. Their version of Athena, goddess of wisdom. Athena is Greek.'* Fitch paused for a moment. *'Minerva is on the California State Seal.'*

After the tables were cleared, Ms. Kaldis, Epicurean Eats owner, brought us dessert. "This is my special baklava. In addition to phyllo pastry, walnuts, and honey, I add my secret ingredient, a layer of fudge sauce. Try it. You'll love it."

I took the first piece. "Puppets. Un-puppy-believable. Out of this world."

Ms. Kaldis continued, "I didn't mean to listen in, but were you talking about Minerva's Mission?"

With Vicki's introduction, I wasn't looking forward to hearing what Ms. Kaldis was going to tell us.

She sat down without waiting for an invitation and poured herself an Ellenikos Kafes. She sipped her coffee and began,

"When I got divorced, my husband stole our daughter Xanthia back to Greece. He thought America was spoiling her. I didn't know what to do. I was frantic."

She took a piece of chocolate baklava and ate it before continuing. "One day, these two central casting toughs visited me. They knew about my divorce and Xan being taken away. They said they were from Minerva's Mission and offered to help. My name is Athena. I thought Minerva was a good omen, but I feared they were human traffickers and didn't want them to have anything to do with my girl. I sent them away."

Tears pooled in her eyes. Cerberus rested his head in her lap, and she scratched his ears. "Those two kept coming back. In desperation, I gave them the last contact information for my daughter, Xanthia."

She sobbed and wiped her eyes. "I never heard from those men, nor anything from my daughter or my ex-husband. I feared the worst."

Two patio heaters ran out of gas, and a cold pall fell over the table.

"Until last week—" She hugged Cerberus, and he licked her face. She reached into her blue-and-white apron pocket and handed me a grease-stained piece of heavy paper, an invitation.

I passed it around the table. It announced, PLEASE CELEBRATE XENA KUNATH ON HER GRADUATION WITH A DOCTOR OF PHILOSOPHY IN AEROSPACE ENGINEERING FROM THE CONTINENTAL DIVIDE SCHOOL OF MINES. Everyone was quiet. We were confused until Mrs. Kaldis handed us a card with the Minerva's Mission logo. "Turn it over."

On the back was a handwritten note that read, MAMA. IT'S ME. I LOVE YOU AND MISS YOU. XOXO, XAN. PS MM SUPPORTED MY EDUCATION.

Now, everyone, including the waitstaff, had wet eyes.

Athena sobbed, "I'm going to Colorado for the ceremony. I don't know how to contact Minerva's Mission to thank them."

'Thank them? Really?' mocked Fitch. 'What about your years of worry? Why didn't Xanthia contact you sooner?'

"Have you heard from your ex?"

She laughed. "That's the strangest part. He sent a letter saying how proud he was, apologizing for wanting Xanthia to be a kalí nikokirá, a Greek trad wife. He hadn't heard from her in over a decade, but he'd be at her graduation."

Ms. Kaldis stood up, and her staff led her away. Her final words were, "On the house."

I left a large tip and headed home. When I arrived at Higgs Haven Garden Apartments, Vicki was waiting for me. "Let's mess up your clean sheets."

This was the best Valentine's Day. I didn't mind that no one had enjoyed my pink banquet.

Dahl purred and rubbed against my leg.

I reached down to pet her. "Yes. You enjoyed the pink banquet."

43. CCTV

A week later, the Sleuth Club gathered to review the Stony Estancia Regional Hospital CCTV footage for October. Four cameras watched the freezers. Thirty days. 3,000 hours of video.

Szilard's Sleuths occupied the first five rows in the Stony High Theater. César and Leticia from *Stony Estancia Surfs* were in the control room. Persey spoke from the stage flanked by Cerberus on her left and her daughter, Dally, on the right. "Ultra-low temperature storage preserves vaccines and biological samples." She pointed to several test tubes and flasks. "These are common. You can ignore them." Next, she held up a variety of small bottles. "These are what we are looking for. The hospital CCTV is 4K. You should be able to zoom in and read the labels."

Louis asked, "Are you certain it wasn't something he ate?"

"Good question. Most alpha-gal syndrome cases are from red meats, dairy, or gelatin. However, Wally was vegan. Those foods weren't part of his diet."

"Could it have been something he ate?" Louis pressed for clarification.

"Yes, of course, but that's not likely in this case."

Hafsa asked, "Do we have to zoom in on every small bottle?"

"No. The bottles we're looking for will be unique. They cost a thousand dollars, and one would be sufficient. If you see many identical bottles, you can ignore them." She signaled the projection booth in the back. "These are reagent bottles." The next slide displayed behind her. It read GALACTOSE-ALPHA-1,3-GALACTOSE. "This is the label we are looking for."

Louis leaped up. "How do we get the video files?"

Vinnie joined Persey on stage. "No problem. You can download the 'WHERE'S MY GAL?' app using your Stony High ID and password."

'How did he get their passwords?' Fitch wondered. He wore a hacker's black hat.

Don't ask, I warned.

"We have the Kwoleks as backup, but let's show those AIs," Vinnie added.

"Hola," César spoke over the PA system. "The *Surf* will post Persey's talk in case these little bottles are somewhere else."

Tish added, "The empty bottles could be in someone's kitchen, mixed in with the spices, or in a school locker, hidden among deodorants and–" She paused. "And whatever else might be in school lockers."

The theater filled with nervous giggles.

"Gracias," Persey replied.

The Sleuth Club cheered and got to work.

'*Good luck,*' Finch said sarcastically. '*If I were the killer, I would have recycled the bottles.*'

Another week passed. The students reconvened in the theater, looking tired and despondent. A Kwolek swarm followed them, buzzing and flying in patterns.

'*The Sleuth Club hasn't found anything,*' Fitch concluded.

Clearly, but the Kwoleks seem excited.

The energy reversed when the Kwoleks projected their discoveries on the large screen.

The students cheered and jeered as they mocked the slides.

"That's COVID-19 vaccine." "Close, but no cigar. Beta-galactosidase." "Are you joking? Not a chemical reagent. Those are pagan spell jars." "Have you been drinking? Mini bottles from minibars."

I enjoyed the fun at the expense of the Kwoleks, but I began to think that Persey had the wrong cause of death. How could these bottles be that hard to find?

'*I trust her,*' Fitch asserted.

GRADUATION

I walked into the Stony High admin building and greeted the sub coordinator. "Mornin, Mr. Sendak. I'm here for Dr. Chandrasekhar, Physics."

He took a deep breath and sighed.

I wasn't surprised by his harried response. Few school days remained, state testing was complete, and seniors had their college acceptances. He had to fill more teacher absences than usual. Attendance wasn't a priority for anyone.

He looked up from his computer. "Sorry. I had to reassign you. Not Dr. Chandrasekhar, Physics. Mr. Chan, AP Mandarin." His smile quirked. "Chandra, Chan, close, right?"

"Are you serious? I know one word of Mandarin. Nihao. Hello. I'm sure my pronunciation is terrible."

Mr. Sendak sighed. "Whatever. I need a credentialed teacher in the room, and you're it."

'Chin up.' Finch was wearing gym shorts. *'Don't make his day any worse. He could have assigned you to girls' PE.'*

I accepted my visiting teacher's badge and headed across the courtyard to the foreign languages building.

"Holmes. George Holmes." I was calling roll in the AP Mandarin class and hadn't seen that name before. I would have remembered. Holmes. Sherlock Holmes was my favorite detective. Few people entered or left Stoney Estancia High School, especially this late in the year. I scanned the classroom for a new face. Everyone searched, bobbleheads turning left and right.

A teen stood up in the back. "I'm George." His gentle voice sounded like a song. He said something in Mandarin. The class responded together, most likely dialogue from their lessons.

'Who's he?' Fitch voiced what I was sure everybody was thinking.

"Welcome, George. Could you please introduce yourself?"

He said something else in Mandarin, and the room laughed. The joke was on me. I accepted the kidding. "Welcome, George."

"Thank you, Mr. S."

'He knows you.' Fitch did not to appear surprised.

"I've been homeschooled." He paused for two beats. "Holmes homeschooled."

Fitch played a rimshot on his cymbals for George's wordplay.

My wide smile appreciated his little joke.

George mansplained, "The tradition at Stony High is that homeschooled students must return in time for the state tests to participate in the graduation activities." His lecture continued, "Those activities include the formal dance, commencement at Bragg Vineyard Arena, and the all-night party."

'Who the puppet does he think he is?' Fitch was costumed as Björn, the Stony High mascot. He made bear claws with his green plush paws.

I glanced around the room. No one else was offended by this presumptuous newcomer. The class accepted his lecture and applauded.

I followed their lead and said, "We're pleased to see you."

He said something else in Mandarin, followed by, "I'd like to speak at graduation."

"No problem," I said. Stony High elected commencement speakers. Oral histories ascribed this to a time when three students tied for the Valedictorian position. "If you get elected," I added, thinking this outsider had stepped over the line.

The class didn't object.

When the buzzer sounded for lunch, Emily and Hafsa put their arms around his waist, and they walked down the alley to Only Donuts with a small student cadre following.

Fitch scratched his head. *'What the puppies is going on? Who's George Holmes?'*

George wasn't the only surprise. Tish and César stopped me on my way to lunch. "The Makers Guild IPO is on. Do you have any comments?"

I had plenty of thoughts. This had been a disappointing year. We hadn't solved Walter Fisher's murder, and Goleta Hardcastle was missing.

'You haven't solved the graffiti conundrum,' Fitch chortled, juggling cans of spray paint.

I was more than a little chagrined that Dr. Telkes was taking her company public before I'd solved any of my mysteries.

'They're not solely your mysteries. Don't forget Szilard's Sleuths and Senior Detective Victoria Yukawa,' Fitch admonished me.

I'm happy to share successes, but I take failures personally.

'It isn't a failure until you quit.' Fitch held up an embroidered meme. *'Have you quit?'*

Puppies. Puppets. No. Now, I'm adding George Holmes to my list of mysteries. Who's he? If he was homeschooled, how does he have so many friends? Will they choose him as the graduation speaker?

"Welcome to Stony Estancia High, home of the Bruins." Jared Sendak, the substitute coordinator, made bear claws with his hands and growled, "Go, Bruins," before registering me on his computer. "You're here for Mr. Leaphorn and World Mythology. No reassignment today." He handed me a visiting teacher badge.

I collected the lesson plan QR code from Mr. Leaphorn's room and retreated to the teachers' lounge, where I could review it without interruption. TEXTBOOK READING. I sighed. ONLINE WORKSHEETS. I frowned.

The last school month is the worst. Your honorary grandkids have senioritis.' Fitch wore a green graduation gown and a gold mortarboard.

"What's wrong, Mr. S? Did you find another lesson plan not to your liking?" Ms. Dupin, my favorite math teacher, sat across from me and pursed her lips.

'Now you're going to get it for ignoring her lesson plan.' Fitch slapped his palm with a ruler.

I was embarrassed. A novice substitute might pick and choose, or improvise, but I was a reliable one. I followed each plan like Moses had delivered it on stone tablets. I knew better. I bowed my head. "Mea culpa, Ms. Dupin. I was having a bad day."

"No problem, Mr. S," she replied in an unexpectedly cheerful voice. "My bad. When I learned you picked up my absence, I should have given you something to teach, not what I leave for the typical sub who doesn't know any math."

"Thank you, but I do know better than to treat any plan as simply a suggestion."

"You know that Benford's Law–" She interrupted herself. "What made you think of that?"

I hung my head. "Yes. Yes. It won't happen again."

"But it's part of the Advanced Placement Stats syllabus." She lowered her voice. "Since your lesson, when they see a data table, they test it and pronounce it, 'Downhill slope, righteous data,' or 'Cross-country trail, bogus.' I intend to use your mnemonic in my future AP Statistics classes."

"That's high praise. Thank you."

"Whose lesson plan is that?" She pointed to the document on my phone.

"Mr. Leaphorn." I made a moue. "Worksheets."

She laughed. "The state tests are complete. Senioritis is rampant. For these final weeks, we're glorified babysitters."

"I know. I shouldn't accept any sub assignments once testing begins. You don't need teachers, just cops." I crossed my arms. "I'm retired. My policing days are over."

"Regardless, to use your words, the lesson plan isn't a suggestion. You should follow it."

<hr />

Loose white flower clusters hung from the California pepper trees, giving the courtyard a festive appearance. A few red berries had ripened, a sure reminder that graduation and summer were approaching.

'Confirmation of the changing climate,' Fitch remarked while carrying a poster, INVISIBLE FRIENDS HAVE NO CARBON FOOTPRINT.

Ms. Dupin sympathized with my dislike for Leaphorn's lesson plan while also counseling me not to change it. I decided to follow the rules. I sat in the shade of a pepper tree, examining the dull, repetitive worksheets.

When the homeroom buzzer sounded, I walked to the science building, but my way was blocked by a crowd marching through the courtyard.

"No air conditioning. Make today AC free," half the crowd chanted. The response was, "There's no planet B."

I recognized Keith Evans from the Stony Estancia Hotel. "Hey Kee, what's happening?"

"Climate action can't wait. Moe and Jax hacked the HVAC system. No air conditioning today."

The students broke the rules. So could I. Besides, with their school laptops abandoned in the hot classrooms, we weren't going to do online worksheets. I grabbed what I needed from

Mr. Leaphorn's room and messaged the class's group chat,
MR S: LEAPHORN'S CLASSES MEET OUTSIDE THE OBSERVATORY.

They sat on the grass. I announced, "Welcome to World
Mythology, the summer edition." Moe looked up from his
phone. Emily stopped stroking Clouseau. Jaxon watched me
out of the corner of his eye.

'Good opening,' jested Fitch. *'Can you deliver on the
implied promise?'*

Easy, peasy.

"All year, you've learned about ancient mythologies. Today,
we'll turn the tables." I handed posterboards to Hafsa and
markers to Louis. "Please, distribute these. I want you to select
a classical constellation and write a modern myth for it."

Hafsa asked, "We're working in groups, right?"

'It's a trap,' warned Fitch. *'You're outside. Without the
classroom structure, you're asking for trouble.'*

I was resigned to some mayhem teaching seniors en plein
air. "No problem. Groups are fine. Presentations are due in
thirty minutes."

My assignment hit the Goldilocks zone between structure
and freedom. The field hummed with creativity.

Moe and Kee, buddies from the Stony Estancia Hotel, drew
a very round cat with a bow in its hair.

"That's cute, or should I say, kawaii?" I waited for them to
look up, wondering why they chose that image. "Did you
understand the assignment?"

Kee smiled. "Easy peasy, Mr. S."

Moe explained, "We're redefining the constellation Leo.
Kittens have replaced lions in the zeitgeist."

I couldn't argue with that. "Purrfect."

Next, I went to Hafsa and Emily. They stayed with the
Japanese theme—an anime princess with large eyes and a long
sword. I knew better than jumping to a conclusion. "What
constellation are you using?"

Emily said, "Cassiopeia, Queen of Aethiopia," challenging
me to question her.

After a silence, Hafsa explained, "We envision the queen as
Ruth Bader Ginsburg, the Notorious RBG, and RBG as a
warrior."

'I'd say this was a successful assignment,' Fitch proudly declared, presenting me with a "Best Sub" trophy.

Jaxon drew a jail with a barred window. "This isn't the best artwork. I wanted to redefine Libra, the scales."

"Why?"

"We studied justice and the balancing metaphor, the idea that there are two sides to every question. This two-sided fallacy has been the 21st century's downfall."

"How?" I encouraged him to continue.

"We need to return to eternal truths like The Golden Rule, and jettison situational ethics."

My respect for Mr. Leaphorn went to the moon. Clearly, he taught them more than to memorize old stories.

I had no trouble recognizing Louis's drawing. "Gemini, the twins, right?"

"Yes and no. This is the gender-transition constellation, male and female, before and after."

I nodded, "A transgender constellation."

Fitch and Finch stood together holding a pink, blue, and white flag. *'We're the trans constellation.'*

The class ended with the buzzer and Tsui on my phone.

"Officer Tsui. Are you calling because you lost Detective Yukawa?"

"What? Uh, no. Sorry." He sounded more excited than contrite. "We have another graffiti report. The senior center this time, during daylight." He calmed down. "Can you accompany me?"

"No, thank you. I don't expect we'll learn anything new from the tenth incident."

A dejected Tsui hung up, and my phone notified me—an alert from the *Surf SE* app. XXX MARKS THE SPOT. MISS U.

I tapped on my phone to bring up the latest map.

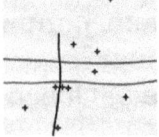

'Does that look like a constellation?' Fitch pondered looking through his Galilean telescope.

46. DITCH DAY

I loved spring in Southern California. Dahl and I stood on the balcony, me barefoot in my pajamas and Dahl meatloaf-style on the rail. A glow behind the mountains signaled morning's arrival in Stony Estancia. Each time a ray of sunrise found a palm tree, its fairy lights blinked off. A jogger's crunch on the gravel path announced daybreak at Higgs Haven. Early birds serenaded Dahl. My phone heralded a group chat. I stretched and yawned before checking it.

HAFSA: SENIOR DITCH DAY [FIRECRACKER][CONFETTI].

'What's senior ditch day?' asked Fitch, wearing his green-plush Björn costume, and making bear claws. *'I don't imagine you're invited.'*

I replied, **MR S:** DID YOU KNOW IM ON THIS CHAT [FROWNING FACE] [CONFUSED FACE].

KEE: NO PROBLEM MR S. JOIN US BEHIND THE OBSERVATORY [SMILEY FACE].

'Time for lesson five. Support them.' Fitch beat on a bass drum to a John Philip Sousa soundtrack.

I had my marching orders. I tapped "omw" and autocorrect sent, **MR S:** ON MY WAY!

Louis bounced like he had a springy tail. "We aren't going down in history as the only Stony Estancia class with an unsolved murder mystery." He circled the group with grand jetés. "Insanity is doing the same thing and expecting different results."

All the phones played *Boogie Woogie Bugle Boy* by The Andrews Sisters.

Hafsa spun Louis around, and they jitterbugged. He slid her between his legs, and she leaped over his back. The audience clapped to the boogie-woogie rhythm.

The music stopped. Hafsa tucked her hair back under her headscarf. Louis shouted, "Find the murder weapon! Think outside the box."

Fitch opened his copy of *The Sleuth Club* and flipped through the pages. *'The book's end is nigh. Revelations are coming.'*

Moe said, "We're going old school." He held a stack of pages. "By the time the homeroom buzzer sounds, these 'alpha-gal reagent bottle' wanted posters will be everywhere on campus." WANTED: THE BOTTLE THAT MURDERED WALLY.

"I'm sure we overlooked some evidence," declared Emily.

'Too many fingers and not enough pie.' Fitch closed his copy of *The Sleuth Club*. *'You won't get any spoilers from me.'*

Everyone grabbed posters and ran down the hill.

When only Hafsa and Emily remained, I asked. "I understand the need to uncover Mr. Fisher's murderer, but why aren't you more concerned about Goleta Hardcastle?"

The two teens looked at each other. "Who?"

"I thought she was your friend, and you barely knew Wally. He was just a Career Day presenter."

"Of course. Sorry. Too much is happening." Emily picked up Clouseau and hugged the flame-point Siamese. "Leeta can take care of herself."

Hafsa added with a grin. "She was smart, straight A's, honors classes, AP Physics, AP Mandarin, president of the Astronomy Club."

'Oh no. Past tense. She's dead.' Fitch reverted to his pessimist persona, dressed in goth black.

"We have posters to distribute." Emily shook her papers, and they both ran away. Halfway down the hill, Emily turned. "There's no more Goleta Hardcastle."

'They're joking. Right?' Finch wore Victorian mourning, all black, a weeping veil, a matte black dress, and a black bombazine cloak. No fur. No lace.

When the seniors entered the Bruin Bistro, after skipping their morning classes, the teachers were somewhere else. Even Mrs. Golding deserted her post.

'You have to love Stony Estancia,' chortled Fitch, dressed as a lunch lady. *'No one wants to catch the seniors ditching class.'*

I collected an avocado and Emmentaler cheeseburger, truffle fries, and a thin-crust jalapeño-and-pineapple pepperoni pizza slice before sitting with Moe and Kee. "How is that old-school approach working?"

"Nothing yet," Kee took a bite of his taco, letting the tortilla crumbs fall back to his plate.

Moe picked up a slice of sushi crunch roll with his chopsticks. "Any school that can make excellent shrimp tempura can solve a murder."

'Non sequitur alert!' shouted Fitch, dressed in the large ruff of an Elizabethan tutor.

The Lunch Ladies approached, carrying a white carton on a cafeteria tray. Dr. Yasmine held up a copy of the poster and said, "I expect this is what you're looking for."

'Doesn't look like a reagent bottle,' Fitch snarked, studying the poster.

The elderly Asian lunch lady bowed with his arms at his side. "We found it in the -20° C freezer behind the chef's truffle supply."

"It doesn't look like that little glass bottle, but Dr. Yasmine says it's important," the third lunch lady murmured as they backed away.

I read the label. 24 UNITS. NATURAL ALPHA-GAL (GALACTOSE-ALPHA-1,3-GALACTOSE) 250 micrograms, STORAGE TEMP. -20° C.

'Twenty-four units!' Fitch gasped. *Over twenty thousand dollars! Welcome to Stony Estancia, the land of money and privilege."*

Moe reached for the box.

I grabbed his wrist. "Don't touch it. It's been stored in optimal conditions to preserve DNA and fingerprint evidence. Coroner Persey will want to examine it."

I pulled an insulated evidence bag from my backpack, secured the white carton, and rushed everything to the morgue.

Persey opened my evidence bag. "Oh, no. Look at that condensation." She rushed the white carton into her walk-in freezer.

"Didn't you say that a single bottle would have been enough to kill Wally?" I asked when Persey returned. "Why twenty-four bottles? These aren't cheap."

"Twenty-four units." She ignored me and repeated, "Twenty-four units." She said it softly. She sang it with a boogie-woogie rhythm. She whistled. She said, "Two layers, stacked, two high, four wide, three deep. Twenty-four."

I opened my bottomless backpack, found a treat for Cerberus, and set up my espresso machine. "Caffè latte and biscotti?" That got her attention.

"Sí, por favor." She sat and dipped her biscotti into her latte, singing "Twenty-four units of alpha-gal in the box," to the tune of *100 Bottles of Beer on the Wall*. She jumped up, shouting, "Intuitively obvious." In her excitement, she tumbled the espresso machine to the floor. Cerberus sniffed the mess. Persey pulled him away. "Here's another doggie treat."

Cerberus took his treat and curled up on his bed.

With the biggest smile, Persey explained. "Yes. One unit could have killed Mr. Fisher. The killer took advantage of the fact that alpha-gal is harmless to everyone else. People consume alpha-gal every day. For non-allergic people, non-AGS folks, virtually everyone, no amount is dangerous. It might as well be water."

'*So?*' Fitch said, unimpressed. He shrugged his shoulders and held his palms up.

"So?" I prompted Persey, eager for an explanation.

"Don't you see? Mr. Fisher loved the baklava, but our murderer couldn't predict which piece he'd choose. The killer laced them all with alpha-gal, both vegan and non-vegan, to be sure. There was enough reagent."

'*We are up against a clever murderer,*' Fitch said, wearing his deerstalker hat and polishing his magnifying glass. '*A worthy opponent.*'

"Whichever piece of baklava Wally chose, it would be fatal, but they were all harmless to the crowd."

"Now we know how Wally was murdered." I high-fived Persey. "Good job."

'Big deal,' Fitch scoffed. 'You don't know whodunit!'

But I have a good idea.

Cocina de Cetto's tables were empty. Straight ahead, Abuela stood behind the counter. To the right was the salsa bar, spicy salsa roja, mild salsa verde, and a reddish-brown salsa labeled muy picante. My salsa was green. I'd never risked the salsa muy picante.

I recognized the young lady behind the counter from Stony High. Despite her name tag, I doubted her name was Abuela. The tag was a joke. Abuela means grandma. I ordered three Carta Blanca beers and a basket of homemade tortilla chips. I ladled green salsa for myself, red for Vicki, muy picante for Tsui.

'I'll have muy picante,' said Fitch, wearing a red firefighter uniform. His hat said, BOMBERO. *'Nothing like Mexican food to solve hot crimes.'*

When our food arrived, I ordered another round of Carta Blancas beers.

Vicki waved her hand at Abuela. "No más cervezas." She turned to me. "No more beer. We have work to do."

Abuela suggested. "Strawberries are in season."

"Bueno," Vicki said, "Tres aguas de fresa." She got right down to business before starting her chile relleno. "Zee, tell us your new evidence."

I recounted how the Lunch Ladies discovered that empty carton of alpha-gal vials. "It had been lost in their -20° C freezer all these months."

Vicki asked, "What's the Bruin Bistro doing with such a freezer?"

"Vee, you aren't going to believe this."

'You should have purchased a cryofreezer, not that AI-enabled fridge.' Fitch adjusted his chef's toque.

Don't remind me. I hung my head in shame. I had freezer envy.

"Try me, Zee. I'd believe anything about that Bruin Bistro." Vicki stuck out her chin.

"Nitrogen ice creams, cryo-shattering, high-end pastries." I sighed. "Imagine next year's pink banquet if I had one."

Our strawberry aguas de fresa arrived. They were a Cocina de Cetto specialty. They came in Margarita glasses.

"We were lucky to find the carton." I abandoned my half-finished beer in favor of fresh California strawberries. "The Lunch Ladies discovered it behind some truffles."

"I should have guessed," Vicki said with maximum sarcasm. "Not."

"Imagine twenty-four vials. Any single one was more than enough to kill Wally." I paused to let that sink in. "Persey called alpha-gal the perfect poison, lethal only to the intended victim." I took a bite of my carne asada burrito.

'What about collateral damage? How could the killer know that Wally would be the only victim?' Fitch said.

AGS, Alpha-Gal Syndrome, is rare in California.

"Persey told us that alpha-gal reagent was the murder weapon on New Year's Eve," Tsui commented. "Since New Year's Eve, I've been pursuing the clues Persey gave us."

"Means, motive, opportunity," Vicki muttered to herself. She cut a piece of chile relleno and covered it with rice and beans. "Means. How many people could have figured out that Mr. Fisher had AGS, and known where to get and how to store the deadly reagent?" She ate her forkful.

"I could think of only one person," I confessed. "Someone who hasn't been bashful to tell everyone about his PhD in Biochemistry. A simple search will find his *Stony Estancia Surfs* interview. Mr. OOP."

"I agree," Tsui interjected. "When Persey named the murder weapon as alpha-gal reagent, I concluded Mr. OOP was a person of interest. I overheard him telling his life story to Mr. Szilard outside the Stony High admin building last October. I did some investigating. His real name is Robertson Drew." He took a long drink from his agua de fresa. "Mr OOP is overeducated, a Biochemistry PhD and an Accounting MBA."

"Good work," Vicki complimented her assistant. "My only problem is money." She sipped her beer. "Remind me, Zee, how much did those alpha-gal vials cost?"

"Twenty-four vials. Over twenty thousand dollars."

Tsui jumped in. "I'm one step ahead of you. Using Persey's clues, I tracked an alpha-gal shipment to the Bruin Bistro, a foam container with dry ice. It was from Allopathic Allergy Reagents. $21,670 and change, including shipping and insurance." He picked up his taco, dipped it in salsa muy picante, and crunched it with a confident smile.

Vicki wasn't convinced. "You guys present an interesting case, but that's a lot of money. I can't imagine Mr. OOP getting paid enough to have a spare twenty K lying around."

Tsui put down his taco. "I've got you covered. In the week before the alpha-gal order, my person of interest, Robertson Drew, made three eight-thousand-dollar withdrawals, all under the limit, therefore not requiring IRS Form 8300, Report of Cash Payments over $10,000."

Vicki pressed for a more complete story. "I see means and opportunity, but what was his motive?"

I helped. "Well, Vee, the *Surf* reported that he blamed Career Day for his son's disappearance."

Tsui held up his phone. "In case you don't recall their clickbait headline." MR. OOP'S SON ABDUCTED FROM CAREER DAY.

'So many clicks. How did he remember that one?' Fitch juggled a tablet and two phones.

Showoff.

Vicki took charge. "Okay, Tsui. Bring the overeducated OOP in."

'Is this Mao's Cultural Revolution? Why is he a suspect?' Fitch slammed a small red book on the table. *'Drew has a biochem doctorate. That doesn't make him a murderer.'*

Vicki and I waited at the Civic Center for Tsui to deliver his person of interest. She pointed to a seat. "Robertson Drew, thank you for joining us. This meeting will be recorded." She put her phone on the table.

Mr. OOP sat down. "Like I had a choice."

"Would you like a lawyer present?"

"Not necessary. In addition to my PhD in Biochemistry and an Accounting MBA, I went to law school online."

'That's absolutely a psychopath's education,' Fitch straightened his gray doctoral robes with a vertical red velvet panel on each side and adjusted his eight-sided doctoral tam at a jaunty angle. *'The background for a criminal bent on world domination, a classic mad scientist.'*

"Please state your name."

"Robertson Drew, but you can call me Bobby."

"Do people also call you Mr. OOP?"

"Yes, but I don't like that name."

"No problem, Mr. Drew. Tell us why you murdered Mr. Fisher."

Mr. OOP didn't respond.

"We have the evidence we need to arrest you and for a jury to convict."

'Liar, liar, pants on fire.' Fitch wore his firefighter suit and bombero helmet.

Our suspect looked surprised. "Maybe I do need a lawyer."

Vicki warned him, "City Attorney Blake will go easier on you if you confess. He doesn't like to waste the city's budget on trials."

Mr. Drew murmured, "I'm not saying anything until Ms. Burgess, Attorney Abigail Burgess, arrives." He pushed his chair away from the table and crossed his arms.

Vicki stood up, leaned across the interview table, and shook her finger at him. "Everyone liked Wally. I doubt she'll defend you for his cold-blooded murder. I can call the public defender."

'What's she thinking? She went over the line there. That's harassment.' Fitch was aghast. He wore white robes and a golden halo while playing a harp.

Agreed. She's frustrated that it took so long to catch him.

I jumped in. "Shouldn't we summon his lawyer?"

Vicki came to her senses and turned to Tsui, "Call Abby and tell her this killer thinks she'll help him."

Since Vicki was playing bad cop, I grabbed the good cop role. "Here are some refreshments while we wait for Ms. Burgess." I reached into my backpack, set the table with silver, crystal, linen, and candles. I served cold drinks along with a fruit tray from Factory and Farm Foods, Stony Estancia's upscale market.

Mr. Drew relaxed, drinking ginger beer from a crystal tumbler and enjoying pineapple chunks garnished with maraschino cherries on multicolored toothpicks. After he'd stacked up four used toothpicks, there was a knock on the door.

Abby took the chair next to Mr. OOP.

'Wow. That was quick. Does she hang out at the police station?' Fitch wore his jetpack.

I wouldn't be surprised. After all, she's Stony Estancia's top defense attorney. I smiled and offered her something to eat.

She took a root beer can and a crystal tumbler. "I'd love a float. Do you have any vanilla ice cream?"

I reached into my multi-dimensional backpack. "Your wish is my command, homemade with fresh Ugandan vanilla beans, shipped in a cryofreezer."

Tsui helped himself to a sarsaparilla and papaya slices topped with fresh, shaved coconut.

Vicki glared at me.

I broke the impasse. "Senior Detective Yukawa, could you please review the evidence for Attorney Burgess?"

'Are you planning to join me?' Fitch sat in a doghouse. *'Are you crazy? She doesn't have actual evidence.'*

She gave me a look that said, "Don't be calling me for midnight second dinners any time soon," and explained about the alpha gal reagent, the box found in the cryofreezer, and Mr. OOP's missing son.

Ms. Burgess listened politely before responding, "You've done your homework. You have means, motive, and opportunity. Unfortunately, it's all circumstantial." She paused to stir her root beer float. With a deep inhale, she said,

"That Ugandan vanilla is heavenly, an earthy aroma with a hint of cocoa."

Vicki spoke through her clenched jaw. "Despite Mr. Szilard's hospitality, we aren't here for a tea party. Would you like to confer with your client?"

When we returned, all that remained of Ms. Burgess's root beer float was some foam, and Mr. OOP had a stack of used toothpicks.

Ms. Burgess said, "I don't expect the trial-adverse Mr. Blake will go to court based on Dr. Drew's education and employment at the Bistro. These facts fit nicely into your scenario but are hardly incriminating."

Vee glared at me while I prepared Abby another root beer float. This time, I topped it with whipped cream and drizzled chocolate sauce.

Abby took a spoonful of fluffy white deliciousness, wiped her lips with a linen napkin, and said, "I don't mean to disparage your investigation. However, this case has lingered for a long time."

Abby was trying to be friendly, but Vicki wasn't placated. Vicki crunched her almond biscotti, crossed her arms, and frowned.

The attorney stirred her float with a reusable straw. "The strongest part of your case is the money, so much money, all cash, mighty suspicious."

Vicki smiled and sipped on her espresso between small bites of almond biscotti.

Abby drank her root beer float. "Thank you. This is delicious." She turned to Vicki, "We've been friends from the first day you arrived in Stony Estancia. We women must support each other." She lowered her voice. "I'm going to make this easy." Attorney Burgess turned to her client. "Can you explain all that cash?"

Mr. OOP emptied his ginger beer. "No problem."

By his relaxed posture, I was sure that the client and lawyer had prepped his answer.

He spoke slowly, affecting a drawl, "Shortly after Robby Junior, Robert Drew, disappeared, I was approached by Athena's Avengers. I won't repeat their outlandish promises. I thought they were a scam, but they were my only hope. I gave them money every time they requested it."

Ms. Burgess prompted him, "Do you think they snatched your son?"

Mr. Drew looked down into his lap, and his leg rocked back and forth. I could barely hear him speak. "My son and I had differences. I wasn't surprised when he ran away. In retrospect, I could have handled it better. Athena's Avengers seemed like a way to make amends." Tears pooled in Dr. Drew's eyes, and he struggled to catch his breath.

Fitch flew around the room like an animated Winged Victory. *'Why do Athena's Avengers keep appearing? What's the connection?'*

Abby put her arm around Mr. Drew's shoulder. "You don't need to say any more about Robby Junior." She spoke gently. "But, perhaps... Can you tell the police where that money came from? No one imagines that Mr. OOP can demand a large salary."

Dr. Drew's drawl became more exaggerated. "Aww shucks."

'Golly gee, give me a break.' Fitch wore a straw hat, bib overalls, and a plaid shirt. He had a wheat stalk in his mouth.

"When I was a biochemist, I invented a tissue adhesive that replaced sutures in pediatric surgeries. I'm receiving royalties." He paused and stretched. "Also, as a CPA, I helped a few start-ups with their IPOs, negotiating with the underwriters, filing their S-1's, etcetera. They were short on cash. I accepted payment in stock. When they went public, I built up a nice nest egg."

"That's a fascinating story, but tell me, what's an S-1? Why did that make you rich?" I asked.

Dr. Drew leaned back and folded his hands behind his head. "Ah, the magical S-1. The registration statement that a company files with the Securities and Exchange Commission. The are no IPOs and no one gets rich without one."

'Mr. OOP is Dr. Money Bags.' Fitch dressed in a top hat and a silk morning suit like that character from Monopoly.

The room was silent except for some chewing and sipping.

Mr. Drew broke the silence. "I understand you're frustrated. To show there are no hard feelings, I can help you."

Everyone turned to Dr. Drew. He had their undivided attention. Teacher's Nirvana. I was jealous.

Vicki gave her first smile. "Yes?"

"I looked at those columns of numbers posted by *Stony Estancia Surfs*." He recovered his composure. "I can tell you that the Kwoleks' attempts to find coded messages were completely wrong." He nodded his head proudly. "Intuitively obvious to the most casual observer."

'Maybe not an evil scientist after all.' Fitch cheered. *'I never trusted those flying Tamagotchis.'*

Dr. Drew stood up, and his voice strengthened. "The patterns are unmistakable to any CPA. The small files are balance sheets, income statements, and cash flows. The big files are transaction journals. By the number of entries in the journal and the dollar amounts, I'd suspect a small company, not retail."

Vicki stood up and shook his hand. "Thank you."

'She thanked him, but what help was he?' Fitch wore a green eyeshade and pulled the crank on an old-fashioned adding machine.

Throughout Stony Estancia, *Surf SE* broadcasted: WINNER, WINNER, CHICKEN DINNER, MR. OOP WINS THE CRACK THE CODE CONTEST.

'That's the clickbait headline for the ages.' Fitch unrolled a papyrus scroll and recorded the event with a reed pen.

George Holmes ran across the football field to the observatory where the Sleuth Club was meeting. He held up his phone, shouting, "They filed! They filed." Simultaneously, *Surf SE* notifications sounded on every phone—a cacophony of discordant beeps and whistles. MAKERS GUILD GOING PUBLIC. S-1 FILED.

Moe's finger swiped across his screen. "Ignore the management discussion, it's hype. Pay attention to the executive compensation."

Jaxon could barely catch his breath as he read the S-1. "Dr. Telkes has twenty million shares and options for ten million more. She's going to be the richest person in Stony Estancia."

'Nothing like a stock offering to turn everyone into Smaug.' Fitch was a dragon perched atop a mountain of gold.

Everyone looked at George Holmes. The students had selected him to speak at graduation. He'd outpolled Emily and Louis. He exclaimed with a whistle. "The underwriters have set the offering price at $27.50. You do the math."

Fitch wore his green plush Björn mascot costume, stepped behind a gold lamé curtain, and Finch reappeared in a green sequined evening gown. She asked, *'What do your grandkids know about George that escaped you?'*

Szilard's Sleuths forgot about graffiti, the missing Goleta, and Walter Fisher's murder. My privileged grandkids, who never thought about money, now thought of nothing else.

"Super yachts," said Jaxon.

"Private jets," offered Hafsa with dreamy eyes.

"Destination parties," murmured Keith.

"Designer clothes," sang Emily, strutting like a model on the runway, carrying Clouseau, her flame-point Siamese. "So many cats. All cat ladies will envy me."

"A new lab with a cyclotron," offered Moe.

"Not so fast." Euclid, the night watchman cum mathematician and cryptographer, walked slowly across the field, his cane sinking into the soft turf. "Didn't you click the

Stony Estancia Surfs link when Mr. OOP won that contest? Those numbers on the USB sticks were financial reports."

Mr. OOP followed him, struggling to roll a cart laden with sweets. "Original Ocean Pirates offers cornucopia cannoli, silver-ingot shortbread, gold-bullion ginger snaps, and credit card chocolate chip cookies. All organic. All kosher. All halal." He distributed the sweets. "Think. Eat. Think. Consuming sugar improves cognitive functions."

Moe shouted, "How did we miss that? Those numbers weren't random. The keys. Identical numbers are in the Stony Estancia Makers Guild's S-1."

My detective instincts went into overdrive. What did the billion-dollar IPO have to do with the keys, as those numbers had been christened by al Mahad?

'Did you have an Islamic institute christening something?' Fitch giggled, wearing a black cassock and a Roman collar.

The teens gathered around Mr. OOP's cart. They switched back and forth between the S-1 and the keys, the numbers from the USB stick.

'This is a novel. There must be a connection.' Fitch reviewed Arthur Conan Doyle's *Silver Blaze* and Agatha Christie's *The Murder of Roger Ackroyd.*

I'm working on it, Fitch. I'm working on it.

"This is a common S-1 pattern. Two companies." Mr. OOP offered. "Makers Guild. Plus a competitor. The underwriter's due diligence, comparing the two." He laughed. "Why were the numbers important? Why were they buried like treasures? Why did al Mahad call them the keys? Especially, since the numbers would be public when the S-1 was filed."

Moe got it. "Have we been chasing these numbers for nothing?"

"Winner, winner, chicken dinner, made with Original Organic Product extra-nutritious GMO flour," Mr. OOP congratulated him. "The keys were a red herring."

Mr. OOP was wrong. I called Vicki, "I solved it."

"Congrats, Zee. Are we talking about Goleta, the graffiti, or the murder?"

"The murder, of course. Meet me at the Stony High Theater tonight."

"It's a date." Vicki asked, "Who else have you invited?"

Who isn't invited? Fitch asked while shouting from the top of the observatory, *Come one, come all!*

Stony Estancia Surfs led with STONY HIGH'S MR S SOLVES MURDER, followed by REVELATIONS TONIGHT AT STONY HIGH THEATER. CLICK HERE.

The crowd streamed into the Stony High Theater.
Attendance exceeded my expectations. I should have sold
tickets to limit the crowd. I had the foresight to reserve the
front row for the VIPs: Vicki, Tsui, and Coroner Persey, who
was accompanied by Cerberus and her daughter, Dally, who
wore her hospital guard uniform with her sharpshooter award
proudly on display. Others in the VIP row included Principal
Golding, Robertson Drew alias Mr. OOP, and smartest-guy-
in-the-room Vinnie Purcell. A Kwolek swarm cut in line, flying
over the crowd to hold seats for Dr. Telkes and the young
engineers from the Stony Estancia Makers Guild. The Sleuth
Club skipped the line by sneaking in the stage door.

Mohamed Manuelito and Keith Evans formed my crew in
the control room at the back of the house, Moe on the
electricals, and Kee on the soundboard. Peggy Mutai and her
paramedics stationed themselves in the side aisles. All eyes
were on me, waiting for what I had to say. Teacher's Nirvana.
"Mr. Walter Fisher's death was easy enough to solve when I
stopped thinking about the keys and those alpha-gal reagent
bottles. We had the answer all along. Watch these Career Day
surveillance clips."

I gave Moe a thumbs up and added, "Video produced and
edited by Mohammed Manuelito."

Emily raised her hand, and Clouseau hissed.

"Yes, Emily? Do you have a question?"

She stood and spoke in a strong voice. "Why are we looking
at Career Day videos when Wally died hours later at the
Halloween Dance?"

Coroner Persey jumped up. "I'll explain it. Take notes this
time."

Fitch flattened a sheet of parchment, sharpened his goose
quill pen, and dipped it into a bottle of iron gall ink. *'Ready to
scribe notes.'*

"Alpha-gal is slow-acting. Anaphylaxis might not develop for four to six hours." Persey held up an epinephrine autoinjector. "Serious reactions can take longer."

Hafsa asked, "Are you telling us that Wally died at the Halloween Dance from something he ate at Career Day?

'By George, she's got it.' Fitch sang dressed as Professor Henry Higgins from *My Fair Lady*.

Moe dimmed the house lights, and the audience watched intently.

Mr. Fisher was saying, "Good morning, guys, gals, and non-binary pals." He opened his eyes with exaggerated excitement. "Do I see the famous Bruin Bistro Baklavas?" He put his hands together and pleaded. "I'd trade my life for one. Vegan, please."

I signaled Moe to stop the playback and announced, "Watch carefully. Little did Wally know that he was literally trading his life for a baklava."

Moe resumed the video.

Mr. Fisher continued to rave about the honey-soaked pastries. "These are my favorites. I look forward to Career Day at Stony High for these sweet treats."

The video cut to a different camera. The screen froze. The scene darkened. The soundtrack played a discordant minor key. The tray that Louis had left behind had a green and gold label, VEGAN.

The crowd gasped, "Uh oh."

When the video returned to Louis, he chasséd up to the stage with a baklava tray without a label.

Another quick cut, some more minor key music, and the screen filled with a green and gold label lying on the ground— BUTTER.

The screen returned to Louis, offering his tray to Mr. Fisher, who took a huge bite of baklava, spraying buttery, flaky pastry everywhere.

The audience understood the mistake. Louis had given Wally the non-Vegan tray. They gasped.

Louis rose from his seat with the Sleuth Club, performed a relevé, and extended his arms, wrists together. "I did it. I killed him. It was an accident."

Tsui cuffed him.

The Stony High Theater reverberated with cheers and shouts of, "Mystery solved," and "Mr. S is the greatest detective."

I took a bow as Tsui walked the contrite Louis away.

County Coroner Persephone Paterson wore her full makeup, kohl eyes, midnight lips, and black fingernails. She strode to the stage in a long black dress. The theater was silent except for the clicking of Cerberus's claws, which were painted black. When she reached the stage, she took the microphone and announced in a deep voice, "I am Persephone, Queen of the Underworld. Let Louis free."

Cerberus barked.

Persey continued, "I explained this before, but you must have slept through that lecture." She made a motion with her hand, and the stage lit up with a flash. She had everyone's attention. "That flaky buttery pastry might have given Wally a tummy ache, but it didn't kill him. Whether Louis gave Wally the butter baklava or the vegan baklava, the result would have been the same." She paused. "All the baklava, vegan or not, was drenched with alpha-gal. Every piece was fatal to Wally."

I retrieved the microphone and said, "Thank you for that clarification." I addressed the audience. "The murderer is the person who doused all the baklava with alpha-gal."

The auditorium went silent, and Tsui uncuffed Louis.

That was the end of my show. I hadn't solved the mystery. The theater devolved into a multitude of small discussions. I was in teacher Samsara—wandering lost without a lesson plan. Chaos.

'You've had your say, and so has Persey. Who's next?' Fitch enjoyed my quandary. *'Who's the culprit? Did you convene this big reveal without knowing the killer?'*

Not exactly. I'm counting on the Sleuth Club.

I signaled Moe and Kee back in the control room, and the house lights came up. "Brief intermission. Mr. OOP and I will be serving refreshments in the lobby." The choices included Oatmeal, Orange, and Papaya desserts from Mr. OOP, French pastries from my backpack, and baklava from Epicurean Eats. No one touched the baklava.

Vinnie and Mrs. Golding helped serve the food.

Mrs. Golding asked, "Are you stuck? I was expecting a big reveal."

"Not stuck," I answered. "My intuition tells me that the keys will point to the killer."

"Al Mahad said as much," Vinnie agreed, "I trust them."

Mr. OOP said. "The keys are accounting reports. Why were they smashed and buried?

Hafsa picked up a mille-feuille. "I couldn't help overhearing. If you'd allow the Sleuth Club to present, we'll clear this up. We've prepared some slides and given them to Moe and Kee."

'Time for lesson five,' Fitch said. 'If you can't control them, you might as well support them.'

Hafsa addressed the theater, "I have never slept through a lecture." She signaled for a slide. "This slide from the Makers Guild S-1 shows a robust business positioned to enter many billion-dollar markets. I call this Case A." She signaled for the next slide. "This is also from the S-1. It reveals a business that's failing in many ways, with poor sales, insufficient cash flow, out-of-control expenses, and on the verge of bankruptcy. I call this Case B."

Louis rubbed his wrist, recently freed from handcuffs. "Case A is the Makers Guild." Dr. Telkes and her engineers cheered and applauded. "Case B is a competitor." The Makers Guild crowd booed.

Emily spoke next. "I was going to show you the Benford's Law histograms." She lost the group. People stopped listening and chatted. She retrieved her flame-point Siamese from beneath her skirts. Clouseau meowed. "Let's skip the fancy math, histograms, ski slopes, and cross-country trails."

The audience returned their attention to Emily. "Here is the conclusion. Case A is made-up. Case B is real."

The audience was in an uproar.

"The Makers Guild is near bankruptcy?" "They fudged the numbers?" "Where do the Case B numbers come from?"

Hafsa took the microphone. "Case B numbers are real. They can only be the Makers Guild. A failed business. A dismal story. These numbers, the keys uncovered by the Institute, al

Mahad, were buried behind the library to hide the true story of the Stony Estancia Makers Guild."

Dr. Telkes stood and sneaked her way to the aisle.

Hafsa continued, "Case A is bogus data. They cooked the books. The financials in the Makers Guild's S-1 are fraudulent. Made up. Fake news. Caught by Benford's Law."

Vicki jumped up. "I got it. Wally buried that evidence in the memorial garden. We've had his fingerprints for a while."

'Wally hid the evidence before he was murdered. The game is afoot.' Fitch quoted Shakespeare wearing his Elizabethan finery with an over-the-top ruff collar.

The adults shook their heads while the Sleuth Club cheered. When the noise settled, Vinnie stood up. "The ladies are correct. The S-1 is fraudulent. No one can argue with Benford."

Then the omniscient *Surf* posted, SECURITIES FRAUD. IPO IS. PERMANENTLY. OFF.

Mr. OOP jumped up. "I see it now. The keys were the key."

At that point, Dr. Telkes ran out of the theater shouting, "I don't know how that buffoon figured it out. He extorted me. I was going to be rich. I couldn't let that clown stop progress. Billion-dollar markets. Many billion-dollar markets."

The Kwoleks circled her in the courtyard like bodyguards.

Persey winked at her daughter and said, "No problem. Dr. Telkes won't get far." She whispered to Cerberus, "Go get her." The chocolate lab sprinted across the courtyard, closely followed by Persey's daughter, Ms. Dalgliesh. As they approached the Kwoleks, the quadcopters sparked to life and attacked with lightning bolts.

Cerberus retreated to lick his wounds. Dally drew her Glock 19 and took out fifteen Kwoleks before she was out of ammo.

'Fifteen kills for fifteen shots.' Fitch held an assault rifle with his bare chest displaying blackwork ink. *'That's a lot of hours at the range.'*

The crowd rushed out of the theater, surrounding Dr. Telkes and the remaining Kwoleks. Every time someone approached close, they were zapped. The confrontation was at an impasse. Dr. T was protected, but she couldn't escape.

"Okay, everyone, back off." Vicki took charge. "I'm calling for reinforcements."

I spoke to the engineers from the Makers Guild. They abandoned their boss, threw her under the bus.

"I had nothing to do with the money." "Can't believe she faked the numbers."

'Rats abandoning the sinking ship,' Fitch laughed.

One engineer said, "I had my head down working on special projects."

"What special project?" I asked.

"Top secret," said an engineer with a short Afro. "But it doesn't matter anymore."

"What was it?"

She smiled. "MegaKwolek. A Kwolek big enough to transport three people."

Another engineer broke in. "We're going to put self-driving cars out of business."

My *Surf SE* app buzzed with a notification: MEGAKWOLEK, THE FLYING CAR YOU'VE BEEN WAITING FOR.

Vicki lowered her phone. "Stony Estancia SWAT arrives in fifteen minutes in their armored personnel carriers." Vicki made another call. "The Marines and their AH-1Z Viper attack helicopter are a few minutes behind them."

Fitch paced back and forth in the no man's land held by the Kwoleks. His bare chest showcased his perfect pecs, covered with geometric blackwork ink.

Back off, buddy. You may be impervious to their lasers and lightning bolts, but you're no help.

'You aren't winning this war.' Fitch banged his chest Tarzan style.

We were at a stalemate. Dr. Telkes stood behind her moat of crackling electricity, ignoring us as she played with a video game controller.

Officer Tsui had his hand on his firearm. "Can I shoot her?"

Principal Golding, Lieutenant Peggoty from the paramedics, Detective Yukawa, and Fitch all shouted, "No!" Coroner Persey said, "Hand your pistol to my daughter and she'll eliminate the remaining Kwoleks."

Tsui pointed to a large quadcopter flying over the Stony High Theater. "But... But... Her MegaKwolek is going to be here before SWAT or the Marines."

Vinnie said, "That thing is way bigger than the Kwoleks. I had no inkling they could manage something like that."

Dally held Tsui's Glock with a two-handed grip. Calmly, she pointed at each Kwolek, closed one eye, and squeezed the trigger. With each shot, another quadcopter fell to the ground. She returned the gun to Tsui when the air was clear.

The MegaKwolek kept coming.

With the lightning bolts eliminated, Louis moved across no man's land, picking up speed, with preparatory chassés. For that moment, everything stopped. Louis launched himself with a Grand Jeté, levitated, hanging in the air, gliding over the disabled Kwoleks, and landing beside an astonished Dr. Telkes. The action resumed with a powerful fouetté. Louis kicked the controller from the mad scientist's hands.

'That was the best tombé pas de bourée and grand jeté ever,' Fitch exclaimed, wearing a pink tutu which he tore off and flung into the air.

Stony Estancia Surfs posted, STONY HIGH'S BARYSHNIKOV FOILS MAD SCIENTIST.

Dr. T's MegaKwolek controller skidded across the brick-paved courtyard, crashed into a circular planter, smashed to pieces, and showered a California pepper tree with electronic parts. The MegaKwolek landed atop the theater, and its rotors spun down.

Cerberus herded Dr. Telkes. Dally handcuffed her until Vicki and Tsui could take Dr. T into custody.

Dr. Telkes kept shouting, "How did that buffoon figure it out? My plan was perfect. I was going to be rich. Billion-dollar markets. Many billion-dollar markets. That stand-up comedian got what he deserved."

The Makers Guild engineers faded into the crowd. The one with the short Afro went over to the pepper tree and collected the controller parts in a pastry box from that wonderful pâtisserie in Warehouse-o-Rama.

The Battle of Stony High was over.

I looked around the courtyard and couldn't find a single sympathetic face. The Stony Estancia Makers Guild engineers chanted, "Lock her up. Lock her up."

"That closes this case," Vicki said with a sigh, "Videos of her confession will be enough for our jury-adverse city attorney to prosecute."

I hugged Vicki. "My place for second dinner tonight?"

"Do you have clean sheets?"

"Oh yes, a satin blend of silk and Egyptian cotton." I winked. "I bought them for you...for us."

"Wouldn't miss it."

Fitch sang, *'Vee and Zee sitting in the tree K-I-S-S-I-N-G.'*

However, Goleta was still missing. And what about the graffiti?

Dahl and I enjoyed salmon for lunch. She had hers poached. I had a blackened filet with roasted pineapple, plantains, and taro. We ate on the balcony, listening to cars honking in celebration of the Stony High graduating seniors. I was proud of my honorary grandkids for uncovering Wally's killer.

'You're up for teacher of the year.' Fitch wore his doctoral robes. 'You taught them Benford's Law, downhill ski slopes, and level cross-country trails.'

A caravan of cars and trucks, led by Hasfa's metallic-blue SUV, stopped below my balcony. They blasted Vitamin C's *Graduation (Friends Forever)* and Kool and the Gang's *Celebration.* Names were written on the windows with white markers.

I waved to them and shouted, "Don't be late."

'You're rewriting history there.' Fitch dressed as an Egyptian pharaoh using a chisel and a mallet to remove earlier rulers from the temple walls. 'Why celebrate them? They didn't find Goleta. You never solved the mystery of the graffiti.'

I responded with more confidence than I felt. *The school year isn't over until after commencement. Don't give up on the Sleuth Club. They have a few hours to find Leeta.*

'Good luck with that.' Finch dressed as Goleta and held Bygul and Trjegul. 'I have the cats.'

When they left, I set out for the Bragg Vineyard Arena, the only venue large enough to hold the graduation ceremony. For the planet and the city, I left my car in the garage and walked.

When I turned onto the Pacific Electric Trail, Fitch taunted me, 'What about the graffiti?'

Forget the graffiti, a fad, ancient history, a red herring.

Finch cross-dressed as The Pythia, Oracle of Delphi, wearing white robes and a veil. 'I don't think so.'

The Pacific Electric Trail was festooned with Stony High colors, golden blossoms exploding from the green honeysuckle, filling the air with the floral fragrances of jasmine and vanilla. The bees buzzed and collected a bountiful harvest. Ahead of me were more walkers, graduates in green robes and golden mortarboards, accompanied by three generations.

This idyllic scene ended when I reached the biggest traffic jam since New Year's Eve. The *Surf* deployed their neon-yellow flying cameras while César and Tish took advantage of the slow-moving cars to interview families. Kwolek directed the traffic to parking spaces, like the home-grown robots in the Democratic Republic of the Congo.

Szilard's Sleuths, wearing their graduation robes, held buckets and carried signs. FESTIVAL SEATING. DONATE TO WOMEN IN STEM. DONATE TO THE FAMILY SHELTER.

I emptied the meager cash from my wallet. The large bills already in the bucket put me to shame. Kwoleks flew the full buckets to the Stony Estancia Community Bank.

Festival seating meant we were on our own—no reserved seats. The chaos left single seats scattered throughout the auditorium. After countless excuse-mes and thank-yous, I took a seat in row K, in honor of the Kwoleks.

The house lights dimmed, and Mayor Shay Cadfael tapped on his microphone. "Please welcome the Stony Estancia High School Graduation valedictorian, Hafsa Khattak."

The audience applauded while the Sleuth Club cheered, whistled, and shouted, "You go, girl." The DJ played *I Am Woman* by Helen Reddy.

Under her golden mortarboard and tassel, Hafsa wore a rainbow hijab.

"In the 19th century, women were abolitionists, and then suffragettes. The 20th century brought women's liberation. I'm proud to join the 21st-century Stony High graduates in their efforts to support justice for all people, all genders, all abilities, and all colors."

After the cheering died down, Hafsa recounted senior year highlights like the Halloween Dance and the New Year's Eve Ball. She made a rookie teacher's error. This self-congratulatory speech went on too long, and the audience began to fidget.

Hafsa read the signal and ended with, "I don't want to leave you with the impression that the Bruins are only interested in partying. I'm proud of Stony High's support for our next speaker."

Mr. Cadfael returned to the stage. "Thank you, Hafsa. The Stony High salutatorian is George Holmes."

The audience was more enthusiastic for George than they were for Hafsa. The DJ played *Born This Way* by Lady Gaga.

George wore a COVID-19 mask. "Thank you for the warm welcome. I have completed the hardest and most satisfying year of my life." He ducked behind the podium. After struggling for several minutes, he appeared dressed in blue snow pants, a pink down jacket, and a white wool hat.

The Sleuth Club went wild.

"These are my souvenirs from my winter of negative temperatures, snow drifts, and frozen lakes, so many lakes. You can imagine the shock I experienced as someone from Southern California." The Sleuth Club responded in unison, "Icy cold, but you were bold."

He pulled on a pair of University of Minnesota mittens decorated with gold M's and clapped his hands together, pantomiming freezing weather. He said, "Minnesota was cold and lonely." The Sleuth Club replied, "All alone, not even a phone."

George pointed to the sky. "I waited for night and my companion, Orion." He held his hands together and blew on them. "During the day, *Stony Estancia Surfs* posted graffiti stories. Those posts assured me that I had support back home." The Sleuth Club shouted, "We risked arrest to send you the best."

'I got it. Those graffiti incidents were signals showing support for George.' Fitch was back grinding lenses in Galileo's workshop. He brought up the final graffiti map from the *Surf*.

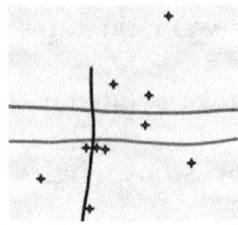

'*Don't you recognize that pattern?*' Fitch looked through his Galilean telescope.

I was baffled.

Fitch was entertained. '*Here's a hint. Look at those three stars in a row.*'

I shook my head.

'*Orion's belt.*' Fitch whispered with a haughty smile and displayed the constellation superimposed on the graffiti sites.

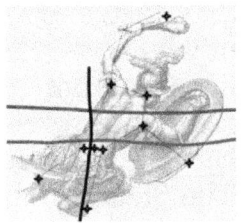

Intuitively obvious to the most casual observer, I admitted.

Fitch wore his doctoral robes and stood beside George at the podium. '*The graffiti incidents were like a flashing lighthouse or a secret handshake. They showed solidarity and camaraderie. They told George he was remembered and loved.*'

He stripped off his snowsuit, paused until he had everyone's attention, and removed his mask. He gave the audience a huge smile. "I want to invite my confused parents to share the stage. Mami, Papi, please join me. It's been a long year of isolation, and I missed you."

No one moved. The Sleuth Club stared at Mr. and Mrs. Hardcastle. After the crowd's susurrations rose to a nervous peak, Emily spoke to them. Mr. Hardcastle shouted, "¡Dios mío!" and Mrs. Hardcastle shrieked, "¡Que Dios nos ayude!" They both ran to the stage.

Mrs. Hardcastle stuttered, "G... G... G..." until she finally said, "George."

Fitch waved a pink, blue, and white transgender flag.

It came together for me. George was their child, and he was in Minnesota for gender-affirming care. The Sleuth Club protected his secret and supported his transition by creating the fiction of Goleta's abduction, allowing him to receive care in peace.

'You've got it.' Fitch hugged Finch, his anima, his feminine side.

Finch wore a white flowing gown, like Athena, and Fitch dressed like Ares, bare-chested, showing off his perfect pecs and blackwork ink. *'With support from Stony Estancia, George had a smooth transition to his true self.'*

Finch cautioned, *'Don't be fooled. This Stony Estancia fantasy ignored many challenges. Standards of Care for Transgender People, in the International Journal of Transgender Health, is over 250 pages. Nothing is as easy as in the fictional Stony Estancia.'*

George hugged his parents.

I hugged Fitch and Finch.

Mrs. Golding came on the stage with Dr. Chandrashekhar, Ms. Dupin, and Mr. Leaphorn. The teachers took turns calling names, and Principal Golding handed out diplomas.

Jaxon Chee was first. He set the pattern, shaking hands with the teachers, high-fiving Principal Golding, and hugging George.

When George's name was called, he accepted his diploma with his parents at his side. After a year apart, they weren't ready for him to step away. The teachers hugged George and his parents.

The final person was Louis Rawlins. He chasséd onto the stage and lifted George like Rafiki presenting Simba at Pride Rock. The DJ played *Circle of Life*, and everyone returned to their seats. There wasn't a dry eye in the arena.

The mayor returned to the podium. "We have one more reunion. I'm honored to recall Dr. Ruth Doyle, who spoke at the Women in STEM Symposium during Homecoming at the opening of the academic year."

'How do you expect anyone to remember her?' Fitch frantically flipped pages to the front of his copy of *The Sleuth Club.*

Surely, they'll recall that she was familiar with Stony Estancia, but the Surf couldn't find any record of her.

Dr. Doyle came on stage to shouts of "No makeup," and "Love pheomelanin."

She wore her hair in a high bun and a sleek, gold-sequined dress accented with large green earrings, a green tennis bracelet, and a green teardrop pendant around her neck.

'Stony High colors,' Fitch shouted, sporting a green velvet suit with a gold silk shirt and his green-and-gold suede dancing shoes.

She held out her arms, "Come on, Dad, Bobby Drew, join your daughter."

Mr. OOP muttered, "Ruth, Ruth Doyle." I read his lips as he mouthed, "Not Robertson Drew, Jr.," like he was teaching himself not to use his daughter's deadname. He stood next to her on the stage, a dazed smile on his face, happy to have his child back.

'Ah ha,' Fitch said with a chuckle.

The DJ played *Respect* by Aretha Franklin.

Finch and Fitch held hands. *'We wish all transitions were as smooth as those in Stony Estancia.'*

After commencement, the party returned to Stony High, where the Lunch Ladies organized first and second dinners with contributions from Chicago and New York Pizza, Cocina de Cetto, Four Rivers, and that wonderful pâtisserie in Warehouse-o-Rama. Everyone ate and danced to music from the Stony High Band until midnight. George danced the dubbelbugg with his parents, who wouldn't let him out of their reach. At midnight, the music stopped, and the Lunch Ladies organized the clean-up.

At two, with few people left, Emily said, "For a fitting end to the year, let's have an early breakfast."

Hafsa said, "Crepes at the mall."

George's mami said, "Sí, muy deliciosa."

His papi added, "Vámonos. My treat."

Emily cut a piece from her maple-banana crepe. "Sorry, Mr. S, the Sleuth Club led you on a wild goose chase."

'For a good cause. George had a smooth transition.' Fitch transitioned to Finch, and Finch returned to Fitch, back and forth. *'I'm genderfluid.'*

Hafsa spooned some whipped cream from her raspberry and huckleberry crepe and plopped it into her latte. "We will grant you a wish. Ask me anything."

'We know about the Graffiti,' said Fitch.

Agree. Lighthouses beaming support to George in Minnesota.

'What about Minerva's Mission and Athena's Avengers?' Fitch suggested.

Waste of a wish. My grandkids wouldn't be involved there.

'Try it,' Fitch taunted.

I couldn't think of anything else. "What can you tell me about Minerva's Mission?"

Emily looked at George, and he gave her a thumbs-up.

Two blue-gray cats took the seat beside me. They purred loudly when I helped myself to the bacon that came with my breakfast crepe. "Two for me and one for you."

The cats grabbed their rasher and took it into the corner under a potted palm tree.

George's mami said, "Tell me, what did Bygul and Trjegul think of winter in Rochester, Minnesota?"

Fitch petted a spectral Dahl. *'That explains what happened to Goleta's, oops, sorry, George's, cats. When George ran away to the Land of 10,000 Lakes, he took the cats.'*

George smiled. "The first time it snowed, they ran outside. Their paws sank into the cold white powder. They shook each paw, put it down, and shook it again. Finally, they dashed for the warm house and never approached the door again."

After surrendering more bacon to the cats, I said, "Uff da. That doesn't tell me about Athena's Avengers."

Emily drank her English breakfast tea, took a deep breath, and said, "There's no Minerva's Mission, no Athena's Avengers. The Sleuth Club created all those stories."

George added, "I didn't want my family, the school, or the police to discover me until I completed my care. The Sleuth Club had one goal, right from the beginning: It wasn't to find missing students, because they knew where everyone was. Their task was misdirection."

'Some detective you are.' Fitch rolled on the floor with glee. *'You let a group of teenagers fool you.'*

It took me a moment to decide whether I should be mad. I decided that I was proud of the Sleuth Club.

"Congratulations. You learned your lessons. It's easier to ask forgiveness than permission. Well done."

'The Sleuth Club didn't need your advice or assistance.' Fitch relaxed in a hammock, sipping iced tea. *'When are you going to tell Vicki that there's no Minerva's Mission, no Athena's Avengers?'*

Not now. Maybe later.

JULY FOURTH

EPILOGUE – THE FUTURE

I revered the Sleuth Club, high school seniors on the brink of adulthood. Legally, they turned eighteen. Puberty was in their past, and brain maturity in their future. When I was with them, I forgot the numbers. Neither of us acted our age.

'Irresponsible, impulsive, and immortal.' Finch was Athena, dancing wildly at a rave at the Mount Olympus Club.

They gave me courage, and I gave them respect.

I sent a text to the Sleuth Club chat. **MR S:** JULY 4 BREAKFAST

After second dinner, a simple meal of cold pork chops, tossed salad, stir-fried veggies, basmati rice, followed by apple and cherry pie, I began breakfast preparations. The first step was bread. I placed sourdough, focaccia, brioche, cinnamon rolls, and doughnuts in the proofer cabinet. Batter for buckwheat pancakes, crêpes, dosa, and latkes came next.

'Are you sure you have enough?' Fitch wore his apron and chef's toque.

No. I'll order pita, yogurt, spanakopita, and baklava from Epicurean Eats. They're open twenty-four hours, and they deliver.

I took a break for espresso and stroopwafels before putting the bread loaves in the ovens. By then, the sun was rising. I put out dishes, cutlery, butter, jams, chutneys, cheeses, and sausages.

Moe and Kee were the first to arrive. I greeted them, "Good that you arrived early. You're in charge of the griddle." I pointed to my bamboo mixing bowls. "Pancake batters are here, and eggs are in the old refrigerator."

George and his parents were next. "Welcome. Can you organize drinks?" I said.

George looked around my multi-dimensional kitchen. "Where are they?"

The new fridge responded, "I'm crazy AI. I have one percent, two percent, whole, goat, oat, and almond milk on the top shelf." The fridge door lit up with a video.

George's mami asked about juices.

Crazy AI responded, "Orange, apple, peach, grapefruit, papaya, and lemonade on the lower shelf. I can order something else if you wish."

George's mami's jaw dropped. "That's fine. Gracias."

The fridge replied, "Da nada."

After that, the apartment filled with the sounds of conversation and eating.

When we finished breakfast, Dahl climbed into Emily's lap. She announced, "Popcorn plans. I'll go first."

"Popcorn, Me." The room went silent. Teacher's Nirvana. "Following the advice of my life coach, I'm off to study political science before law school."

Fitch waved a placard, ELECT EMILY.

"When I run for President in twenty years, I expect all of you to vote for me."

Everyone applauded. She shouted, "Popcorn, Louis."

Louis chassé to the dining table and did a grand jeté over it. "I applied to several dance companies." He frowned. "Stony Estancia has an excellent academic reputation but lacks stature in ballet."

The group became silent. The only sound was the hiss of the espresso machine and the stirring of the milk frother.

He did a relevé. "No problem. Go, Bruins. I'm off to study psychology to help people who have been traumatized by misinformation, like I was when I believed I'd killed Mr. Fisher. My accountant advises that with my middling dance skills, it will be a better career." He closed with, "Popcorn, Jax."

Jaxon leaped from the sofa over the coffee table, and with a forward flip, he landed in front of the new fridge. "I'm headed to the national skateboard training center. Look for me in the next international competition."

This received a polite response.

He laughed. "Psych! I'm going for a dual major in college for mechanical engineering and physics."

Jaxon continued the ritual with, "Popcorn, Keith."

Kee began with, "George and I are going to address a billion-dollar market, rapid housing for the massive coastal population displaced by climate change. I'm enrolled in a contractor/project manager apprenticeship, and George is going to architecture school. Keep watch for Evans and Holmes Homes profiting from rising oceans." With a big smile, he said, "The real billion-dollar market."

Everyone laughed.

"Popcorn, Hafsa"

Hafsa stood. "Has anyone wondered about the fate of Stony Estancia Makers Guild now that the CEO is indicted?"

The Sleuth Club broke out in laughter like this was the best joke ever.

"Dr. Telkes will spend her time in prison with only 20,000 shares."

The crowd seemed puzzled.

Mohamed shouted, "Inshallah. If God wills it."

Hafsa replied, "Mashallah. What God has willed." She lowered her voice. "I have decided to defer college."

The Sleuth Club collectively held its breath.

"With the help of my financial and legal team, I recruited investors to restructure the bankrupt Makers Guild— a 1000:1 reverse split, and stock options canceled. The new name is Stony Estancia Election Reformers, SEER, a non-profit. I'm the CEO, and Moe is the CTO."

'Moe and Hafsa are sweet on each other.' Fitch made kissing sounds.

With that announcement, I was certain that the excitement echoed off the mountains. The *Surf SE* app posted, HAFSA NAMED CEO OF SEER. CLICK HERE FOR THE DEETS.

Hafsa stood taller and spoke with newfound authority. "SEER is an AI non-profit. Our AI engine, Big Sister, will fact-check all media." She paused. "What will make us different?" A longer pause. "Big Sister will file suits for fraud, slander, and libel. I expect millions of suits for starters, but as individuals and corporations clean up their acts, the number should fall."

She smiled. The audience smiled back.

"Otherwise, SEER will end up owning all the fake news outlets."

On that cheerful thought, we finished breakfast with a group hug. How lucky I was to spend my retirement years with the Stony High seniors.

By noon, the students had left, the kitchen was in order, both dishwashers were running, and Vicki sat beside me in the car. When I stopped at a red light, I squeezed her hand. "It's nice you have the July Fourth holiday off."

"The last time I wasn't on call was when we chaperoned the Senior Trip to Washington, DC. What do you have planned?" She leaned over the center console and kissed my cheek.

I merged onto the Desert Freeway before answering. "It's going to be a surprise, but I can show you these." I reached into my coat pocket and handed her the tickets. "These were a gift from the Hardcastles."

She read, "Fourth of July Cruise. Watch the coastal fireworks from Malibu to Palos Verdes from the comfort of a super yacht." She whistled. "Very nice. Will we see any whales?"

"I hope so. The cruise includes a twelve-course dinner paired with California wines, a cabin for after the fireworks, and a champagne breakfast to watch whales. The dinner will make up for the pink banquet you missed on Valentine's Day."

"That sounds romantic. Perhaps, we'll have our own private fireworks."

"Sounds perfect, and I have another surprise."

'When are you going to ask her?' Fitch got down on one knee.

I'm thinking. At dinner or breakfast. Maybe during the fireworks?

I received a text message. **CRAZY AI:** TIME TO BUY MILK.

Vicki asked, "What's that?"

"Nothing," I said. "I'm turning off my phone." I showed her my black screen.

In a breathy voice, she replied, "Mine also. It's just the two of us."

I concentrated on the LA traffic. A green sign, ENTERING ALTA MESA, announced we'd left Stony Estancia and were on our way to the coast. The traffic let up. I put on autopilot and listened to Vicki's gentle breathing during her well-deserved nap.

***

When the fireworks started, Vicki asked, "Didn't you have a surprise for me?"

'Now,' said Fitch, shooting confetti cannons into the air.

I dropped down on one knee and offered her a small package from my backpack. "Victoria Yukawa, will you marry me?"

She untied the white ribbon, ripped off the white tissue, and brought the wooden box to her nose. She pulled me to my feet and gave me a warm hug. "Oh, Zarand. Redwood. I love it. It's beautiful."

"Open it."

While she admired the diamond in a bezel setting, I removed the ring from its white velvet nest. Wordlessly, she held out her left hand, and I slid the ring onto her fourth finger. It was perfect. The internet hadn't led me astray.

She moved her hand, and the diamond sparkled in the reflected light of the fireworks. "How traditional of you." She furrowed her brow.

'Uh oh. Her tell.' Fitch wore a black evening tailcoat, a white waistcoat, a white bow tie, and black patent shoes. Dahl rubbed against his legs and purred.

She seemed lost in a daze. "Did you consider an emerald?" She paused. "Or an opal? I love the iridescent colors."

"I can exchange it."

She snapped out of her reverie and gave me a wet kiss. "No. Never. I love it."

I was confused. "Are we engaged?"

She gave me another hug. "Give me some time to think about it."

Fitch laughed. *'That's a teaser for the next book.'*

To the Reader

Please accept the author's gratitude for finding and reading this book.

I'm an independent author and appreciate how difficult it is to select my books from the flood of offerings. I'm dependent on reader-to-reader recommendations.

If you enjoyed my novel and wish to support independent writers, I appreciate posts on social media, especially the all-important Amazon rating. A review on Goodreads or StoryGraph also helps.

Even better is a recommendation to your friends. Thank you.

If you would like to correspond with the author or receive infrequent updates about Zarand Szilard, substitute teacher, you can send an email to Zarand (dot) Szilard (at) gmail (dot) com.

You might also be interested in the first two books in this series, Mr. Szilard, Substitute Teacher Mystery #1, *The Ecology Club: A Cozy Mystery (and How to Save the Planet)*, and Mr. Szilard, Substitute Teacher Mystery #2: *The Library Club: A Cozy Mystery, Representation Matters*. Available from most online booksellers.

Omega Cat Press books can be found at:
https://www.amazon.com/shop/influencer-20171115075/

Thank you,

Dr. O.

CHEERS, CREDITS, AND EASTER EGGS

Many people and organizations (knowingly and not) contributed to this work of fiction. Acknowledgment here doesn't imply an endorsement, review, or knowledge of this book.

Special thanks to https://www.critiquecircle.com/ and my partner in crime, Joy, who was with me through the many rewrites. Any remaining problems belong to me.

Also, thanks to Jason for consulting on the cover design.

Those interested in learning more about Lynn Conway, American computer scientist, electrical engineer, and transgender activist, can read the excellent biographical entry on Wikipedia, the free online encyclopedia.

Is Zarand food-obsessed? Are you? Overeaters Anonymous (https://oa.org/) is a community of people who welcome everyone who feels they have a problem with food.

Every author must invent names. *The Ecology Club* draws on scientists' names. For example, Mr. Szilard is named for Leo Szilard, a Hungarian-American physicist who wrote the letter that inspired the Manhattan Project. *The Library Club* used authors' names. Zarand's cat received her name from children's author, Roald Dahl. This book's names came from fictional detectives.

CHAPTER NOTES

Chapter 2, Women in STEM
    The chemicals listed by Dr. Doyle are real. The last one, dihydrogen monoxide, is H_2O or water. Here are some of the papers Dr. Doyle used to write her (fictional) dissertation: Jablonski, Nina G. (2021) The evolution of human skin pigmentation involved the interactions of genetic, environmental, and cultural variables. *Pigment Cell Melanoma Research* 34: 707-729 and Wakamatsu, Kazumasa, et al., (2021) Chemical and biochemical control of

skin pigmentation with special emphasis on mixed melanogenesis, *Pigment Cell Melanoma Research* 34: 730–747.

Fitch is compared to a hydrogen electron circling its proton for fourteen billion years. This is no big deal for hydrogen, with a theoretical half-life of between 10^{28} and 10^{36} years.

Chapter 3, Egg Drop Challenge

The Egg Drop event is popular at many STEM events, as your favorite search engine will reveal. I've never seen Goleta's bouquet and stone approach. If you see this, please email the evidence to Zarand (dot) Szilard (at) gmail (dot) com.

Title VII is in the Civil Rights Act of 1964. It prohibits employment discrimination based on race, color, religion, sex, or national origin.

Chapter 5, Graffiti

Fitch wears a leather jacket to copy Arthur "Fonzie" Fonzarelli from the 1970s, 1980s TV show, Happy Days.

I had associated second breakfast with the Hobbits. Second breakfast predates J.R.R. Tolkien. It's traditional in Bavaria, Poland, Slovakia, and Hungary.

Chapter 6, Kwoleks

Dr. Telkes, CEO and Founder of Stony Estancia Makers Guild, named her AI drones to honor chemist Stephanie Kwolek, the inventor of Kevlar.

When Fitch defends Dr. T, he wears the minimalist CEO uniform popularized by Steve Jobs: a turtleneck and jeans.

Vicki refers to Dora the Explorer's backpack. Dora's backpack's name is "Backpack," or "Mochila" in Spanish.

The string theory reference is pure foolishness. Even if string theory were proven, those extra dimensions are small, something like a trillionth, trillionth, trillionth of a meter—nothing that can explain Zarand's backpack, which is also pure foolishness. This is a cozy mystery, not science fiction.

Chapter 7, Unmarked Graves

Mr. Mbacke is confident his union will prevent Dr. Telkes from getting him fired. Even though unions protect employees, U.S. union membership has declined over the last seventy years.

Chapter 8, Career Day

Recruiters are giving away condoms. In California, anyone can buy condoms. Attempts to have schools provide free condoms have failed.

Y2K was a prediction that society would collapse on January 1, 2000, because computer software couldn't transition from 12/31/99 to 1/1/00. Nothing happened.

Non-binary is a term for genders in addition to male and female, such as transgender, no gender, shifting gender, or two genders.

Chapter 9, Assassination

Fitch carries a towel and says, "Don't Panic," in a homage to Douglas Adams and the Hitchhiker's Guide to the Galaxy series.

The Beanie Baby bubble began in the 1990s.

Peggy and her EMTs traveled to Australia as part of the USDA Forest Service bushfire mission starting in 2019. The Forest Service has had an ongoing relationship with Australia and New Zealand since the 1950s.

Chapter 11, Szilard's Sleuths

Zarand's first lesson for sleuths, "It's easier to ask forgiveness than permission," has been attributed to many people. I was told it came from Jesuits. The internet prefers Grace Murray Hopper, a U.S. Navy Rear Admiral and a pioneering computer scientist.

The name, Björn, assigned to the Stony High bear mascot means bear in many northern European languages.

Chapter 12, Trace Evidence

The Bodleian Library is at Oxford University and dates to the 15th century, one of the oldest in Europe. It holds many rare volumes. Fitch is not a threat to these antiquities.

Chapter 13, Golding's Gym

While stranger abductions grab headlines, the FBI reports they're rare, one in a thousand. More than 95% of missing children are not abductions, but runaways.

Zarand recalls *The Child Buyer. A novel in the form of hearings before the Standing Committee on Education, Welfare, and Public Morality of a certain state Senate, investigating the conspiracy of Mr. Wissey Jones, with others, to buy a male child* by John Hersey, 1960.

Fitch discounts Chandra's observation that all three missing students were good students using Bayesian analysis. Bayesian analysis evaluates evidence based on what's known. In this case, if Stony High had few good students, finding three would be an important clue. However, since Stony High has many good students, finding three is no big deal.

The Taurus Statue is awarded at the annual Taurus World Stunt Awards to honor stunt performers. Categories include the Taurus Lifetime Achievement Award, the hardest hit, and the best overall stunt by a stunt woman.

Chapter 14, Four Rivers

There are many ways to drive from Southern California to Northern California, from Los Angeles to San Francisco, from Hollywood to Silicon Valley. The fastest is Interstate 5. The north-south Interstate highways start in the West with 5 and progress to 15, 25, …, all the way to 95 in the East. The most scenic route is the Pacific Coast Highway, also known as State Route 1 and US Highway 101.

Zarand's Halloween costume is Father Brown, a Roman Catholic Priest and amateur detective created by G. K. Chesterton in the early 20th century. In addition to Father Brown, Chesterton is famous for writing, "If a thing is worth doing, it's worth doing badly."

Chapter 15, Halloween Dance

During the second century CE, Galen promoted the four humors theory, which posited that the balance of black bile, yellow bile, blood, and phlegm explained all diseases, supported bloodletting, and ultimately misguided Western medicine for over a millennium. Galen wrote, "All who drink of this remedy recover in a short time except those whom it doesn't help, who all die."

Chapter 17, Firehouse Barbecue

The EMTs were watching a *Blues Brothers* movie. Two action musical comedies, a niche genre.

Chapter 21, Coroner's Inquest

Idiopathic is a Latin medical term for "I don't know." When you want to take a nap, claim idiopathic sleepiness. When you want a second slice of pie, blame it on idiopathic hunger.

Chapter 23, Only Donuts

The four food groups were promoted by the U.S. Department of Agriculture in the 1950s and 1960s. Rather than being based on nutrition, they represented major agricultural interests: dairy, livestock, grains, and produce. In the 1980s, the more scientific Food Pyramid was introduced, followed by My Plate in the 2010s.

Zarand pays homage to the classic Steven Seagal film, *Under Siege*, where Admiral Bates says, "If I can't control you, I might as well support you." Earlier in chapter 5, Mr. Mbacke says, "I also garden," paraphrasing Steven Seagal's character in the same movie.

Chapter 25, Black Ops

Jodi Picoult's book, *Nineteen Minutes*, explores high school shootings and bullying.

The SECRET meeting name is an acronym for Stony Estancia Computer and Radio Encryption Tech.

Chapter 26, Pauli Falls

Facial recognition and Large Language Models (LLMs) are trained on internet data and reflect the biases endemic to the internet. Facial recognition accuracy for white males exceeds other demographics.

Charlotte Brontë published *Jane Eyre* under the male pseudonym Currer Bell in 1847. She went on to write several other novels. Her sisters adopted similar pseudonyms. Emily Brontë published *Wuthering Heights* as Ellis Bell, and Anne Brontë published *The Tenant of Wildfell Hall* as Acton

Brontë. They kept their true initials, as did many characters in this book.

Chapter 27, Bad News

Vicki has Japanese ancestry and was disturbed by an accusation of disloyalty. During World War II, xenophobia spread across the United States, targeting Japanese Americans. President Franklin D. Roosevelt issued Executive Order 9066, relocating 120,000 people of Japanese ancestry. Most were U.S. citizens. They were held in concentration camps from 1942 to 1946.

Srinivasa Ramanujan was a self-taught mathematician from India. He was ignored until G. H. Hardy at the University of Cambridge recognized his work in 1913. He published thousands of results before he died at age 32 in 1920.

Chapter 29, Calling in Favors

Keith Evans brags about Skara Brae, the Neolithic village on the Orkney Islands in northern Scotland. The village is over 5,000 years old, making it older than Stonehenge and the Great Pyramids of Giza.

Chapter 32, Al Mahad

Stockholm syndrome is a theory that hostages bond with their captors, famously associated with Patty Hearst as a hostage of the SLA, Symbionese Liberation Army, in 1974. Fifty years later, the theory is unproven.

The patent number, 7657076, is U.S. Patent *Characterizing biological stimuli by response curve,* awarded to the author and others on February 2, 2010.

Chapter 33, Elizabeth on Trial

Fitch mocks Elizabeth's trial by dressing as Pooh-Bah, Lord High Everything Else. Pooh-Bah is from Gilbert and Sullivan's comic opera *The Mikado*.

Chapter 35, New Year's Eve

"Intuitively obvious to the most casual observer," is an ironic statement often attributed to math professors. It means that something was anything but obvious. For example, a professor might fill the whiteboard with a complex proof that ends with laughter from the three super smart girls in the front row when the professor says, "QED. Intuitively obvious to the most casual observer." The rest of the class is lost.

The -20° C medical freezers used to store alpha-gal reagents and COVID-19 vaccines are colder than home freezers and more precisely controlled.

Chapter 36, Pink Banquet

Fitch explained Zarand's expanding backpack and kitchenette by alluding to dark energy. This is mixed up with the cosmological constant, introduced by Albert Einstein. If you're interested, read *The End of Everything* by Katie Mack.

The one-way link is a technique that many espionage organizations use for secure communication. An example is a *numbers station,* an automated radio station that repeats the same numbers. Since the signal is broadcasted, counterintelligence forces can't figure out the intended recipient's location.

The statues in Nobel Square, Cape Town, South Africa, commemorate the end of apartheid. The Nobel Peace Prize winners were Albert Luthuli, Desmond Tutu, F.W. de Klerk, and Nelson Mandela.

Chapter 38, Benford's Law

The Harvard University "computers" were low-paid women who made important discoveries, including classifying and cataloging stars, laying the foundation for stellar evolution, and proving that stars were primarily hydrogen and helium.

Europeans learned about zero during the Islamic Golden Age from the House of Wisdom, supported by the Abbasid Caliphate in Baghdad. Muslim scholars learned about zero from the work of the 7th-century Indian mathematician, Brahmagupta. For simplicity, zero is credited to Asian mathematicians. For more on the Islamic Golden Age, read the novel, *The Murders, The Mosque: Justice in the Golden Age of al-Andalus* by J. and D.R. Oestreicher.

The national area graph uses actual data.

Samsara contrasts with Nirvana. Both Buddhism and Hinduism use Nirvana to describe a state of peace. Simplistically, Samsara is the cycle of death and rebirth marked by suffering and pleasure, while Nirvana is release from this cycle.

Chapter 42, Epicurean Eats

The non-alcoholic Ouzo is fictional, but someone should make this.

Chapter 45, Modern Mythology

The Goldilocks Zone is borrowed from the search for habitable planets. The Goldilocks Zone is that distance from a star that supports liquid water. Too close and the water evaporates. Too far and the water freezes.

Kawaii is a Japanese word for "cute." It often refers to Anime characters with large heads and eyes.

Chapter 47, Putting It All Together

The Tamagotchis were "digital pets" released in the late 1990s. Users wore them and cared for them. If they provided excellent care, the digital pet matured, but if they ignored it, it died. These were a major fad. Over 90 million have been sold.

The little red book Fitch slammed was *Quotations from Chairman Mao Tse-tung*, widely distributed in China during the Cultural Revolution.

Chapter 48, S-1

Smaug is a gold-hoarding dragon from J.R.R. Tolkien's *The Hobbit*. Northern Europe has ancestors to Smaug in the Germanic and Norse sagas, and the epic poem *Beowulf*.

Mr. OOP encourages the students to eat sweets to help them think. A paper in *Neuropsychology Review* states, "A transient improvement in cognitive performance can be observed following the ingestion of [sugar]." Peters, R., White, D., Cleeland, C. et al. Fuel for Thought? A Systematic Review of Neuroimaging Studies into Glucose Enhancement of Cognitive Performance. *Neuropsychology Review* 30, 234–250 (2020).

Chapter 49, Revelations

Mikhail Nikolayevich Baryshnikov, the Latvian and American dancer, was the preeminent male classical ballet dancer of the 1970s and 1980s.

Chapter 50, Reunions

The idea for traffic robots comes from Therese Izay's company, called Women's Tech. Traffic and corruption in Kinshasa, Democratic Republic of the Congo, were well known, but appropriate solutions were not. Women's Tech's traffic robots blend the functions of traffic lights and human traffic agents. Robot traffic agents don't ask for bribes. They're a good example of local tech solving local problems.

George dances the dubbelbugg with his parents. This is bugg, a Swedish dance, with three people instead of two. Bugg is a swing dance where acrobatic moves aren't allowed.

Other Acknowledgements

I must acknowledge these editors who believe this book, and all books, are about cats.

Chapter graphics

School by Mike Wirth, US from the Noun Project 54581. Pupils by David Khai, US, from the Noun Project 2023631. Cat by Yanti 2212636 from the Noun Project. Paid licenses.

Stony Estancia Map

The map incorporates the following from the Noun Project. These are the required attributions (all CC BY 3.0):

Church by Gregor Cresnar. Fire Station by ATOM. High School by Muhammad Ikraam. Hills by eljot. Hospital by Alvida. House by Dian Chandra Lesmono. Mall by Blangcon. Police station by mynamepong. Small house by Iconiqu. Townhouse by Muhammad Fadli Rusady. Tropical forest by

Olena Panasovska. Warehouse by Aimmatun Fitria.
Waterfall by Ishaq_hmad.

Cover art
The cover was designed with Photopea.com, an advanced online photo editor. Ivan Kutskir is the creator of Photopea. He was born in Ukraine but lives in the Czech Republic.

ABOUT THE AUTHOR

I (he, him) grew up on Long Island, NY, and attended MIT as an undergraduate. After graduate school in Salt Lake City (Computer Science), I worked at Silicon Valley startups. Like Mr. Szilard, I returned to school after retirement to get my California teaching credential. As a substitute, I wrote Dr. O. on the whiteboard at the start of each day. Today, I live in Southern California with my wife and writing mentor, together with a variable number of cats. We enjoy our grandkids, international travel (COVID-19 willing), reading, and writing.